# WILLIAM

## AUTHOR OF THE

# SHADOW
## ❧ OF THE ❧
# WATCHING
# STAR

They sought the path
to power in a world
of blood and ice....

BANTAM BOOKS

ISBN 0-553-56029-8

US **$5.99** / $7.99 CAN

9 780553 560299

50599

S

# DRIVEN BY DESPAIR, DIVIDED BY TREACHERY, THEY SCANNED THE HEAVENS FOR A NEW STAR TO GUIDE THEM

**Cha-kwena**—A shaman obedient to the spirit voices of the Ancient Ones, he is sworn to prevent the slaughter of the sacred white mammoth, totem of his tribe. But now, alone beyond the edge of the world, he aches for the loving embrace of his woman—a desire that could spell doom for the future generations of the People.

**Mah-ree**—Her brazen defiance of Cha-kwena and of the laws of the Ancients has brought tragedy upon her tribe and shame upon herself. Abandoned by the one man she loves, she has lost all hope, escaping into the primeval forest, seeking only her death.

**Kosar-eh**—A great hunter and proud warrior, he has seen the Four Winds sweep through his life, leaving behind death and disaster. From the ruins of shattered dreams he struggles to build a new life for himself and his family . . . but the Four Winds are threatening to overtake him once more.

**Warakan**—A boy in whose spirit resides the final transcendent hope for peace between warring tribes, he is the keeper of the sacred stone talisman, the key to power . . . but he is also the bearer of an age-old hatred, a secret and bloody desire for revenge and human sacrifice.

**Jhadel**—The last surviving member of the ancient priesthood, he has long had a vision of a great alliance between the tribes. Now he has in his care a boy, Warakan, who can choose to fulfill that dream—or to destroy it.

Bantam Books by William Sarabande

# THE
# FIRST
# AMERICANS

# SHADOW
# OF THE
# WATCHING
# STAR

## WILLIAM
## SARABANDE

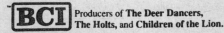

**BCI** Producers of **The Deer Dancers,**
**The Holts,** and **Children of the Lion.**

*Book Creations Inc., Canaan, NY • Lyle Kenyon Engel, Founder*

BANTAM BOOKS
NEW YORK • TORONTO • LONDON • SYDNEY • AUCKLAND

SHADOW OF THE WATCHING STAR

*A Bantam Book / published by arrangement with
Book Creations Inc.*

*Bantam edition / May 1995*

*Grateful acknowledgment is made to the following publishers for
permission to use quotations from copyrighted works:* Lakota Myth,
*by James R. Walker, edited by Elaine Jahner, by permission of the
University of Nebraska Press (copyright 1983 by the University of
Nebraska Press); and* The Florentine Codex: General History of
the Things of New Spain, *Book II, by Fray Bernardino de Sahagun,
edited by Arthur J. O. Anderson and Charles Dibble, by permission
of the School of American Research and University of Utah
(copyright 1950–69 by the School of American Research and
University of Utah). Also,* The Chuckchee, *by Waldemare Bogoras
(copyright 1904–09 by Leiden and the American Museum of
Natural History Memoirs);* The Old North Trail, *by Walter B.
McClintock (copyright 1920 by Macmillan and Co.); and* Peoples of
the Earth, *Vol. 16,* The Arctic, *by Douglas Botting (copyright 1973
by Danbury Press).*

*Produced by Book Creations Inc.
Lyle Kenyon Engel, Founder*

ISBN 0-553-56029-8

*Published simultaneously in the United States and Canada*

*Bantam Books are published by Bantam Books, a division of Bantam
Doubleday Dell Publishing Group, Inc. Its trademark, consisting of the
words "Bantam Books" and the portrayal of a rooster, is Registered in
U.S. Patent and Trademark Office and in other countries. Marca
Registrada. Bantam Books, 1540 Broadway, New York, New York
10036.*

PRINTED IN THE UNITED STATES OF AMERICA

OPM     0 9 8 7 6 5 4 3 2 1

# DEDICATION

To Pat Jones, Dean Allen, and Donna Caltrider of Edelweiss Books, Big Bear Lake, California, with thanks for all the goodwill, good talk, and good books sent my way!

To Charles Cline, for all the black bean soup!

And to Mary Ward—for concern shown, for offers of assistance, and for seeing the spirit of the white "buffalo" in the mammoth!

# THE THREE TRIBES

## People of the Red World

Kosar-eh–headman
Ta-maya–his second woman
Gah-ti*, Ka-neh, Kho-neh,
Kiu-neh, Klah-neh–his sons
Doh-teyah–his daughter
Siwi-ni*–his first woman,
mother of his children

Cha-kwena–shaman
Mah-ree–his woman
U-wa–his mother
Joh-nee–his sister

Tla-nee–sister of Mah-ree and Ta-maya
Ha-xa*–mother of Ta-maya and Mah-ree
Kahm-ree–grandmother of Ban-ya

## People of the Watching Star

Tsana–chieftain
Ban-ya–priestess; once of the Red World · Jhadel–shaman
Warakan–son of fabled Mystic Warrior
Indeh–Land of Grass warrior · Hrak, Unai, Xanahay–warriors
Ysuna*–daughter of the Sun; priestess

## People of the Land of Grass

Shateh*–high chief and shaman, grandfather of Warakan
Xohkantakeh, Zakeh, Ranamal, Ynau–warriors
Shan, Neeracheela–Zakeh's women
Lahontay*–old warrior, hunt master
Axwahtal–headman of the northern bands of this tribe, once
ally of Shateh, now chieftain in his place
Ika, Xree, Lana–preadolescent daughters
of the northern bands

* deceased

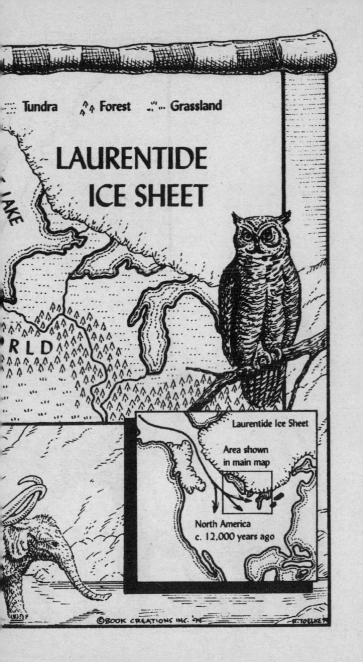

:::: Tundra    ʌ Forest    .ꞏꞏꞏ Grassland

# LAURENTIDE ICE SHEET

Laurentide Ice Sheet

Area shown
in main map

North America
c. 12,000 years ago

©BOOK CREATIONS INC. '9E

E. TOELKE

*Owl comes,*
    *Hay yah! Out of the black robe of Night,*
*Death comes,*
    *Hay yah! In the shadow of Watching Star,*
*Spirit Sucker comes,*
    *Hay yah! On the wings of Four Winds, the People*
    *scatter.*
*Owl comes,*
    *Hay yah! Now Mouse and Man must be afraid!*

# PROLOGUE

"So she sang,
    'A young man would be wise.
    A young man would be brave.
    He left the place he knew.
    He came to death's valley . . .
    He broke the living stone . . .
    He slew my friend the bear . . .'
  "And Iya said, 'Ho, sing what you will. It
is your death song and it is music that will
make my heart glad.' "

—Bad Wound (Taopi-sica)
*Lakota Myth* by James R. Walker

"Shaman!"

The spirit of the wind called from the black depths of the Ice Age night. It moaned across the storm-savaged highlands, keening in the way of a wild beast mourning a lost mate until, at last, the sleeping boy's eyes opened in cold darkness.

Warakan's heart was pounding, and his thoughts ran as wild as the wind. *It has returned to the forest, the thing that cries in the winter dark! The sad-voiced spirit that clothes itself in the invisible skin of North Wind as it*

*haunts the abandoned village of the dead to which Jhadel
has forbidden me to return!*

Knuckling the residue of dreams from his eyes, the
boy remained flat on his back upon the jumble of dried
ferns, feathers, and strips of crudely cured animal skins
that served as his mattress. He held his breath and listened, trying not to be afraid as he remembered, *All that
is bad comes from the north . . . all that is dark and cold
. . . all that has to do with death and danger.*

Beside him lay the sleeping old shaman and the
orphaned cub of the tawny she-bear whose thick, shaggy
pelt now clothed his own thin, furless hide. Beyond the
vaulted confines of their hide-covered, sapling-braced
lodge of bark and brushwood, North Wind was no
longer moaning; it was howling through the forest like a
gut-wounded dire wolf.

The lodge creaked, straining against its hardwood
anchor pegs, then trembled violently. Warakan trembled, too, but although he was wary of the rising wind,
he did not fear the storm that spawned it. His shelter
had endured worse weather since White Giant Winter
had come down upon the world. The size of the lodge
was nothing to boast of, but its location on a bench of
broken woodland beneath an overhanging streamside
bluff would grant protection from the full fury of the
storm. He and Jhadel had dug the broad, circular foun-
dation of the lodge knee-deep into the skin of the earth,
surrounding it with bark and brushwood to prevent the
intrusion of all but the most tenacious drafts of cold air;
even these were baffled by a ring of heavy stones that
held the bottom edges of the lodge covers in place.
Now, snug as a wood rat in his winter den, Warakan was
confident that his shelter would survive this latest on-
slaught of weather; but he was less sure of other things,
of more elusive things potentially far more dangerous.
Of these intangibles he *was* afraid.

He lay motionless in the dark, breathing softly as he listened for the spirit to call again. Moments passed. Outside, North Wind continued its rampage through the trees, but if it spoke in the language of men, the boy could not understand its words. He closed his eyes, as though by depriving himself of one sense he might sharpen another, and gradually he became aware of other sounds: the soft rubbings of thong against wood; a loose section of hide flapping near the apex of the roof; the erratic snortings of the dreaming old shaman, Jhadel, sloppily sucking air through broad, camel-like nostrils; and the low, whistling snores of the yearling bear as it slept its winter sleep in a grass nest well away from the central fire pit, where the heart-ember of sacred Fire smoldered in a mound of ash lest it grow cold and lifeless before dawn.

The boy shivered, not against cold but against frustration. The latest snowstorm had kept him lodge-bound with Jhadel for more than three days and four nights. Not wanting to worry the old man, Warakan had not told him that the only reason they had meat in their boiling bag, fat for their tallow lamp, and kindling for their fire was because he had recently begun to replenish their supplies of dried meat, burnable twigs, grass, and fat from the many carefully placed hunting caches they had assembled at the beginning of winter. The boy's frown became a scowl as he wondered if the old man knew anyway; there was little in the way of secrets that a youth who had not yet seen the end of his tenth winter could keep from a shaman of Jhadel's years, even if the youth was Warakan, grandson of the war chief Shateh and son of the fabled Mystic Warrior, Masau.

*They are both dead, and you are here beyond the edge of the world, cast out from among the People with only an old man and a bear to care whether you live or die. So much for the powers of Jhadel!*

A sigh of bitter acquiescence to this unwelcome truth brought the scent of the lodge into Warakan's nostrils. It was an appalling invasion. The rancid stink of soiled bed furs and clothing, of charred wood and dung and bones, and of moldering hides mingled with the smell of the unwashed old shaman and the young bear.

*Too long has White Giant Winter kept us in this lodge! Will Warm Moon never rise again? Will the forces of Creation never send the sweet breath of South Wind to speak to us of spring?*

As though in answer to the boy's unspoken questions, the wind rose again to slap at the exterior thonglacings of the lodge, and suddenly Warakan's head went up in the darkness. He opened his eyes. His heart was pounding. It was there again—not the voice *of* the wind, but something crying *in* the wind, a distant unarticulated sound of such unspeakable sadness that the boy yearned to howl back in sympathy . . . and in fear.

*What is it? Why does it cry? And if Jhadel is truly a shaman, why does he not hear the spirit summoning him on the wind?*

Stung by suspicions he dared not ignore, Warakan sat up. The old dread was back in his gut. The voice of the spirit was already fading. He strained to hear it, but movement had roused a sharp, all-too-familiar pain in his battered rib cage, and he found it difficult to concentrate. Hissing through clenched teeth, he reproached himself for his weakness.

*Someday I will be a warrior!* Warakan reminded himself sharply as he glared into the blinding-black interior. *Someday, no matter what Old One says, I will leave the dark deeps of this winter-cursed forest into which he and I have been forced to flee from our enemies. Someday I will turn my back to the rising sun and strike out for the*

*stronghold of those who have beaten me and scarred my
face. I will return their "gift" of pain. And I will bring to
them a gift of my own. Strong in the power of the sacred
stone talisman of the Ancient Ones I will bring it. With my
face and body painted with the blood of Life Giver, the
white mammoth that is totem of the People, I will bring it.
Wearing the skin of Yellow Wolf, the Red World shaman
who turned the hearts of all but Jhadel against me and
made my grandfather name me Outcast, I will bring it. I
will bring Death to all who are responsible for the slaughter of my father, grandfather, and sister!*

"Someday . . ." The whispered exhalation flowed
from Warakan's mouth like blood from a wound. He
pressed his lips together, deliberately stressing the
newly healed gash that ran from his upper lip into the
right nostril of his broken nose. This time when pain
flared, the boy welcomed it and named it Teacher. In a
world of warring tribes in which few boys lived to be
men, he knew he must learn from pain the most important lesson of a future warrior—how to command his
body to submit to the will of his mind.

Gritting his teeth against the hurt in his sides, he
reached forward and fumbled for his winter foot gear.
He could see nothing in the darkness, but he could hear
great tides of air surging and shifting restlessly beyond
the lodge as he realized the voice that wept in the wind
was silent now. Frustration pricked him. Soon the storm
would be over. Once North Wind went its way, only the
forces of Creation could say how long it would be before the spirit called to him again, if ever. And if, as he
feared, its cries warned of approaching danger, he
might be too late to take heed.

*Be it a spirit of the wind or, as Jhadel claims, only a
wounded wolf or lion or fang-toothed leaping cat, if a boy
can snare it, this Warakan will do even though the Old
One has forbidden it! I will go into the night. I will extend*

*our traplines. And if I catch it, be it beast or spirit, then will I know if I am right to fear it!*

Finger-fishing for thong laces, he located them, pulled the attached moccasins onto his lap, and reached forward again; this time his hands hunted the two long, thin, feather-stuffed buckskin liners that he would wrap around his feet and calves before pulling on the heavy, trisoled, knee-high moccasins Jhadel had fashioned for him from two thicknesses of smoked elk hide. Moments later, the insulating liners were in his hands and his feet were wrapped. He put the moccasins on, cross-lacing the thongs to prevent trespass by the carnivorous, toe-eating frost spirits he would surely encounter on his forbidden journey across the frozen land.

*As silently as Night Hawk winging across the face of Moon I must go,* he cautioned himself. *For if I wake Little Bear Brother, the cub will follow to ruin the hunt as he so often does, and if I wake Jhadel, he will never let me go. But if I do not, and the spirit is crying in the wind to warn us of . . .*

Unnerved, Warakan cut off the query before a full mental image of his fear took form. On a night like this, he had no way of knowing what invisible forces from the world beyond this one lurked in the dark, waiting to carry the careless words and thoughts of a fearful boy upon the wind to the forces of Creation.

Warakan attempted to swallow his rising apprehension as, slowly, making considerable effort to move without rustling the bedding, he stood erect. His cautiousness saved him from bumping the top of his head when it came into contact with one of the framing posts. In a burst of happy enthusiasm, he wondered whether he had grown taller since dusk; the realization that the lodge was once again sagging under the weight of new snow, only making him *seem* taller, left him momentarily dispirited.

A wolf began to howl in high, baleful dissonance. Warakan frowned as it occurred to him that old Jhadel could have been right when he credited spirit song to wolves. Warakan knew wolves when he heard them, and this one was close. Very close.

He tensed. Wolves were not the only carnivores hunting the winter woods in the vicinity of the lodge these days. He and Jhadel had found the spoor of wild dogs and of larger, more dangerous predators: a pair of good-sized lions, a leaping cat that favored its right hind limb, and before the first heavy snows a bear with paw prints broader than the width of the old man's shoulders.

Warakan's hands flexed at his sides. Somewhere within the lodge were his bone lances, gloves, and leggings, his luck-bringing golden eagle feather, the deerskin sack that held his extra spearheads, and the waterproof rawhide carrying bags within which he stored his fire-making supplies and sinew snare lines; he needed at least some of these things to set his traps, much less venture alone through the surrounding forest with any hope of safety on a trek that might take him more than a hand count of days if he went all the way to the gorge and back. But how, the boy pondered, was he going to retrieve his belongings without tripping over the scattered debris of everyday winter confinement that he and the old man had strewn haphazardly across the hide-covered floor?

*Carefully,* he thought as he swallowed hard and advanced slowly.

Determined not to wake Jhadel, Warakan did his best to recall where the little mounds of remnant marrow bones and splinters of half-worked stone tools and spearheads lay amidst cast-off clothing and piles of animal skins. His best was not good enough. The ball of his right foot came down on something unexpected, and before he could arrest his forward movement, the object rolled under the arch of his foot. He remembered too late the bear-bone lance he had been mending by the fire pit. An instant later it was under his heel. Taken off balance, he grabbed for thin air, found no purchase in it, and went sprawling.

Somewhere close by, the cub sighed and made low sounds of settling more deeply into slumber, but the loud smacking of seamless lips told Warakan that he had awakened Jhadel. Infinitely annoyed with himself, the boy lay on his belly, waiting for Old One to drift back into dreams. It was not to be.

"I will not allow you to go alone into the storm, Warakan." The shaman's voice was a phlegmy scrape in the darkness.

Disgusted, Warakan clambered to his knees. "Then come with me. The storm will soon be over."

"Will it?" The old man's question hung in the air, sharp as a double-edged stone lancet.

Warakan could feel Jhadel's eyes fixed on him, not in the way of a man trying to pierce the shroud of night but like a hunting animal that sees by dark as well as by day.

"Dawn will be long in coming, Warakan," Jhadel said. "Return to your sleeping place and to your dreams."

Warakan knew a command when he heard one; he also knew that he was not going to obey. Rising, he declared, "The lodge is again heavy with snow!" The statement came in a rush; there was no need to lie, not when he could mask deception with truth. "I must remove the added weight before the roof braces are overstressed. No need for you to be disturbed while I seek my gloves and scraper and—"

"And when you have done this, Warakan, what *else* will you seek?"

The boy knew that Jhadel had already unmasked his intended deception. He could hear movement in the lodge now, the sighings of bed furs and skin garments as Jhadel drew himself into a seated position and wrapped his bony, tattooed arms around his folded knees.

"There is a wolf singing in the forest," observed the Old One.

"I am not afraid of wolves."

Silence filled the space between them. Jhadel allowed it to settle before he said, "The wind blows from the north again tonight, from the cold heights of the high gorge, from the ruins of fallen lodges, and from the abandoned village where the bones of the dead follower of the Red World shaman, Yellow Wolf, lie beneath the shadow of the Watching Star." He paused. "That which you have heard crying in the wind will not easily be found, Warakan, nor will the snares of a mere boy confound it. You will *not* go into the storm in search of it."

Warakan's face expanded with resentment as he realized the old man had not only trespassed into his thoughts but must have been awake all along. Pain knifed across the boy's mouth, cheekbones, and the broken bridge of his nose, but this time when Warakan hissed air through his teeth, his uncontrolled reaction was not to pain; it was in open, angry defiance of Jhadel. "I *will* go!" His voice cracked with fear. The old dread was fully alive in him now, festering like an infected wound under the protective scab of his hard-won self-control. "The spirit calls to you, Jhadel! If you were not losing your powers, you would hear and answer!"

"A shaman does not respond to tricks of the wind."

"And if it is *more* than that?"

Again silence settled between them. Somehow it was darker than the interior of the shelter, heavier and more threatening than the weight of the latest accumulation of snow upon the lodge. At last Jhadel said calmly, in the way of an all-knowing, imperturbable seer, "No man may know the secrets of the wind, Warakan. Nothing under the black robe of Father Above is certain, but for now, as shaman, I tell you that we are safe here in this little lodge beyond the—"

"If you do not know the secrets of the wind, then you cannot know this!" The boy had not intended to shout. "What if the spirit is crying a warning to us, Jhadel? What if it is trying to tell us that those who have driven us beyond the edge of the world are still hunting us? They will find us if we stay in one place—that much *is* certain. And if the warriors of the People of the Watching Star find us, we will die—that too is certain. You are an old man, and it may well be that you are ready to die, but I am only a boy, and I am *not* ready! I will seek the secret of the wind! If the spirit *is* a spirit, and if it *is* warning us, then we must flee once more before the warriors of the Watching Star, for you are not fit to fight them, and I cannot win against them yet. Not until I am a man and a warrior and—"

"Old, am I? Lost my powers, have I?" Jhadel boomed in sudden anger. "The forces of Creation have placed you in my care, Warakan! To assure the continuance of your life, I have betrayed the will and confidence of my people! For your sake, I am named Enemy by those who would have taken your head and flayed the skin from your body even though you were one of us, a child born and consecrated to the Watching Star until the Four Winds swept you to a new loyalty and a new people among the warriors of the Land of Grass and—"

"I swept myself!" Warakan interrupted with hot belligerence. "The ways of our people were not my ways. I betrayed them with open eyes and a proud heart."

"Hmm. As have I. And so now, for your sake,

never again will there be a place of honor for Jhadel in the fire circles of those who once honored him above all others. Yet the sacrifice of this shaman of the People of the Watching Star has been well made, and not without purpose. Once the People were one, Warakan! The People of the Watching Star, the People of the Land of Grass, even the lizard-eating People of the Red World —all were of one tribe, one blood, one spirit. So it will be again. But not until we have found the shaman Yellow Wolf, who has stolen the sacred stone of the Ancient Ones and driven Life Giver, the white mammoth totem of the ancestors, beyond the edge of the world. To find that man, to seek that totem—this will be a lifetime quest. So I say this to you now, boy: The someday for which we *both* yearn is far from this moment. Go back to your sleeping place and to your dreams, Warakan, for as long as Jhadel lives, you will be many things, but you will *not* be a warrior!"

A tremor of indignation shook the boy, intensifying into pure righteous wrath. "Then *die*!" he shrieked. He was not struck by the full impact of his words until, impelled by fear-driven anger, he plunged recklessly from the dark confines of the lodge into the windswept vastness of the night.

He ran.

Without gloves or lances, with no thought of his luck-bringing eagle feather or the deerskin sack that held his extra spearheads or his rawhide bags, Warakan pounded forward into wind and darkness. Although the forest was thick around him, he had no trouble seeing his way. The snow-covered land and trees emanated a thin, cold light of their own, and North Wind had swept the sky free of clouds. The storm was indeed passing. Stars glinted through the wind-riled canopy of the forest like chips of ice sparkling in moonlight.

His forward progress slowed by dunes of crystal, Warakan looked up as he slogged northward into the wind. There was no moon. Now and then he caught glimpses of the vast, shimmering curve of the Sky River and knew that somewhere above the treetops, the Great Bear in the sky sprawled across the black robe of Father Above toward the group of stars his people called the Great Snake. And there, close to the head of the serpent, was the one star around which all the others turned—the Watcher, the North Star—and the boy cringed as he remembered, *All that is bad comes from the north . . . all that is dark and cold . . . all that has to do with death and danger.*

Warakan went deeper into that part of the forest from which the spirit had called. *If you are there, I will find you. I will make you speak. I* will *know why you weep and cry in the winter dark!*

Emboldened by resolve, he lengthened his stride, the skin of the great she-bear keeping him warm. Although he missed his luck-bringing eagle feather, Warakan found that just thinking of it gave him courage. It had come to him as a gift from the sky spirits on the day of his grandfather's death, as though Shateh himself had come to strengthen and affirm a relationship that could not die. The golden eagle was solar, Brother of the Sun, mediator between earth and sky, his grandfather's helping animal spirit. And now—along with the spirit of the great she-bear—his.

He went on under the winter stars, refusing to allow himself to be afraid. Now and then he heard the long, threnodic call of a wolf, and twice he crossed starlit tracks that told him the beast was running just ahead. After a while he could no longer see the animal's footprints, nor hear its song in the forest, yet Warakan *was* afraid. Try as he might, he could not forget the words he had spoken against the old man. They circled in his brain like riled pack dogs, biting and nipping at his conscience with every step and rasp of breath.

*Then die! Die! Die! Die!*

"No!" he cried, stopping in his tracks, staring into the wind at the sky. "May the Four Winds and all of the forces of Creation behold and heed this boy. Warakan takes back his words against Jhadel. May that old shaman live as long as the mountains, and may he never hear a hostile word from Warakan again!"

He ran, darting between trees, closely watching where he stepped in the new snow. He leapfrogged over fallen branches, around and over scrub growth and boulders that might snare a carelessly placed foot. Was it possible to take back an utterance once it was loosed to run free upon the wind? Jhadel had warned that this was not so easily done. And had he not heard the old women of his boyhood village say that careless words and unjust curses could circle around like tail-chasing foxes to bite the tongue of the one from whose mouth they had sprung? Guilt stabbed him. He regretted his words against Jhadel but not his disobedience of the old man. *If our enemies are out there, I must know. I will not let them come upon us unaware!*

He was moving uphill, slipping occasionally on wide sections of wind-exposed ice and now and then going to his knees in shoals of soft powder. Rubbing and blowing on his hands to keep them warm, he was soon breathing hard from the exertion of his run. He longed for his gloves and willow-framed, sinew-webbed snow walkers, but he could not return to the lodge for them. *Not until I have found some sign of the spirit will I return. Not until I know if it is real and am certain that it is not warning of approaching warriors of the . . .*

His thoughts ebbed. Something strange was happening all around him. Slowly he realized that the snow beneath his feet had turned red. Amazed and puzzled,

the boy stopped again, stared down, then found his gaze
drawn upward. His breath snagged in his throat. The
sky was afire! Vast, throbbing rivers of red light were
undulating above the trees, drowning the stars. And in
this livid auroral glow, the world was the color of blood.

"The Northern Dancers!" Warakan exclaimed, all
at once confused and frightened by a phenomenon that
he had heard of but never seen. His eyes widened as he
recalled ancient tales and portents. What was it that he
had heard the old ones say long ago in the days before
the great raid that had devastated his boyhood village
and made orphans of him and his half-sister? *When the
Northern Dancers turn the sky to flame, then there will be
a great wind, the wind of war that brings Death to the
People!*

"Aiee!" Warakan turned and started back toward
the lodge, certain that all of his fears were about to be
realized. *I must warn Jhadel! I must . . .* He paused in
midstep, surprised to find that his mad race through the
night had brought him into an unfamiliar part of the
forest and that, only partially visible under a layer of
fresh powder, the tracks of some sort of large animal lay
at his feet. Elongated, distorted in shape, they were
made by no beast that Warakan had ever seen. Flustered and afraid, he turned to his right, then to his left,
all the while straining to pick up familiar landmarks;
there were none that snow had not conspired to hide
from his view.

Then, as he stared ahead, Warakan saw something
big and furred hulking away into the trees. The thing
was clothed in tattered mists, and for an instant, just
before it disappeared into the woods, it looked back at
him over the curve of a hairy shoulder, and the boy saw
the hideous, half-human, half-animal face of the spirit
of the wind! It vanished as suddenly as it had appeared,
and as Warakan stood transfixed and terrified, he knew

that the thing had been wailing in the wind not to warn him of danger approaching from the north, but to lure him into a confrontation with his worst nightmare.

In body paint and war feathers, with their ankle-length hair loosened for battle and streaming in the wind, the tall, tattooed warriors of the People of the Watching Star were advancing toward him through the trees into which the wind spirit had just fled. With their war dogs in full battle array at their sides, they menaced him with massive spears and leered with deadly intent while their gaunt, silent, hollow-eyed priestess walked before them under the burning sky.

Warakan attempted to turn, to run, to at least raise a warning to Jhadel, but he was frozen in place, a dumb-struck hostage to the terror of the moment, and of the past.

He saw himself a captive once again. Beaten and cowering within the vast, firelit cavern that was the stronghold of the People of the Watching Star, Warakan saw the priestess approaching with her many warriors and attack dogs at her heels. Clad in a cape fashioned from the skin of his slain sister, with a ceremonial collar of human hair and finger bones around her neck, her face was that of a slant-eyed weasel. She clutched a fat-faced, greasy-skinned, gluttonous infant close to her bare breasts. Her skin reeked of putrid milk and the foul-smelling oil extracted from crushed female sex glands cut from the same wolves whose matched skins garbed her skeletal flanks. She was holding a dagger outward toward him, the length of the blade laid flat across the tattooed palm of her bloodied hand.

Warakan's eyes fastened on the blade. He could not look away. He knew this knife; he had seen the long, sleek, exquisitely carved span of mammoth bone pierce and flay his sister and other captives during ritual devotions from which he had once believed himself exempt. But he was not exempt. He knew that now as surely as he knew that the knife in the hand of the priestess was named Death, and that he was about to be opened and skinned by it.

"Warakan!"

The boy winced at the sound of his name. Had *she* spoken? Had *they* spoken? Was the spirit of the wind calling his name? He could not say. Nor would he wait to find out. Commanding his body as well as his mind to submit to his will, Warakan whirled around and broke for the nearby cover of a thick, snow-weighted stand of mixed evergreens and hardwoods.

Bending low, he ran wildly, circling back through the trees, heading toward what he hoped was the lodge. Perhaps the enemies had not yet found the little shelter and fallen upon Jhadel; perhaps there was yet a chance of warning the old shaman, of bringing him and the sleeping cub to safety. Warakan's gut constricted as he ran on. If they could not wake the cub, how could they carry it? At nearly twelve moons of age, "Little" Bear Brother outweighed them both.

*Ah, Old One, the spirit of the wind is real! And for all our sakes you should have listened to the fears of this boy!* Suddenly his thoughts scattered like rabbits fleeing the flare of torchlight.

One moment the boy was racing across solid snowpack, the next he was cresting what appeared to be the broad, flat top of one of many snow-mantled boulders that lay here and there within the forest as though placed by the hand of some great giant, who had left them behind to mark his trail. Warakan leaped up and out, expecting an easy vault of a few feet before landing on the other side, but to his shock there was nothing there. The boulder was a sheer-faced monolith, and his leap took him straight over its topmost edge into thin air. Too horrified to scream, he fell, instinctively flapping his arms like wings as though they might bear him away from what seemed certain catastrophe.

His effort was valiant but in vain. Warakan landed on both feet midway down a steep incline of wind-channeled new snow that cushioned the impact of his fall. His limbs automatically flexed to distribute his weight, and for an instant he was certain he was going to walk away from the incident unscathed. But when he tried, his leading moccasin sank through fresh powder, penetrated a subsurface encrustation of ice, and plunged straight downward into a boy-eating drift.

Before he could stop it from happening, Warakan's body followed his leg into an immensity of cold, suffocating whiteness. Stunned, buried alive, he flailed wide, twisted hard to his right and left. Once, in another world it seemed, he had been buried in snow—an unproven boy made to lie naked and flat on his back in a snow pit with a breathing reed his only link to air and life; it had been a test of courage and endurance for one who had presumed to go forth with the other boys of his adopted band to hunt and kill his first bear.

*"If you would take on the power of Walks Like a Man, you must become a bear. You must go into the earth. You must fast. You must dream. You must endure the cold embrace of the winter womb of Mother Below before you come forth reborn."*

The words of a long-dead elder seemed as clear to Warakan now as they had then. And now, as then, the boy found strength in them. His bare hands cleared a breathing passage for his face as he burrowed upward, cursing the invisible frost spirits that bit into his fingers, all the while reminding himself that he had survived his ordeal in the snow pit. Naked, without gloves or moccasins or so much as a loin cover to protect his precious male member, he had survived. And he had come away intact from his ordeal! Against appalling odds, he had

killed the great she-bear whose warm, thick hide now
kept his body from succumbing to the freezing embrace
of the killing-cold snow. Warakan thanked the spirit of
the slain bear. Her death had given him life many times.

"Be with me now, Great Spirit Bear!" he implored,
clenching his teeth to prevent snow from invading his
mouth. "Remember that, although this boy has killed
you, he has honored your flesh and meat and bones and
hide and has become Boy Mother of Bear for the sake
of your cub. Grant to Warakan your strength to escape
this snowdrift, Great Mother of Many Bears, because
the spirit of the wind has sent the enemies of Warakan
over the edge of the world to kill him! I must warn the
Old One and your child, or surely they will also be
killed!"

Warakan felt a rush of wind move over the up-
wardly questing fingers of his left hand. His flesh
burned with the contact, and he suspected that his fingers were shredded; he did not care. He had penetrated
the surface of the drift! Overwhelmed by gratitude, he
was certain the spirit of the slain she-bear had answered
his prayer. In a moment he would be on his way to the
lodge again! In a moment he would be running beneath
the burning sky behind the ranks of his enemies to warn
Jhadel of impending danger! In a moment he and the
Old One would find a way to rouse the sleeping cub—
even if they had to jab a stone awl up its backside!

A wave of almost euphoric relief swept through
Warakan. Taken off guard by its sweetness, he sighed.
This was a mistake. With the intake of breath came an
invasion of snow that seared his nasal passages and
shocked his lungs. He gasped, choked, fought to
breathe again, but his lungs refused to function. On the
verge of fainting for want of air, he forced his right arm
upward and, desperate now, pushed with his legs, willed
himself to "swim" upward through snow as he had often

seen river otters rise to the surface of many a deep, clear streamside pool. Then, just when he knew that he was about to succeed, the grip of strong, hard hands closed on his wrists.

This time when Warakan gasped, his intake of breath had nothing to do with relief; it was drawn in response to pure terror.

Someone had taken hold of him.

Someone was lifting him from the snow with strong, hard, bone-crushing hands.

Choking and sputtering, he was pulled through the top of the drift into the red glow of the burning night sky. He screamed, or tried to. His cold-shocked lungs would not allow him enough air to expel the sound. Hoisted high, with all his oxygen-starved senses imploding toward delirium, Warakan felt as helpless as a small animal drawn from a snare by its forelimbs. He was in the grasp of his enemies, and there was nothing he could do about it. The warriors of the People of the Watching Star would kill him now; indeed, killing was the least they would do to a boy who had been born of their blood but had betrayed them twice. Memories flared, of other deaths, of his sister, Neea, flayed and dismembered and . . .

Warakan sobbed. He was grateful when unconsciousness claimed him.

"Warakan, awake!"

The boy opened his eyes, amazed to find himself alive. But he was not at all sure that he should be glad of his condition. Someone was standing over him, a masculine form visible only in silhouette, a dark, hulking storm cloud of a man wearing heavy furs and holding a spear upright against the burning sky.

Suddenly, although the figure remained motionless above the boy, something of enormous weight pounced on Warakan's chest. He shrieked against pain and fright as he felt paws all over him. The wide, warm snout of an animal rooted hurtfully at his face and neck. Then he felt teeth slip against the line of his jaw. Large teeth. Sharp, fanglike canines at least twice the length of his thumbs.

A mind-wrenching horror overcame Warakan. The fur-clad man must be a warrior of the Watching Star, for he had loosed a war dog on his hapless victim. And this was surely the largest of its pack, the biggest, heaviest dog in all this world and the world beyond! Instinctively, the boy assumed a defensive posture, forced himself to lie rigid as a corpse, closed his eyes, held his breath, and made no movement that might rouse the beast to intensify its attack. As the animal sniffed and slobbered over him, Warakan wondered what kept it from the kill. Perhaps it waited for the rest of its pack. He had no doubt in his mind that this was how his enemies intended to finish his life, for among the People of the Watching Star there was no greater way to dishonor a captive than to turn the dogs on him, and then mock his weakness as he screamed for mercy while being torn to pieces and devoured alive.

Anger replaced horror within Warakan. *I am not a man. I am only a boy! But I will not beg. And I will not scream again. I am Warakan, grandson of Shateh and son of Masau! Their life spirits live on in me! Although Jhadel has sworn that it will not be so, Warakan will be a warrior. Fighting his enemies to the end, Warakan will go boldly to his death! Or perhaps . . . may yet escape?*

The latter premise set Warakan's mind and blood aboil with desperation. He arched his slender torso violently upward beneath the body of the dog. Grabbing fistfuls of the animal's wide furry face and twisting hard, he shoved the beast's head upward with all of his strength and shouted, "Away, Dog of the Watching

Star! Away, I say! Warakan knows no fear of you! If you would eat of this boy, know that his bones will pierce your innards, and by his death you, too, will die and—"

His words were cut short when the animal loosed a bellowing, thoroughly undoglike roar. A moment later, with the boy still clinging to its face, the beast stood erect. It arched its back and roared again. Then it shook its head so violently that, for the second time this night, Warakan found himself flying through air, this time landing not on his feet but hard on his buttocks. Splay-legged and stunned, he stared back at the riled form of an animal that did not, from his new perspective, in any way resemble a dog.

"Little Bear Brother?" Warakan could not believe his eyes. Nevertheless, distance and the glow of the red sky gave him a clear and indisputable view of the year-ling cub. It was standing upright between the trees, paw-ing pathetically at its abused face and bawling like a confused, mistreated human child.

"Arise, great warrior who flees from shadows and cannot tell a bear from a dog!" The voice of the man was a low, contemptuous scrape of sound as he stepped into Warakan's line of vision, jammed the butt end of his spear into the snow, and with a gloved hand drew back a face-concealing cowl of dark fur.

"Jhadel!" The boy nearly swooned. Old Wise One was an amazing sight in any light; in the red glow of the aurora his unexpected presence was positively intimi-dating. His small, squinting round eyes, placed close on either side of a massive beak of a nose, fixed Warakan like those of an appraising condor. With his pale, thin-ning hair free of the browband of raven's feathers that usually held the strands close to his head, his prominent skull, set on a long neck that seemed far too thin to support its burden of skin and bone and muscle and brain, appeared larger than usual. It swayed back and forth in the manner of a predatory bird sighting for prey. His entire face—including his ears, eyelids, lips, and the hulking massif of his nose—had been tattooed a solid black.

"I told you that I would not allow you to go alone into the storm, Warakan," reminded Jhadel.

The boy was all at once relieved, incredulous, and monumentally embarrassed as he realized that it had been Wise One, and not a warrior of the Watching Star, who had rescued him. Then gratitude flooded him. "You have driven them away! How? By what magic, Jhadel, have you made them—"

"Of whom do you speak, boy?"

*"Them!"* Warakan revealed in a frightened whisper as, scrambling to his feet, he pointed off. "There, above and beyond the tall boulder. Before I fell I saw the spirit of the wind and the ones whom the spirit has been summoning against us—warriors of the People of the Watching Star! They called my name and chased me with their spears and dogs. We must flee now, before they return with their cursed priestess and—"

"We are alone in this forbidden part of the forest, Warakan." Jhadel growled, as was his way when vexed. "It was I who called your name. It was I who pulled you from the snow into which you leaped like a panicked rabbit."

Warakan rubbed his bruised wrists. "But you are old, no longer strong, no longer—"

"Fit to fight my enemies? Hmm. There are many ways of besting an enemy, Warakan. And I am strong enough to dog your heels and heft you from a snowdrift, pup that you are. In this place of death it is no wonder that you have seen manifestations of your fear. Come! Let us be gone from here before the spirit of the abandoned dead follower of Yellow Wolf rises up in anger at our presence in this place where his bones were left to look upon the sky forever."

For the first time Warakan recognized his surroundings. He looked around, aghast. His race through the forest had brought him into the larger of the two small abandoned villages that he and Jhadel had encountered on their journey eastward. Snow softened the contours of the lodge frames and small, open-ended structures of poles and branches beneath which lay the charred skeletal remains of a one-armed man. The boy shuddered. The dead man was no stranger to him. The one-armed skeleton could only have been that of the young man Gah-ti, son of Kosar-eh of the Red World. Warakan had known him well. Indeed, he had known all of the followers of the Red World shaman Yellow Wolf and for a brief time had lived among them when they had shared the hunting camps of Shateh, his grandfather.

Now, under the burning sky, the place of the abandoned dead man seemed awash in blood as memories brought images of familiar faces rising from the past—laughing children, handsome women, strong men and youths anxious to learn new ways, a bright-eyed, impetuous little girl-of-a-woman who named the shaman My Man, and the shaman himself, Yellow Wolf, called Chakwena by the Red World people, Trickster by his enemies—young, clever, as wary-eyed as a captive coyote, and as dangerous.

The old man was growling again, this time less with annoyance than nervousness as he turned his face upward. "I have not seen such a sky since . . ." He paused, stared long and thoughtfully at the aurora, then looked down at Warakan. "The omens *are* troubling. You have *not* been wrong to fear them. Come. We cannot stay in this place. I have brought your gloves and snow walkers. The red glow of the campfires of the

Northern Dancers will light our way as we follow Little
Bear Brother back to our shelter."

"But the spirit, the voice in the wind?" Distracted,
Warakan saw that the cub was indeed ambling off
through the trees, still bawling and muttering unhappily
as it headed back toward the lodge and its nest by the
fire pit.

"The cub tells us what we must do," the old man
observed. "And you must learn to use fear wisely, boy,
or it will continue to drive you unthinking into snowdrifts, rather than guide you safely away from them.
You have roused your child from his winter sleep un-
necessarily. White Giant Winter still roams the world.
In the distant hunting grounds of our enemies it is the
time when jackrabbits whistle songs of hunger to the
Starving Moon. It is the time of deep snow and short
days, a time of freezing wind and wailing spirits. Those
whom you fear *cannot* follow us now, Warakan. They
too must endure the passage of White Giant Winter.
We are safe from them, for we have fled far beyond the
very edge of the world."

Unconvinced, Warakan scanned the abandoned village of the People of the Red World shaman. "Yellow
Wolf was not afraid to come here with his followers.
After betraying all who trusted him, after luring my
grandfather and his people into the country of their enemies and setting the tribes to war once again, he came
as surely as those whom he has betrayed will follow
him."

"All men seek the power of the sacred stone,"
Jhadel conceded. "Without it, no tribe can long be victorious in war. All hunt the white mammoth; when it is
slain, those who eat of its flesh and drink of its blood
will take its life-sustaining power into themselves and
live forever."

"Yet when we sighted what was left of this Red

World band traveling westward out of the forest several moons ago, Yellow Wolf and the mammoth were not with them. The followers of the Red World shaman follow him and the totem no more. Why is this, Jhadel?"

"I have told you before, Warakan—no man may know the secrets of the wind! But I can assure you that if the onetime followers of Yellow Wolf have strayed into the winter hunting grounds of warring tribes with neither shaman, totem, nor sacred stone to protect them, then perhaps the spirit you have heard crying in the wind weeps for them, for only the forces of Creation can say what will befall them."

Warakan frowned. Again he thought of familiar faces. Aside from Yellow Wolf and his little girl-of-a-woman, Mah-ree, they had been a good and caring people. Now, as the boy stared at the snow-mantled shelter within which the charred bones of their dead had been arrayed with infinite care, he remembered the shaman's woman, Mah-ree, and his thoughts gentled. For all her troublemaking ways, hers had been a kind and caring spirit—and a pretty one, too. Cha-kwena had not deserved such a woman. Had Yellow Wolf betrayed her and abandoned the one-armed man as he had abandoned and betrayed all who had ever trusted him? Warakan's frown deepened, and with a start he noticed that the bones lay free of snow and undisturbed by predators. How could this be? Unless someone—or something—were guarding them. The premise seemed ridiculous until, shivering with revulsion and dread, he thought of the thing of mist and fur that had disappeared into the trees.

"Come, Warakan!" Jhadel's command broke the boy's concentration. "The wind rises from the north again, and we have far to travel before we can rest safely."

Warakan was surprised when the old man deposited his gloves and snow walkers at his feet before turning away to stride off after the cub. The boy's eyes widened. The light of the red sky was pooling in the footprints of both man and bear—as though they left behind a trail of blood. He caught his breath at the horror of the omen and hurriedly pulled on his gloves, then knelt to lace on his snow walkers, thinking: *The spirit of the wind is real. With my own eyes I have seen it. We* are *in danger in this place. But I will come back. I will set my traps, and if the forces of Creation have not abandoned this boy and his shaman, Jhadel will soon know and see the truth!*

The wind *was* rising again, and the air had turned bitterly cold. Warakan looked up. Above the bent and broken canopy of the storm-exhausted forest, the night sky was beginning to fade toward dawn. But as Warakan rose, he could see that the Great Bear still stretched its star paws toward the Great Snake. Close to the head of the serpent, the North Star stared down at him—the Watching Star, the one star around which all the others turned and beneath whose shadow his enemies had always grown strong.

*All that is bad comes from the north . . . all that is dark and cold . . . all that has to do with danger and death.*

The words were unwelcome hauntings, and Warakan, alone in the abandoned village of the dead, had no desire to deal with them. As he hurried after Jhadel and the cub, the boy turned his face to the rising sun. Someday those whom he feared would come over the edge of the world for him; he had no doubt of that. But the spirit that had drawn him from his dreams was silent now. Perhaps Jhadel was right. Perhaps it wept for others now. In any event, there was nothing he could do to help them. Someday was far away, and for now, at least, Warakan was glad.

# PART I

$\blacklozenge\!\!-\!\!\!-\!\!\!-\!\!\!-\!\!\!-\!\!\!-\!\!\blacklozenge$

# NORTH WIND

$\blacklozenge\!\!-\!\!\!-\!\!\!-\!\!\!-\!\!\!-\!\!\!-\!\!\blacklozenge$

"He ascended by himself, he went of his own
free will to where he was to die."

—*The Florentine Codex*
by Fray Bernardino de Sahagun

# 1

Sunrise at last

The big man stared eastward across the snow-whitened badlands. The wind was down. Last night's unexpected storm had blown away to the east. Kosar-eh was relieved to find the sky free of clouds, but he was troubled as he stood watching the sun rise over faraway hills. The eye of Father Above appeared huge, swollen, and as darkly veined as the belly of a woman about to give birth. Kosar-eh's broad, painted face tightened within his hood of thickly furred badger skins. He was a man who no longer believed in omens, but he did not like the look of this morning's sun. There was something obscene and unnatural about it.

"Kho-neh! Kiu-neh!" He spoke to a nearby brown hillock of curly-haired bison hide beneath which two of his young sons were still sleeping. "Awake! We must be on our way back to the encampment. We have been too long away. Our women, your brother Ka-neh, and the little ones will be worrying."

The hillock moved. A single black-haired head peered up, squinted toward the sun, and made a face of strained forbearance before ducking away to join his younger brother beneath the bison robe. "Let us sleep a

while longer, my father." The boy yawned from underneath the hide. "The others know that we are safe with
you, Man Who Spits in the Face of Enemies."

"But who, save your brother Ka-neh, will keep
*them* safe while we are away, eh, Kiu-neh?" Kosar-eh
responded darkly, thinking of the thirteen-year-old he
had left behind to look after the others. Ka-neh was
bold and eager to assume the responsibilities of manhood, but he was still an untested youth.

A lion roared somewhere to the south, a sound
that Kosar-eh found profoundly unsettling. His gloved
right hand flexed around the feather-adorned shaft of
his spear. Ten-year-old Kiu-neh's use of his battle name
had focused his worry. He was, indeed, Man Who Spits
in the Face of Enemies, a bold and proven warrior
among the ever-battling northern tribes, but he was not
of their lineage. Many a long summer ago war raids had
brought Kosar-eh, along with a good-sized band of Red
World people, north from his village by the Lake of
Many Singing Birds. It had been his hope to become a
fighting man of the plains until misplaced loyalty to a
shaman kinsman had set Kosar-eh of the People of the
Red World forever apart from hard-won allies and hunt
brothers among the People of the Land of Grass, as
well as from the main body of his native band, and his
age-old enemies, the People of the Watching Star. And
so the big man wintered alone with the few surviving
members of his family in the desolation of these badlands, grateful for the solitude of broad, lonely hills and
uninhabited valleys. He doubted if there was now a man
among either of the great northern tribes who would
not kill him and enslave his tiny Red World band on
sight.

*Where are my enemies now?*

The unspoken question sent a wave of apprehension advancing like a column of stinging ants across

Kosar-eh's back, along his arms, and beneath his scalp. Working his shoulders to calm his nerves, he told himself that he was being foolish. His enemies were not in this land. He turned from the rising sun to stare westward. The mountains there had been hidden under a hulking cloud cover for most of the last two moons during which his little band had been hunting its way steadily homeward—until White Giant Winter had forced them to settle in their latest and least satisfactory winter camp. Kosar-eh speculatively arched his brow as he observed the immense range of white, shouldering ridges and soaring, glacier-ridden massifs. So much snow! It hurt his eyes to look at it, yet he kept on staring, realizing that he had indeed come far, for the nearest peaks loomed much closer than he would have thought possible. Stark, white, and gleaming sharply in the light of dawn, the crenellated summits made him think of teeth jutting from the lower jawbone of some long-dead carnivore.

He frowned; the comparison depressed him. The land of his ancestors lay beyond the most distant range. *Far* beyond, in another world it seemed. And between that country and the badlands stretched the vast high hunting grounds of his enemies. Again he wondered where they were: the victors and vanquished in the last great war between the tribes; his onetime friends among the victorious clansmen of the magnificent Shateh, high chief of the People of the Land of Grass; and the tattooed terrors known as the People of the Watching Star, whose warriors had come howling out of hidden mountain strongholds to slaughter and enslave the sons and daughters of lesser tribes—until they themselves were at last slaughtered and enslaved, their once multitudinous ranks broken and scattered like so much dust before the wind.

Kosar-eh's brow worked with further speculation.

He had seen no sign of either tribe since breaking company with his shaman and leading his band homeward out of the eastern forests. Logic told him that Shateh must have taken down his lodges and returned with his many followers through the mountains to the rich, golden grasslands of the chieftain's northern ancestors; this was what Kosar-eh would have done had the choice been his to make. No country had pleased him more than those broad, high, perpetually wind-combed plains of sweet grass and good hunting that would now and forever be a province of his enemies. As for the remnant bands of the People of the Watching Star, he saw no threat in them now; devastated by war and decimated by the many sanguinary raids Shateh had continued to conduct against them long after the last great battle of the war was over, the survivors among the People of the Watching Star were most likely hiding in small packs among the distant ranges, licking their wounds like the dogs they were.

Kosar-eh's thoughts should have soothed him. They did not. Far from the warmth of his lodge, he listened to the roaring of the lion. As the only adult male in a band composed of a handful of females, children, and a single adolescent, he knew that he faced dangers apart from those posed by vanished enemies.

His gut tightened; the ants were marching beneath his skin again. If anything were to happen to him, what would happen to his band? The answer was painfully obvious, as was his following concession: His loved ones' only hope of long-term survival lay far to the southwest in the parched Red World of their ancestors, where men spurned the ways of war and aged happily with their women, content to pass their days in endless pursuit of seeds and grubs and dry-land berries, and of every imaginable species of reptile and rodent that formed the bulk of their miserable diet.

Kosar-eh grimaced. The ways of his native tribesmen had long revolted him. It had been a good day when he determined to leave his homeland forever.

His fingertips sought old hunt and battle scars at his mouth and brow, then traced the layer of chalk-matted greasepaint that marked him as a warrior: three angled lines, one black, one white, the other grass gold, forming a single broad stripe that crossed his face from right temple to left jaw. The pattern and colors—uniquely his own—adorned his spear and blazoned across the knee-length winter hunt shirt of camel skin, which he wore with the hair side in for extra warmth. Now, with the lion still roaring, they emboldened his spirit.

Kosar-eh glared at the mountains. When the Warm Moon rose and great bears crawled from their dens, when the sky darkened with waterfowl returning from their wintering grounds, then he too would respond to the coming of spring. He would cross the mountains. He would take his followers to warmth and safety in the country of their peace-loving tribesmen. He would find his way across the land of his enemies without being discovered or threatened by them. This he *would* do. But for now spring was far away, and Kosar-eh—whose Red World name, Clown Man, revealed the position that circumstances beyond his control had once forced upon him within his native band—was still a warrior.

*Let the lion roar!* His thoughts were pure defiance. *Man Who Spits in the Face of Enemies is not afraid. He has slain the lion kind before. And will gladly do so again!*

The big man's dark, angular eyes narrowed as unwelcome memories flared behind his lids. Memories of a labyrinthine cavern within a mountain valley where a sacred white mammoth had gone to die, and where warriors of opposing tribes had done final battle. Memories of Gah-ti, his disobedient firstborn son recklessly tracking and cornering a cave lion in firelit darkness. Memories of blood, of a cherished youth forever maimed . . .

Kosar-eh could not bear further retrospection. The cavern in the mountain valley had long since been abandoned. The cave lion was dead, as was his son. And now the wind was rising again, gusting out of the south, carrying and intensifying the soundings of the lion. Again his gut tightened, this time in response to the deep, hollow reverberation that he knew could only be coming from the massive chest cavity of a large male. Clearly, the animal was speaking of hunger.

Kosar-eh frowned. The rising wind and roaring beast reminded him that, warrior though he was, when the voice of the lion was heard in the land, a solitary hunter far from his encampment with two young boys in his care would indeed be a foolish clown if he failed to remember that he was potential meat, as were his sons.

"Up!" Kosar-eh commanded his boys. Suddenly restless almost beyond bearing, he turned to observe the taut, white folds of surrounding hills that told him he was nearly a full day's walk from his band's hidden encampment. He shook his head, regretting having been forced by a prolonged scarcity of game to travel so far across open country in search of fresh meat; nevertheless, the risk had been well worth it.

He turned his gaze to a nearby mound of snow beneath which the unbutchered carcasses of a large pronghorn antelope, several hares, rabbits, and nearly a full double-hand count of grouse lay buried. In the pale glow of the rising sun, the cache glistened a watery yellow, but the color was not caused solely by reflected sun glow. The previous night, before welcoming his sons under the impromptu tent he had contrived of his weatherproof bison-hide robe, Kosar-eh had joined them in urinating upon the snow-covered cache.

His restlessness eased a little as he resisted a smile

at the memory. With the storm blowing hard and erratically at their backs, he had shown his boys how to spray
downwind in such a way as to create a veneer of encap-
sulating ice over the snow mound; once this was down
and frozen, the death scent of the buried game was effectively trapped within. The boys, swell-headed after a
day of hunting that had won them a full stringer of
grouse and rabbits each, had found the lesson amusing.
They insisted upon making a game of it, until to their
dismay both had learned that pissing with any accuracy
in a gusting, subfreezing wind could be as much of an
art as setting snares for small game, stalking a pronghorn, or striking a usable flake for a spearhead from a
stone core. Kosar-eh allowed himself the smile. Kiu noh
and Kho-neh would soon suffer for their flippant approach to learning with scoldings and laughter at their
expense when those in the communal family lodge
caught "wind" of them at their return. In the meantime,
he was satisfied that they had learned the main lesson
well; no predators had been drawn to last night's hunt
camp by the blood scent of a poorly made cache of
meat.

Kosar-eh's smile expanded with pleased satisfaction as, with a start, he noticed that the lion had
stopped roaring. The welcome silence lifted his spirits.
He was also relieved to see that the sun was assuming
its normal size and appearance. Well above the horizon
now, it shone forth in an unblemished sky that seemed
to promise a clear day ahead.

"Up, boys!" the big man commanded again, eager
for them to be on their way. Tonight those who looked
to Man Who Spits in the Face of Enemies for sustenance would feast for the first time in nearly a moon.
Tonight two of his sons would be feted within the communal family lodge as bringers of meat, and young
Ka-neh would be congratulated for boldly serving as

protector of his band in his father's absence. And tonight when the boiling bags were drained, and the best of the marrow bones were picked clean, and well-banked coals collapsed into ashes within the central fire pit, Kosar-eh would rest content when the eyes of Tamaya, his beautiful beloved, looked upon him with love and pride as she opened her body to his and invited him to enter.

*Ta-maya!* Her name was warm and sweet as sunlight to him. *Most Favored Daughter of Tlana-quah of the village by the Lake of Many Singing Birds. Ta-maya! Most Beautiful Beloved Woman.* Many a warrior and hunt chief had fought to possess her. Dakan-eh, Bold Man of the Red World, had wanted her. Masau, Mystic Warrior of the People of the Watching Star, had taken her. Shateh, hunt chief and shaman of the People of the Land of Grass, had claimed her and made her his own. But when at last the days and nights of war had ended, she had come to Man Who Spits in the Face of Enemies —*chosen* him to be her man above all others. And Shateh had let her go.

Kosar-eh's heart quickened with gratitude to the chieftain, who had since become his enemy, and with love for his woman. His man bone hardened at the thought of coupling with her again, for although Tamaya lay warm and loving in his arms each night, they had not mated since leaving the eastern forest.

The big man's mood shifted. Darkened. For more than two moons he had denied himself the pleasures of his woman while he mourned the death of Gah-ti, the cherished son who had survived the loss of his arm only to succumb to the fever spirits that preyed upon his band within the dark forest—the forest into which their shaman had led them with false promises of a better life. Ta-maya had mourned with him, not only for Gah-ti, but for Ha-xa-ree, their newborn daughter, and for little Piku-neh, the only surviving member of old Grandmother Kahm-ree's family. Neither shaman, nor totem, nor the reputed power of the sacred stone had been able to save these precious loved ones or ease the grief of those who survived them. Kosar-eh tensed with the memory of the roaring, shaking earth, the steaming, foul-smelling springs, and the great trees that had fallen upon his lodge to crush the life out of his infant and shatter the arm of his beautiful beloved.

And now Ta-maya awaited his return in a distant, hungry camp with only addle-witted old Kahm-ree, middle-aged U-wa, and Ka-neh, a boy of thirteen summers, to guard her and the children against such predators as that which had been roaring in the southern hills. He contemplated the distance that lay between him and his band and gauged it to be much greater than he would have preferred.

He was suddenly overcome by anger as his eyes fixed on the bison-hide hillock. It had not moved. His boys continued to disobey him.

"Up, I say!" Kosar-eh's voice seemed an echo of the lion's as he took hold of the bison hide and with one strong yank exposed to the light of morning two prone, fully clad boys, a collection of spears, and three neatly rolled traveling packs. "Kiu-neh and Kho-neh, Third Son and Fourth Son of Kosar-eh, this man will return to his women and children. With or without disobedient sons he will go! And he will go *now*! Stay! Sleep! If Lion comes for you, it is not likely that he will wish to feed on such lazy boys as Man Who Spits in the Face of Enemies will gladly leave behind him now!"

The boys were visibly startled by the insult but did not seem to take seriously his threat of abandonment until, without further words or so much as a glance in their direction, Kosar-eh upended the wooden sled that had served as a windbreak during the night, kicked it free of snow, and set it purposefully on its runners. A moment later he was using the butt end of his spear to crack open the frozen shell of the cache. When he began to toss stringers of rigid rabbits and grouse randomly about with no apparent intention of loading them onto the sled for transport, the amazed boys scrambled to their feet as one.

"We have killed that meat!" Kiu-neh protested.

"As you see, I will not take it from you," Kosar-eh responded with a coldness he did not feel.

"B-but you cannot just leave our kills here!" Kho-neh stammered, as was his way when nervous or upset.

"Would you presume to tell this warrior what he may or may not do, Fourth Son?" Kosar-eh snarled at his seven-year-old like a riled cougar, then declared contemptuously to both boys, "And to think that Man Who Spits in the Face of Enemies thought you old and bold enough to hunt at his side. Ha! Look at you—a pair of infants bawling for your mother's teats! Your father will not carry your kills for you!"

Hard words. And effective. Already dressed for traveling, the boys exchanged stunned and troubled looks, then hurriedly reached for the hooded fur robes upon which they had been lying. By the time the garments were on, Kosar-eh was successfully maneuvering the dead pronghorn from the cache. From the corner of his eye, he saw the twosome scramble for the snow walkers that had been placed upright in a nearby drift the previous night. Nervously fumbling with lacings that were pliable only because Kosar-eh had insisted that the thong ties be disengaged from the webbing and kept warm beneath the boys' doeskin undershirts while they slept, Kiu-neh and Kho-neh strapped on their snow-shoes, while their father deposited the antelope on the sled along with a stringer of hares. He was strapping on his own snow walkers by the time the boys had finished.

A few moments later he rose, slung on his bison-skin robe, hefted his backpack, and stalked off with his spears in one hand and the lead rope of the sled in the other.

He was only a few strides away when he heard his sons hastening after him. Kosar-eh did not look back, nor did he slow his pace. When two flustered, breathless boys took their places at his side, each carrying his own pack, spears, and stringer of hastily collected rabbits and grouse, it was not easy for the big man to resist a smile of satisfaction. His ploy had worked. Disobedience had led to Gah-ti's death; it was a trait Kosar-eh had allowed in his firstborn, mistakenly equating it with boldness. He would not make that mistake again with his remaining sons; they were too precious to him.

His eyes rested on Kiu-neh and Kho-neh. They must have felt his gaze, but they did not look up in hope of winning their father's approval or pity. Like all his sons by his deceased first woman, Siwi-ni, they were headstrong, hardy striplings whose character promised admirable future growth. Did they truly believe he was capable of abandoning them? Apparently so. He watched them strain with dogged, uncomplaining determination to keep up with him and thus make up for their earlier disobedience. Pride stirred within his breast, deep and sweet, a father's pride in well-made sons.

*What warriors you would have made!* Kosar-eh thought with infinite regret as, remembering the bleak and life-threatening conditions that had brought him to this moment, he lengthened his stride lest frustration overwhelm him. Some things were beyond a man's control; he could not undo the mistakes and tragedies of the past, but he could work to assure a more prosperous future. Alone in the badlands with neither shaman, totem, nor the imputed power of the sacred talisman of their ancestors to protect them, the members of his family might not be prospering, but they *were* surviving. And of one thing Kosar-eh could be sure: With Man Who Spits in the Face of Enemies to lead them, in the passive Red World of their ancestors, the sons of Kosar-eh would *all* be chiefs!

A smile touched his mouth. His thoughts were arrogant and blasphemous, and he knew it; he did not care. In the sunstruck shadow of snow-weighted mountains, the lion was no longer roaring. The sled was laden with meat. The encampment of his hungry band lay ahead. And Ta-maya, his beautiful beloved, was awaiting his return in a land without enemies.

The baby's cry startled Ta-maya into wakefulness.
"Bad things come! Bad things! *Bad!*"
"No, little one, no . . . hush. You were only dreaming. Here now." She placed the fussing two-year-old girl to her breast; Doh-teyah began to nurse hungrily. Naked save for the rabbit-skin sling that bound her broken left arm, Ta-maya lay quietly on her side beneath the bed furs that she shared with the baby and her man inside the communal lodge of their band. On any other morning she would have been soothed and relaxed back into sleep by the sweet, sensory pleasure of the little one's cuddling close to draw nourishment from her body; but Doh-teyah, who was not by nature a fretful child, had been irritable all night long. Ta-maya worried about this and was further distressed to see that Kosar-eh had not returned from the hunt. Her sleeping place seemed cold and empty without him. Having no desire to linger in it, she sat up and drew her sleeping robe with her as she supported in the fold of her one usable arm the fretful suckling of her man by his deceased first woman.

"No need to get up, Ta-maya," said U-wa, kneeling

beside the central fire pit. "Be warm. Suckle the little one. Ka-neh heard ravens calling one another to feast in the light of dawn. He has gone out to check the snares and deadfall traps."

Ta-maya found little comfort in U-wa's words even though she knew the presence of ravens around the band's traplines almost always signaled that some sort of "meat" had been caught, sometimes the ravens themselves. Her brow arched at the prospect of purplish, stringy flesh; even in the homeland of her Red World ancestors it was not desirable meat, except to those who had no other. And had she not heard the old women among the People of the Land of Grass say that the wings of Raven were the first to shadow the world before the coming of Spirit Sucker, Eater of Life, Maker of Death? *Yes.* Clearly she remembered old Xama and Unal say that in days of war, as well as of good hunting, Raven gathered his black-winged clan to fly high above the villages, cawing to announce the arrival of the great herds to their spring and autumn feeding grounds or to betray the advance of enemy warriors. In either event, regardless of who won or lost, Raven reddened his beak in the flesh of bison or of men; it mattered not to Raven. Where there was Death, there also were the black-winged children of Spirit Sucker waiting for the feast. And so the People of the Land of Grass ate not the flesh of Raven.

Although Ta-maya was no longer one of them and her belly was tight with want of food, she said to U-wa, "The meat of Raven is not good meat, and it is not a good thing for a boy to hunt alone, especially when Kosar-eh has forbidden Ka-neh to leave the band during his father's absence from it. The boy is supposed to watch for predators, bring back the children if they stray, and help us at our tasks, not—"

"The storm has delayed the hunters," U-wa reminded her. "The search for meat must have taken them far. Man Who Spits in the Face of Enemies did not plan to stay away all night, but we both know he would not risk the fingers and toes of his boys to the flesh-eating frost spirits that feed in bad weather. Nor, I think, would he have his women and little ones go without a chance of at least some small snare meat while he is away. Soon he will return. When he does, it will lighten his heart to know that in his absence a son of his has brought meat to his women and little ones."

Ta-maya could find no real flaw in the woman's logic, especially in her comments about the dangers of frost spirits. To this day she suffered a slight limp because a careless encounter with them during a storm had cost her a portion of her right heel.

Ta-maya wondered what Ka-neh would find in the snares. Winter had kept the band too long in this winter camp. They had exhausted the local game. At this time of year, even Red World people, accustomed to foraging for survival on the most minimal fare, could find little to sustain them in an unfamiliar land.

Troubled, Ta-maya took in the familiar gloom of the conical shelter she shared with her family. Old Grandmother Kahm-ree was still fast asleep, snoring profoundly at the back of the lodge. The children, too, were lost to dreams under the piled skins beneath which they slept. Ta-maya could not see Klah-neh, Kosar-eh's youngest boy; the four-year-old tended to make a fist of himself and disappear beneath the covers when he slept. The two six-year-old girls—her own youngest sister, Tla-nee, and U-wa's daughter, Joh-nee—lay in a sisterly embrace, their shared paternal lineage evident in their fine, even features.

Ta-maya's brow furrowed. The girls were usually up and about at first light: Joh-nee, always eager to help with Doh-teyah's swaddling and feeding; Tla-nee, al-

ways ready to tease young Ka-neh and thwart his adolescent attempts at dignity. But these days hunger
sapped the children of their enthusiasm for any activity
other than eating and inspired them to linger long and
deep within their dreams of better times.

Ta-maya glanced at U-wa. Kneeling by the stone-
banked fire pit, the older woman prodded the coals with
a wooden poker; as sparks flared, she bent over and
judiciously added small bits of precious kindling and
blew on the newly risen flames. The flames soon caught,
and when the kindling was burning well, U-wa hoisted a
small boiling bag.

Ta-maya watched the woman's strong, steady hands
secure the bag to the bone cooking tripod. Just what did
U-wa intend to cook if Ka-neh found the snares empty
and Kosar-eh did not soon return? she wondered. Or
was the woman's meticulous, almost ritual preparation
of the fire pit and raising of the boiling bag a deliberate
display of optimism and faith in the ability of the hunters to bring meat to the People? If so, perhaps the spirits that watched over men and beasts upon the hunt
would reward her effort and belief.

Ta-maya looked at U-wa, who was working with visible enthusiasm. With her graying hair falling in a single, thong-wrapped braid over one shoulder, she moved
with a smooth resiliency that belied her years. Ta-maya
was impressed. She knew that U-wa would need to hold
up all of her fingers more than three times if asked to
count the number of winters she had seen. Not that she
would do so willingly. The widow did not like being
thought of as an old woman, and indeed, compared to
Grandmother Kahm-ree, she was not.

Ta-maya smiled to herself, remembering that in the
hunting camps of Shateh, U-wa of the Red World had
accepted suitor gifts from Ranamal, one of the Land of
Grass chieftain's best trackers. The older woman had

taken great pride in his attentions, for he was a widower a good hand count of years younger than she and much desired by the other women of the tribe. When rumor whispered through the village that a wolf had been seen stealing from the Red World widow's lodge into the mists of dawn, neither U-wa nor Ranamal deigned comment; but Ta-maya had seen them look at one another with shared secrets in their eyes. All knew that Ranamal called Wolf his helping animal spirit, and that he wore the skins of that animal for ceremony. U-wa's girl, Joh-nee, had confided to Ta-maya that she had been awakened one night by a terrible dream in which she had seen her mother naked and howling beneath a great, hairy, man-sized wolf. It had placed a human-looking paw across U-wa's mouth while it growled at Joh-nee and commanded her back to sleep.

Now, looking at U-wa, Ta-maya knew that it must have been no easy thing for the widow to leave her handsome wolf-lover behind. But she had been given little choice in the matter. When tragedy had struck Shateh's tribe, the chieftain had blamed her only son, the Red World shaman Cha-kwena, and his lawbreaking woman for all their troubles, and the Red World people —U-wa among them—had been given the choice of seeing Cha-kwena slain or fleeing with him into the eastern forests.

Ta-maya's smile vanished with the memory. She began to rock the baby and croon softly to the child, making tender faces of love, and tried not to think of the past or to remember that the little one at her breast was blind and not her own.

She did not want to think of Cha-kwena, the grandson of the Red World shaman Hoyeh-tay. Cha-kwena was now shaman himself, all that Hoyeh-tay, Wise Old Owl, had ever been and more. Kosar-eh had followed Cha-kwena—called Yellow Wolf by some—until he could no longer bear the grief and suffering that his loyalty was costing. Even U-wa had turned from the shaman in despair. Now only Mah-ree, Ta-maya's law-breaking sister, remained at Cha-kwena's side as Shaman's Woman; and now all said that together they conspired with the Four Winds to turn the forces of Creation against those who had trusted and loved them.

*No!* Ta-maya closed her eyes. *I will not believe it. Despite all that has happened, I will not!* Tears burned beneath her lids; she tried to will them away, but it was no use.

Doh-teyah's small mouth parted from Ta-maya's breast, as if she had sensed the young woman's sadness. The little one reached up. Although the child's eyes had been made sightless by fever spirits in the first months of her life, she found her milk mother's tears with searching fingertips and wiped them away. "Bad things come?"

Ta-maya's eyes opened at the baby's question. "No, little one, no bad things. Not now. Not anymore!" Her assurance had been meant to soothe, but she had spoken with such passionate intensity that the baby stiffened and began to whimper. Instantly contrite, Ta-maya dipped her head to place a kiss upon the child's brow, then straightened and smiled down at the round, worried little face. "No bad things are coming to us now, Doh-teyah, daughter of Kosar-eh. No bad things!" This time her words, though intense with hope, were as soft and loving as the kiss that followed them. *May it be so! Ah, Mother Below and Father Above, hear this woman and grant that it be so!*

Ta-maya drew the child close and felt the suckling take her breast again. Remembering her own infant, Ha-xa-ree, she trembled at the depth of her loss and then at the intensity of love that she had come to feel for this child who had not been born of her body. She closed her eyes; the forces of Creation had seen fit to take her newborn daughter from her, but in this beautiful blind child of her man and his first woman, she had found another.

*Is it wrong of me to love her so?* she wondered, then opened her eyes, distracted.

Doh-teyah was fussing again. Her small fingers were working agitatedly at Ta-maya's breast. "There is not much milk for you now, Blind Daughter," Ta-maya conceded. *But our Kosar-eh will soon bring meat. Then this woman's breasts will swell again, and Doh-teyah will not fuss for want of more than this hungry woman can give her now. You will see, soon he will come!*

Comforted by hope, Ta-maya smiled again. In consideration of an ancient proscription, she had not given voice to her longings, for unlike her headstrong, law-breaking sister, Mah-ree, Ta-maya knew better than to speak of things which were yet to be; malevolent spirits might be listening.

She began to hum, rocking the baby, working her breast to stimulate the flow of remaining milk until the sound of footfalls reached her from beyond the lodge. From her place by the fire, U-wa looked toward the door skin as it was swept aside. Light flooded the interior. Ka-neh, bending low, was entering the lodge with a dead, bleeding raven dangling by its feet from his hand.

Ta-maya's heart leaped—not in repugnance at the sight of the raven or in gladness to see the returning youth, but because as Ka-neh held the entrance hide aside, she saw that he was not alone. "Kosar-eh!" She cried the name of her beloved in joyous welcome, then, startled, caught her breath.

The man who was entering the lodge was not Kosar-eh. Clad in the skins of wolves, he stooped as he entered the lodge.

U-wa dropped the bone fire prod and uttered a high, plaintive cry of happy recognition. "Ranamal!"

"He was waiting with Raven at the snare, and so I, and not just this bird, was caught!" snarled Ka-neh, throwing back his hood to reveal a bloodied, battered face as he blurted in an angry, near-hysterical shriek, "Would you greet Death with joy, you stupid woman? Run before the others come! *Run!*"

The warning came too late; a look of shock expanded across the youth's face as he was shoved forward by the force of a blow struck to his back by the man behind him. Staggered, Ka-neh flung up his arms, released the raven, and dropped to his knees.

Ta-maya blinked, confused, as the dead bird "flew" across the fire pit to land at the foot of her sleeping place.

A terrible sound came out of Ka-neh.

Ta-maya met the youth's gaze. He was shivering. His face had gone unnaturally pale and his eyes were very wide. Although he was looking directly at her, Ta-maya knew that he was not seeing her; strange things were happening to his pupils, and blood was welling at the corners of his mouth.

"Motherrrr?"

Ta-maya winced at the sound of Tla-nee's mewling cry for a parent who could not come to her now; Ha-xa was long dead.

Ranamal could not quite stand to his full height within the interior; he leaned forward, adjusting his eyes to the lack of light. He wore no paint. His hair was wild and unkempt, as were his once fine wolfskin garments. He held a short, stabbing spear in his right hand, his mittened fingers placed well up along the shaft, just back from the long, lanceolate, blood-darkened projectile point.

U-wa seemed not to have cognizance of the bat-

tered face of the boy or the bloodied spearhead. She
continued to stare at him in rapturous bewilderment.
"Ranamal! Ah! You have followed this woman across
the long days and nights! Ah! How I have longed for
you! How it grieved my heart to leave you to follow my
son and his band, but a mother's heart is . . . is . . ."
She paused, her attention taken by Ka-neh as the youth
slumped facedown onto the matted floor; blood showed
on the perforated fur of his rabbit-skin robe.

U-wa frowned. Still on her knees, she went to him,
touched his bloodied back with blank-eyed incredulity
before reaching to his neck, searching for a pulse that
was not there. Her face showed dismay and confusion
as she looked up at her onetime lover. "The boy . . .
there was no need for you to harm—"

"The boy is nothing to me!" Ranamal interrupted
with a rumble of disgust. "*You* are nothing to me, old
woman. *Never* anything to me. The stone, the totem, the
power of your shaman son—the favor of these things I
wanted for myself through a mating with you, but Yellow Wolf has stolen the power from my people and seen
fit to run with his followers like the coyote he is, luring
us into the hunting grounds of enemies we thought long
dead and vanquished, causing us to be taken by surprise
and broken in battle and—"

"My son was *made* to flee for his life by those who
lost faith in his power!" U-wa interrupted with righteous indignation, her handsome face transformed. Her
pride betrayed, she looked old now.

"A part of the trick," accused Ranamal with a contemptuous sneer. "But we have seen the extent of the
guile of your Yellow Wolf. It was not enough for him to
cause the death of Shateh's newborn son and contrive
to set the chieftain's heart forever against his foundling,
Warakan, so that the boy was driven from the tribe to
die; nor was it enough to lure Shateh and many of his

best warriors and women to their deaths. Your son has seen fit to further our grief and shame by conspiring with White Giant Winter to fill the passes with so much snow that the survivors among us could not return to our ancestral hunting grounds beyond the mountains. And so the raiders of the Watching Star come at will from their stronghold to strike our camps until now there are only a handful of us who are not dead or enslaved! But this was a mistake on the part of Yellow Wolf. *Yes!* By all of the powers of this world and the world beyond, I tell you, Mother of Cha-kwena, your son has gone too far. He has offended the forces of Creation! Raven and the Four Winds have become our brothers and have led us to the one we seek. We are no longer afraid of the magic of Yellow Wolf, for what have we to lose when we have already lost everything because of him?"

Ta-maya was stunned. Shateh dead? The great hunt chief's people broken in battle? Red World people slain? The warriors of the Watching Star formed into a cohesive force again? "This would be the last thing that Cha-kwena would wish, that any of us would wish . . . for your people or for ours," she said.

His eyes fixed her as rapaciously as the talons of a hunting bird piercing its prey. "I will have the sacred stone of the ancestors! I will take the meat and blood of the totem and claim its power for myself and my tribe! Where is Yellow Wolf? Now he and his followers will pay for—"

"Cha-kwena is not with this band. We have only Kosar-eh to hunt for us," blurted Klah-neh. "When my father comes back, he will hurt *you* for hurting my brother!"

The proclamation of the guileless little boy hung in the air.

Ta-maya knew that if she had been standing, her

knees would have given way at the child's inadvertent blunder. Now Ranamal knew what Ka-neh would never have told him—that he had come upon a shamanless band of women and children who relied on one man to protect them. And that man was now away from the encampment.

"The totem is far away, and the sacred stone is no longer ours!" declared U-wa, her voice tight with bitterness and the pain of damaged pride. "Go! Apparently there is nothing for you here!"

"No?" Ranamal turned the question as softly and sinuously as he might once have stroked the older woman's breasts and thighs preparatory to lovemaking. "You left me to follow your coyote son, old woman. If Yellow Wolf is not with you, then you will tell me where I may hunt him."

U-wa did not hesitate to spit compliance. "My son and his lawbreaking woman follow the totem in cursed forests that lie beyond the edge of the world! Go! Follow them! It matters not to me. They have brought nothing but disappointment and suffering to all who ever trusted them. So it is with you, *Wolf*! How are you better than Coyote? Go, I say. And may you and yours fall off the edge of the world into the sky to burn forever in the face of the rising sun!"

Silence filled the lodge. It settled, suffocating those within.

Then Ranamal exhaled, and the low hiss of sound was more dangerous a declaration of intent than the warning hiss of a viper.

"Bad things come now? Bad things?" Doh-teyah's baby voice whimpered softly.

"Yes, bad things, *very* bad things," Ranamal vowed as he responded to U-wa's provocation with a hard kick that sent the woman sprawling.

Ta-maya held the little one close, too frightened to

form an answer as she recalled Ka-neh's words: *"Run before the others come! Run!"* She felt sick. *Others*. Any moment she would hear their footsteps. Any moment they would enter the lodge. They would surely kill old Kahm-ree and the younger children, and if she and U-wa and the girls were fortunate, they too would die; otherwise, the fate of slaves awaited them. She flinched against dread—and against the invasiveness of Ranamal's stare.

His eyes were fixed on her now, on her face, then on her bare breasts, and then on her face again. When he moved forward, sidestepping the slain youth and threatening U-wa with the tip of his spear as he slowly circled the fire pit toward her, Ta-maya saw the heat of sexual fire in his eyes and knew what must happen now.

Slowly, she put Doh-teyah down, rose to her bare feet, and placed herself between the man and the child. Head high, Ta-maya shook back her hip-length hair and allowed her sleeping robe to slip from her shoulders as she stood naked before Ranamal.

She knew that she was beautiful; the knowledge had nothing to do with vanity. Even before she had first come to a woman's time of blood, men had looked at Ta-maya, firstborn and Most Favored Daughter of Tlana-quah, chieftain of the village by the Lake of Many Singing Birds. Old men had offered wonderful gifts for the privilege of being first with so fair and potentially fecund a child; young men and boys had done the same. Her father, being chief, had allowed her to choose the man she would have in her own time, and that choice had taken her far from the land of her people, had brought war to her tribe. Later other men had wanted her, fought for her, and—her throat tightened— died for her. In the Red World, among the People of the Watching Star, in the Land of Grass, in peace or war, it was always the same: When men looked upon the face and body of Ta-maya, they had only one need, and now, for the sake of the children, she would use that need to serve her own intent.

She saw the look of wanting on Ranamal's face. She met his gaze, held it. "There need be no further bad things between us," she told him and, lowering her face, looked up at him through half-closed eyes as she smiled provocatively. "Death can be such a waste, yes?" She sent the tip of her tongue along the half-closed seam of her lips, moistening, still holding his gaze as, folding her right forearm beneath her breasts, she lifted them, offering them to him, and spoke a low, steady command to U-wa. "Look to the children now, U-wa. You have enjoyed this wolf. Now, before the others come, let him be a wolf with me."

Ranamal's face split with a wide, white, purely predaceous grin. "Yes, old woman," he mocked. "Look to the children."

Ta-maya was shaking. She heard Doh-teyah sobbing; it was not a sound that was easy to ignore. But Ranamal was before her now, hungrily appraising what he was set to take. With his spear in one hand, he splayed the other across her breasts and began to work them with a bold, hurtful provocation that told her how it would be with him. She allowed the trespass, moved into it, encouraging more as, fearing that he would use his spear to silence the baby, she again commanded U-wa to look to the children.

"Bad things!" cried the little one.

Her heart pounding, Ta-maya was aware of movement in the gloom. Would U-wa respond rationally, or would jealousy make it impossible for the older woman to see the reasoning behind Ta-maya's behavior? Having heard no footfalls or voices coming from beyond the lodge, she dared hope that if U-wa acted quickly, there might yet be a chance for her to save herself and the children before the others came. Perhaps she might even find Kosar-eh, warn him and the boys, caution them in their return lest their lives be forfeited before they even had a chance to understand what had befallen their band.

Ta-maya looked directly at Ranamal as he pulled her close. She knew his kind. She had faced him before and had always survived. Now, however, with the wings of Raven lying crushed beneath her feet, she knew that she was in the embrace of Death; when Eater of Life sated himself, he would leave her as he had left Ka-neh and would surely leave the others if they did not manage to escape. And so she took his hand and guided it to pleasure; for the sake of the children of her beloved Kosar-eh, she would not shrink from Death now.

The sun was well up, but the morning remained bitterly cold. Kosar-eh stopped and scanned ahead. Last night's storm had piled snow deep on the mountains, but here in the badlands it had left only a shallow, wind-blown layer of white that lay dry as sand over the snowpack. For travelers on snow walkers, movement was relatively easy. The big man was grateful; if the weather held and his boys could continue to keep up with him, they would be settled and feasting within the warm, sheltering confines of the lodge long before the sun came down.

He headed steadily northeast toward the encampment with Kiu-neh and Kho-neh lagging behind but still moving at an admirable pace, given the distance they had come. It occurred to Kosar-eh that soon he should pause to thank the Four Winds and forces of Creation for allowing him this easy homeward journey; the traditions of the Ancient Ones dictated as much, and he was bound to set some sort of example for his boys. Yet, he asked himself, had not those same powers of earth and sky brought the storm that delayed their homecoming in the first place? His mouth compressed against his teeth. He would not pause to thank them! Instead, he lengthened his stride, comfortable with a recalcitrance that had nothing to do with lack of respect for the spirit forces that swept the world; he had simply ceased to believe in their ability to perceive, much less care about, the thoughts or needs of men.

Squinting against the morning glare, he was aware of dark specks moving on the horizon. Ravens? Teratorns? Or the first dangerous tricks of snow blindness? Kosar-eh pulled his hood forward and lowered his head lest his eyes be seared by the sun's glare on the vastness of unblemished snow. He told his boys to do the same. They must have done so instantly, for their eyes were downcast when he looked back.

Kosar-eh smiled. Did they still believe him capable of leaving them behind? He shook his head as he trudged on with an image of the twosome in his head— each boy bent nearly double beneath the weight of his pack and stringer, plodding along in obvious misery, breath ragged and misting in the subfreezing air. He had driven them hard since leaving the night camp. They had uttered no complaint even though he had not stopped to take food or drink or allowed them so much as a moment's pause to relieve themselves. He decided that it was time to grant this now and signaled them to stop.

Kho-neh dropped to his knees. Kiu-neh staggered a little on his feet but stoically held his ground in the way of the warrior he longed to be. After quickly removing their gloves and opening their robes and loin seams, the threesome emptied their bladders in unison, forming three straight, steady streams that steamed in the subfreezing air and melted miniature canyons in the snow.

"Well done," said Kosar-eh to his boys in good-natured allusion to their failure of the previous night as he shook dry and tucked himself back into the protection of his clothing.

Kiu-neh's face tensed resentfully; clearly the reminder had stung him.

Kho-neh, on the other hand, was so relieved at having been able to free himself of a nearly bursting burden—and so proud of himself for not having lost control of it before—that he collapsed backward into the snow with a long, loud sigh of bliss.

Kiu-neh eyed his younger brother with disapproval.

"We will eat," Kosar-eh announced. He reached for the small leather food pouch that hung from the topmost tine of his antlered backpack, just above his stringer of hares.

The two boys hunkered in the snow next to Kosar-eh close to the unloaded sled, still fully weighted by their pack frames. They ate hungrily, each from his own pouch, each relishing the sweet, oily putrescence of small, pale balls of rancid fat studded with a meager but much appreciated assortment of dried berries, painstakingly gleaned by the women before the first snows.

Kosar-eh squinted off as he chewed. Sun dogs were forming on either side of the sun, the small, circular halos of luminous ice crystals glinting pink and yellow in the late morning sky. Their appearance promised a change of weather, always for the worse, he knew. He was not cheered by the thought of another approaching storm, or by the realization that a teratorn was definitely circling with ravens high above the scabrous, snowy hills in which his encampment lay.

The big man frowned. The wings of the enormous, condorlike bird were so wide and broad that they shadowed the sun and earned it the name of Sun Eater. Somewhere under the shadowing wings of the teratorn, an animal was most likely dead or dying. Kosar-eh thought of the lion he and the boys had heard roaring in the dawn; the scent of blood could entice such predators across the land—and if the dead or dying creature lay close to the lodge of his band, his family could be at risk.

"Eat quickly," he told his boys. "We have a long way yet to go."

"Old Kahm-ree says that when Sun Eater flies with ravens, it is a bad sign," said Kho-neh, gulping a fat ball, then pulling off his left moccasin and rubbing his toes.

"Old Kahm-ree sees bad signs in everything!" retorted Kiu-neh.

The younger boy shrugged, then confided in a lowered voice, "Sometimes I wish Cha-kwena were still with us to tell us about omens and things. Do you think he is alive out there in the dark forest, my father?"

Kosar-eh stiffened; the emotions that ran through him were so intense that they shook him as he said, "The bones of the great white mammoth totem, Life Giver, lie in the Valley of the Dead, where the final battle in the war between the tribes was fought! This I have seen. The herd that Cha-kwena follows is only that —a herd of mammoth, a gathering of tuskers, no more, no less. They—and he—are nothing to us now!"

"But he swore that the white mammoth calf was Life Giver reborn," the younger boy said. "And old Kahm-ree says that as long as the white mammoth lives, so too will the People live and be strong forever in the power of the totem."

Kosar-eh's voice was hard as he asked, "Did you or anyone else beside the shaman trickster, Cha-kwena, ever set eyes on the newborn totem?"

"I . . . no, but Cha-kwena said that he had seen it in the sacred grove, a little white mammoth calf standing close to the spring, and—"

Kiu-neh interrupted his brother with a cuff to the shoulder. "The sons of Kosar-eh have no need of shamans or totems or talismans when their father is with them!"

"But we left the village without Cha-kwena!" Kho-neh protested, revealing a heretofore unspoken concern. "Cha-kwena would have returned from his Vision quest! With his woman to burden him, he could not have stayed away much longer. We should have waited for them. Mah-ree could have made good, healing salves for my toes. Look, I think the frost spirits are biting."

Suddenly irritable, Kosar-eh told the boy to put his moccasin back on. "White Giant Winter was returning to the forested land of death into which Cha-kwena led us. I warned him that I would not stay in it. If he had wanted to keep company with me and my family, he should not have stayed so long away. And if he did return to the village, he could have followed us, as surely as his troublesome little girl-of-a-woman has always followed him. As for your toes, Kho-neh, yes, Mah-ree claimed to be Medicine Woman, a shaman in her own right. But that foolish little girl-of-a-woman could not banish sickness from our camp or blindness from your sister Doh-teyah's eyes any more than she could keep herself from defying the laws of the Ancient Ones and bringing the wrath of the forces of Creation down upon us! Even though she is a sister of my Ta-maya, I say that we are well rid of her and a shaman whose own mother, U-wa, has turned her back on him forever and chosen to return with us to the land of our Red World ancestors!"

Kho-neh was scalded by the unexpected heat of his father's words and embarrassed by having been so thoroughly rebuked in front of his older brother. In an effort to maintain his dignity, the seven-year-old took his

time pulling on his moccasin as he said with quiet petulance, "Joh-nee still fears that Cha-kwena's spirit will
hunt and punish Kosar-eh for abandoning him and his
woman."

"And since when does a son of Kosar-eh listen to
the babblings of a girl who has barely seen the ending of
her sixth winter? Joh-nee would be wise to forget her
shaman brother!" snapped Kosar-eh. "Yellow Wolf and
his woman have brought misfortune to all who ever believed in them. Because of Cha-kwena's treachery and
Mah-ree's lawbreaking ways, we are outcast forever
from the lands in which I hoped to live out my days in
honor as a hunter and warrior of the chieftain Shateh!"

Reacting strongly to his father's words, Kiu-neh
popped into his mouth the last ball of fat and eagerly
spoke his heart out of a full mouth. "Perhaps now that
my father has broken with Cha-kwena, Shateh might
agree to take us back. Others from the Red World have
made new lives within the protection of his great tribe. I
have no desire to return to a land where men do not
know the ways of war and are content to eat lizards and
ants because herds of big meat are wise enough not to
bring their calves to feed in a parched land of little
grass. We should seek Shateh, my father! We should—"

"Shateh has by now led his many followers over the
mountains to their tribe's ancestral hunting grounds
within the Land of Grass," said Kosar-eh.

Kiu-neh was not deterred. "We could follow them
instead of—"

"We cannot!" Kosar-eh interrupted. The boy's
echo of his own longings bruised him to his spirit and
beyond. "Have you forgotten that when Cha-kwena and
Mah-ree fled from Shateh's wrath after bringing death
to the chieftain's lodge, Shateh decreed that they and
all who chose to remain loyal to them were to be hunted
and slain? Have you forgotten that on that night, all

Red World people who wished to remain within Shateh's tribe were commanded to prove their loyalty to their chieftain? Have you forgotten what was asked of this man?"

The boys looked up at their father, silenced by the depths of sadness in his eyes.

Kosar-eh knew they had not forgotten; he reminded them anyway, and himself. "It is the command of the ancestors of the People of the Land of Grass to deny sustenance to the physically unfit. For the followers of the shaman, Yellow Wolf, exceptions were made. Until that night."

Kosar-eh paused, shaken by recollections that shadowed his mood more darkly than the wings of the teratorn now shadowed the snowy ground. Man Who Spits in the Face of Enemies—although he had fought beside the Land of Grass warriors in the great war and been a part of their final victory—had been told that if he were to remain a warrior of Shateh, he must turn his one-armed son from his lodge and feed his blind daughter to the village feast fire. He wondered what his boys would think of him if they knew how close he had come to conceding to the chieftain's demand. In consideration of his own ambition as a warrior, as well as of the many benefits gained by his family while living within the large, sheltering community of Shateh's tribe, he had summoned the strength of will to do the unthinkable. Had Ta-maya not succeeded in touching his heart with her despair over the fate of his children, Gah-ti would not have lived long enough to succumb to fever spirits in the cursed forest, and Doh-teyah's tiny spirit would now be blindly walking the wind forever.

The big man closed his eyes. Unable to deny his beautiful beloved anything, his only recourse had been to defy Shateh. And so Kosar-eh had fled the village with his family and followed Cha-kwena into an autumn snowstorm, knowing that his action would mark him as a traitor to the one tribe with which he had ever felt true affinity. And what had been his reward for loyalty to the shaman Cha-kwena? Hunger, the alienation of friends, the threat of annihilation by old enemies, the deaths of his eldest son and newborn daughter.

He opened his eyes. His mood was blacker than before. He wished that Doh-teyah and not the newborn Ha-xa-ree had perished in the forest. Or better still, he reasoned, if his blind child had failed to recover from the sickness that burned away her sight in infancy, and if Gah-ti had not survived his ordeal with the lion, then his band might still be members of Shateh's tribe.

A terrible longing shook Kosar-eh. Under the shadowing wings of the teratorn, he surveyed the cold, inhospitable vastness of the badlands and fervently wished that Doh-teyah would die. *Now.* The sooner the better. Without his blind child's presence in his band, he would not fear reunion with Shateh; he would seek it. Given his proven talents as a hunter, hand-to-hand fighter, and worker of stone, he had every reason to believe that the war chief would forgive him his Red World weakness on behalf of his disabled offspring and permit him to dwell once more among the People of the Land of Grass. Then his women and little ones would once again be safe from wild beasts, and . . .

Even before the wind gusted hard from the north, Kosar-eh was chilled by the appalling nature of his thoughts. He could never have abandoned Gah-ti! And now his love for little Doh-teyah shook him so deeply that he was momentarily afraid the forces of Creation had seen into his thoughts. If so, would they fulfill his death wish for his sightless child?

The question startled him. Once before he had wished another dead. Siwi-ni, his first woman, the mother of his sons and of Doh-teyah, had been old and weakened by childbearing. She had begged the forces of Creation to free her spirit to walk the wind forever. And so, he doubted if his wish had been answered regarding her, for it had been her time to die. Now, feeling foolish, he castigated himself for fearing the intangible powers of the spirit world. The forces of Creation had never before demonstrated concern for his longings; why should they do so now?

"Rise now," Kosar-eh commanded his sons. "We will return to the encampment. Forget the lives you once led as members of Shateh's tribe. We cannot walk with them again. And forget Yellow Wolf and Medicine Woman. This man has learned the hard way that all those who claim to walk the Vision path of a shaman's dreams are deceivers who seek advantage only for themselves."

"But Shateh believed in the magic of Yellow Wolf!" Kho-neh reminded him, staring down while doing concentrated battle with the lacings of his moccasin as he attempted to tie the securing knot correctly. "Enough so to hunt him and name him Enemy and try to kill him!"

"And in the end Shateh wisely abandoned the hunt and returned to the land of his ancestors, as you must abandon your fear while we return to ours. Cha-kwena has nothing you need. A man should not seek his strength and courage in the powers of others, or in totems or talismans, my sons. For these things you must look into your own hearts and spirits, and to the wisdom of the Ancient Ones. Armed with the knowledge and skills of those who have hunted and survived in this world before you, you will need neither shamans nor totems nor sacred stones to interpret the signs of *true* portending."

"And what may these true signs be, my father?" asked Kiu-neh, on his feet and ready to travel.

Kosar-eh pointed upward to the sun dogs and saw that they had now spread and stretched themselves into a single thin ring of refracted light encircling the sun. "There, the sun in its lodge . . . a sign you must mark well. It portends a change of weather, the coming of another storm."

"Maybe Joh-nee is right," suggested stubborn little Kho-neh, standing now but still working to secure his laces. "Maybe Cha-kwena is using the powers of the totem and sacred stone to send the storms of winter against us because we abandoned him in the forest."

Losing all patience with his sibling, Kiu-neh kicked the boy down, only to have Kho-neh take hold of the offending foot and pull the older boy down with him.

Kosar-eh shook his head. Resting his spear against his shoulder, he took both boys by their pack frames and pulled them to their feet. "We have enough enemies in this world without fighting one another. Come! Put an end to your bickering. Speak no more of the 'power' of Cha-kwena. Our women and little ones await us in a hungry camp. And you have much to boast of when we return with these gifts of meat that your skill—and not the magic power of any shaman—has won for us!"

There would be no boasting. There would be no feast or joyous reunion with loved ones.

Kosar-eh knew this the instant he and the boys came within sight of the encampment.

"Smoke . . . so much smoke!" exclaimed Kho-neh, pointing toward it. "Is it a grass fire, my father?"

"In the dead of winter with snow covering the land?" Kiu-neh snorted derisively. "But it does seem to be too much smoke for a cooking fire raised in a camp of little wood and no meat worth roasting."

"Be still!" Kosar-eh stopped and stared ahead. The

sun had long since slipped past noon. The ravens and teratorn had vanished from the sky. The boys had set a remarkable pace. Until this moment, the big man's spirit had been singing with gladness in this good day. Now his eyes fixed on the wide, irregular column of brown smoke rising from the hills in which his encampment lay, and he was filled with such dread that he could not breathe.

Kosar-eh had seen similar plumes of smoke before. As Man Who Spits in the Face of Enemies, he had participated in creating them after every raid on the scattered encampments of his vanquished enemies among the People of the Watching Star. He remembered weeping women, screaming children, bloodied spears and war clubs, and burning lodges.

A terrible hollow opened inside him, cold and dark, and he shivered as his thoughts fell away into it, rationalizing: *All that I did before was not without just cause against those who slaughtered and enslaved and fed young women captives to their tusked god of the sky. The People of the Watching Star brought war and death to the tribes. But my band has done nothing! My family is . . . is . . .*

"Vulnerable." Kosar-eh gasped the word; it nearly staggered him. Fighting hard to steady his nerves, he cried, "It is not possible! Not a raid, not here . . . not in a land without enemies! It cannot be!" Yet even as he spoke the wind was rising, bringing across the land the unmistakable scent of burning hide and hair. An instant later, when a cloud of ravens rose skyward above the encampment and a single teratorn ascended to shadow the sun, Kosar-eh recalled his earlier wish to see his blind child dead. Had those powers in which he had lost all faith of communion heard and answered his prayers after all? There was only one way to be sure.

"Stay here," he commanded his boys. "Guard the

meat . . . and keep yourselves alert and well hidden
until I return."

It was nearly sundown when Kosar-eh reached the
burned-out ruins of his encampment. U-wa, haggard
and exhausted, stood alone amidst the carnage.
Stunned, the big man went to her, listened intently as
she spoke. Her words were so appalling that they barely
penetrated his brain.

"Grandmother Kahm-ree and little Tla-nee dead?
And Ka-neh? All slain?" Kosar-eh's mind and body had
gone numb. He shook his head, stared hard at U-wa,
and scowled. She was not the one he wanted to see.
"Ta-maya?"

U-wa began to reply, hesitated, then went on in a
rush, "It was the sight of ravens circling our snares that
drew the war party from the mountains. Ka-neh's tracks
in the snow led them to our camp. First Ranamal, then
other warriors of Shateh came. They took Ta-maya and
your youngest boy away with them."

"Where? How long ago?"

"Long before the eye of Father Above was at its
highest." U-wa gestured toward the far hills with swollen, burn-blistered hands, then hung her head in abject
sorrow. "I have done the best I could. There was no
warning, no time to do anything other than what I have
done! Ta-maya told me to look to the children.
Ranamal did not care about them, or me; his eyes were
only for her. So I commanded the little ones to come
from the lodge with me. Once outside, I saw that only
my own Joh-nee had obeyed. I wanted to go back for
the others, but I knew it would be no easy thing to wake
old Grandmother Kahm-ree and little Klah-neh, or to
convince Tla-nee to leave her sister. The rest of
Ranamal's war band was approaching. We were left no
choice but to flee into the hills, where we hid, watching

them until we could look no more. At last they went away, leaving the lodge in flames, and . . ."

The numbness within Kosar-eh was expanding; it took all his concentration not to be overwhelmed by it as he focused on felled and looted storage huts, on broken, scattered drying racks, and on the smoking rubble that had once been his family's spacious communal lodge. He cocked his head. U-wa was still talking, gesturing with scorched hands, but her words were a distant, undifferentiated hum at the back of his head, even though he now understood that she must have been burned while dragging what she could of the bedding and belongings from the flaming lodge. His narrowed eyes focused on familiar things, which now appeared strangely grotesque: his painted, feather-adorned willow backrest, Doh-teyah's quilled cradleboard, Ta-maya's favorite buckskin pillow, his parfleche of knapping tools, Tla-nee's favorite doll, and several bed furs spread out together in a mounded heap.

"To keep the birds away," explained U-wa when she saw where his gaze rested. "Wait, Kosar-eh! No! Do not look beneath the robes! I could not bring the bodies from the lodge before the fire had done its worst. Do not—"

Kosar-eh ignored her. He knew what he would find when he used the killing end of his spear to fling back the skins, but he did not anticipate the extent of his horror upon confronting the sight. Burned almost beyond recognition, the mutilated bodies of his loved ones stared up at him, blackened skulls in which teeth had been smashed and eyeballs shrunken or exploded by heat, and across which skin lay like sun-blackened strips of jerked meat. His gorge rose, and dizziness took him to his knees. Leaning on his spear, it was all he could do to maintain his balance as he saw that before being left to incinerate within the lodge, the bodies of old

Kahm-ree and the children had been scalped and dismembered; of the three corpses, not one possessed a complete set of arms or limbs.

"When the lodgepoles and cover skins have cooled, we must search for the remains," said U-wa. "We cannot leave our loved ones like this . . . blind, unable to eat or find their way upon the wind as their spirits wander the world beyond this world forever."

Kosar-eh fought back a wave of nausea and shook his head. The humming was intensifying, stinging now, hurting. He closed his eyes. Never in any raid upon the camps of his enemies among the People of the Watching Star had he intentionally slain, much less mutilated, a woman or child. Others had done so. And afterward, by way of justification to the Red World fighters among them, the warriors of Shateh had explained that such mutilations were necessary because even the females and children of their enemies were capable of banding together after death for the purpose of taking revenge upon those who had slain them. But, he reasoned, old Kahm-ree and the children of his band were not of the People of the Watching Star. They had lived in the villages and camps of Shateh, eaten of the same meat and slept by the same feast fires, laughed and cavorted with the chieftain's own wives, daughters, and foundling son at many a stream and river crossing. They wished only one thing of the great chieftain of the People of the Land of Grass—to live in peace with him or apart from him, according to his will.

Kosar-eh was shaking. "How could a man who once named me Hunt Brother do this to my children? I have raised no hand against Shateh! I have fought with him in war and hunted the great herds with him and—"

"Shateh is dead." U-wa pressed her bruised rib cage with her folded forearms to alleviate pain as she told Kosar-eh all that Ranamal had revealed about what had transpired with the People of the Land of Grass since Kosar-eh's band had left them to follow Cha-kwena.

Kosar-eh looked up. The woman's words fell upon his spirit like an icy rain, chilling him to the very center of his being as he realized that everything he had feared, and more, had come to pass.

"They are convinced that my shaman son has turned the Four Winds against them." U-wa's chin quivered, but although her face contorted with anguish, she restrained her tears. "Now, as the People of the Land of Grass are again hunted by the People of the Watching Star, they seek the power of the totem and sacred stone that Cha-kwena, my only son, has stolen from them! And so they have come into this camp and done all that you see because we are Red World people, and they were certain that he would be with us." Her attempt to maintain dignity had been bravely made, but she had suffered too much this day; tears spilled onto her soot-blackened cheeks as she sobbed, "Aiee! At least you and two of the boys were not in the encampment, Kosar-eh, for not even Man Who Spits in the Face of Enemies could have fought off so many! If I had not run away, my body—with my own dear Joh-nee's and your sweet Doh-teyah's—would be there at your feet! Aiee! If only we had understood and heeded the warning of your blind child. Doh-teyah said that bad things were coming. She—"

"They would never have found us if we had stayed in the forest with my brother."

The sharp declaration of the little girl startled Kosar-eh. He looked to his right and saw Joh-nee emerging from behind a snow-encrusted tangle of iron-woods within which she had been hiding. A wisp of a child with tangled black hair and dark eyes enormous in an oval face gone pale with shock, the only daughter of

U-wa was clad in a sagging bed fur and a pair of ill-fitting moccasins that were obviously not her own. The child advanced toward him with such a hateful, single-minded stare that he did not notice she was carrying something heavy in her arms beneath the makeshift robe.

"Kosar-eh was wrong to abandon my brother!" Joh-nee was emphatic as she stopped and glowered down at him. "Where is Kho-neh? Have you abandoned my friend, too?"

"He is with his brother . . . *safe*." Kosar-eh's voice sounded distant, weak, as though it rose not from his throat but from the cold, empty place that had opened within him when he had first glimpsed smoke rising from the encampment.

Joh-nee's brow furrowed. "This girl told Fourth Son of Kosar-eh that Cha-kwena would punish his father. And so he has. Look at what my brother has done to the one who stole his sister from him, who abandoned him to walk forever alone with his woman in the dark forest with the totem and the sacred stone of the ancestors and—"

"It was I, not Kosar-eh, who forced you to leave the forest, my daughter!" protested U-wa. "And though my shaman son has brought bad luck upon us, I know that your brother would not wish death to any member of his family."

"His mother and sister are not dead," the child reminded her darkly. Kosar-eh flinched, but not only at the girl's remark. Something was moving in her arms. A moment later "something" turned out to be "someone" as Doh-teyah peeked from beneath the bed fur.

"Koshray?" The two-year-old spoke her father's name as best she could, smiling her dimpled smile and reaching blindly outward for him.

The big man's reaction to the sight of this daughter

he had wished dead appalled him. He looked up at Doh-teyah, then down at the burned bodies of Kahmree, Tla-nee, and Ka-neh, then up again at the sightless suckling. He laughed, but there was no merriment in the sound. It was a loud, harsh bark of a laugh at the obscene joke the forces of Creation had seen fit to play upon him. Staring skyward, he said accusingly, "So you *do* listen! So you are *not* deaf and blind to the needs and thoughts of men! So you *do* speak . . . in the *blood* of my family!"

Overcome by the cruel perversity of the moment, Kosar-eh jumped to his feet and glared at Doh-teyah with absolute revulsion. "By all the spirit powers that rule this world and the world beyond, I will not accept this most worthless of my children when the others are dead or stolen from me, along with my woman!"

Joh-nee's haggard face tightened as she pulled the uncomprehending Doh-teyah into a ferociously protective embrace just as U-wa exclaimed, "Kosar-eh, look! All is not lost to you! Your boys come!"

Kosar-eh whirled around. Kiu-nch and Kho-nch were indeed trudging campward, two small, heavily burdened figures highly visible against the snow as they made an obvious and thoroughly uncharacteristic effort to work as a team while dragging the meat-laden sled. The big man's hand tightened on the haft of his spear. He was not glad to see them. He had commanded them to remain behind, to keep hidden, to guard the meat, to obey their father. Instead, they defied his will. *Always* his boys defied his will!

Shaking with anger, Kosar-eh wondered if there was some intrinsic flaw in his nature that engendered this continuous and deadly disrespect on the part of his sons. Or was the defect in his sons themselves? If so, then perhaps the forces of Creation were not sadistically playing with their lives, but were gleaning them from his band with the same brutal indifference that they gleaned unfit calves from the great herds.

The supposition was devastating. The darkness within Kosar-eh was all-pervasive now. As he observed his approaching boys, his body spasmed against truths too terrible to bear: The unwillingness of Kiu-neh and Kho-neh to rise and greet this morning's sun had delayed his return to the band, and while he had been away, Ka-neh's blatant disobedience had led raiders into this camp. Now, of the five fine sons that his first woman, Siwi-ni, had birthed, only three were alive, and the youngest of these had been stolen from him along with his woman.

"Ta-maya!" The name of his beautiful beloved ripped from Kosar-eh's heart, and suddenly nothing else mattered to him. He had been on enough raids with the warriors of Shateh to know how they would use his woman until they returned to their own females; if Ta-maya survived the ordeal, she would be a spirit-broken slave for the rest of her days. Again he found it difficult to breathe. His love for Ta-maya—the gentlest, kindest, and most beautiful of women—was the core of all meaning in his life; the thought of her brutalized and taken captive by men whom he once trusted and sought to emulate was more than he could stand.

Jabbing his spear in defiance at the setting sun, Kosar-eh cried, "I will not allow it! With your light or without it, I will find my Ta-maya and bring her back to her band!"

"Ta-maya is long gone, Kosar-eh!" U-wa reached to lay a calming hand upon his forearm, but there was nothing calm about her expression as she realized that in his grief he was as blind as Doh-teyah and less rational than any child. "You cannot leave us! The little ones and I need you now more than ever! The sun is nearly down. You have no hope of finding Ta-maya in the dark. And even if you did, you are only one warrior, and she is with many. Besides, it was she who enticed my Ranamal, and afterwards, when the others drew her naked from the lodge to pleasure themselves upon her, I did not hear her scream or see her shrink from them before I turned away in shame and—"

He struck her—hard—and roared down at her as she fell, "My woman is the daughter of a chieftain! Ta-maya would not scream, or beg for mercy, or allow words of dishonor to foul her mouth as you have just done!"

U-wa made no protest. Shocked as much by the terrible, mind-shattering force of the big man's blow as by the malicious words that had poured from her mouth on a wave of uncontrollable jealousy, she sobbed, bereft, "Forgive me! I live only because the woman of Kosar-eh sacrificed her pride by using her body to distract a wolf from his prey long enough for me to lead the children to safety. If I failed to save them all, the fault is mine, not hers! Forgive me, Kosar-eh! If not for my sake, then for the sake of the children, please forgive me!"

Her apology came too late. Kosar-eh turned and stalked away.

"Go into the hills and seek shelter until I return," he commanded over his shoulder. "With the meat my sons are bringing, you will not go hungry." It did not occur to him to wonder what would happen to them if he did not return; he did not care. He had found the bloody, brazenly laid footprints of the marauders, and now, spear in hand, the madness of grief was upon him as he set himself to the pursuit.

He would find Ta-maya and rescue her. Or he would not come back.

*        *        *

"I hope he dies," said Joh-nee, shivering in the cold wind.

"Take back your wish!" commanded U-wa, rising shakily. "If he dies, *we* die."

The little girl shook her head in disagreement and planted a rebellious kiss on Doh-teyah's brow. "Chakwena will never allow harm to come us! Our shaman will return from the far forest now that the one who abandoned him has left us. You will see. My brother will come with the sacred stone and the totem and—"

"You should not seek your strength in the power of others, or in talismans, or in totems that do not exist, little girl!" Kiu-neh's echo of his father's advice was spoken with surprising authority for one so young. With the sun settling low over the western mountains, he came into the ruined camp with a visibly shaken Khoneh.

The younger boy dropped his end of the sled's guide rope, looked around, and—as U-wa explained what had befallen the encampment—stared at the bodies that lay in the gathering shadows. "My father was wrong," he whispered, trembling. "We *did* see bad omens."

Kiu-neh eyed the sky. Long skeins of cloud were advancing from the northwest. Without flinching, he moved to cover the dead, then looked toward the hills into which Kosar-eh was rapidly vanishing. The boy's voice was as cold as the rising wind when he said, "He was right about one thing. Another storm *is* coming. And he has left us to deal with it alone."

"No!" U-wa would not believe it. Her ears were ringing, and a bright, hurtful, disconcerting light pressed behind her eyes. "The spirits of anguish feed upon your father. He must run until they are purged. Then he will come back. Before dark. You will see. In the meantime you are now the oldest of his sons, Kiu-neh. Until your father returns, we must stand together to protect this woman and these children."

Young Kho-neh's mouth turned down. He did not appreciate being referred to as a child, especially in front of Joh-nee. Embarrassed, he stood to his full albeit meager height in a pathetically overstated imitation of manliness. "You must not be afraid, little girl," he assured Joh-nee. "The sons of Man Who Spits in the Face of Enemies will protect you!"

Joh-nee appraised young Kho-neh and, out of kindness to one whom she considered a friend, offered no direct challenge to his well-intended bravado. While pulling her robe more closely around herself and Doh-teyah, she replied to his brother through chattering teeth, "Believe what you will, Third Son of Kosar-eh. Now that your father is gone, my brother will send his power across the land to help us."

U-wa was suddenly furious. "Be silent, Daughter! By his own choice your brother has placed his concern for a herd of mammoth above that for his own band and has followed a gathering of tuskers over the edge of the world to—"

"He follows the *totem* into the light of the rising sun," the girl responded passionately. "He walks in the power of the sacred stone. The spirits of the Ancient Ones and of all the animals have called him to be guardian of the totem. He told us to walk with him. Kosar-eh refused. And now we are—"

"And now, in this place of death, I curse the day I ever bore him!" U-wa threw up her burned hands in despair.

Joh-nee's eyes went so round that they looked like moons in full eclipse. "You do not mean that!"

"I do!" U-wa shouted at her daughter. "Cha-kwena lied to us. The totem is dead. The sacred stone has no power."

The baby stiffened in Joh-nee's arms. "Bad things come!" exclaimed the little one, her face raised skyward, all of her senses save that of vision obviously alert.

U-wa tensed as she saw Joh-nee kiss the child and make soft assurances that now that Kosar-eh was gone, surely all that was bad had already come their way. Hackles rose along the woman's neck. She felt sick. The last time she had heard such words spoken to that baby it had been moments before the raiders came. "Come," she said to the children. "We cannot linger here. A storm is coming. Kosar-eh has commanded us to take shelter in the hills. We must obey."

"Are we to abandon our dead, then, as he has abandoned us?" Kiu-neh turned the question as he might have twisted the point of a sharpened stick in the wound of prey that he held below contempt. "My father does not care about us. But are we not to mourn our loved ones in the way of our ancestors so that their maimed spirits will at least have some chance of wandering the world beyond this world in honor?"

U-wa was torn. In the deepening red glow of sunset, the wind was intensifying and storm clouds were definitely gathering. Her brow furrowed; her head hurt. She was nauseated and dizzy, but the boy was right. They could not just walk off and leave their dead without so much as an invocation to the spirits on their behalf; surely Kosar-eh would not want this. Before the advent of darkness and weather, with Kiu-neh, Kho-neh, and Joh-nee working together, it would not take long to search the burned-out lodge for previously unfound body parts. Once placed with the deceased, the dead would be more or less whole again. Then, with care and luck, enough kindling might be found to raise a prayer fire so that, in the way of the ancestors, words of final parting could be sent on consecrated smoke along with invocations to the spirits on behalf of the dead.

"I do not think we should make fire," said Joh-nee when U-wa declared her intent. "The smoke may be seen and smelled by more than spirits."

"The raiders have come and gone, girl!" U-wa reminded her.

Joh-nee sighed, obviously uneasy as she put Doh-teyah on her feet and turned eastward to wonder aloud, "Ah, Cha-kwena . . . Where are you now, my brother?"

"What difference?" slurred Kiu-neh. "Come. Help us with those who, because of him, are now dead."

# 2

Cha-kwena came to the lake alone.

For four nights and four days the shaman had been fasting. Now the fourth day was ending with the sun's descent into the immense white wastes of frozen water that lay before him, confounding his spirit as surely as they had confounded his every effort to find a way around or across them and back to his band.

Twice had Moon turned her full face to the earth since the only son of U-wa had awakened half-drowned on a partially submerged gravel bar somewhere along the deeply indented shoreline of this body of water. Now, as then, from horizon to horizon, winter-iced deeps claimed the land as surely as they had claimed his body after a pack of wild dogs had driven him into treacherous breaks of open water, which would have taken his life had the mammoth not dragged him unconscious onto dry land.

For endless days and nights Cha-kwena had traveled up and down this monstrous shore, desperately searching for the spot from which he had emerged from the forest to glimpse the lake for the first time. But every cove and inlet appeared much the same, and all he found was one of the red-and-blue-banded spears he had thought lost to the lake. With an unceasing cloud cover, every effort to find his way back through the trees to the village where he had left his people was frustrated. Soon, hungry and exhausted and compelled to seek shelter by the arrival of White Giant Winter, he had reluctantly followed the mammoth northeastward toward a sobering range of black hills and gray, forbidding mountains of ice.

*Wherever the mammoth find browse, there, too, shall the People find meat.* The teachings of the Ancient Ones had given strength and solace as he followed the small herd of tuskers along the lakeshore to the floodplain of a great river. From there they went upslope across a cold, windswept plain of glacial rubble, broken in places by strange, stunted woodlands and broad tracts of spongy turf. There he had indeed found game—small, broad-bellied brown horses; hook-nosed antelope; massively antlered stag moose; towering, long-legged camels; and even a pair of shaggy mastodon. All had been browsing at the neck of a canyon. With them were many a beast Cha-kwena had seen only in his mind's eye, for they were the creatures of legend: musk ox—Black Old Man Who Wears Horns as a Hat; yak—Hairy-Bellied Brother of Ox; caribou—Little Deer Who Eats Only Moss; and rarest of all, rhinoceros—Horn Nose, huge and granite gray under his woolly hair, his puny eyes glinting arrogantly in his regally held head.

Now, carrying his spear and clad in the furs and hides of those beasts of legend that had consented to die by his hand, Cha-kwena paused on a stony beach at the tip of one of many glacially eroded peninsulas that intruded into the frozen vastness of the lake. He wondered if it was possible to feel so alone and not die from the anguish of it.

He was a small, leanly muscular man, young for a shaman but, with nearly twenty winters behind him, far from youth. His face was painted blue in the way of the holy men of his tribe when they sought communion with the sky spirits. Over his roughly made winter shirt and leggings, he wore the heavy cloak of twisted rabbit pelts that his woman had made for him many a long moon ago. Upon his head was his time-battered sacred head-dress, fashioned from the eviscerated body of a great horned owl. These cherished belongings warmed Cha-kwena's body but not his spirit; now, more than ever, they made him long for home and band.

The wind was in his face. Cold wind, North Wind, enemy wind, bringer of storms and death. It hissed and spat airborne grit as it ruffled the feathers of his head-dress and invaded the protective projection of the hood to make his skin burn and his narrowed eyes smart with cold. He turned from it, hunkering on his heels, and stared westward to the horizon, where the setting sun glinted through thin bands of gathering storm clouds like the hungrily malevolent eye of a carnivorous bird.

Cha-kwena scowled, but not entirely in despair of the approach of yet another storm. The look of the sun made him think of bloody-beaked ravens and teratorns circling within the dark and hideous dreams that had been plaguing him of late. Somewhere, somehow, something was wrong in the world. He knew it, *felt* it. There were dangerous, shifting elements of change stirring in the very air he breathed, and deep within the marrow of his bones he sensed that his people were in danger.

"How can I help them when the land conspires with the forces of Creation and White Giant Winter to hold me captive on this far shore beyond the edge of the world?"

Cha-kwena's scowl deepened. He had committed himself to a fast in hope of clarifying the exact meaning of his dreams, but the nutritional deprivation that usually did so much to sharpen his senses and focus the power of shamanic vision had given insight into nothing save hunger. As his belly lurched and growled, frustration brought him to his feet.

The sun was sinking rapidly beneath the cloud-banded horizon. The shaman stood transfixed, watching as mist formed far out on the ice. Red mist, bloodred, it was spreading, and phantoms were taking shape from its vapors. Human but faceless, shrouded in the red haze of distance, they stood in a long line before, suddenly, they came surging toward him. Instinctively he stepped back and cried out, then watched with relief as the specters were dispelled by the sound of his voice.

Or had they merely transposed themselves to another place?

Cha-kwena stiffened. He was no longer alone. His backward step had brought him into contact with something bigger than a boulder and as solid, but very much alive, if he was to judge from the heat of its breath at his back. Every hair follicle on his scalp and at the nape of his neck bristled as he leaped forward. Spear ready, he whirled around, expecting to confront man-eating phantoms—and saw instead something that made him burst out laughing at his foolishness.

The shaggy "little" white mammoth calf growled a happy greeting as it sidled forward, sagged heavily against the shaman's side, and slung a winter-furred trunk around his knees. Cha-kwena steadied himself for an elephantine hug that nearly took him off his booted feet; the calf was not yet a yearling, but, nourished by the rich milk of the huge, freckle-skinned matriarch of its herd, it had more than tripled in size since birth; its strength was, quite literally, staggering.

"Ah, little one, why do you follow me instead of your mother? Do I look like a tusker to you?" Cha-kwena leaned into the young mammoth's embrace and, soothed by its warmth and nearness, removed his glove

and allowed the calf to pull his hand into its mouth as it
liked to do when seeking comfort in a friendly suck as
though at the nipple of a surrogate mother. The shaman
smiled, touched deeply by the affection of the totem
animal of his tribe; nevertheless, his throat constricted
as a wave of remorse rose in him. His obedience to the
command of the spirits of the Ancestors to remain at
the totem's side had cost him all that he had ever loved
and held dear.

"If only Kosar-eh and the rest of my people could
see you now, they would know that they were wrong to
doubt this shaman's word and to refuse to follow me—
and you—into the face of the rising sun! The spirit of
the great white mammoth totem *has* been reborn in
you. The power of Life Giver, Grandfather of All Mammoth, *is* returning to the world and to this shaman
through you. It grows stronger as you grow stronger,
and soon—"

His words were interrupted by the ear-splitting
trumpeting of the great cow mammoth. Seeking her
calf, she came pounding from the canyon in which she
and the rest of the herd were wintering, close to the
shelter of driftwood, cast-off antlers, bones, and hides
that Cha-kwena had erected. The shaman turned
toward the sound as the little white mammoth released
his hand to trot eastward in dutiful response to its
mother.

Cha-kwena scanned ahead of the calf, upward
across the broad, shouldering sweep of a terminal mo-
raine toward the entrance to the canyon. He could just
make out the herd—the great freckled cow, massively
made, towering above the other females, adolescents,
and older calves. The shaman's head went high in re-
spectful recognition. These tuskers had saved his life as
surely as he had taken the life of the great white bull of
their herd, the ancient totem, after finding it mortally

savaged by coyotes and wild dogs in a place that his tribesmen later came to call the Valley of the Dead. It still hurt him to think of it, that act of compassion, especially now. Though he was certain that the spirit of the totem had been reborn in the little white calf, he was equally certain that he would be an old man before the calf attained the full and awesome power of totemic maturity. And it was sobering, indeed, to realize that the herd of mammoth upon which he now gazed might well be the last of its kind in all the world.

*When the last mammoth vanishes from the earth, with the passing of its kind, so too shall the totem perish and the People die forever.*

The shaman's brow furrowed. The prophecy of the Ancient Ones of the Red World never failed to disturb him. In the lands across which he had led his band, mammoth had been hunted until only bones and tusks remained to speak of their passage. Yet, although men had been turned by expedience to hunt other game, the elders of the northern tribes still held that a warrior who failed to wet his spear in the blood of a mammoth would never be a man. And Cha-kwena knew that, among these ever-battling tribes, there were chieftains and shamans who would give everything to know the whereabouts of the little white calf, for a legend persisted that the man who slew the white mammoth, who ate of its flesh and drank of its blood, would become totem, gaining immortality for himself and invincibility for his people.

Cha-kwena shook his head. Not so long ago many believed that *he* had become totem, with his slaying of Grandfather of All Mammoth. Shateh, high chief among the many tribes of the People of the Land of Grass, had been so convinced of Cha-kwena's totemic power that he had put aside his old hatred of Red World people to forge an alliance with Cha-kwena's

band and assure triumph in war against their mutual
enemy, the cannibal People of the Watching Star. When
this had been accomplished, the enemies had scattered
like broken leaves upon a rising storm wind. Then the
war chief renamed Cha-kwena Totem Slayer, shaman of
his own tribe, and looked to him for advice in all things.

Until Cha-kwena, following the sacred herd of
mammoth in the way of his ancestors, led Shateh's people eastward into land that was dry and barren as the
genitals of an old woman.

Until increasingly hungry, thirsty times fell upon
the chieftain's people, and in a land of little rain and
less meat, Shateh's hunters began to eye the sacred
herd and, salivating, wonder why Totem Slayer forbade
its flesh to those who—before joining with him—had
been mammoth hunters.

Until, in those last strained days and nights together, the breast milk of nursing mothers began to
wane, and little ones spoke longingly of past feasts while
old women whispered suspiciously about the infallibility
of their new shaman's power.

Cha-kwena would have left the northerners then
had the choice been his. But even if Shateh had allowed
him to go, the men of his band had by then no wish to
abandon their new lives. Their alliance with warriors
had changed them; their ways had become the ways of
the fighting men of the distant Land of Grass. Had they
known that Life Giver mated before its death and the
real totem lay vulnerable within the belly of the great
cow, they would not have listened to an increasingly
powerless Red World shaman. They would have found a
way to separate the matriarch from the herd, weaken
her with spears, and stalk her until she dropped; then,
led by Shateh, they would have cut the living fetus from
her body so that they might all eat of its flesh and drink
of its blood and claim totemic power for themselves.

Cha-kwena trembled. He gazed at the pale, shaggy creature as, bleating now, it continued toward its mother with its tail up and its trunk extended. When it reached the great cow and was lost to view inside an encircling gathering of tuskers, the shaman's mood went as gray and cold as the dusk.

He listened to the howling of distant wolves, placing the origins of the ululations well to the north. He could discern distinct voices: several young animals, each eager and highly nervous; three mature females, one much larger than the others, her voice steady yet tentative, clearly awaiting command. And a single mature male, his call deeper, longer, more sonorous than the rest. With darkness, this was the animal that would bring the others together in a location of his choosing, and then the endless search of predator for prey would begin across a desolate land that granted favor to neither.

The shaman's right hand tightened around the hardwood haft of his spear. He had little fear of wolves. Only in starving times did they look hungry-eyed at such potentially dangerous prey as men or mammoth. Indeed he envied the pack, longed for the ordered camaraderie of a family working together for the survival of all. With his heart yearning to cross the ice and return to his band, Cha-kwena stared westward once again.

*Mah-ree! Ta-maya and Tla-nee! U-wa and Joh-nee! Old Kahm-ree and Kosar-eh and all of his rowdy boys! Are you still waiting for me in the forest village?* The shaman doubted it. The unfairness of his situation struck Cha-kwena hard. The totem was warm and secure within the embrace of its mother and family. But what of the shaman who was sworn to protect it?

"Am I never again to know the companionship of my own kind, or be comforted by my mother, or rest warm in the loving embrace of my Mah-ree?" Cha-kwena's voice broke. His need to return to his people and little girl-of-a-woman was so intense that tears smarted beneath his lids. "Mah-ree!" He cried the name of his beloved and cursed the night he sent her back to the village without him.

His eyes closed, Cha-kwena conjured Mah-ree's dimpled smile, her sweetly impudent laughter, her eager lovemaking, and found himself trembling with wanting and regret. She could have been with him now had he not turned from her in anger! It was her place to be at his side as his woman! She had said it more times than there were ways to count the words: *Always and forever! Cha-kwena and Mah-ree! Mated for life in this world and the world beyond, like swans and wolves and eagles, like First Man and First Woman in the tales of the Ancient Ones!* If only Mah-ree's flagrant disobedience of the laws of the ancestors on their last night together had not made it impossible!

He opened his eyes, stared ahead, and saw nothing but the past. Even as a child, Mah-ree's bright, questing nature had sent her trespassing boldly around the corners of tradition. Her intent was to be another First Woman. She would hunt with a spear! She would travel across unknown lands astride the twin-domed head of the great white mammoth totem! She would sit as Mother of Medicine in council with the forces of Creation, a full equal with First Man and the animals and all green growing things and with every spirit of the Earth and Sky! All this was, of course, impossible. Since time beyond beginning, there was, and could only be, one First Woman. The use of spears was allowed only to males; all knew that the handling by female hands of such weapons could result in the man bones of every male in the band becoming permanently flaccid. Females did not sit in council, unless it was with one another, and then only to discuss those subjects that directly related to their gender. And no one rode astride mammoth!

Yet Mah-ree, second-born daughter of Tlana-quah, chieftain of the Red World village by the Lake of Many Singing Birds, had not been dissuaded from her intent. Time and time again she was chastised; time and time again she went her own stubborn way. Until, on that sunstruck day when the great bear had come marauding toward Shateh's village, startling the chieftain's women at their creekside bathing and surprising the men who had been appointed to guard them, Mah-ree's forbidden and secretly acquired skill with a spear had enabled her to kill the beast with a lance that one of the men had thrown wide. She had saved her own life with that throw, and that of one of the chieftain's women. But according to the traditions of her adopted tribe, Mah-ree had also offended the ancestors, humiliated the hunter whose spear she had used, and shamed the spirit of the great slain bear. Later, when the chieftain's wife lay near death after shock-induced premature labor forced the birth of a stillborn son, all blamed the law-breaking Red World woman for depriving Shateh of that which he wanted most in all the world, and the last shred of faith that the chieftain held in the Red World shaman was gone forever.

On that night Mah-ree's life was to have been forfeited as punishment for her disobedience to the laws of the Ancient Ones. On that night the warriors of Shateh declared their intent to hunt the sacred herd. On that night Cha-kwena fled with his lawbreaking little girl-of-a-woman. With Kosar-eh and the others following, the long trek that eventually brought him to this place of solitude had begun.

He sighed, despondent, for to this day he did not know why he had expected her to change, much less obey him on that fateful night when he had commanded her to remain with the others while he went alone in search of the sacred herd, intending to drive it back to the village. Mah-ree had taken the sacred stone of the ancestors from the sanctuary within which he had left it —to grant his people courage during his absence—and had selfishly used the talisman to embolden her own heart as she followed him through the dark woods in the reckless hope of seeing the little white calf. But her presence had sent the mammoth deeper into the forest, and Cha-kwena had been so enraged that he accused her of putting the totem at risk, of being the source of their people's misfortune, and of threatening his shamanic power. Ignoring her tearful promise to be obedient, he commanded her to return immediately to the village with the sacred stone and had gone on alone after the herd.

The sacred stone! If only he had the talisman! That small, fang-shaped, fossilized stone that was, somehow, not stone at all, but the last remaining fragment of the bones of First Man and First Woman. It had been in the care of the holy men of his tribe since time beyond beginning when First Man and First Woman, Father and Mother of all the generations of the People, followed Life Giver, a great mammoth, out of the world of spirits into the world of living beings. It was said by the Ancient Ones that the spirits of First Man and First Woman resided within the talisman. And surely Cha-kwena knew this to be true, for the stone spoke to those who would hear the voices of the ancestors that dwelled within.

The power of the talisman had waned with the ebbing life of the ancient totem mammoth, and when Life Giver had died, the power of the stone died, too. But only briefly. The rebirth of the totem awakened the sleeping spirits within the talisman; now, safe in the care of the band, they would speak to guide his people

and keep them strong and safe from all who would
come against them.

Why then, he wondered, could he not envision
Mah-ree safe within the band? And why was he disturbed by ill-defined visions and dreams that threatened
not only him but her and his people? Perhaps, he
thought, it was not only longing for his band but lingering love for his lawbreaking little girl-of-a-woman that
haunted him. For surely, in the long days and nights
after leaving her, Cha-kwena had often looked back,
half-hoping to see Mah-ree's small, slender, high-
breasted figure stubbornly dogging his trail. But he had
seen no sign of her and, to his profound disappointment, had finally realized that she had actually obeyed
him. Perhaps, under Kosar-eh's stern, pragmatic, and
unyielding leadership, this most stubborn and adorable
daughter of the Red World had mended her ways at
last. But he, the one who loved her most of all, was not
there to see and celebrate the change in her.

Consumed by longing, he stepped boldly onto the
ice and shouted to the gathering dusk and storm clouds
and to whatever spirits of the wind would hear him. "I
never asked to be Shaman! On the night I left my people and woman to follow the herd I never intended to
keep on going *forever*! Show me the way by which I may
return to my band! The totem and the mammoth kind
have survived since time beyond beginning in this world
without my help. Surely they will be able to do so now
in this place of desolation to which those who would
hunt them will never come!"

"Will they not?"

The question startled him. He looked around, puzzled. Who had spoken? Far beyond the curve of the
western horizon, coyotes suddenly raised a high, frenzied yapping that silenced the wolves. Cha-kwena
scowled. Since following the sacred herd through the

forest into this land of desolation, he had not seen or heard a single coyote. He had no love for their kind. Coyote had come to him in his boyhood dreams, had appeared as though out of nowhere to run at his side in times of need, to guide him along the paths of life, and along the vision trails that confirmed his calling to be shaman; but they had also tricked and confounded him into dangerous mires of indecision, then mocked the failures to which they had brought him. Yellow wolves had run with wild dogs to savage the great white mammoth.

"Why do you call to me now?" he shouted angrily. "You have not seen fit to come from the forest to show me the way by which I could return to my band. Nor have you come to comfort me in my solitude. Now you sing to the dying day with those of your own kind while I stand here alone to face the coming of yet another storm. Ah! Come closer! Let the spear of Cha-kwena speak to those who so brazenly mock him!" His heartbeat quickened as suspicion flared. "Or do you *warn* me?"

Again he sensed that something was wrong in the world. He knew it, *felt* it. His people *were* in danger. His mother, his sister, his *woman*!

"I must go to her, to them!" he cried.

"They are far from this place, in a land of blood and death where men of faith still hunt the totem. You cannot return to them! Listen not to Trickster! Turn away, away! Now, before it is too late, remember that you are Cha-kwena of the Red World, Grandson of Hoyeh-tay, Brother of Animals and Guardian of the Totem . . . Shaman!"

Startled, Cha-kwena could have sworn that the wings of a large bird brushed the top of his head as again he looked around to see who had spoken. The coyotes were no longer barking. The wolves were still.

The mammoth were plodding toward the entrance to the canyon. But well out on the frozen lake stood a blue-faced old man in a bonnet of tufted grass. His scrawny body was clad only in summer sandals of pounded sagebrush, a breechcloth of antelope hide, and a short, rabbit-skin cape. A great horned owl perched on his shoulder.

"Hoyeh-tay?" Cha-kwena spoke the name of his long-dead grandfather, then closed his eyes in disbelief. When he opened them again, the ghosts of the old man and his helping animal spirit, Owl—whose skin Cha-kwena wore upon his head—were gone, but mist phantoms were forming on the ice again, taking the shape not of many but of one, this time not human . . . but animal.

"Bear!" Cha-kwena named the phantom and knew that he had seen this beast before—hanging on a drying frame in Shateh's village after Mah-ree had slain it, and in many a nightmare vision since.

"If you return across the ice, Shaman, who will guard the totem when you are slain and the sacred stone is taken by enemies and your people are scattered like seeds upon the wind?" asked Bear. "The ravens of your dreams are gathering, Brother. Other shamans awake to other needs than yours. Soon they will join with lions and follow you. They seek the sacred stone. They hunt the totem. *I* will hunt the totem. And when the white mammoth dies, so too will you and the People perish forever!"

The wind was very cold. The great cow mammoth was trumpeting in the canyon. Cha-kwena shivered as he saw the phantom fade into mist again; he felt drained, weakened by hunger and the knowledge that he had experienced the vision he had been seeking through days and nights of fast. If he was to assure the lives of his loved ones, he must continue to put his concern for the mammoth above all else.

Now, in the ebbing light of the dying day, with a storm rising at his back, Cha-kwena turned and followed the mammoth. As long as the totem lived, so too would his people live. They would grow stronger as the mammoth grew stronger, and in the meantime, as long as Kosar-eh kept his followers faithful to the way of the ancestors, the band would remain in the protection of the sacred stone that Mah-ree had returned to them.

"Will they?"

Again words born of no visible source invaded Cha-kwena's senses, but he plodded on toward the canyon, keeping his back to the lake and to the misted phantoms of the past. After four days and nights without food, water, or sleep, he was weary of Vision; he needed to eat, to quench his thirst and his need for sleep. And so, with a snarl of defiance to the forces of Creation that had drawn him beyond the edge of the world to his solitary fate, he replied, "They *have* to!" and stalked on, refusing to consider the alternative.

# 3

Kosar-eh cursed the night.

He stopped, glared at the sky as though he might will back the day, then, conceding to the impossibility of such a feat, hurried on.

Until now he had been able to track the raiders with ease across the snow. They were moving quickly into the hills, and for a while Ta-maya's footprints were clearly visible among those of her abductors—small, rough-soled winter moccasin tracks, one indenting the ice-encrusted snow slightly more than the other because she favored her frost-scarred right foot. If Klah-neh was with them, he was either being carried or his weight was so meager that there was no mark left by the press of his feet. But he had not seen his beautiful beloved's footprints for some time now and knew, from the deepening imprint of the tracks of the largest man in the raiding party, that she was also being carried.

"That man will be the first to die!" he vowed, his heart hardening as he was forced to slow his pace to accommodate the increasingly steep and stony terrain.

Thickening cloud cover soon obscured the first stars of evening, and in the gathering darkness a coyote yapped somewhere close ahead. The sound had a distractingly human quality, and Kosar-eh found himself thinking of Cha-kwena. "I will not let you turn me from my purpose!" he declared, cursing the shaman Yellow Wolf for having brought him to this moment.

He was not sure just when snow began to fall. Desperation drove him now. If he failed to find the raiders before their trail was covered, he had little hope of ever finding his woman and youngest boy. Fighting increasing exhaustion, he kept steadily on, growling with frustration as now and then—but always just out of spear range—a coyote appeared ahead, laying its tracks over those of the raiders as though attempting to lead the way . . . or obliterate the trail Kosar-eh sought to follow.

Fatigue had long since cooled Kosar-eh's rage but not his intent. Spear in hand, he entered a level clearing and stopped. The coyote was gone. Wind-driven snow clouds briefly parted, granting enough starlight to illuminate his surroundings. A tremor went through him, followed by shock, dread, rage, and terror. In the snow were man-made impressions not yet fully covered by the new snowfall. Some sort of gathering had occurred in this place . . . and violence. Despite wind and snow he caught the stink of blood and the musk of recent matings. And there, at the center of the clearing, was a castoff fur and something else, something small and all too familiar.

"No," he said as he moved forward, slowly, afraid to confirm his worst fears. A moment later, there was no denying them. He went to his knees and stared down at Ta-maya's sleeping robe and at one of the two feather-adorned bone hairpins he had made for her. His hand reached out, touched with tentatively questing fingertips that which he could not bear to touch . . . her blood on the fur, long since gone cold and now frozen.

Then he heard laughter: deep, male, a gurgling mockery.

Kosar-eh stiffened, turned, glared through intensifying snowfall, and saw what he had failed to see when he entered the clearing—the snow-covered form of a fur-clad man propped against the fallen tree.

"I told them you would come for her," the man said.

Kosar-eh was shaking. He knew the voice. It was weak, breathy, and there was something oddly thick about the way it bubbled out of the speaker's throat. "Ranamal!"

"Ah, yes . . . so you have not forgotten this Wolf. Good. Yes. It *is* good. Now, Red World Clown, you will give this Wolf that for which I have been waiting . . . what I need. Yes."

Kosar-eh was on his feet. "Where is my woman . . . my son?"

Again there was laughter, low and wheezing. "Be grateful, man of the Red World, that the boy will forget his lizard-eating father as he is raised to be a warrior among the People of the Land of Grass. Is this not what you wanted for all your boys, eh? Yes. You should thank me. All your fine sons, save the mewling pisser whose life I ended in your pathetic, unguarded rat's nest of a lodge . . . they will be no good to any tribe now, eh? And your woman, Ah . . . how tight she was when I pierced her! Has your filthy diet of lizards and vermin made your man bone so small, or have you not enjoyed her as fully as every man in my raiding party has just—"

Kosar-eh's spear flew. Even as it left his hand, he knew that its stone head would plunge not into Ranamal's heart but into his groin. As it did, Kosar-eh was grateful for the lack of light that had caused him to misjudge distance and send his lance in a shorter arc than passion intended. He wanted Ranamal dead, but not until he learned from him what he must know; besides, seeing the head of his spear embedded in this man's pelvis gave Kosar-eh a profound albeit momentary sense of retribution.

As he advanced to stand over Ranamal, the moment passed. "You will tell me where the others have taken my woman and son!" he demanded, his voice cold with barely controlled rage.

Ranamal, hands around the haft of the spear, stared in blank-eyed shock as he sagged sideways.

"You *will* tell me!" Kosar-eh demanded, kneeling as he impatiently took hold of the man's furs in order to pull him back into a seated position; it was in this moment that, with a start, he saw that Ranamal's back was wet with blood from another wound. "What?"

Ranamal laughed, an ugly, bitter gurgle, made at his own expense. "The old grandmother . . . snoring all the time, pretending to sleep. . . . Then, even as I came hot into your woman, she came into me with a prod from the fire still burning as she drove it deep. . . . Ah . . . who would have thought that she could make such a killing wound on this Wolf, eh? Or that my fellow warriors would leave me here to die of it alone?"

Kosar-eh was not moved to pity. With his hands curled into the fur at Ranamal's shoulders, he hefted him into a seated position and shoved his injured back hard against the stump. "Where is my woman? You will tell me, or I will hear you howl as you beg for death, Wolf!"

Ranamal stared long and hard at Kosar-eh, his face twisted with pain. Then, with open contempt, he spat in the Red World man's face in derision of the battle name that Kosar-eh had won among his people. "I will hear you howl first, would-be warrior, when I tell you this: Ta-maya, woman of Kosar-eh, was enjoyed here . . .

by every man in my war band until she slipped a skinning dagger from its sheath at Ynau's side and would have stabbed him with it. Weak, whimpering woman. We had finished with her by then. With her broken arm and limping leg, what good was she to us, eh, when we have our own women, whole and eager, waiting for compliance in our camp by the—no, I will not tell you that. But I will say that we gave to your woman what she chose for herself—Ynau's blade. While we ate and rested for the journey ahead, she staggered naked into the hills . . . bleeding . . . crying for you, Red World man. But you were not present to watch her die . . . there . . . or was it there?" Ranamal gestured weakly off in all directions, deliberately frustrating Kosar-eh's hope of finding his beloved woman's body until, suddenly, the howling of coyotes arrested the movement of the man's hand. "They will find her before you do."

Kosar-eh was impaled by the truth of the statement. "*Where* did she fall?"

Ranamal's breathing was shallow now, strained; yet through intensifying pain and the slow, killing effects of the internal hemorrhage that had been sapping the life from him for hours, he smiled. "Forget the dead, would-be warrior. As you snivel over a lost woman, the smoke and stink of your burning lodge will have drawn other raiders to what we left of your camp. Now the warriors of the Watching Star will hunt your band instead of mine! And if you have again left others in an unprotected camp with neither shaman nor sacred stone nor totem to protect them, they will be long dead or enslaved when you return to them. But do not despair, Kosar-eh. The days and nights spent in this world of the living are short for all men, eh? Ah, yes. It *is* so. The spirits of the dead of your camp, and of your woman, Ta-maya, will wait for you on the wind! I will soon be with them. And I will enjoy her body there, in the world beyond this world, as I enjoyed it in the land of the living until you come to—"

Kosar-eh's rage was so immense that when he silenced Ranamal's vindictiveness with a blow to the mouth, his closed fist half-lifted the man off the ground and sent his head backward over the top of the stump, effectively snapping his neck. Death found Ranamal with a leer of spiteful satisfaction still on his face.

Kosar-eh heard and smelled the life go out of the man as Ranamal's body sagged upon the stump. Shaking, rubbing the bruised knuckles of his right hand with his left, Kosar-eh felt his rage dissolve into an agony of frustration. This was not what he intended! As he watched snowflakes fall onto the dead man's face, into his open eyes and grotesquely smiling mouth, he knew that he had just given Ranamal exactly what he had been hoping for: a quick death, an ending of pain, not a reprieve from it.

Again rage overwhelmed Kosar-eh. He stood. With one foot braced on the dead man's belly, he jerked his spear free from Ranamal's groin. Again and again he plunged the long stone projectile point into the body, piercing the furs that encased him, disemboweling him, severing his genitals and further mutilating his corpse until there was no hope of Ranamal's twisted spirit ever emerging whole from his body to ride the wind to the world of spirits. This Wolf had raped and slain the woman and followers of Kosar-eh when alive; he would not further humiliate them in the land of the dead.

Now, with coyotes howling in pack, despair overwhelmed Kosar-eh as he turned his face to the wind and snow and howled with them, releasing the demon of his agony. Klah-neh had been stolen; Ta-maya and Ka-neh were dead. And with a storm rising all around he knew that he had no chance of tracking the abductors of his youngest boy or of finding the body of his beautiful beloved. Bereft of all hope for them, he was chilled by a sudden recollection of Ranamal's words: *"Now the warriors of the Watching Star will hunt your band instead of mine! And if you have again left others in an unprotected camp with neither shaman nor sacred stone nor totem to protect them, they will be long dead or enslaved when you return to them."*

For the first time since Kosar-eh had so thoughtlessly turned his back on the smoking rubble of his encampment, he remembered those whom he had left behind: U-wa and Joh-nee, his bold Kiu-neh and brave Kho-neh, and Doh-teyah, the blind daughter whom Ta-maya loved so deeply that she had been willing to face exile and risk death rather than see the child slain.

Shame overcame Kosar-eh, and disgust for his callousness toward the blind child he had wished dead and the others who trusted and depended upon him. He raised his spear, impatiently cleansed its stone head in snow, then turned from the corpse that he had made and went to his beloved's discarded sleeping robe.

He knelt, fingered through a rapidly accumulating layer of snow, and withdrew Ta-maya's hairpin from where he had last seen it. Placing it to his lips, he closed his eyes, conjured her beautiful image—radiant, smiling as she held Doh-teyah to her breast, her hip-length black hair parted in the center of her head and pulled back from her exquisite face, secured high above each temple with the adornments that he had fashioned for her with such love and care: two bifurcated pins, each the length and width of her forefinger, both carved from deer antler, each engraved and painted with the same black-and-white lateral striping that decorated his own body, and each festooned with a single black, iridescent magpie feather that shone lustrous green in the light of the sun or moon or stars.

"Forgive me," Kosar-eh implored the spirit of his

slain woman, and suddenly he wept—for her, for himself, for the love and joy they had known together and would never know again.

The continued howling of coyotes drew his thoughts away from his self-consuming misery. He listened. The yellow wolves were much closer than before. Again he thought of Cha-kwena; again he cursed the shaman for bringing him to this place and yet another moment of tragedy. Then his brow came down. The yapping of the coyotes told him that the pack had divided and was on the move, one or more of the animals heading on into the wind, the rest running south and east in the direction from which he had come.

*Toward the encampment!*

With Ranamal's threat burning in his brain, Kosar-eh rose to his feet, reached under his hood, and secured Ta-maya's pin to the forelock of his own hair. Drawing strength and resolve from the possession of even so small a keepsake of their love, the big man knew what he must do: what his beautiful beloved would have had him do if her gentle spirit were here to guide him now.

"I will go back. For the sake of the children, I *must* go back!" And although his heart would have had him continue the quest for the slayers of his woman, he committed himself instead to return to the encampment.

With the wind at his back, Kosar-eh had little difficulty finding his way through snow-lit darkness. Across long, familiar miles, coyotes loped ahead, laying their tracks in fresh powder, now and then pausing to circle and yap as though impatiently encouraging a slower member of the pack to hurry onward.

"I am no brother of your kind," Kosar-eh murmured, troubled by their presence and behavior. His mind filled with images of circling ravens and teratorns, of sun dogs and smoke, of lions roaring in the livid glare of a swollen sun, and of the mutilated faces of his murdered sons. His gut tightened. He assured himself that —despite the vindictive threats of Ranamal, and even if warriors of the Watching Star *had* come together to hunt old enemies within this land—what had befallen his people in the light of this morning's sun could not possibly happen to them twice under the same sky.

Yet Kosar-eh was filled with dread as he hurried on, for he remembered the elders of his distant Red World tribe counseling young hunters to avoid at all cost the high mesas during times of storm. Lightning could strike again and again, singeing the earth and shattering stones, fingering living creatures with white-hot veins of fire. Kosar-eh had witnessed the feeding frenzy of lightning when it struck without warning on the vast, golden plains of the Land of Grass, when it bolted out of whirling winds that sucked men, trees, lodges, and entire herds of bison into the sky.

*Long ago and far away,* he thought. *In another world. There are no mesas in this land!* But he knew that he had brought his people into hunting grounds where they were vulnerable to lightning storms of another kind—to enemies whom he had mistakenly assumed dead or long gone across the mountains.

Kosar-eh went on until, at last, with the ruins of his gutted camp just visible ahead, he stopped. The coyotes were silent. The wind was down. Snow was falling straight to the ground. The world was quiet, so quiet that he could hear individual flakes of snow settling upon him and all around him. Instinct and a lifetime of experience as a hunter told him that it must be close to dawn. U-wa and the children would be sleeping in the boulder-strewn hills into which he had commanded them to go and hide themselves. Relief went through him like a draft of long-fermented blood and berries. They were alive! He would go to them in the morning. Now he would rest and try not to think of all that he must tell them when . . .

His thoughts stopped. His head went high. Something was wrong, different about the camp. His hand tightened around the haft of his spear. A good double handspan of snow had fallen since he had left, but well away from where the main lodge had been burned, he saw that another structure had been raised. He stared through falling whiteness and made out a wide sweep of what had to be snow-weighted skins lying across a brace of poles.

Anger replaced his relief. Certain that yet another of his commands had been disobeyed, Kosar-eh advanced without caution. He would rouse the sleeping woman and children and drive them into the safety of the hills! He would make them obey him! He would . . .

Again Kosar-eh's thoughts ceased. He stopped dead in his tracks, stared with disbelief at an assemblage of tall, massively headed spears upended in the snow in front of the lodge, ranked as though standing sentinel. Even before he heard the murmuring of several men, and the low sounds of a little girl softly crying, he knew that all that he had feared had come to pass.

*"The smoke and stink of your burning lodge will have drawn other raiders to what we left of your camp. Now the warriors of the Watching Star will hunt your band instead of mine!"*

Hackles rose on Kosar-eh's back as the words of a dead man mocked him even as he heard Doh-teyah's frightened, quivering baby voice coming from the interior of the lodge.

"Bad things! Bad things!"

He caught his breath, but not at the sound of his

daughter's voice. He was suddenly aware of someone standing behind him. In the next instant something sharp and hard pressed into the small of his back. Kosar-eh bolted forward with a rapid and violent twist to his right that he intended to bring him full circle with his spear levered and at the ready. It was not to be.

Tripped from behind, he fell to the ground, and someone kicked him—hard—and snatched his spear from his hand. Fighting for breath, he stared up at two tall, fur-clad, facially tattooed warriors. One of them had Kosar-eh's spear in hand. The other held the one that had evidently been pressed into Kosar-eh's back; it was pressing his belly now.

The sun was rising somewhere beyond the snow clouds, granting light enough for him to recognize his assailants as warriors of the Watching Star—as they, no doubt, recognized the colors that patterned his body, garments, and spear. Would they remember him from past raids upon their encampments? Kosar-eh had a sinking feeling that had nothing to do with the blow he had just received; any man who had ever seen him in battle and come away to tell the tale was unlikely to forget him.

"Use your weapon or withdraw it," he challenged them and, not caring whether he lived or died, braced himself for what would come.

"At our discretion, not yours, man of the Red World!"

Kosar-eh scowled; puzzled, he recognized the speaker as Indeh of the Land of Grass. Indeh had abandoned the ranks of Shateh's warriors long before the last war to join the raiders of the People of the Watching Star. Kosar-eh had never trusted, much less liked the man. "So you are still alive? A pity."

Indeh's broad, meaty-lipped face contorted with resentment. "For you!" he shot back and would have impelled his spear forward into Kosar-eh's gut had his companion not stayed his hand.

"Wait. Look at this!" insisted the other, appraising the exquisitely knapped projectile point of Kosar-eh's spear. "Do you know this man, Indeh? Has he made this wondrous spear, or has it been brought forth from the stone by the magic of the shaman we seek? Ah, with our best stoneworkers dead, to again have—"

"This man has worked the stone," Indeh conceded, pushing the projectile point of his own spear deeper into Kosar-eh's midsection. "He learned the skill from my own tribesmen many a long moon ago. His reputation as a knapper was well known among us . . . as was his loyalty to the shaman, Yellow Wolf. His face paint has faded, but look at his hunt shirt and spear. Many a man among our scattered bands has spoken of the black-and-white warrior . . . of the lizard eater pretending to be a man!" His eyes fixed Kosar-eh as sharply as his spearhead stressed him. "Where is Chakwena of the Red World now—and the sacred stone, and the totem? You will tell us! You will lead us to them! Or—"

"Why do you still hunt these things? There is no power in the stone or in the shaman, and the bones of the totem lie in the Valley of the Dead," replied Kosar-eh as a terrible weariness that had little to do with fatigue overcame him. It was the cold, bleak, emotionless weariness of a man who saw that his own death was not only imminent but unavoidable. He did not care. His children and all others who trusted him were slain or enslaved; his beloved Ta-maya was dead. He was certain that when the raiders quit this camp, they would add the bodies of U-wa, Joh-nee, Kiu-neh, Khoneh, and blind Doh-teyah to the corpses their enemies had made this day.

"Why seek Yellow Wolf among the followers of

Kosar-eh?" he continued. "That powerless shaman has abandoned this equally powerless band and taken a worthless talisman over the very edge of the world, where by now he and his precious mammoth and Bad-Luck-Bringing Woman may well have fallen off the land into the sky. Go! Join him. This world will be well rid of you!"

"He echoes the woman." A frustrated Indeh swung the butt end of his spear upward.

Kosar-eh was stunned by the resultant blow. With his head spinning and blood welling in his mouth, he did his best to steady his gaze on Indeh's face as he spat to one side to indicate his contempt for the man; the effort cost him consciousness, but only for a moment.

"You, warrior from the Land of Grass! You will look at this man and heed what he will say to you now."

Kosar-eh opened his eyes at the cold command of a stranger's voice. He looked up. Another tattooed warrior stood before him. The newcomer was taller than the other two, broader of shoulder and longer of arm, impressive in finely stitched and fitted furs, physically powerful, and—with a desiccated human hand hanging from a thong around his neck, and a long gray scalp lock attached to the forelock of his own hair—dangerous looking.

"I am Tsana, slayer of Shateh and warrior chieftain of the People of the Watching Star," said the stranger. "On this dawn, in the light of the rising sun, though snow and cloud mask the sky, I unmask my heart as I say this to Man Who Spits in the Face of Enemies: Lead me in the way in which the shaman Cha-kwena has gone with the totem and sacred stone, and I vow on the Watching Star and on the lives of my people that I will forget that you have fought against us and brought death into our camps. Yield to me what I will have of you, and the captives I have taken this day will not be harmed, and Man Who Spits in the Face of Enemies will live to be a warrior at my side as together we hunt those who have taken your woman and slain your sons."

Kosar-eh heard the words; he did not believe them.

Seeing his reaction, Tsana nodded. "Indeh, Hrak, bring the others so he may see the truth of your chieftain's words."

The two men bowed deferentially, then hurried to the shelter.

Kosar-eh watched them go, saw a hide pulled back, and squinted as light flowed from the interior. Then Kiu-neh and Kho-neh were brought from the shelter, escorted by Indeh and Hrak and several other good-sized men. Joh-nee was with them, and Doh-teyah was safe in the girl's embrace.

Kosar-eh was stunned. The children appeared shaken but otherwise uninjured by their captivity. He did not know whether to rejoice or lament until he noticed that U-wa was not with them. Suspecting the worst, he spoke her name.

"A brave spirit," said Tsana. "She was honoring your dead when we came upon her. Fearlessly she faced us. Boldly she warned us away. And then, when we approached, she fell to the ground like a cornered doe that sees no way of escape from advancing hunters. She has not moved or spoken since."

A tremor went through Kosar-eh as, remembering Ta-maya, he accused, "You killed her!"

"No, my father," Kiu-neh informed him. "It happened exactly as he has said. They have raised medicine smoke for U-wa, and bathed her face and hands and feet with melted snow and—"

"Your son speaks true words," interrupted Tsana. "The warriors of the Watching Star do not squander the lives of females who are potential life bearers, or of children who will grow into warriors. War against those with whom you have so unwisely allied yourself has left no true healers alive within my tribe, so there is no one in this camp with knowledge enough to bring the woman U-wa's spirit back into her body from wherever it has wandered. I regret this, but if the woman dies, you cannot lay the fault of her passing from this world on me or mine."

Kosar-eh spat a fragment of broken tooth. "In another place, many a long moon ago, my woman was taken into your country by men of the Watching Star. Had I and my people not come after her, and had the warriors of the Land of Grass not allied themselves with *me,* she would have been given as gift meat to the cannibal spirit your people call Thunder in the Sky. And she would not have been the first female to die in such a way!"

Tsana did not flinch. "Such a sacrifice has been made in times of lingering cold and war and hunger, when Great Spirit has shown need of it. But rarely have we found cause to offer the meat of our own."

"No . . ." The word bled from Kosar-eh's mouth, thick with hatred and revulsion. "You have offered 'meat' stolen from other tribes, and while the women of your enemies wept for their lost daughters, you devoured their flesh and—"

"You know nothing of our ways, or of the needs of the great tusked spirit!" Tsana eyed the sky. "Now is a time of lingering cold and war and hunger. Now White Giant and his women, the Cold Sisters—Snow, Ice, Hail, and the Great Nagger, Howling Wind—feed upon the world. Now, with the passes through the mountains blocked by snow, the People of the Watching Star shelter far from the hunting grounds of our ancestors, and find our strength, not in the meat of mammoth, but in scrapings from the bones of a dead totem." He paused, fixed Kosar-eh with long black eyes. "There is *another.*

The totem has died, but its spirit is alive, growing in the world. This we *know*. This we *feel*. This we have been *promised* by the forces of Creation that have spoken through our shamans! And for the sake of finding the totem, we are forced to do that which would, save for starving times, be abhorrent to us." His face was rapt. "So I say again: Join with us now, Spits in the Face of Enemies. Lead us to the power and to the one who has stolen it, if not to avenge the death of your woman and sons, then for the sake of the children who look to you now for the continuance of their lives."

Kosar-eh's head was pounding; he had not missed the threat. Slowly, shakily, he got to his feet and saw Tsana gesture to Hrak. The subordinate warrior stiffened and immediately handed Kosar-eh his spear, which he accepted with no word of gratitude or display of emotion. He felt strangely devoid of feelings, as if something had died in him. His face hurt; he did not care. The wind was cold; he was inured to its chill. Yet with his badger-skin hood now lying loosely around his shoulders, the wind gusted erratically to send snow and the feather that was attached to Ta-maya's hairpin fluttering across his face. The contact was shattering. Her scent was on the feather. Warm, redolent of her smooth, sweet skin and of her favorite fragrances—sage and sweet grass and meadow rue—it brought memories of his beautiful beloved welling in Kosar-eh like waters from a cool, clear spring. He closed his eyes, trembled as though in her embrace, and then, with a start, opened his eyes, refreshed and renewed.

"Koshray!"

The big man stared into the face of his blind child. Doh-teyah was reaching out to him from Joh-nee's arms. His brow furrowed. Ta-maya had loved this little one; indeed, she had put the value of the child's life above her own. Was her spirit with him now, reminding him of this, imploring him to do the same? He moved forward and, to Joh-nee's visible surprise, took the toddler in one arm as he demanded of Tsana, "Shateh would have denied life to this blind child. What fate does Tsana hold for Doh-teyah, daughter of Kosar-eh, if this warrior agrees to lead him in the tracks of Yellow Wolf?"

"No, Kosar-eh! Do not!" Joh-nee's frightened cry made a mockery of her next words. "This girl is not afraid to die!" Her chin was quivering; indeed, within the bed fur that clothed her, her entire body was shivering as though in a gale. "Never will Joh-nee betray her brother and tell his enemies where he has gone! *Never!*"

Tsana eyed the girl thoughtfully, then looked back at Kosar-eh as he pointed his spear arm at Doh-teyah. "Shaman's Sister has said that twice this blind child called out to warn her band of approaching warriors long before they were seen, heard, or near enough to be scented. Such a child is a gift to her people from the forces of Creation. Speak what words you will to me, Spits in the Face of Enemies. Live as a warrior and avenge the death of your woman and children, or die now, along with the last of your sons; the choice is yours. Either way, Sees the Wind will be cherished by the People of the Watching Star. And this girl, Joh-nee, will in time be made to reveal to us what she remembers about the whereabouts of her shaman brother."

"I will lead you there!" volunteered Kiu-neh, eyes shining as he looked up at Tsana with the adoration of a pup eager to be accepted by the new leader of its pack.

"I seek a *man's* eyes, whelp," replied Tsana, scalding the boy with his disdainful tone. "To get them, perhaps you will be the first to die. Then your father will know that my threats are as sincere as my offers of friendship."

Kosar-eh was beaten and knew it. Kiu-neh's willingness to transfer loyalty to another cut him to the quick; nevertheless, his son had good cause for losing faith in his father this day. He would not stand by and allow the boy to be slain, or allow stubborn little Johnee to suffer for his sake out of concern for Cha-kwena. The shaman had no power. The totem was dead. The sacred talisman was only a piece of stone. If the warriors of the Watching Star chose to believe otherwise, why should he attempt to dissuade them when their misguided faith in intangibles could be used to save the lives of his children?

"The one you seek has gone the way he has always gone," he said to Tsana, "over the edge of the world, following the mammoth into the face of the rising sun. I will show you the way."

# 4

"Go! Go *now*!"

Cha-kwena awoke with a start, stared up at the thong-laced snarl of antlers and bones that formed the underpinning of his shelter, and fought back a scream. Caribou and elk, deer and stag moose were locked in mortal combat above his head! He heard the clash and scrape of horn, the chink of stones clattering beneath cloven hooves, the groans and whistling shrieks of mortal contest, and saw and smelled the sweat of bodies testing one another until antlers were ripped away and blood flowed down upon him.

The shaman sat up, gasping. The antlers and bones above his head were only that now. He touched them to be sure. His nightmare had dissolved, as had so many others before it. Cha-kwena scowled; the voice that had called him from his dreams lingered in his thoughts as the stink and heat of his own sweat lingered in his nostrils and upon his body.

Suddenly desperate for cold, clean air and open space, he clambered on his knees to the ox-hide baffle that kept the weather at bay and crawled outside.

Beyond the shelter was nothing but whiteness—vast mounds of snow heaped upon the earth for as far

as his eyes could see through the veil of falling flakes
that dimmed the light of the clouded dawn. He could
not tell where the land ended and the sky began. He
would be snowbound for many a long day and night. His
shelter was still abundantly stocked with meat, but his
caches had been robbed repeatedly by wolves and foxes
and other carnivores more clever at stealing than he was
at stashing; if White Giant Winter did not soon leave
the land, his abilities as a shaman hunter would be
tested once again, and he had seen no game in over a
moon.

The growling of nearby mammoth caused Cha-
kwena to squint in their direction. He knew that he was
looking into the heart of the canyon, and he visualized
the defile as he had first seen it at autumn's end: dark,
ice-scoured walls soaring against a cloudless sky, the
sheer granite faces cleft by the arm of a great, gray,
tumultuously frothing river whose voice boomed and
roared as it muscled its way through the stony depths.
Frost-browned ferns, stunted conifers, and leafless,
lichen-festooned hardwoods had filled the forest along
the riverbanks; waterfalls, solidified by a sudden early
freeze, plunged in glistening, white, translucent silence
from the heights. Now even the great river was stilled by
the subfreezing press of White Giant's hand.

Again a mammoth growled, a sound of restless,
bored complacency. Cha-kwena could just make out the
herd. Well into the canyon, it formed a protective circle
around the calves, close against a wind-breaking but-
tress and near what was left of a stand of scrub spruce
upon which the animals had been foraging.

"Where the mammoth kind find browse, there, too,
will Man find meat," Cha-kwena reminded himself, but
his vocalization of the oft-recalled promise of the Ancient Ones did not comfort him. "If only this man could
subsist on trees, or feed upon lichens and grasses tusked

up from beneath the snow!" He knew from the depth of the snowpack and from what he had last seen of the spruce grove that soon the mammoth would be forced to seek other browse. But where? Farther east, deeper into the canyon? They might find fodder there, but what was a man to eat?

The question was sobering. Cha-kwena had been to the heights of the canyon and glimpsed what lay beyond —a mountain range of solid ice, stretching as far as he could see. It had been the most singularly glorious and appallingly desolate vista he had ever set eyes upon. Now, staring into all-encompassing whiteness and visualizing the surrounding landscape into which the sacred herd had led him, he shivered as a voice from the past rose within his mind to mock him.

*"Is this not what you have always wanted? Have you not yearned to journey beyond the edge of the world to see lands that no men have ever seen before?"*

"Not alone!" cried Cha-kwena in response to the conjured cajoling of his grandfather. "Not cut off forever from my band!"

It was in this moment that Vision struck him; like a great, whispering wind, it staggered him and invaded his senses. An inner light burst white-hot behind his eyes. With spirit voices suddenly sighing all around, the shaman stared *through* snow and cloud—through time itself —and saw, not the canyon that lay before him but another defile, a vast, Red World chasm. It was a huge, darkly vaginal cleft in the earth. As he stared at it, it appeared as though the skin of Mother Below peeled back and laid itself bare of its own accord. And there, deep within the very womb of the earth, Cha-kwena saw himself as a boy walking with his grandfather beneath the cold, piercing light of the eternally Watching Star. An owl flew before them, following in the wake of Life Giver, the great white mammoth totem, as it sloshed knee-deep through a river of blood—with Mah-ree perched like a little brown bird atop its towering head.

Cha-kwena sucked in a startled breath. His little girl-of-a-woman was not as he remembered her. She wore a cape of raven feathers over some sort of darker robe, a moldering, ill-made thing that hung upon her skeletal frame. Her eyes were fixed ahead, sunken in a pallid, haggard face that would have been unrecognizable had she not reached out to him and moaned his name.

"Cha-kwena . . . my shaman . . . always and forever . . ."

And then he saw the sacred stone. She held it in the curl of her palm. It was bleeding as she released it and allowed it to fall.

He gasped, wanting no part of this vision; nevertheless, it had him and would take him where it would.

Wolves were howling now. He heard them clearly, and the clash of antlers somewhere far away to the west. Then, slowly, the boy in his dream became another boy entirely, and his grandfather was transformed into a black-faced, tattooed stranger. As the pair sloshed across the river in pursuit of the mammoth, the boy became a bear. The animal caught the sacred stone in its mouth. And the stone was sobbing—in the voice of Cha-kwena's little sister, Joh-nee!

Cha-kwena cried out, shook his head to be free of Vision, but his effort was in vain. The bear was charging the totem, attacking the great white mammoth, killing it. The shaman willed himself into his vision and hurled an imagined spear. The weapon flew in a screaming arc. Hearing it, the bear turned, inadvertently exposing its breast just as the lance descended to pierce its heart. But the animal did not die; it rose on its hind limbs. With paws that bore the look of human hands, it pulled the spear free of its flesh and then, with its left forelimb, threw it back at Cha-kwena.

The shaman stood as though rooted. He could not move. He could not cry aloud to fend off impending death. Everything around him seemed to have come to a stop: the river, the bear, the mammoth, the boy, the black-faced, tattooed stranger, and the specter that was his woman, all were as though encased in invisible ice. Only the spear moved. And in the cold light of the Watching Star, Cha-kwena focused on the forwardly hurtling projectile point—and saw that it was the sacred stone of the ancestors.

It drove straight through him, cleft him in two; the halves of his body folded outward, then coalesced, allowing him to whirl around in time to see the spear land in the midst of the feeding mammoth. He screamed. The totem was struck. He knew it, *felt* it, even before he saw the little white mammoth fall.

In that moment Vision shattered. Stunned and confused, Cha-kwena stared into falling snow and, seeing the mammoth browsing unperturbed, nearly collapsed with relief. Everything was as it should be. The herd was safe, the totem unharmed. Had all that he had just seen been Vision, or was it merely the fearful conjuring of a lonely man who had seen too much of war and the all-too-often murderous aspects of human nature? Longing for the clarity of mind that had been his when he possessed the sacred stone, Cha-kwena's right hand drifted upward to his throat as though, by making contact with that part of his body against which the amulet had so often lain, its powers might somehow be his again. He closed his eyes. Longing for home and family, he silently implored the forces of Creation to keep his people safe.

Far away within the canyon a crested jay called to its mate. Cha-kwena opened his eyes and listened, remembering a night when he and his little girl-of-a-woman had bundled together under their furs, close to a warming fire kindled with downy blue feathers collected from the castings of mountain jays. The memory was as warm and welcome as the fire had been. The shaman retreated into his shelter and, sitting on his mattress of piled skins, drew around himself the rabbit-skin robe that Mah-ree had made for him.

"Mah-ree . . ." Cha-kwena sighed, her name soothing his spirit. He wondered what she would say if she knew how much he had come to miss her. She would dimple; she would tease. And then she would tilt her pretty face skyward and say with a pout that this was as it should be, for he was wrong to have gone his solitary way without her.

But the warmth of the shaman's mood was short-lived as he recalled the way his woman had appeared in his vision. He shivered. *So thin! So haggard! A ghost of her former self!* Was she in danger? Had she been injured? Had she fallen victim to the fever spirits that haunted the distant forest? Was she even now calling to him across the very edge of the world? *If only I could be sure! If only I could go to her, see her, hold her in my arms again!*

Cha-kwena glanced dejectedly around the confines of his shelter until his eyes fell upon his spear. It lay as he had left it, close to the weather baffle, ready to be taken up at a moment's notice. He observed the banded haft and long, exquisitely made projectile point, which Kosar-eh had fashioned for him before they had gone their separate ways. How, with such a powerful, strong-willed, and skilled man as headman of his band, could Mah-ree and his people *not* be safe?

*They have the sacred stone.*

*They have each other.*

*And as long as the totem lives they will survive.*

"But how shall I survive without them?"

Cha-kwena could hear the mammoth huffing and growling as was their way when content. The great matriarch had her family about her, and the white calf was safe and warm in her shaggy, hot-breathed, mothering embrace. As for the shaman who had sworn to protect the totem and the sacred herd, he was warm in his shelter of bones and antlers and hides; his parfleches were well stocked with meat, and not all of his caches were empty. Nevertheless, he knew that he would soon die of loneliness.

He chewed on his thoughts, reconjured the visions that had come to him with the dawn, saw blood and battling beasts and men who became animals while their females wept and moaned and the totem was hunted in a river of blood. And then, suddenly, he understood. This was the world that he had put behind him! A world of endless war and death. A world where men were indeed transformed into beasts, where women wept for the slain and children whimpered in the shadow of the Watching Star. Surely Kosar-eh, who placed the welfare of his woman and children above all else, would not long continue to put his band at risk in such a world! With the rising of the Warm Moon, the scars of the big man's grief over the death of his newborn daughter would have healed, and, realizing that he had been wrong to lose faith in his shaman, Kosar-eh would lead his followers back through the forest. Strong in the ever-growing power of the sacred stone, they would rejoin their shaman and put their enemies behind them forever.

Cha-kwena smiled. He would wait for them here at the edge of the world; he would wait with the totem. He closed his eyes. Beyond the confines of his shelter, the little white mammoth uttered a high, thin squeak meant to pass as a trumpet; the great cow replied, her voice rolling like thunder in the canyon. The shaman's smile broadened. The calf *was* safe in the care of the sacred herd. Soon White Giant Winter would release his hold upon the land, and Kosar-eh would come. With Mahree, U-wa, Ta-maya, old Kahm-ree, and the children he would come! Cha-kwena would raise beacon fires along the shore of the great lake; light and smoke would guide his people to him. And when Kosar-eh set his eyes upon the totem at last, the big man would know that he had chosen the right trail when he turned his back to the Watching Star and on the warrior ways of the ever-battling northern tribes and opted instead to follow his shaman, his hand extended in friendship once more.

# PART II

# WEST WIND

"Our father, the Sun! It is now time you were
   rising.
I want to dance with you."

—Mad Wolf
*The Old North Trail* by Walter B. McClintock

# 1

The wind had turned at last. It blew steadily from the west, from the home of the Thunderer, and in the light of morning Warakan awoke and knew that the storm was over.

And then it was there again—the howling, the sobbing on the wind—but this time the boy was not the only one to hear it.

"Again it cries," observed Jhadel. "Close this time. *Very* close."

A wave of excitement rippled through Warakan's lean young body. He cocked his head. The spirit was back. Perhaps now Jhadel would see with his own eyes the huge, furred thing that Warakan had glimpsed hulking off into the trees under the bloodred light of the Northern Dancers! And it *did* sound close, so close that, given the direction from which the cries were coming, Warakan suspected the creature might actually have been lured into the trip snare he had set early yesterday. He was suddenly worried; until this moment, he had not fully believed he would be successful, and so it had not occurred to him to consider what he would do with the spirit if he did ensnare it. How would he approach such a being without falling under its spell? How would he take it from the snare without being harmed? And, even more troubling, what was the old shaman going to say when he discovered what his apprentice had been up to?

Jhadel was sitting cross-legged on his bed furs, listening intently, his tattooed eyelids lowered. "It sobs like a woman in pain. And its cries are weak, like those of a dying thing." He fixed the boy with his condor eyes. "It has blundered into your trap."

Warakan flinched. "I—"

The old man signed the boy to silence with an impatiently raised hand. "Your spirit that cries on the wind has been wise and wary until now, content to stay in the hills, close to the high gorge. I do not know what has drawn it here, unless it has found your snare irresistible. Tell me, just what did you use for bait?"

"Prayer song. Smoke of burning sage and sweet grass. My little bone-and-stone stringer that makes music when hung in the wind. And it is not 'my' spirit! And since when do you admit that it is more than a wolf or lion or leaping cat or—"

"Since realizing that nothing will keep you from answering its summons!"

At that moment, the wailing on the wind stopped with a piteous sob, then cried sharply, "Shaman! My shaman!" before falling silent.

Warakan's features expanded with amazement. "There! Did you hear? It is as I have said. It *is* real! And it calls to *you*, not to me!"

"Hmm. We will see. Now, because of your disobedience, we *must* seek it. If it is ensnared, we must free it. And if it is dying, we must end its suffering and beg its forgiveness lest, after death, it return from the world beyond this world to make an end of us."

Warakan was aghast and confused. "But how do we kill a spirit?"

Jhadel appeared worried. "Let us hope that we do not have to find out."

Together they went into the bright light of morning, wearing snow walkers and carrying bone lances, the boy in his bearskin with his luck-bringing golden eagle feather inserted into his plaited hair and Jhadel in tawny, moldering furs. A browband of raven's feathers encircled the old shaman's head, his body bent under the weight of his medicine pack. He leaned on his sacred cottonwood staff with its streamers of pounded mammoth hide, tufts of woven mammoth hair, and many tiny beads of bird bones clicking in the morning wind. Chanting they went, the words offered first by the old shaman, then echoed by the boy.

"We come!"

"We come."

"Spirit of the wind, we come!"

"Spirit of the wind, we come."

"On the shaman path, we walk!"

"On the shaman path, we walk."

"Seeking the crying spirit, we come! Extending aid of Man to one who, though all wise and powerful, may have come unknowing into the snare of this foolish boy, we come!"

Warakan glowered up at the old one. "Seeking the crying spirit, we come, extending aid of Man." He would not say the rest of it.

Jhadel paused and scowled at the boy. "The spirits of this world and the world beyond know all things. To them, Man is as transparent as clear water; by your silence, the one that cries sees into your heart. It sees the disrespect of Warakan."

"If it were all wise and powerful, it would not have blundered into my snare!" the boy snapped defensively.

"Which you should *never* have set!"

Warakan could not deny the truth. And now the

spirit was wailing again, its voice trembling through the surrounding woods; indeed, it sounded trapped and disconsolate. He remembered the furred and hulking thing he had seen on the night of the burning sky and wondered how the sinew and fiber lines of his snare could hold a creature so monstrous and dangerous looking.

Perplexed, his thoughts formed into a question he had not pursued before: If the spirit *was* a spirit, a thing of mist and air and power, how could it be trapped at all? His brow furrowed, and pain slithered across the broken bridge of his nose; he took no notice. Instead, he wondered—with no small measure of dread—if the spirit was only pretending to be trapped in order to lure into the trees the foolish boy who had been audacious enough to imagine that he might dare to trap it!

Despite the warm skin of the great she-bear that clothed him, Warakan was suddenly cold. He turned to the shelter he and the old man had left behind; he could just see it through the trees. Small as it was, and resembling nothing if not a pack rat's nest piled high with snow, it looked warm and welcoming to him. "Perhaps we should go back," he suggested eagerly.

"We cannot! Come. Show this man where you have laid your cursed snare."

"But . . . I . . ." Warakan did not want to admit to being afraid, so he offered the first excuse for turning homeward that came to mind. "What will happen to my sleeping cub if we do not return? There are predators in the forest. If Bear Brother wakes and we are not there to protect him from—"

"Enough!" Jhadel snapped; he had seen straight through the boy's skin into the heart of his intent. "You have good cause to be afraid. For *yourself,* not for the cub. The forces of Creation do not deal kindly with those who dishonor and deceive the spirits!" He shook his head. "Boy Mother of Bear, the days of your cub's dependence upon you will soon be at an end. Do not worry over its fate; it will soon go its own way in search of its own kind. As for you—"

"Bear is my child, my brother!" the boy interrupted, cut to the quick by a premise he had never considered. "I *am* his kind. He needs no one in this world but Warakan! When I am a man, Bear Brother will walk at my side. Together we will be warriors! Together we will make our enemies and even the spirits tremble when they—"

"Arrch!" Jhadel snarled disapproval of the boy's audaciousness and was about to speak when the spirit screamed.

Warakan tensed. On a rising draft of wind, a high, sharp tinkling came chittering through the trees. "My music maker!" the boy exclaimed, visualizing the sinew-strung lengths of perforated pebbles and hollow bird bones that Jhadel had attached to a wooden wand and presented to him as a gift to help ease the boredom of midwinter days. Waved in the hand, or placed where the wind could rattle or comb through the stringers, the contrivance made unique and pleasant music. Thinking that it might intrigue the spirit enough to draw it through the woods, Warakan had hung the wind chime from the topmost branches of the sturdy young conifer from which he had then fashioned his trip snare. Judging from the intensity of the chiming, he knew that someone—or something—must be shaking the tree very hard. He was certain that it was the spirit fighting to be free of his snare until the unmistakable screech of a fang-toothed leaping cat ripped the air.

The shaman stiffened.

So did Warakan.

The wailing of the wind spirit had stopped; the chime was still tinkling madly, and although the big cat did not screech again, there was something ominous in its silence.

"If you have snared a spirit from the world beyond this world and made it vulnerable to the predations of the carnivores of this earth, you will not live long enough to be a warrior, nor will—"

Jhadel did not finish his warning. Warakan, a bone stave hefted and ready, was already moving forward through the trees.

Staring into the west wind, they stopped when they saw the spirit, lying with its back to them in the snow, sprawled on its side beneath a young conifer. One hairy limb was extended upward, hopelessly snarled in a sinew line secured to a branch high above. From this branch, swinging with the wind and even the most subtle stresses of the creature's movement, hung the wind chime. All around the tree and the trapped spirit were the fresh tracks of a large feline.

Warakan heard Jhadel suck in his breath, then whisper, "Is this what you saw in the light of the Northern Dancers?"

"It is!" replied the boy, but his enthusiasm was short-lived; the "thing" did not appear to be made of mists or air or power, nor was it even half as large as he remembered it.

"Your 'spirit' . . . it looks like a bear," observed Jhadel.

"The bear kind have yet to come from their winter dens. Even my own Bear Brother still sleeps. And it is not 'my' spirit. We both heard it call *your* name." Despite his words, the boy was unsure of how to respond to what he was seeing. The thing in the snow *did* appear to be a bear, a very small, old, and sickly bear, its dark fur grayed and visibly patchy, its hide sagging over its bones as it strained with pitiful weakness to free its furry limb. Warakan felt confusion settle upon him like a massive robe too heavy to wear. Was the creature only an animal after all, or was its appearance a trick designed to lure him forward to his death?

"Be it of this world or the world beyond, we must free it or put a quick end to its suffering before the fang-toothed cat returns!" said Jhadel, slinging off his medicine pack.

Warakan was distraught. When he had long ago killed the great she-bear, survived on her meat, clothed himself in her skin, and taken her cubs, he had sworn never again to kill or eat of the bear kind. Yet the spirit of the wind had called him to this place, and now, holding staves made of the she-bear's bones, he was contemplating doing just that.

Until, on the far side of the snare, a fang-toothed cat emerged from the trees. Massive head down and extended, short ears back, stumpy tail tucked and flicking, Smilodon growled deep in its enormous chest, warning Warakan and Jhadel away from what it had evidently chosen to be its next meal.

The spirit did not move.

Warakan took an inadvertent step back. The cat was impressive. Looking a great deal like a cross between a lion and a lynx, it was nearly as large as the former, and even with its mouth closed, its protruding fangs were visible. The boy's mouth gaped. The stabbing teeth of the beast were longer than his forearms.

Jhadel held his ground. "A stave . . . hurl one now." His words, low, even, and betraying no emotion, formed an imperative command nonetheless. "Your aim is good. Throw short. Do not strike the animal. Merely return its warning with our own. If the forces of Creation are with us, it will turn away."

Warakan found it impossible to obey. The fang-toothed cat was magnificent. As he stared into its golden eyes, he wondered if the forces of Creation were not staring back at him out of the body of the great carnivore. He cocked his head as it occurred to him that he was the one who should turn away. If he did, the animal would leap upon the thing in the snare and tear it to pieces. If the spirit was truly a spirit, it would be able to defend itself; if not, then better to be killed by a leaping cat than by a mere boy. Be it bear or spirit, if it was old and near the end of its days, perhaps, the boy reasoned, instead of holding him accountable for ensnaring it and making it vulnerable to death, it would find the wondrous cat worthy of its meat and consider its life spirit honored when consumed by a predator of such inordinate power and beauty.

"Warakan!" Jhadel's voice held a nervous edge.

The cat heard it.

The boy caught his breath. The muscles along the feline's snout and upper jaw bunched and rolled back as it snarled. Warakan stared into the red maw designed for killing. And then, as the animal drew all of its power into itself preparatory to hurling out of the trees in an arc of death that would descend upon the helpless thing in the snare, an appalling event happened.

"Keep away!" shrieked the thing in a young woman's high, frightened voice, its ensnared limb deliberately tugging on the lines that held it captive. The wind chime clattered violently.

Undeterred, the cat leaped.

"Aiee!" screamed the spirit.

Warakan blinked, disbelieving, as he saw the thing in his snare produce a heretofore unseen, feather-adorned, black-and-white spear. Already in midair, the great fang-toothed cat saw it, too. The animal screeched, stiffened, and twisted hard away from the lanceolate projectile point of stone, which the spirit extended upward to greet its fall.

The cat came down well to one side of its prey, facing in the other direction; from the moment its paws touched the snowy ground, it kept on running.

Stunned, Warakan and Jhadel watched it vanish into the trees, then stared, speechless, as the thing in the snare lowered its spear and collapsed, sobbing with relief.

Staves at ready now, Warakan advanced slowly behind Jhadel toward the creature that now lay silent before them until, coming as close as he dared, he stopped beside the old man and stared down at a small heap of shivering, bearskin-covered bones.

"Talking Bear?" Jhadel gave a name to the thing as he addressed it with awe. "Why have you called to this shaman, appeared as a bear to threaten a leaping cat with a spear, and spoken with the voice of a woman?"

"Because I *am* a woman!" growled the spirit. Turning weakly on one side, it looked up out of large brown eyes sunken in a haggard, youthful, but fully human face made skeletal by starvation.

It was a moment before Warakan recognized her. Then, amazed and inexplicably delighted, he cried, "Mah-ree of the Red World!" and swept forward immediately to free her shaggily booted leg from his snare.

She stared at him, her features contorted by confusion. "Cha-kwena? You are a boy again! How can this be, my shaman?"

"Yellow Wolf is not here. I am Warakan," he informed her proudly, in his best imitation of a manly tone. "Surely you have not forgotten *me*. I am son of Masau, grandson of Shateh!"

Mah-ree did not appear to have heard him. She smiled wanly, closed her eyes, relaxed within her hideous furs, and allowed the boy to fumble at the snare lines as she weakly sighed, "I was certain you would not leave me forever alone within this dark and cursed for-

est." Her eyes opened again; there was panic in them
and in her voice as she gasped, "You told this woman to
return to the band, my shaman. And this time she did
obey you! She *did*! But the village was deserted, her
people long gone. How could she follow them alone
through the dark woods? And so she stayed and tended
poor Gah-ti's bones and waited for her shaman to return. Bear came instead, old and hungry, and would
have eaten this small woman! But Gah-ti's spirit came
to her, and with the spear that Kosar-eh left for Gah-ti
to take with him to the world beyond this world, this
woman, this lawbreaking woman—" Her voice broke.
With a sob, she shook her head. "Again and again under the ever-changing face of Moon, Mother of Stars,
this woman has called to her shaman upon the wind!
And now, at last, he is here!"

Her eyes closed again; she was calmer now, but
much weaker than before. "Soon the others will return.
They are coming even now. The wind has brought to me
the scent of my dear sister Ta-maya's favorite fragrances
upon the smoke of Kosar-eh's lodge fire—sage,
meadow rue, sweet grass! Ah, soon we *will* be a band
again. Then you will lead us to the totem, and Kosar-eh
will know that all you have said is true and—" Again
Mah-ree paused, opened her eyes, and looked straight
up at Warakan.

The boy knew that in her weakness Mah-ree was
seeing another when she looked at him; he did not care.
He had freed her from his snare and knelt above her
now. How small she was, how vulnerable. Now, when
she smiled at him, her expression was one of such radiant and absolutely unconditional love, he was shaken.
Never in all his life had anyone looked at him with such
love. Not mother, not father. And certainly not Jhadel.

"I have kept this safe for you," Mah-ree whispered

in the tone of a conspirator as she reached for the boy's hand and guided it to her throat.

"What? I . . ." Though Warakan was flustered, bewildered by her intent, he was so entranced by her nearness and touch that he offered no resistance as her gaunt hand pressed his fingers around a familiar object —hard as stone, rough as old bone, no larger than the thumb of a man, and as gracefully arched as a stabbing tooth taken from a small feline.

"The sacred stone of the Ancient Ones!" he said, shocked. He tried to pull his hand away, but Mah-ree would not allow it. Her hand rose with his, and the worn length of braided sinew to which the talisman was attached snapped.

"Yes! Take it. It is for you, my shaman," she insisted on a fading sigh.

Warakan felt her hand go limp around his own, and then her arm fell. She had slipped into unconsciousness.

Stunned, the boy kept his hand upraised and stared with disbelief at the talisman, which shone white in the light of the new day. "Wise One?" He looked to Jhadel.

The old man threw a long shadow as he stood between Warakan and the sun. He came forward slowly, thoughtfully, then rested his staff against his shoulder and leaned down. His own two hands closing the boy's fingers into a fist around the sacred stone, he said, "Now it begins."

"What?"

"All that I have ever dreamed . . . more than you have ever wanted!"

# 2

U-wa was dead. Her spirit had wandered from her body with the first light of dawn, and Joh-nee, having fallen asleep exhausted at her side, had not been awake to stop it. Now the little sister of Cha-kwena sat beside her mother with fixed and watchful eyes. She shed no tears, nor did she respond to the needs of Doh-teyah, whose care she had abandoned to Kosar-eh and his boys. She simply sat in the full light of morning, held her mother's hands, and wished for the spirit to return to her body.

"This time I will not let it wander away from you. Please, my mother, come back. This girl did not mean to fall asleep. She will watch you more closely!"

Kosar-eh appeared beside her and said kindly, "Come. The others prepare to move on."

Joh-nee looked up at him. "I do not care what they do. I will wait for my mother."

"Her spirit is gone. It will not return." The big man was sorry there was no gentler way to say it. For the last three days U-wa had lain like a corpse as she was transported by Tsana's warriors on a litter contrived of hides secured to four cross-braced spears. Not once had Joh-nee allowed that her mother might not awaken from the trance into which she had collapsed on the day of the twin raids upon the encampment. All the while, the girl had walked at her mother's side by day and kept vigil over her fur-covered pallet by night, clutching the buckskin doll that had belonged to Tla-nee, her slain half-sister.

"If you had not abandoned Mah-ree in the forest, her medicine would have made my mother better, and her spirit would not have wandered away!" Accusation and resentment burned in Joh-nee's eyes.

Kosar-eh was too emotionally fatigued to argue with the child. He knew that she blamed him for her mother's death, that she would never forgive him for striking U-wa and then leaving her and the others vulnerable to the second raid. He did not fault the child; he would never forgive himself. "Come," he said again, extending a hand.

"No!" Joh-nee glared at him defiantly. "Cha-kwena will not let our mother's spirit walk the wind forever. My brother is strong in the power of the totem and the sacred stone! He will send U-wa's spirit back to us upon the Four Winds. I will wait for her—and for him! Riding upon the great white mammoth, he will come with the sacred stone to drive our enemies away and bring back the spirits of my mother and sister and—"

"It is we who will go to him!" slurred a surly Kiu-neh from where he stood nearby, aloof from his father. He was ready to travel and offered no assistance whatever to Kho-neh, who was attempting to secure a fussing Doh-teyah into her cradleboard. "Cha-kwena is our enemy now!"

"Never!" Joh-nee's upturned little face was tight with grief and determination as she glared hatefully at Kosar-eh. "You will be sorry if you betray my brother to those who would hunt him and slaughter the totem and steal the sacred stone of the Ancient Ones for themselves!"

Kosar-eh shook his head; the girl was as stubborn as her shaman brother. He could not understand how she could still believe in Cha-kwena after all she had seen and endured, but her love and loyalty touched him nonetheless. To save such a valiant child from Tsana's threat, he would gladly betray her brother.

"If Cha-kwena were with us now and it was his will, your mother *would* still be alive."

Kosar-eh was startled by the warrior chieftain's statement. The words had been flung like stones—hard, unforgiving, cruelly directed, ostensibly to the child but actually to him. He was both bruised and irritated by their impact as he turned to see a frowning Tsana, obviously distracted by Joh-nee's outburst, part company from the ranks of his fellow raiders of the Watching Star. A moment later the chieftain was beside Kosar-eh, and their eyes met. Cut by the cold sharpness of Tsana's gaze, Kosar-eh defensively raised his head. The chieftain's frown became a smile with no warmth in it; it did not reach his eyes until he tucked the human hand pendant that he wore around his neck into his furs, then knelt before Joh-nee.

"Do not despair for the one you call U-wa, Shaman's Sister," Tsana said, his tone gentle now, warm and smooth with compassion. "We will honor her life. We will raise a bier for her in this place and join into a sacred circle and raise our voices to the forces of Creation so they will remember U-wa of the Red World! This we will do before we journey on. Death must come to us all, little one, but you must not imagine that your mother will not be with you. As the daughter of U-wa, you have only to invite your mother's spirit to enter your body, and she will live within you until the end of your days. This is the promise of the Thunderer, the Great Ghost Spirit of my people. Do the spirits of the

Red World not promise the same to the children of your band?"

Joh-nee's eyes had grown wide. Her face was paler than usual. Tsana was Enemy to her, and his tone and manner obviously confused her. The hostility she had just displayed to Kosar-eh was not evident in her voice as, clutching Tla-nee's doll more tightly than before, she conceded in a whisper, "They do. . . . Yes, it is so."

Kosar-eh was not surprised by the change in the girl. Tsana had a way about him; it was as though he could at will exude an invisible salve that soothed and benumbed the spirits of those whose favor he intended to win.

Now the chieftain was reaching out to Joh-nee, touching her face with benignly questing fingertips and nodding with tender reassurance. "Yes, I see the spirit of U-wa smiling at me from the eyes of Shaman's Sister. She is with you, little one . . . even now."

Kosar-eh saw tears well within Joh-nee's eyes as, bowing her head lest Tsana or anyone else see her cry, she whimpered softly, "It is not the same!" And then, suddenly, she convulsed with sobs. "Cha-kwena! Why have you not followed us out of the far forest, my brother? We would have forgiven you. And Mah-ree, why are you not here to work your healing magic upon my mother and—"

"We will find her, little one," promised Tsana, taking the weeping child into a paternal embrace. "It will not be in time to heal your mother. But if, as you say, the one you call Medicine Woman is with your brother, we will find her with the help of Spits in the Face of Enemies. We have need of a healer and shaman among our people. No harm need come to them from us."

Kosar-eh was not sure what astounded him more: the unexpected turn of the man's words or the sight of Joh-nee, not only allowing but clinging to Tsana's embrace. He understood the little girl's desperate need of someone to hold—someone strong, someone upon whom she could depend, who would keep her from being swept away by the gales of tragedy that had shattered the last fragments of order in her life. But Tsana? Had she forgotten the man's threats against her, his promise to kill Kiu-neh and Kho-neh if Kosar-eh failed to accept his "friendship" and lead the warriors in the tracks of Yellow Wolf? *"No harm need come to them from us."* Indeed! Could she not sense the deception that underlay the chieftain's every word? As though Cha-kwena would stand by and see the totem slain, or use the sacred stone to determine favorably the destiny of his most ancient enemies—

Kosar-eh stopped his thoughts. *There is no totem,* he reminded himself. *The sacred stone has no power. Cha-kwena allied himself with other enemies when it served his ambition to do so, then betrayed the Land of Grass chieftain just as easily as he turned his back on his own band. And it was warriors of the People of the Land of Grass, not of the People of the Watching Star, who burned my lodge and slew my woman and children!*

Kosar-eh observed Tsana holding Joh-nee and wondered if the girl's instincts about the man could be right. The premise was sobering; it presented a possibility that Kosar-eh had not considered before now. By judging Tsana and his tribesmen by all that he had ever heard about them from their enemies, could he have been misjudging them all along?

"Come now, little one." Tsana held a thumb under Joh-nee's chin and raised her tearful face to his. "The wisdom of Spits in the Face of Enemies has made us one band now, Shaman's Sister. Do not be afraid. The sun rises on a new day. The traveling provisions and meat that your people have shared with us are nearly gone. It is time to move on again, toward the stronghold of my people. Will you not come consenting with this man of the Watching Star, little one, to that good place where you will be welcome and warm, and where there are milk women who will give nourishment to Sees the Wind? Surely your mother would not be happy to know that because of her death, and by your refusal to go on, you have caused the one called Doh-teyah to go hungry?"

Joh-nee blinked, looked to where Doh-teyah was still fussing as a red-faced and frustrated Kho-neh did his fumbling best to adjust the last of the ties that held the child within the bondage of her cradleboard. "I . . . no, but—"

Tsana interrupted the girl by scooping her into one strong arm as, in a single fluid motion, he rose to his feet, turned, then called to Indeh and Hrak and several others. "Prepare to raise the scaffold upon which we will leave and honor the body of the woman U-wa." He paused, looked at Kosar-eh, and said, "There is no dry firewood or oil in this winter place to burn the dead in the way of your tribe, so this must be done in the way of mine."

"A death honoring a lizard eater from the enemy People of the Red World?" Indeh slurred.

Kosar-eh stiffened at the insult, but it was Tsana who answered it.

"This woman, U-wa, was mother of a shaman!" declared the chieftain. "The spirits honored her in this world. Tsana of the People of the Watching Star will do no less! Would Indeh, onetime enemy from the Land of Grass, challenge his chieftain in this?"

Indeh withered at the query and suffered in morose silence the disapproving glares of the warriors of his adopted tribe.

Kosar-eh was pleased. His hand moved to his battered face. He had not forgotten his earlier encounter with the defector from Shateh's tribe. Someday, he vowed, he would find a way to make the man pay for the pain and humiliation he had endured because of him.

Tsana directed his next words to Joh-nee. "Now we will close the circle of your mother's life. Now her spirit will live in Shaman's Sister and give you courage as you come consenting to the Watching Star."

Kosar-eh noticed that this was the second time the man had used that phrase to the child: "come consenting." What difference did it make to the chieftain whether the girl consented to her fate or not? He could not say why this disturbed him, nor did he have a chance to think more about it. Doh-teyah was suddenly squalling like a little storm cloud, and Kho-neh, having had enough of the toddler, was dragging her in her cradleboard toward her father.

It was done, quietly and reverently. Four straight young cottonwoods were found in the streamside gully within which the raiding party and their captives had passed the night. After a brief ceremony in which the spirits of the trees were asked to give up their lives for the honoring of U-wa, they were felled and debranched with stone axes, then carried to the site where the honoring was to take place. Here, with skilled hands working quickly together, a simple four-sided platform was raised, with each corner set to acknowledge the power of one of the Four Winds. Upon this was placed the bier of the dead woman, her feet facing west so that her eyes might look forever toward the land to which all spirits would make their last journey, following the setting sun over the edge of the world to that mysterious place from which the People of the Watching Star believed it would someday never return.

After Tsana intoned the final words, he encouraged Kosar-eh to speak briefly of U-wa to the forces of Creation so that her life would be honored by one of her own, but Kosar-eh's throat was tight, and few words would come. Soon the circle of mourners broke apart. The men of the Watching Star, anxious to be away from a camp in which someone had died, prodded their captives back to where they had abandoned their traveling packs and impatiently urged them to prepare to move on.

Only Joh-nee was allowed to remain by the bier. She stood there alone, a solemn little figure clutching a doll, until Tsana himself came to tell her it was time to go. She obeyed without a word, trudging beside the chieftain until, tugging at his robe, she looked up at him and said, "What you said about the sun not coming back . . . in the Red World it is told that as long as Life Giver is with the People, the sun shall go to sleep in its lodge to the west every night, and rise again from its lodge in the east every morning, and the People will live forever."

The chieftain stopped and looked down at the child for a moment, then dropped to one knee and said, "That is why we must find the white mammoth. That is why we must bring Life Giver back to the People from wherever it is your brother has taken the totem."

"The totem *leads* the shaman—away from those who would hunt it and eat it and steal its power for themselves!"

"Is that what your brother has told you?"

"Yes. Cha-kwena has been called by the spirits of the ancestors to keep the totem safe."

"But who keeps him safe beyond the edge of the world?"

"The sacred stone! And Medicine Woman. And the spirits."

"Is he not lonely there, in the face of the sun, with only ghosts, a single woman, a stone, and a herd of mammoth to keep him company? Do you not miss him, little one? Do you not long to walk at his side, as you now walk at mine?"

Joh-nee's chin quivered.

Tsana smiled kindly, reached to touch her face. "I, too, have lost a brother, Shaman's Sister. Many brothers. A woman. The mother and father who named me Son. All of my family. War with the People of the Land of Grass and of the Red World has left its marks upon my spirit as well as upon my body and face. Here, do you see the scars across my cheek? I know what it is like to be hunted by enemies, to live in a world where all you love and care for has been taken from you. And I also know that if I had a little sister like you and a brave mother like U-wa, I would not abandon them."

Tears smarted in Joh-nee's eyes. "The spirit of my mother is with me! You *promised*!"

"Tsana does not break his promises." His fingertips caught her tears and wiped them away across her cheeks. "Do not cry, Shaman's Sister. This man of the Watching Star will be your brother now."

"This girl has a brother."

"He is far away. He does not care about you, or he would be with you now—and your mother would be alive, and the son of Kosar-eh would not be walking the wind forever with the little friend whose spirit you keep close to you inside the doll you carry."

Joh-nee caught her breath, amazed at his insight. "Tla-nee is my sister," she told him in a whisper. "Our father was Tlana-quah, chief of the village by the Lake of Many Singing Birds, second man of U-wa after the father of Cha-kwena ate bad mushrooms and walked the wind forever." She paused. Her eyes had gone very wide. "This girl took Doh-teyah from the lodge and followed U-wa. Tla-nee did not follow. This girl wanted to go back for her, but U-wa would not let her go! Even when this girl heard her sister shout and scream, U-wa would not let her go. And so they left my sister in the burning lodge, but later this girl ran and found her. Now I keep her spirit safe with me until . . ." The unspoken thought was so disturbing that the child could not bring herself to articulate it. "I keep it safe!" she cried, and drew the doll from her breast and held it before Tsana. "See! Tla-nee is here!"

Tsana appraised the limp and much-loved thing—a folded swatch of soiled buckskin cut and sewn to resemble a human form. It was stuffed with lichen or some sort of bird down and clothed in a fur dress and hat, with cross-stitches of horsehair forming a neat little face. A few tufts of ash-darkened braided fiber served for hair.

"Ta-maya made it for Tla-nee," explained Joh-nee, her head cocked thoughtfully to one side as her mind momentarily drifted to happy memories. "She made a doll for me, too, a doll without a hat—because I do not like hats. But my doll was burned in the lodge, and so I have taken Tla-nee's doll and told Tla-nee's spirit to hide inside it, and . . . and . . ." She stiffened and frowned. "Ta-maya will never make another doll. They hurt her. They took her with them when they went away! Kosar-eh followed. He said that they . . . they . . ."

Tsana's brows arched. No man who had ever set eyes upon Ta-maya of the Red World could ever forget her rare and perfect beauty; he was no exception. He shook his head, regretting that he had not had a chance to sate himself upon her before she had been taken and used by others until all that remained of her was as limp and dead to a man's passion as Joh-nee's spiritless little doll. Smiling gently at the girl, he was amused to think of how shocked she would be if she knew his thoughts. "Hush, little one. There is no need to speak words that burn your heart. It is good to remember that men from the Land of Grass burned your lodge and took the lives of your sister and the woman of Kosar-eh. The warriors of Tsana have not done these things to you. Indeed, have we brought harm to you at all?"

Joh-nee's head swung from side to side. "No harm," she conceded.

The chieftain rose and extended a friendly hand down to the child. "Come, little one. Take my hand. Your brother has left you vulnerable to all that you leave behind, but Tsana will care for you now. Will you not ease the loneliness in this man's heart as he would ease the grief in yours? Will you not consent to call this man Brother?"

She looked at him long and hard. "You will not hunt the totem?"

One dark brow arched upward across Tsana's handsome face. "This you will never see me do."

Joh-nee frowned as though sensing evasiveness in his reply; indeed, in everything he said there seemed to be either a question or an underlying meaning that never quite managed to be expressed by his words. She chewed her lower lip, as was her way when nervous or indecisive, and looked ahead to where the others had donned their pack frames and were staring watchfully at her and Tsana, no doubt waiting for the chieftain to signal them on. Kosar-eh was carrying Doh-teyah on his back; this was good, Joh-nee thought, a sign that he was no longer rejecting his blind daughter, perhaps even emerging from that terrible state of grief madness that had turned him into someone she neither knew nor liked. Nevertheless, she was touched with sadness when she saw that Doh-teyah was fast asleep in her cradleboard. Had the toddler forgotten her so quickly?

As her gaze took in Kiu-neh and Kho-neh standing next to their father, it struck her that, despite all that had happened, they were still a family, while she stood apart with no one left alive in the world to call her own except the brother who had—no matter how she tried to make excuses for him—gone his way over the edge of the world without her.

"Come, Shaman's Sister," invited Tsana.

This time she took his hand. "This girl *will* name Tsana Brother now."

# 3

It was a mistake.

Joh-nee knew it the moment she saw where they were leading her, and yet, somehow, Tsana made it all seem right.

Soon the sun would set. Long shadows lay across the land. And the entrance to the high, stony pass that led into the Valley of the Dead lay before them.

"There are bad spirits in that place," she told him.

"There are bad spirits everywhere!" remarked the chieftain.

Joh-nee could find no cause to disagree.

All day they had walked, heading always toward mountains—those far, white, tangled western ranges that she remembered so well. Now and then Kosar-eh paused and looked longingly back across the hills they had left behind. Joh-nee watched him. She knew that he wanted to be free, to leave her and his boys again and, uncaring of Doh-teyah, take his spear and run once more across the land seeking those who had stolen his youngest son and slain his beautiful beloved.

It was not to be. The warriors of the Watching Star kept their captives under close scrutiny every moment of the day. Somewhere along the way they had stopped to eat; Joh-nee did not remember when or where. Tsana had gone off alone to hunt, and even before he returned empty-handed, a warrior named Unai brought soft bits of aging pronghorn meat for Doh-teyah to chew on, and Joh-nee did her best with the limited supplies to change the toddler's swaddling. After the little one had been allowed to stretch her legs and totter about for a short while, Joh-nee offered to carry her when the raiding party moved on. Tsana, however, was determined that Kosar-eh should carry the blind child himself. A sullen Kosar-eh did not seem to mind or even care what was done with or for the little one, and Joh-nee, believing that his heart had not softened toward his blind daughter, had grown hostile toward him and refused to help him with his child at all. Nevertheless she kept a close eye on the little one, for besides her doll, Doh-teyah was the only sister of her band left to her now, and Joh-nee knew that the spirits of U-wa, Tla-nee, Ta-maya, and old Kahm-ree would expect no less of her.

At last, observing Kosar-eh's continuing backward glances, Tsana came to the big man's side, and Joh-nee, trudging nearby, heard the chieftain say, "Your longing is wasted, black-and-white warrior. You would not be able to track the Land of Grass raiders in the snow that has fallen. And how far would you get with this child on your back? Even if you were to abandon her, do you not think that those whom you hunt will be watching for you, waiting for you, expecting you to come for them?" The chieftain stated his opinion without emotion. "When prey is alert and waiting for the hunter, that is the time for the hunter to rest, to sleep, to grow strong in his hunger. Then, when the prey has relaxed and passively returned to its feeding, the hunter may strike and be sure of success."

Joh-nee saw frustration run through Kosar-eh like

wind moving through tall grass, invisible but present, a
latent power that made her remember the rippling muscles of a stag elk she had once seen run to exhaustion by
Shateh's hunters. Wheezing and sweated, the animal
had been driven straight into the Land of Grass village,
where it had come to a dead stop. Head up, sides heaving, eyes wild, nostrils flared, and tongue lolling, it had
circled and stared madly. Everyone thought the animal
as good as dead when the hunters closed for the kill.
But the stag had reared up and leaped straight over
them, breaking for the freedom of the plain. Shateh had
been so impressed by the beast's unexpected strength
and unprecedented daring that he had commanded the
hunters to stay their spears and let it go.

She could tell by the way Tsana and his warriors
watched Kosar-eh that they were unsure of him and half
expected him to run. Perhaps, she wondered, this was
why they burdened him with Doh-teyah, making his
blind daughter's weight upon his back a constant reminder that his children's lives depended on his actions
and obedience. Her mouth compressed as bitter
thoughts rose within her: They were wise to guard him;
Kosar-eh had abandoned his children before and with
apparent peace of mind was willing to betray her
brother.

They went on, heading into the shadows of the dying day. With every step the warriors of the Watching
Star went out of their way to ease the journey for
Kosar-eh and his children until, at last, a runner was
sent ahead into the narrow pass, and Joh-nee heard him
calling in the way of a wolf. Soon other "wolves" answered. Though warm in her heavy robe and extra
clothing, which Tsana had so carefully gone out of his
way to contrive for her, the girl shivered.

\*          \*          \*

"We will be in sight of the stronghold by moonrise," said Tsana.

And Kosar-eh, walking uphill beside the chieftain in the gathering dusk, smiled against irony. With his eyes slitted against the rising west wind, he told himself that he should have known all along that his captors would lead him here, back toward the despised Valley of the Dead, where the great white mammoth had perished, where the bones of generations of tuskers littered the land.

The crest of the pass still lay well ahead; a heavy mist was rising from the far side, obscuring all within its path. The air smelled of clouds and snow and cold stone. Kosar-eh was not sure just when he saw the first of the trail markers. Looming through mist, it was there one moment and gone the next. Then suddenly it was right in front of him. Tsana and the others gathered around it, and Joh-nee, now sitting astride the chieftain's hip, turned her head away with a moan.

"My father . . . l-look!" Kho-neh's exclamation was reminiscent of the high-pitched squeak of a frightened mouse trying to sound bold in hope of bluffing away the rodent eater that has just slapped a paw over it.

Kiu-neh heard the vulnerability in his brother's voice and chided, "Have you never seen a dead man before?"

"Yes!" the younger boy snapped defensively. "But not like this one!"

A low rumble of laughter rose from the ranks of the warriors of the Watching Star.

"What do you think?" Tsana asked Kosar-eh.

But Kosar-eh stared ahead and said nothing. He had seen dead men many times before, but never one that looked quite like this. And while he had been told of this man's death, he had not fully believed in it. Until now.

Before him, sheened with ice and robed in mist, the head of Shateh and his naked, eviscerated corpse were impaled on a mammoth-bone stake.

Kosar-eh experienced a complete absence of emotion as he observed the remains of the Land of Grass chieftain. *So this is how it ends, for even such as you,* he thought, and felt neither gladness nor remorse for this man who had once named him Hunt Brother and then turned against him and his people when the forces of Creation ceased to favor his tribe.

Kosar-eh's eyes narrowed. Perhaps he had simply seen too much of death to be shocked by the condition of the corpse. Save for the head, neck, and shoulders, there were no bones, no hands or feet; the man had been flayed and set to dry like the hide of an animal. Wind and weather, birds and small gnawing beasts had been at the face; what little skin was left was in shreds. Were it not for Shateh's war collar, fashioned of the primary feathers of a golden eagle, the man would have been unrecognizable; the collar itself was in ruins, the feathers tattered, and one of them, the most central to the design of the adornment, missing entirely.

Shateh's long, graying hair had been removed from his skull along with his scalp. Kosar-eh, having lived among the northern tribes, knew this had been done to dishonor and mutilate the dead man's warrior spirit, for it was believed by them that the essence of a man's soul lingered for many days after death in his hair and the nails of his hands and feet. To deprive him of these things was to prevent the departure of his spirit from this world to the world beyond.

"All those who fell before us in the last battle are like this," Tsana informed him proudly. "The remains of the warriors of Shateh line the approach to the strong-
.

hold of the People of the Watching Star, a statement to all who would come against us that this is how they will end their days—their bones and flesh meat for our dogs, their skins food for the wind, their faces turned to a sky they will never see again and to a world beyond this world that their spirits will never enter!"

The fire in Tsana's words burned Kosar-eh. And now, as the cold mist played upon the grotesque and shriveled remnants of what had once been a powerful man whom others both feared and admired, a sudden understanding burst so brightly within Kosar-eh's head that he winced. Startled, he moved his gaze to Tsana. *It was Shateh's spear hand that the chieftain of the People of the Watching Star wore around his neck, and Shateh's scalp that adorned his forelock.*

Tsana, seeing his understanding, nodded in grim affirmation. "Yes. *His* fighting hand! *His* hair! Both *mine* now." He opened his robe, drew out the shrunken medallion, and held it on his extended palm like some sort of five-digited, semiflattened spider. When Joh-nee moaned again and pressed her face more deeply into his shoulder, he bent his head and, holding his trophy close to the child, urged with softly spoken passion, "Look bravely, Little Sister! Do not turn away! Because of the man who once owned this hand your mother and sister and most of those whom you love are dead. Rejoice in seeing this hand in my possession! Tsana holds the spirit of Shateh captive in this world, dishonored forever before the spirits of his ancestors. Never again, in this life or any other, shall he bring pain and suffering to my people. Or to yours." His glance moved to Kosar-eh. "So shall it be for you, Spits in the Face of Enemies, when, strong in the power of your new tribe, you reclaim your stolen son and with your own hands do to the one who took your woman as I have done to Shateh!"

"I have slain that wolf and left him to be meat for carrion eaters," said Kosar-eh. The statement gave him no satisfaction. As he stared fixedly at Shateh's corpse, he realized that his killing of Ranamal had done nothing to ease his agony over the loss of his woman or lessen the pain of his memories of the carnage wrought upon his loved ones by followers of Shateh, whom he had once trusted and emulated above all others.

The wind gusted, sent mists flurrying all around. Kosar-eh's feelings of bitterness and betrayal were absolute. Chilled, he scanned ahead through momentarily fragmented clouds. Rising from the snow and stretching to the crest of the pass at irregularly spaced intervals, like so many branchless trees, were the staked remains of those members of Shateh's war band who had shared their chieftain's fate.

Kosar-eh's eyes narrowed. "So many!" Now, at last, he felt satisfaction, but it was a dark, cold, half-shadowed thing that brought no pleasure and made him restless to achieve that which he had set out to do. He turned his gaze to Tsana and said, "There are *others*. Even now they put distance between us, traveling across different hills, into another portion of the mountains through which, at the first sign of White Giant's leaving, they will flee into a land where we will have little hope of finding them if we do not follow now!"

"We?" Tsana turned the word, taking thoughtful measure of the man who had spoken it; he needed no shamanic insight to see the longing for vengeance in Kosar-eh's eyes, the purely focused hatred on his battered face. "Are we, then, truly of one tribe now?"

They continued on, Kosar-eh trudging forward while Doh-teyah slept in her cradleboard on his back. Higher into the pass they went, along an avenue of corpses, deeper into wind-tattered mists and the ever-thickening grays and blues of evening.

With darkness the wind dropped. The mists thinned, then vanished entirely. Now, cresting the pass at last, Tsana signaled a pause so that the children could rest before they began the long descent into and across the Valley of the Dead.

"This boy is no child!" Kiu-neh protested. He was embarrassed and ashamed to see his brother already seated on a stump, allowing Joh-nee to help him pull off his moccasins so that he could rub his feet. "This boy is not like *them*! Kiu-neh, Third Son of Spits in the Face of Enemies, does not need to rest. Nor does he complain of aching feet."

"I do not complain!" countered Kho-neh, petulant and resentful.

"He makes war on frost spirits," Joh-nee explained, glaring at Kiu-neh. "Look, if you doubt. They *have* been biting at his toes. And he has not said a word to anyone but me until now."

Tsana raised a contemplative brow as he looked from the twosome to the youth who was trying so hard to impress him. "Have you no consideration for the needs of your younger brother, or for the concerns of the girl I have named Sister?"

Realizing that he was being politely but firmly rebuked, Kiu-neh seemed to shrink inside his furs. "I . . . I . . ."

"When you have become a warrior of the Watching Star, Third Son of Spits in the Face of Enemies, you will know to think first of the good of the weakest. The strong man can always be counted on to take care of himself, but what of his women and children or, in times of war, the wounded warriors of his band? They are vulnerable and not able to hunt or defend themselves or travel long distances unassisted, yet it is they who hold the future for us all! One man cannot keep the enemies of his people at bay! And someday even the strongest of men must die. But the tribe lives on . . . *forever*!"

The warriors murmured their agreement among themselves, proud in the wisdom of their chieftain.

Young Kiu-neh's eyes went round with awe. "When I am a warrior of the Watching Star . . ."

Joh-nee looked up and observed Tsana as though she had never really seen him before. Slowly, a radiant smile rearranged her dirty, haggard little face.

Kosar-eh, however, stared across the miles and wondered if the chieftain's words had been intended to strike so cruelly at his heart. He had left his women and children vulnerable. With no thought of their safety had he struck out alone, following his own purpose, with no concern whatsoever for the survival of his band. He frowned. Dogs were barking somewhere in the distance.

Suddenly the past came crashing down upon him. No longer did he see the snow-blanketed valley glinting coldly in the light of a rising winter moon. Instead he saw it as it had looked long ago under the sunstruck wings of a circling pair of white-headed eagles: broad hills, tall stands of evergreen forest to the west, grassland to the east; a lake sparkling blue in the golden light of a late summer sun; hardwoods tinged with the first flaming colors of the season. He heard the whistling calls of rutting elk and the rustling of waving grasses as great wedges of waterfowl flew from the north to feed and settle upon the lake.

Within his mind's eye Kosar-eh saw herons and egrets and plumed cranes high stepping through the shallows of the lake as, disguised as clumps of vegetation in tall reed hats, his boys followed him well out from the shore to insinuate themselves among gibbering rafts of black, red-eyed coots. How boldly they kept up with him, floating amid the unsuspecting coots and then, at just the right moment, grabbing the foot of the nearest bird with one hand and breaking its neck with the other. How proudly they returned to the cave encampment in the hills, his fine, strong boys, their stringers sagging with as many as six fat coots apiece! How happily the women greeted them! How the dogs barked and wagged and salivated in anticipation of a meal!

A tremor went through him. The remembered laughter of women and children ripped his heart—his slain women, his dead and missing children! Who could have known then, during those first sweet days and nights within the valley, that it was the legendary place where mammoth came to die, a place where a cave lion was waiting to mutilate his eldest son and where insidious, disease-bringing spirits would feed upon his people, blind his daughter, madden his dogs, and drive the great white mammoth totem into the lake to die forever? And who could have known that ancient enemies were even then in pursuit, that war would soon come to the valley and send the band fleeing to the very edge of the world to virtual annihilation and . . . to this moment.

*Cha-kwena was shaman! Cha-kwena should have known!* Kosar-eh grimaced at the unspoken words, then shook his head. *And I should have seen that he had no power! I should have killed him for the lying yellow wolf he was long before his lies led my people to* . . . He let the thought drift; he could not bear for it to continue.

A terrible weariness shook him, left him empty and weak on his feet. Then, suddenly, with the west wind gusting across the Valley of the Dead, he breathed in cold, bitter air and felt inexplicably strengthened as, looking ahead to a high range of hills that stood like a dark wall at the far side of the benighted valley, he saw a light glowing midway up the wall. Orange as a midsummer sun, steady as the watching eye of a hunting raptor, yet shivering like the Morning Star, it could be only one thing.

"The stronghold!" Tsana informed him, pointing ahead. "They have raised a fire of welcome in the outer cave!"

The sound of barking dogs was erratic now, as though the animals were on the move and coming closer, but this was not the sound that took Kosar-eh's attention. He stiffened, turned, stared back through the pass, back across the long miles. Something had cried out—a single shout. And for an instant he could have sworn that he recognized the voice. *Ta-maya!* His heart leaped with hope of the impossible. He waited breathlessly for the cry to be repeated, and heard instead the high, frenzied yapping of a single coyote.

"The meat eaters of the night are awakening. We should go on," urged Hrak. "Coyote summons his pack to the hunt. He and his kind are not the only long-toothed ones to prowl these hills. There are lions here."

"A yellow wolf . . . is that what you heard?" pressed Kosar-eh. "Only that?"

"What else did you imagine?" asked the hunter, shrugging.

At that moment hope, all hope, died in Kosar-eh. He had not heard Ta-maya call his name. He would *never* hear her call to him again, except within his dreams and longings. His hand drifted upward to touch the feathered hairpin of his beloved, and as he listened to the shrill chorus of distant coyotes, hate centered itself within his spirit. Coyotes had mocked him with their yappings on the night that Ta-maya had met her death, then mocked him again as he followed them to the encampment where U-wa lay dying and his children were enslaved. He thought of Cha-kwena, the shaman who named Coyote Brother. Remembering the avenue of corpses along which he had traveled to reach this place,

Kosar-eh trembled with the certainty of how good it would be to see that shaman's head impaled upon a mammoth-bone stake as penalty for all that Chakwena's deceit had brought to him and his people.

"Come," said Tsana. "We will go on. Third Son, help your brother with his moccasin. Unai, carry the smaller of the brothers when he is ready. If frost spirits have been at his toes, I want no further damage to come to him; he has a brave heart for one so small and, like his older brother, will make a warrior someday. New Sister, will you not walk with your brother awhile? And you, Spits in the Face of Enemies, come, I say, while your blind child still sleeps. Our people await the return of these warriors of the Watching Star, and a new life awaits you and your children. Until White Giant leaves the land, we will winter together. Do not look back! Surely there is nothing there for you now!"

"Do you see it, Axwahtal?" The giant's voice was as deep and resonant as rolling thunder. "There, across the dark valley in the far hills. A light! It looks like feast fire in a big camp . . . *their* camp."

"Yes, Xohkantakeh," replied Axwahtal, leader of the raiding band of warriors from the Land of Grass. "A blind man could see it."

"They must have decided to winter in the cave that the Red World shaman abandoned before the last war . . . in the Valley of the Dead."

"Then we must move on," said a third man, worried.

"Why? They are not following us," stated a fourth.

"Not now! Not yet!" said a fifth.

"I had no idea we were still so close to the entrance to the Valley of the Dead," said the fourth man, yawning.

"Too much time on the captive woman has sapped

your brain as well as your man bone, Ynau!" growled the giant Xohkantakeh.

"It was not I who took the gag from her mouth!"

"She could not breathe. And anyway, I do not think she was heard."

"Perhaps she was. Perhaps she was not. Either way, my sounding covered her cry." Ynau raised his head and uttered the best imitation of a coyote that Ta-maya had ever heard.

She sat hobbled apart from her captors with Klah-neh shivering on her lap. "Do not be afraid," she whispered to the child. "I will not call out again. I will not give them cause to hurt you because of me. But you must be still, and brave." She grimaced against anger. Ynau had just broken the little finger of the boy's left hand, and Ta-maya had not the slightest doubt that the hawk-eyed warrior would inflict more of the same upon the child if she displeased him again.

"Your father has not forgotten us," she said, as much to assure herself as the boy. "Kosar-eh will come. I *know* he will. Twice before he has come through storm and battle and many dangers to bring this woman safely home. And now, knowing that you are at my side, he will surely come. You will see."

Klah-neh buried his head in Ta-maya's breast. Still shivering even though she warmed him against her bare skin within the heavy bison-hide robe the giant had placed around her when her own thin, bloodied bed fur proved inadequate against the night's chill, the little boy snuffled through restrained sobs as he sucked on his swollen, aching finger.

Ta-maya used her good hand to stroke the top of his head. She was certain that, although the child was vulnerable to minor injury, he was not in mortal danger. She had overheard the raiders say as much. Once Klah-neh reached the hidden village of the survivors of the

People of the Land of Grass, the women would vie for the honor of being the one to mother him. Klah-neh, child of lizard eaters though he was, would be raised to forget his ancestors as he became a cherished member of a tribe that had lost all too many sons in war. Irony was bitter in Ta-maya's mouth. Was this not what Kosar-eh wanted for his sons, to see them grow to be warriors and hunters of big game on the golden plains of the Land of Grass that he so loved?

*Not like this!*

Ta-maya's eyes burned with tears as she stared into the night. She did not look at the raiders sitting huddled together in a talkative circle. To look at them would be to risk drawing their attention, and she had no wish to do that. She cringed. Was there one of them who had not pumped the wet heat of his passions into her at least once since she been mauled by Ranamal? *No.* All of them had taken her. *All.* Again she cringed. The light of tomorrow's sun would reveal her battered face and body, and her fractured right arm, reset so tenderly by Mah-ree in the far forest, ached so that she knew the bones had been sundered by those who had taken pleasure in savaging her. Feverish and in pain, Ta-maya closed her eyes, thought of Ranamal, and wondered if she would also be abandoned to die if she proved a hindrance to the men of this war party.

Now, as their low talk came to her, she was startled to hear that this was indeed on their minds.

"The woman has a bad leg . . . and the right arm is broken. She will slow us down now, I think, and if we take her as far as the encampment, she will be of little use to the other women."

The words of Axwahtal, leader of the raiding party, caused Ta-maya to tremble as hope flared within her. *If they leave me behind, I will make my way back to my man. I will . . . somehow, by the forces of Creation, I will!*

"She has breast milk. A useful thing."

Ta-maya flinched at the observation of the giant.

"She still has other uses, better uses," Ynau slurred lecherously. "To force a woman like that to spread herself in any way you demand . . . anytime you demand. Hmm. It has been good with her. She was Masau's woman once, you know. The great and legendary Mystic Warrior of the Watching Star himself! And Shateh looked at her with covetous eyes when her band walked with ours, and—"

"And now they are both dead men!" Axwahtal reminded him caustically.

"Not because of her." Xohkantakeh almost seemed to be defending her.

"No," agreed Axwahtal. "Women have no power."

"It was because of the cunning of the shaman of the Red World woman's band that they are dead, and that war has broken us!" Again the giant.

Ta-maya closed her eyes. How they hated Chakwena, blamed him and her poor, lost band for everything that their own war-making ways had brought upon them.

"Yellow Wolf walks in the power of the sacred stone, and of the totem. All know this," rumbled Xohkantakeh.

"I am sick of talk of absent stones and vanished totems!" Axwahtal sounded profoundly annoyed. "Listen to yourself, Xohkantakeh, sitting here burbling about power and magic like a boy longing for Vision before his first hunt! Bah! Like you, I am far from youth, and I tell you now that my people were doing well enough before we came from the north into the country of Shateh in search of bigger and better game. True enough, there were no more mammoth in our land, and all the enemies worth fighting had been slain or enslaved, or had come here, but the spears of our hunters were often red with the blood of bison and elk, and we had many women and many fine sons. Now, in this far country, too many of my sons have died, and I am weary of war. My dreams are often of the women and hunt brothers I left behind in the ancestral hunting grounds of my people. When White Giant allows, I will return with my followers to the Land of Grass. I will take back my women. I will lie on them and make new sons. And in the lodges of my old hunt brothers, I will tell many good tales of war and victory."

"Victory?" drawled Ynau.

Axwahtal harrumphed. "To survive, this is victory enough. You, Ynau, and all others who have allied with my fighting band since the death of Shateh may return with me to the land of my fathers, and yours. Or stay. The decision is not mine to make."

"And the Red World woman?" asked Xohkantakeh.

"You think too much of her, Xohkantakeh, for one who was hesitant to pierce her even once. You would think that . . ." Axwahtal paused.

Ta-maya tensed. The sound of drums was coming from the distant valley, deep and steady, and somehow dangerous.

"They celebrate a raid . . . *our* raid!" exclaimed Ynau. "As though we left them anything worth taking!"

"Their stronghold *is* close," Axwahtal observed with noticeable concern. "It is good that we have made no fire. Rest. We will leave before the dawn. As for the woman, I do not care what you do with her. As long as she does not slow us or threaten to alert our enemies again."

Ta-maya sat very still and held her breath, hoping they would seek sleep now and leave her to her rest, and then go their way, abandoning her tomorrow. Her heart was racing as she made a silent prayer, *Ah, Chakwena, wherever you are, hear this woman! Remember your people, old friend! And if the power of the stone is still yours, and if the totem has, in truth, been reborn, forgive my man for refusing to wait for you! Forgive us all! Look to us in your dreams and see—*

"Again. *Now!*"

Ta-maya looked up to find Ynau standing over her, his robe thrown open to free that which he sought to pleasure now at her expense. With the eyes of a hawk and the body of a cougar, he was working himself, readying himself, but he was alone, and she told herself that she should be grateful for that. Suddenly he snatched Klah-neh from her arm; before the child could make a sound, he was roughly gagged and bound.

"The boy is worth something to our women." The cautionary reminder came from the darkness. "Give him to me! I will keep him still."

Ta-maya thought she recognized the voice of a raider named Zakeh, but she could not be sure. Ynau was kneeling before her, still working himself, preparing to force her to take him again; of all of them, he was the cruelest, the most insatiable, the one most excited by his ability to inflict pain and rouse fear. She pitied his woman. And now, as he shoved her onto her back, pulled wide her robe, and positioned himself for rape, she pitied herself.

Hurting and burning with fever, Ta-maya closed her eyes again and willed herself to think only of tomorrow. If she lay passive and open to the violence of Ynau's rutting, if she made no complaint, gave no indication of fear or pain, even this most avaricious and sadistically sexual of men might finally weary of her and go his way with the others. She would make her way back to her band . . . to Kosar-eh, gentle lover, powerful and unforgiving warrior. Surely he was hunting for his stolen woman and son, hunting as steadfastly as the beat of drums was now pounding across the ever-deepening night.

# 4

*Drums!*

Kosar-eh wondered if they would ever stop. Like the heartbeat of some invisible giant, they pulsed in unison, a constant, rhythmic cadence throbbing across the night, guiding the raiders home.

At last, with the moon in full ascendance, men and dogs came through the darkness to greet the travelers. Soon, in the dull, sparking light of burning, oil-impregnated tree moss and strips of hide, Kosar-eh found himself high in the far hills, climbing a ladder of bones and passing through an arch of enormous mammoth tusks into the firelit cavern of the People of the Watching Star.

Now, as the big man paused beside Tsana, the beat of drums ceased abruptly, and with the cessation of sound fatigue rocked Kosar-eh, but it was shock at the scene which met his eyes that stunned his senses.

He was aware of Doh-teyah fussing on his back; he barely heard or felt the child. Kiu-neh and Kho-neh pressed against his limbs, like a pair of saplings seeking shelter against an oncoming gale in the shadow of the tree that had spawned them; he was only vaguely aware of their presence. Little Joh-nee peeked wide-eyed from behind Tsana's robe; he was oblivious to her. Kosar-eh stared ahead and could not keep himself from gaping like an awed youth.

Before him, a great pyre of wood and fat burned within a circle of mammoth vertebrae. On either side of the flames, the cave was crowded with people and dogs pressing forward from the depths of the cavern. *So many people! So many dogs!* War had not weakened the People of the Watching Star; it had drawn them into a cohesive force more threatening than before! In painted hides and furs and feathers, they stood boldly before him. Out of tattooed faces they stared at the black-and-white warrior and his children. Even the dogs were adorned, and several of them were growling. Kosar-eh ignored the animals and stared back at the people, stunned by the immensity of this clan, which he had so wrongly assumed to have disbanded forever.

He was not sure when he noticed the slaves among them. Females all, women and young girls. He knew their status by their cropped forelocks, minimal clothing, cowed postures, and lack of tattooing. And he knew *them*. Shoved forward, no doubt to impress—or intimidate—him was Vral, first woman of Shateh's right-hand man, and Neela, Bhandi, and Cheelapat, Shateh's three youngest women, as well as Tinah, Khat, and Oni, the chieftain's adolescent daughters. He wondered if they had been captured in a raid or after being abandoned—often the penalty for being the wives and offspring of men who led their people to defeat in war.

Kosar-eh's brow furrowed as he scanned the assembly for Vral's brood of young boys. He found them standing, not as slaves, but with the other boys of the tribe, their hair uncut and neatly combed, their faces well oiled.

"So shall it be with the sons of Spits in the Face of Enemies!" declared Tsana, observing where Kosar-eh's gaze had wandered. "As this man has vowed, they will be warriors of the Watching Star!"

Kosar-eh was aware of Kiu-neh relaxing a little against his leg. He looked down. A moment ago his boys had been intimidated by the scene that greeted their exhausted eyes. Now Kiu-neh forced himself to stand to his full height as, with head held high, he puffed out his meager chest. Kho-neh looked up at his father and did his best to manage a wan smile.

Kosar-eh saw the chieftain usher Joh-nee from hiding behind the sweep of his winter robe. The girl's obvious shyness and trepidation brought a smile to Tsana's lips as he lifted her into his arms and, hefting her on his hip, declared, "Behold the sister of the shaman Yellow Wolf . . . now the sister of the Watching Star!"

A surprised sigh went up from the assembly.

"The child has consented to this?" asked a middle-aged woman, elbowing her way forward to the front of the throng as she eyed Joh-nee with a disbelieving scowl. Her round face was a knot of purplish scars.

"Yes, Oan. She has *freely* named Tsana of the People of the Watching Star to be her new brother," the chieftain confirmed.

Kosar-eh saw that the ugly woman appeared pleased. Joh-nee was blushing fiercely, and again he was struck by the apparent importance that Tsana and his people placed upon the consent of captives who were not to be slaves to accept their new lives of their own free will.

At a single gesture from Tsana the clan moved away from the fire, allowing Kosar-eh to see into the depths of the cave for the first time. Its contours were as he remembered—a vast, arching space upon which his people had once placed their sleeping mattresses and raised their drying frames and cooking fire—but nothing else was the same. The ceiling had been deliberately darkened and adorned with a great black star. Painted hides and intricately fringed banners were raised here and there to define the dwelling spaces of the hunters. And the bones of Life Giver, the great white mammoth, had been brought from what Kosar-eh had assumed to be their eternal resting place within the shallows of the lake in which the totem had been slain by Cha-kwena. He frowned. A grotesque vaulted pathway of vertebrae, grinding teeth, and upended ribs led to the very back center of the cave. There, where the ceiling met the floor of the outer cavern, seated on a dais composed of the intricately carved molar of a mammoth, was . . .

"Behold Spirit Woman, high priestess of the Watching Star!" invited Tsana.

Startled, amazed, and incredulous, Kosar-eh caught his breath. He knew this woman! Once before—long ago and in another world, it seemed—he had glimpsed Spirit Woman, Ysuna, Daughter of the Sun, intermediary between the People of the Watching Star and the great tusked god, Thunder in the Sky. All claimed that she was immortal, that when her body failed to serve her will, Ysuna would be reincarnated into the flesh of Sheela, her brother's child. But with his own eyes Kosar-eh had seen Sheela slain. And now, although the garments of this Spirit Woman were in many ways the same as he remembered the other two wearing, Kosar-eh saw that the specter on the mammoth-tooth throne was neither of the women who had carried that name. She was another entirely! And he knew her all too well.

"Ban-ya . . . ?" He spoke her name as though the very utterance of it fouled his mouth. He was aware that Tsana was watching him as he stared at her as intently as she was staring at him. He did not care. He could not take his eyes off her. Adorned in a robe of prime, matched wolfskins and wearing a collar of woven hair and human finger bones, Ban-ya—daughter of the distant Red World and of Kosar-eh's own native band—appraised him out of the tattooed face of a slant-eyed weasel.

Dumbstruck, Kosar-eh gaped at one whom he had long thought deservedly dead. The last time he set eyes on this woman, she had been stripped of all belongings, denied winter garments, weapons, or food, and abandoned to die alone in the Valley of the Dead even though she claimed to be carrying the unborn child of Shateh. It had not been the first time he had seen Ban-ya scorned or named Liar. Indeed, in the Land of Grass as well as in the Red World of her ancestors, this only granddaughter of old Kahm-ree had brought her people nothing but trouble. Always too bold, ambitious, and self-serving, Ban-ya had been given away as a gift to Shateh by her own man, who had despaired of her ways, though he had kept the son he had made on her. Her insidious manipulations for advancement among the chieftain's women had ultimately resulted in several deaths, including that of Shateh's last surviving son. With her own hand Ban-ya had fed the man baited meat.

Kosar-eh's jaw tightened. How had this most despicable of women not only survived her banishment but come to be taken in and elevated to the status of high priestess among the ancestral enemies of both her native and adoptive tribes? Was this, then, another obscene joke played upon him by the forces of Creation—that he should be enslaved by enemies and brought to stand before a living Ban-ya when his own most worthy of women was slain? He was shaking.

"Come forward, Spirit Woman!"

Kosar-eh flinched at the sharpness of Tsana's command.

Spirit Woman obeyed it instantly. Slowly, as though

entranced, she rose and walked under the arch of mammoth ribs, emerged to pass to the right of the fire, then came to stand before Kosar-eh and his sons.

Kosar-eh grimaced against irony. Ban-ya's addlebrained old grandmother, Kahm-ree—who would have been abandoned to die along with Ban-ya had it not been for the kindness of his band—had not been mistaken in her stubborn belief that the condemned murderess had survived against all odds and would eventually be reunited with her people. If only the poor old woman could have lived to savor this moment at his expense!

"Is the face of Spirit Woman not familiar to you and the children of your band?"

Again Kosar-eh flinched at the sharpness of Tsana's voice. To his surprise, Ban-ya did the same. Yet her face remained set, her body rigid, her eyes wide and strangely vacant.

"She does not often speak." Tsana's voice was gentler now, his words softly phrased goads directed, not to Kosar-eh, but to the woman. "She does not know Spits in the Face of Enemies, or his sons, or his Blind Daughter, or my new little sister. But then, she could not, could she?"

Distracted and confused by the meaning of the man's query, Kosar-eh looked at Tsana and was startled to see the chieftain smiling at Ban-ya in the manner of a predator observing a prey animal. Suspecting that there was more between these two than met the eye, he felt instinctively—and not without a rising sense of satisfaction—that while Ban-ya had become high priestess of the People of the Watching Star, somehow she was also a captive in this place.

Still staring at Ban-ya, Tsana said in the same mellifluous tone as before, "When we first found Spirit Woman howling in this cave, Indeh, once a warrior of

Shateh, recognized and named her as Ban-ya, Red
World woman of Shateh. But he was wrong. Out of her
own mouth the truth was spoken. And now, in this form
that you see before you, she dwells among us, the reincarnation of Ysuna and Sheela, mysteriously embodied
in the flesh of a Red World woman. But who among us
dares question the will of the forces of Creation? If the
Daughters of the Sun, Ysuna and Sheela, have chosen
to take form and live again in one who was abandoned
in this place to die, who will say this cannot be? Spirit
Woman bore two male infants in this cave. On the meat
of one she survived, in order to suckle the other until
we came. And on that day, naming her infant a son of
Shateh, she offered that child as bait to be used to lure
that man here to his death."

The words brought a resounding acclamation from
the crowd.

"And so we owe Spirit Woman our victory in war!"
exclaimed Tsana. "By her sacrifice of the flesh of the
sons of Shateh, she has finished forever any hope that
man's spirit might have had of returning to live again in
this world . . . even if we had not done this to him!"
He raised the hand, smiled broadly as his people gave
voice to their praise once again. "Now to the breasts of
Spirit Woman are all infants of the Watching Star
brought to draw the first milk of life! And now, behold,
for the forces of Creation have smiled upon us, and all
good things come to the people of Tsana!"

Stunned, Kosar-eh saw a muscle working high in
Ban-ya's jaw; otherwise, there was no response from
her. He wanted to ask how she could have fed upon her
own child, but given her history, he told himself that he
should not be surprised; this woman would do anything
to survive.

His attention turned to Doh-teyah, who was suddenly squalling on his back. He reached up to loosen

the straps of the cradleboard and sling the child forward into his arms when, to his surprise, in a most brotherly fashion, the chieftain set Joh-nee on her feet so that he might offer assistance. In a moment the baby was freed of her confinement and held high in Tsana's hands.

"Behold the daughter of the black-and-white warrior!" Tsana exalted. "Behold this blind child who is able to see the wind to know what will come to her people! Now, as she is nurtured on the milk of Spirit Woman, the blood of Sees the Wind will be transformed into the blood of the Watching Star!"

It happened before Kosar-eh could react, much less speak against it. Ban-ya's hands rose, parted her wolf-skin robe, and held forth her breasts to the hungry child. Kosar-eh stared. In the Red World of his youth, the breasts of Ban-ya, daughter of Xhet-li and granddaughter of Kahm-ree, had been the envy of every woman and girl in the band, the objects of every man's lust. No woman, and certainly no girl, in the memory of the tribe had breasts as big as Ban-ya's huge, smooth, wondrously elongated orbs. And how she had flaunted them, enticed with them, until all gave credence to the rumor that her widowed mother had sent her to dwell with old Kahm-ree when Xhet-li's new man was caught fondling what he had wrongly assumed to be his. Now, as then, the breasts overflowed the confines of Ban-ya's small hands. But they were no longer beautiful.

Kosar-eh grimaced at the sight of the milk-engorged mounds of flesh marred by stretch scars. He saw Ban-ya's fingers tighten. The nipples swelled; milk spurted. And in that instant Tsana lowered Doh-teyah, who, scenting the breasts—if not the woman—as a source of much favored nourishment, reached out, took hold, and burrowed in to feed greedily as she was placed into the arms of Ban-ya.

"Ah!" exclaimed Tsana. "She accepts the life we

offer! Now Sees the Wind is a daughter of the Watching
Star!"

Kosar-eh felt betrayed by the child. How long had
it been since Doh-teyah had been nursing at Ta-maya's
breast? He closed his eyes, remembering the two of
them together in his lodge, the smiling face of the
woman, the baby at her breast. Now his beautiful beloved lay dead, and already this blind, uncaring child
was happily pulling the milk of life from another.

Tsana was gesturing his people forward. "Come,
welcome the new children of the Watching Star. And
behold Spits in the Face of Enemies, an enemy no
longer. He will lead us to hunt the Yellow Wolf and the
absolute power of the totem and sacred stone."

"But—but you promised that you would not hunt
my brother!" Joh-nee's protest sounded like the whimper of an injured pup.

Tsana responded by scooping the little girl into the
crook of his arm. "Tsana is your brother now, and all of
the People of the Watching Star will name you Sister!"
He began to move forward into the assembly. "Come!
All! Show this girl and her family that the words of
Tsana are true. Welcome them! This night let us celebrate a union of bands. As in time beyond beginning, let
the People be one!"

The chieftain's words echoed in Kosar-eh's head.
*As in time beyond beginning, let the People be one!*
The drums were sounding again, their rhythm
lighter and more careless than before. A pair of youths
made bright, spontaneous music upon reed whistles,
and someone was blowing with mad merriment upon a
flute. Seated before the fire, in the place of honor, closest to the chieftain's right hand, Kosar-eh could not see
the flutist. A great wall of people circled the fire,
women and children to one side, men to the other,

some seated, others standing, all happily engaged in conversation as the slaves passed horns of drink and bone plates piled with meat. The high priestess was ensconced across from him on her mammoth-bone "throne," intermittently nursing and fondling Doh-teyah and constantly surrounded by doting female attendants who fussed over her and the bewildered toddler. Joh-nee sat watchfully on the ground at Spirit Woman's feet, clutching her doll, her eyes on the baby as though she had made herself Doh-teyah's guardian.

Kosar-eh could not help but notice that the toddler had been bathed and clothed in clean garments, and that Joh-nee had been washed and combed and given new moccasins. His boys, too, had suffered their faces to be scrubbed. The scar-faced woman, Oan, had seen to it that Kho-neh's feet were slowly warmed and packed with compresses of moist leaves chosen for their ability to draw blood to the surface of the skin and, by so doing, banish any lingering frost spirits before they could inflict serious damage.

Indeed, Kosar-eh had to admit that the women of the Watching Star had gone out of their way to provide generously for the needs of his family. Without so much as a word from Tsana, they had brought moistened rabbit skins with which he had been able to refresh and cleanse his face, then had carried sleeping skins, woven mattresses, and winter clothing to the place that the chieftain had designated to be for the exclusive use of his family. A prime location, it had good access to the central fire and the entrance of the cave, but was not in the path of errant smoke or unduly drafty or wet on rainy days, when the wind might occasionally gust from the south.

His mind and body numbed by weariness and whatever it was he had been quaffing from the drinking horns, Kosar-eh found himself amazed by the willingness of Tsana's people to take him and his family in. After all, as an ally of the man whose remains they had spitted to a mammoth-bone stake, he had been an active, if not infamous, participant in raids on the scattered encampments of their tribe. Granted, Kosar-eh knew that in a time of their choosing he would be made to lead them to the totem and the sacred stone. But he was still the black-and-white warrior, Man Who Spits in the Face of Enemies, and until this night *they* had always been his enemies. As they had warred on his tribe and allies, so he had warred on them—viciously, without mercy or consideration. And now, with the lives of his children in their control, they could just as easily have cinched the collar of a dog around his neck and leashed him in the meanest place in the cave, and he would still do their bidding—not to please them, not out of concern for his own life, but to save the lives of the children.

Kosar-eh frowned. Seeing them in their own stronghold, hearing their laughter, seeing their children at play and their women with infants at their breasts, he remembered Tsana's words: *"You know nothing of our ways!"* The chieftain was right.

*"As in time beyond beginning, let the People be one!"*

This time the statement drifted across his mind like the cooling mists through which he had traveled to reach the apex of the pass. This clan—this most hated of clans—was not totally different from his own. He, who had lost all faith in the imputed power of shamans, talismans, and totems, now realized that one aspect of the legends told by the Ancient Ones *must* be true: The People of the Red World, People of the Land of Grass, and People of the Watching Star *did* share a common genesis. Somehow, in time beyond beginning, when First Man and First Woman followed the great white mammoth from the world of spirits into the world of living beings, the forces of Creation shaped the lives of their many children in different ways until, perhaps in some great wind, they were blown across the world to far lands, within which they formed separate and unique entities, destined to become strangers.

It was a shattering epiphany. As Kosar-eh continued to appraise the warrior People of the Watching Star, he remembered that in the days before war first came to his Red World tribe, the thought of raising a spear against another human being would have been unthinkable to him. Yet now, recalling the ease with which he had not only taken the life of Ranamal but mutilated his body, he asked himself how he differed from these warriors of the Watching Star, whom he had so long held in contempt. If given the opportunity, would he shrink from flaying the bodies and spiking the heads of those who had slain his woman and children?

He trembled. Staring at his onetime enemies, he saw them prospering in this valley within which his own people had suffered so much sadness. He could not find it in his heart to wish them ill, even though the continuing sound of the flute touched a cord of agony within him.

"Black-and-white warrior, you must eat and drink and celebrate our new brotherhood. How else will you remain strong and committed to the purpose that unites us?"

Kosar-eh opened his eyes. He stared at Tsana, who was offering the ram's horn. He accepted it and again drank deeply of the fermented liquid that tasted of blood and fungi and berries gone green with mold. His vision was momentarily impaired as a slave came and knelt before Tsana, her head down, her upraised palms proffering the scapula of a horse; the bone plate was laden with chunks of some sort of boiled meat that gave off strong essences of the sage and mint and juniper berries with which it had been seasoned. Kosar-eh, his vision clearing, eyed the meat and the woman. He could see enough of her downturned face to recognize Cheelapat, youngest of Shateh's wives. Vindictive, hot-tempered, manipulative Cheelapat. She had never failed to be less than cruel and contemptuous to him and his people whenever Shateh's back was turned. It did his heart good to see her on her knees before Tsana.

"Your eyes look long and thoughtfully at this slave," the chieftain said to Kosar-eh. "She is yours for the purpose of pleasure and service if this is your need. And meat. Take meat! You must eat, Spits in the Face of Enemies!"

Kosar-eh's mouth tightened. Had he ever in his entire life felt as morose as he felt now? "This man and his children are in a warm and welcoming camp, but others close to his heart are not with him, nor will they be with him again. This man mourns for them. He will not eat for the passage of four days and four nights, this to honor the Four Winds upon whose wings their spirits ride to the world beyond. And he will *not* have the slave. Nor will he know pleasure again until those who slew his woman and son and abducted another son are like Shateh and his warriors . . . gutted, meat for dogs, their heads impaled, and their skin fringed by the wind!" The words set something loose within Kosar-eh. Suddenly, angrily and with open frustration, he declared loudly to Tsana and the entire gathering, "Is there not power enough assembled here, among the warriors of the Watching Star, to hunt those who have dared to take captives in a place that Tsana claims to have won for his people? This man was not afraid to hunt these raiders alone, but Tsana of the Watching Star has turned his back to the wind and allowed them to escape. What perverted sense of pride allows you to take your ease when, in the camp of the raiders from the Land of

Grass, there are men who must be mocking you and your ancestors for your weakness?"

Tsana was on his feet.

Cheelapat looked up at Kosar-eh in gape-mouthed incredulity and nearly dropped the scapula.

A ripple of amazement shivered through the assembly, followed by silence. Absolute silence. Not a drum, flute, or whistle sounded. Not a dog barked or growled or whined, and even the laughter of children fell away. All eyes were on Kosar-eh.

He rose to glare unflinchingly at the crowd. Would they condemn him for challenging their chieftain and insulting their warriors, or admire the courage with which he had spoken? A sick, sinking feeling opened in his gut. What had made him speak without first analyzing the possible consequences of his words? How had he come to forget that the lives of his children depended on his ability to please these people? A cloying, mucilaginous sweetness at the back of his throat made him remember the amount of fermented liquid he had quaffed from the horns. His tongue felt thick and furred; whatever he had been drinking had loosened it.

Tsana's face was set, his eyes cold as he said, "Does Spits in the Face of Enemies dare to spit in this man's face? And in the faces of my warriors and people?"

A resentful murmur went through the crowd.

Kosar-eh knew that he must stand to the moment and win back the favor of the chieftain and his people or lose everything. There was nothing for him to do now save speak his heart. "Forgive the words of one who cannot see past grief. We have all known war. We have been enemies in these wars. Now this man asks if there is one among you who has not felt the pain he feels, who cannot sympathize with his need to find and punish those who have slain his woman, his children? With this man's last breath would he make his way through cold and dark to find those whom he would see staked beside their tribesmen as penalty for what they have done to his woman and band, and to your people more times than can be counted!"

"And when you have breathed your last, who will guide the People of the Watching Star beyond the edge of the world to the power of Yellow Wolf and the sacred stone and totem? The children of your band? No. They see with the eyes of youth and will not remember the way." Tsana's eyes had narrowed as he turned to his people and pointed at Kosar-eh. "This man is here because he placed the value of one member of his band above the value of his band as a whole. Now he and his children are captives . . . or brothers and sisters of our tribe, according to the will and generosity of one who knows the responsibilities of leadership and would never leave his people vulnerable." He shook his head. "Even if Tsana possessed the clarity of vision of the shaman Yellow Wolf and walked strong in the power of the sacred stone and vanished totem, in consideration of the needs of these captive children Tsana would have returned to this place where they could be tended, and fed, and given respite from the terror and tragedy that have befallen them. What are the lives of a handful of interlopers from the Land of Grass compared to the value of two strong boys who will someday be warriors, a potential life maker, and a child who can see the wind?"

The assembly stirred with restless approval and whispers of affirmation.

Tsana, his eyes on Kosar-eh again, seemed to be measuring him and coming to a sum of which he was unsure. "If it is the will of the forces of Creation, then you *will* stake the bodies of those who have slain your woman beside their tribesmen along the route to this stronghold! It may not be tomorrow, or for many a long moon, but I tell you now, Spits in the Face of Enemies, that the Four Winds have brought us together for a much greater purpose. It has been foretold by the Ancient Ones that a day will come when the People of the Watching Star will be as the great herds, our numbers uncountable, the sound of our passage across the land like thunder in the sky, until—strong in the power of the sacred stone and totem to which you will now lead us—all tribes will fall before us. All! And on that day the mammoth will return to graze once more in the land of our fathers. The People will be one once more!"

Tsana waited until those assembled quieted before he turned to Kosar-eh and said, "You are a fighter of much valor. Your skill as a worker of stone is of immense value. Why be a slave humbled by threats when you can be a warrior of the Watching Star instead? Perhaps this has been the will of the forces of Creation for you and your bold sons and your blind daughter and New Sister all along."

Kosar-eh found Tsana's supposition numbing. As his gaze scanned the cave, he observed the various assemblages of mammoth bones—the arch of tusks, the fire ring, the pathway that led to the high priestess's dais —and knew without being told that these were the bones of Life Giver, the great white mammoth. The bones of no other animal could be so massive. Staring at them, he could not understand how his captors could believe that the totem still lived when, with their own hands, they had dragged its bones and tusks from the lake, hefted and assembled the remains of its skeleton here in the cave. They must have heard Cha-kwena's lie about the rebirth of the white mammoth, he reasoned, perhaps from Shateh and his warriors before they met their deaths. Since the fable of the great white mammoth's immortality was part and parcel of their ancestral belief, they must have accepted it without question.

Kosar-eh would not question it either; though he knew that it was a lie, he dared not challenge it again as long as it promised to keep his children alive and someday lead him to vengeance.

"Behold!" A woman's sharp command centered the attention of everyone in the cave.

All eyes moved to Spirit Woman.

"She speaks!" one of the warriors whispered in surprise.

From the warrior's tone and the reaction of the crowd, Kosar-eh surmised that it was rare for the high priestess to address her people. Now he saw that she had risen and handed Doh-teyah into Joh-nee's eager embrace. With arms and face upraised, Spirit Woman spoke in a voice that he recognized instantly as belonging to Ban-ya of the Red World, but it was a thinner, drier voice than he remembered, as though her vocal chords had been scarred.

"There *is* a way to assuage the black-and-white warrior's grief!" she proclaimed. "Let it be done now, to affirm his place among us, and to determine if he is, indeed, worthy to be one of us!"

Kosar-eh was aware of Tsana tensing beside him. When he looked at the chieftain, he saw that the man's face had tightened as though he had been dealt a blow.

"Are the women and daughters of the dead chieftain Shateh not among us?" queried Spirit Woman, staring straight at Tsana. "Why should they live, when the woman and children of Spits in the Face of Enemies are dead because of their man?"

A shiver of excitement ran through the assembly, like a barely perceptible wind that presaged a rising storm.

Hackles rose at the back of Kosar-eh's neck. Spirit Woman was looking at him. There was recognition in her eyes, and more: hatred, a need for retribution. She had neither forgotten nor forgiven him for turning his back to her the day that Shateh and his people had abandoned her to die. And she knew him well enough to determine the best way to make him suffer for that callousness.

Tsana's expression had changed. He turned his attention back to Kosar-eh and appeared pleased, yet more tense than before. "Spirit Woman speaks wisdom. The woman of Spits in the Face of Enemies was taken and used and slain by the men of the Land of Grass. The woman of their chieftain, Shateh, is here, at your feet. Take her. In her body and blood and suffering, you will soothe your pain as you enter onto the warrior path of the People of the Watching Star."

Cheelapat dropped the bone plate.

Kosar-eh, appalled, stared down at the woman. What Tsana was suggesting was an affront to the spirits of his ancestors. Never in all the raids in which he had participated had he intentionally harmed, much less mutilated, a woman. How could he do so now? And with his sons looking on!

Tsana took a handful of Cheelapat's hair, jerked her to her feet, and pulled her against him, twisting her head so that she was forced to look at Kosar-eh.

He saw terror in her eyes. She was a small woman, young, still pretty enough to arrest and hold the gaze of any man; but Cheelapat imagined herself to be clever— and was not intelligent enough to know that she was wrong. In a misguided attempt to dissuade him from harming her—and perhaps hoping that Tsana would be impressed enough by her courage to change his mind about consenting to her death—she boldly spat in Kosar-eh's face.

"Lizard Eater! Grub Sucker! This woman spits in the face of one who is not fit to be her enemy!" Cheelapat shrieked the invectives at him. "You are not wor-

thy to take the life of this woman, much less stand in the
shadow of Tsana or any warrior of the Watching Star!"

Startled by the unexpected insult, Kosar-eh backhanded spittle from his face and, considering the
woman's bold attempt to grease the pride of the others,
wondered if she was not without some small measure of
intelligence, after all.

Cheelapat was about to prove him wrong. "Why do
you grieve for your woman, Lizard Eater? Do you not
think she died praising those who favored her by blood-
ying their man bones in the body of a creature as vile
and unworthy of their efforts as she?"

The words were pure provocation. They ignited
rage within Kosar-eh—sudden and violent.

Seeing the other man's reaction, Tsana shoved the
woman toward him.

An instant later, Cheelapat was dead, her neck broken, her body a crumpled heap at Kosar-eh's feet. He
looked down at the corpse he had made, at the woman
of Shateh—whose followers had slain one son and
taken another along with his beautiful beloved and fired
his lodge and left his followers to burn within it—and
all that had ever been gentle and loving in him died.

"Now let it be finished in the way of a warrior of
the Watching Star! If a man born of the Red World has
the stomach for it!" The goad came from Spirit Woman.
"If not, let him go his way into the night, a man free to
pursue his enemies—although what he will do with
them when he finds them is questionable, for he will
have proved that he has no place among the fighting
men of the People of the Watching Star. Regardless of
his decision, his sons will live on with us to be warriors.
His blind daughter will be suckled on the milk of the
tribe. And New Sister will fulfill her destiny among us."

Tsana's face convulsed. "And who will lead us over

the edge of the world in pursuit of the totem and sacred stone?"

"Third Son of Spits in the Face of Enemies will show you the way!" volunteered Kiu-neh, standing forth boldly and eager to please.

Kosar-eh did not flinch. He knew that he had lost his son to new loyalties. And he knew Ban-ya was baiting him. She did not believe him capable of what she was demanding of him now—to mutilate the body of a woman, to flay and dismember her, to feed her flesh to dogs and impale her head upon a stake beside that of Shateh. She wanted him to quail in revulsion at a deed of such hideousness to one of their native Red World tribe; she wanted him to choose freedom instead and to abandon his children, and by so doing be lessened forever in the eyes of all who were watching him so fixedly now.

Kosar-eh pinioned her with his eyes. He knew that Ban-ya wanted this as much to demean Tsana's judgment as to punish him. He also knew that he was not going to allow her to have her way. The Red World was far away. His remaining two sons would survive with or without him. His beloved Ta-maya was dead, and his youngest son most likely walked the wind with her. Who was left in this world to care what Kosar-eh did now?

And so, when the skinning knife was brought, he did not turn away.

Ta-maya opened her eyes to cold silence. Ynau had long since left her. Another had come to sate himself on her since, and then he too had gone his way. She lay on her side, covered by the heavy fall of Xohkantakeh's robe, listening for sounds of the camp. All was silent. Moon, Mother of Stars, had gone to sleep in her lodge to the west. Even the wind was down. It was a moment before she realized that the raiding band must have gone their way without her. She was free! Her heart leaped, then sank. What good was freedom? They had left her bound and gagged, vulnerable to even the smallest predators of the night.

Frightened, she attempted to move to a seated position, but she had been left lying on her broken arm, and movement roused such excruciating pain that she screamed through the gag, then sagged into unconsciousness. Pain woke her a few seconds later, or was it hours? She stared at the sky. The tail of the Great Snake had shifted around the ever constant eye of the Watching Star, and from where she lay, she could perceive a faint thinning of darkness to the east. Soon it would be dawn.

Drums were sounding now. She listened. The sound was different from before: deeper, more invasive, the rhythm faster and somehow imperative. Above the drums, barely discernible across the miles, came the sound of chanting. Ta-maya recalled another dawn, other drums and chants, a great dais of mammoth bones, ceremonial fires burning high, and her own near death by sacrifice at the hands of the People of the Watching Star.

Shivering, Ta-maya remembered Ysuna, Daughter of the Sun, and Masau, Mystic Warrior and shaman of the People of the Watching Star; he had given his life to save hers in the bloodred light of that distant dawn. Tears stung beneath her eyelids. *For what purpose did that brave man and my first love die? There was never a child born of our love, and so the life spirit of Masau is dead forever. If my life ends now, when the only child of my body lies dead beyond the edge of the world, then I too will die forever. What, then, has been the purpose of my life at all?*

A terrible, aching misery rose in Ta-maya until she remembered, *You have bought the others a chance to es-*

*cape! U-wa and old Kahm-ree, Joh-nee and Tla-nee and the boys! And Doh-teyah, daughter of my heart if not of my body. And . . .* "Kosar-eh!" she sobbed his name. "Man of My Heart will have kept them safe! And . . ."

The gag made speech impossible, but hope burst brightly within her breast. Perhaps Kosar-eh was coming for her and his son even now. Yes! Surely it must be so! Once her beloved had seen to the safety of the others, no matter how long it took, no matter how far the journey, he *would* come for his woman!

"Kosar-eh!" Again, despite the muffling, hurtful restrictions of the gag, Ta-maya spoke his name, this time not as a sob but as a cry of hope and need.

And then she heard the sound of approaching footfalls.

She opened her eyes. Her heart leaped with joy, with gratitude. Despite pain, she willed herself to sit upright, and this time, strengthened by hope, she bore the agony induced by the effort and succeeded.

A tall man was coming toward her; she saw him moving in silhouette against the fading stars.

"Kosar-eh! Man of My Heart!" Ta-maya tried to say through the gag.

A moment later she sobbed with disappointment as she recognized the massive form of the giant Xohkantakeh hulking toward her like a great, black-maned bison.

He knelt before her on the snow-covered ground. Ta-maya wished for death and knew that she would have rape instead. The thought of opening herself to the invasion of this huge warrior, of bearing his weight, of being tusked by the probings of his massive, engorged man bone, of being torn again and made to bleed was too much for her. When he placed his huge, ursine hands on her shoulders, she screamed and shook her head against the gag as she attempted to lurch away. It was no use. Pain coupled with terror of what was to come and made her swoon.

Xohkantakeh grumbled with annoyance as, roughly and impatiently, he pulled the robe—not away from Ta-maya's trembling body but more closely around her. "The others do not want you anymore. They say that you are a tired, broken, too badly battered thing, and it is best to leave you behind to be meat for wolves and lions, or for any raiders of the Watching Star who may still be trailing us. They have no need to care about one female when they look forward to returning to a winter camp in which they will be welcomed by their women and children. But Xohkantakeh sits alone at his fire cir-cle these days." He shook his head and scowled at the woman whose shoulders he held tightly in his grasp.

Ta-maya was shaking in fear of him. Even if she had not been gagged, she could not have spoken to ar-ticulate her dread as, slowly, the giant raised one hand and sent his fingertips moving across her battered fea-tures in slow, sensual, purely proprietary trespass.

"I, too, mourn for slain loved ones," he told her huskily. "My woman. My daughters. It is not good to be alone. So I have come back for this Broken Wing whom the others have cast aside. They do not care, as long as I carry her burden alone. At the winter camp there is one who can mend your arm and dull the pain and fever spirits that weaken your heart toward life."

Ta-maya gasped, startled as, with one sudden, downward movement, the giant pulled her gag away.

"Do not cry out," he warned. "Now you will be Xohkantakeh's woman."

"I am the woman of Kosar-eh of the Red World, always and forever the woman of your enemy. Let me return to him, or finish me now . . . here . . . for this woman will *never* be your woman, and this woman is *not* afraid to die!"

Again the giant shook his head. "Do you not hear the drums, Broken Wing? They speak of captives taken and of a tribe strengthened in the blood of the slain. I think that your man has died this night, and your band with him. I think it is their blood that gives voice to the drums and renewed purpose to our enemies. Soon, wearing the skins of their slain captives, the People of the Watching Star will dance in the light of the rising sun. This is their way. Then, in days to come, when White Giant leaves the land, they will hunt the totem. If they find it before my people do, they will kill it and consume it and grow even stronger on its power. Then, I think, they will hunt my people and finish us both! But now I say, while White Giant lingers on the land, this man has seen enough of blood and death. Xohkantakeh will not allow Broken Wing's spirit to join those of her band on the wind this night. She will become part of a new band, of a new people." He rose, lifted Ta-maya, and strode off with her in the direction from which he had come.

She did not speak; she knew there were no words capable of turning him from his intent. She did not resist; she was too weak and broken of spirit to even try. The stars were fading in a night sky slowly growing gray. Ta-maya's gaze was drawn upward as a single bright spear of light blazed out of the alignment of stars that her people knew as the Great Bear. She followed the flight of the flaming star eastward until it disappeared beyond the horizon, and for a moment she found comfort in thoughts of Cha-kwena and her sister, Mah-ree, safe together in that far land beyond the edge of the world, where Kosar-eh had refused to remain with his people.

*May you two, at least, remain strong in the protective power of the sacred stone and of the totem! Remember me! Remember all who may have died this day! But look back no more upon this world of war that you have so wisely put behind you!*

Now, with Xohkantakeh taking her into a narrow defile and hurrying on after his raiding band, Ta-maya's heart went cold when she saw the steady, gleaming eye of the Watcher—the North Star—glinting malevolently down upon her. She closed her eyes. The drums in the Valley of the Dead were silent. East Wind was rising with the dawn. In the gathering light of the new day, Ta-maya feared that she would never see her beloved man or any of her loved ones again. Nevertheless, as she turned her face into Xohkantakeh's fur-clad chest and yielded helplessly to whatever the Four Winds would bring to her, she curled the fingers of her left hand around all that she had left to cling to of the past—one of a pair of feathered bone hairpins given to her by Kosar-eh in long-gone days of hope and happiness—and she was comforted.

Yet even as a captive among her enemies, Ta-maya of the Red World knew that although her own life might well be at its end, all was not lost for her people. Xohkantakeh was wrong about her band and her man; he *had* to be wrong! As long as Cha-kwena walked strong in the power of the sacred stone and the shadow of Life Giver lay upon the world, her people would live forever.

In that very moment, far beyond the edge of the world, a meteor burned a white-hot arc across the gray vault of the dying night. For a time span of many heartbeats the way of its passage was branded in the very flesh of the sky. Cha-kwena, having risen early to greet the dawn with solemn meditation, sat cross-legged on the shore of the great frozen lake and could not help but perceive the falling star as a sign from the forces of Creation.

"From out of the west . . . into the east . . . leaving a trail that my eyes can follow! That my *people* can follow to me . . ." The supposition drifted. Perhaps it was loneliness that turned it and set him on the course that would change his life forever. Cha-kwena would never be sure. With the little white mammoth totem sleeping safely within the canyon in the protection of the herd, his eyes fixed across the vast wastes of frozen water that stood between him and his band, then strayed back to the star trail in the sky. "Or, perhaps, it is a path that *I* may take to *them*."

The shaman could not have defined the emotions that ran wild in him at that moment. Later he would recognize in them far too much frustration and eager anticipation of a return to the company of loved ones, and far too little wisdom. But now, marking the fading star trail's position in the sky, Cha-kwena sought its point of origin. "While there is still ice thick enough to hold the weight of a man on the great water, I will return to my band! My people will be there, under the Great Bear, waiting for their shaman! The forces of Creation have at last shown me the way!"

# PART III

# EAST WIND

"I saw the 'master' of the voice and spoke with
him. He subjugated himself to me . . .
[and now] the small gray bird with the blue
breast comes to me and sings shaman songs
in the hollow of the bough . . ."

—Chuckchee shaman
*The Chuckchee* by Waldemar Bogoras

# 1

Warakan stared into the dawn.

He could not say what had drawn him from the lodge just in time to see the meteor flame across the fading night. Never in all his life had the boy seen a shooting star of such brilliance. Entranced, he had quickly retrieved his moccasins from the lodge and without a word to the sleepers within had hurried through the trees, seeking the familiar boulder-strewn rise that allowed a view eastward over and through the trees. He was not sure what he expected to see. The star had flown beyond the edge of the world by the time he scrambled to the heights, but for many a long moment the mark of its passage hung like a luminous filament cast across the sky from the spinneret of some huge, invisible spider.

Now it had faded and vanished with the night. Only a few stars were visible; Warakan knew that soon they too would be gone. Save for a few bands of clouds striating the horizon, the sky was clear. The promise of morning was soft and new, its colors neither purple, blue, nor gray, but a combination of all three. The boy usually found the world to be beautiful in these first tenuous moments of daylight, but now, with his hands enfolding the sacred stone of the ancestors, he could find no loveliness in the morning. Indeed, the sky appeared bruised and battered by the shooting star's passage.

And then he saw it. Another star, an even brighter one. The Morning Star shone above the horizon, a livid red aura forming around it as though its sharp-edged incandescence was somehow burning through the clouds and causing the sky itself to bleed.

Warakan's frown turned into a scowl. He did not like this star. It made him recall things he would as soon forget. Somewhere, far to the west, if his people were feeling the need to propitiate the forces of Creation, they would be doing so now in the blood of their captives, in the light of this star. The boy's mouth twisted. He remembered his sister, Neea, saw her stabbed, her young body flayed, her hair and fingers hacked off to become adornments on the sacred collar of Spirit Woman.

The boy shivered. Again the old longing rose in him. *Someday I will be a warrior . . . someday I will return to them . . . someday I will dance in their skins!* And, with the yearning, Warakan was impelled to reach up with his left hand, clutching the sacred stone tightly in the other, to try to pluck the offending point of light from the sky.

The Morning Star shimmered as brightly as before, and Warakan, feeling foolish, withdrew his upraised hand. With a sigh he looked down at the sacred stone. Ever since the woman from the Red World, still intermittently delirious, had given it into his care, the boy found testing its powers irresistible. So far, however, its magic remained elusive.

He turned eastward again, fixing his eyes on the star. He knew it would soon slip below the horizon; with its disappearance the sun would rise, and a new day would be born. Hunkered on his heels, Warakan watched and waited, wondering where the star went and wishing on the powers of the sacred stone that it would die there and never return. Just wishing lightened his mood, and as the moments passed and the star disappeared, the boy felt an immense sense of gratification until . . .

"It will return soon enough!" Jhadel warned him from below the rise, beckoning frantically. "I have been searching everywhere for you. Come now! Your cub is awake. And Talking Bear has once again been taken by bad spirits!"


Death!

Mah-ree saw Spirit Sucker staring at her out of darkness, huge and furred and menacing within the cover of tall trees, its body and breath stinking of the world of moldering decay.

Spear in hand, she stood her ground and attempted to stare Death down.

Death was not impressed. From the darkly furred face of a sick and ancient bear, Spirit Sucker stared back at her.

"Why do you wait?" Mah-ree cried. "Come, Spirit Sucker! This woman who deserves to be meat in the jaws of Walks Like a Man sees you hiding in the eyes of Great Paws. Come, I say! This woman is ready to walk with you forever in the world beyond this world! Her death will be a good thing. Never again must Lawbreaker and Bad-Luck-Bringing Woman bring bad spirits to her people, or block her shaman's way to Vision along the path of dreams that has led him to the totem!"

"So the cave painting on the inner wall of the cavern in the Valley of the Dead *did* speak truth!"

Mah-ree blinked, startled by a young boy's happy

exclamation and by light suddenly dispelling the near darkness that surrounded her.

"Yes, yes, Warakan, but that is not important now. Hold the weather baffle aside so we can all see exactly where, and *who,* we are!"

Mah-ree frowned at the sound of an old man's voice as her eyes narrowed against the invasiveness of morning light. She could see him now, a grotesquely tattooed figure moving slowly but steadily around from her right.

"Give me the spear, Mah-ree of the Red World," invited the old man kindly. "There is no danger to you from the one you call Great Paws. This bear is not the same beast that attacked you long ago in the winter forest. It is only the yearling brother of this boy, Warakan. The animal will do you no harm if you do not provoke it. As you can see, it is still half asleep."

Mah-ree's hand tightened on her weapon. The hideous old man was advancing toward her slowly. She knew him—and yet did not know him. Confused, she looked across the shadowed interior of a cluttered lodge —not a dark forest—and saw not a marauding, sickly old bear but a young, healthy animal sitting groggily on its haunches in a nest of grass.

"Truly, Bear Brother will not harm you, Mah-ree of the Red World."

Once again startled by a voice behind her, Mah-ree turned, looked at the boy who had spoken, and was suddenly appalled to see what he wore around his neck. "The sacred stone! Give it to me! It is not for you! It is for my shaman! I have kept it for him, only for him!" Still holding her spear, she lurched forward and, before the boy could stop her, took hold of the talisman with her free hand and pulled it so hard that the mended thong to which it was attached snapped with such force that the boy fell backward.

A growl filled the lodge, deep, threatening.

Again Mah-ree turned. This time when she saw Death menacing her, she knew that it was not a figment conjured from her nightmares. The bear, surprised and angered by the sudden violence of her movement against the boy, was standing upright. She had not the slightest doubt that it was real. Her mouth dropped open. Yearling though the animal might be, as it rose to its full height its head rammed against the inner thatching of the lodge skins and kept on rising. The shelter began to sway and creak.

"Aiee!"

Mah-ree heard the boy's outcry of alarm. As the bear began to shake its head—and shake the lodge down around it—she prepared to hurl her spear.

A moment later, a resounding war whoop stayed her hand as the boy leaped across the room, tackled her from behind, and brought her to the ground as he screamed, "You will not kill my child!"

They were the last words she heard before the lodge and the bear crashed down around her.

The distress cries of Bear Brother drew a stunned Warakan upward through the tangled wreckage of the lodge. Jhadel was sitting beside him, holding his head but apparently unhurt. It was the same with Mah-ree. The boy glared at her. "If you have hurt my brother, I—"

"Your brother is a bear!" she interrupted. "It is good that he has run away! He might have killed us all and—"

Warakan cut off her words with a snarl. He did not want to listen to her. Not now. Not ever again! Over the past days and nights during which he had helped Jhadel tend to Mah-ree of the Red World, the boy had been touched by her frail, feverish vulnerability in ways that

had softened his heart toward her. All such feelings
were gone now. He had seen her raise a spear to his
child! She had driven Bear Brother into the forest!
Even now Warakan could hear the distant bawling of
the cub. Suddenly he remembered the traps he had set
in hope of snaring the wind spirit. Dread came to him
like a physical blow. Since "catching" the woman in the
woods, he had been so distracted that he had forgotten
to check the remaining snares; and now he knew that
Bear Brother must have come afoul of one of them.

"Warakan! Wait. Where are you going?"

The boy did not reply; he would not be deterred by
Jhadel's command or query. Without staves or protection of any kind, he bolted into the trees and ran wildly,
calling out to the cub, assuring his child that he was on
the way. When he heard the old man shouting after
him, warning of danger from an injured animal of such
size, he would not listen. Bear Brother was not an animal! And Warakan, Boy Mother of Bear, could not ignore its cries.

It was a simple snare contrived of fiber lines securing the top of a bent sapling to the ground and held in
place by a single bone trigger pin. On its rampage
through the woods, the bear had run straight across the
snare, tripped the pin, snarled its forelimb in the lines,
and somehow managed to skewer its forepaw with the
trigger.

Warakan saw his child sitting in the snow, still
bawling like a baby, holding up its bleeding paw as
though, by staring at it, it might convince the trigger pin
to extract itself.

The boy went forward without thinking. "Ah, Bear
Brother, I will help you!"

"No, Warakan!" shrieked a panting Jhadel.

Warakan looked over his shoulder and was surprised to see the old man gasping after him through the trees. The boy shrugged and shook his head, thinking Wise One foolish indeed to imagine that his cub would ever harm him. He said as much and turned back to his child.

"No!"

This time Jhadel's shout was so loud and sharp that both boy and bear winced simultaneously. Apparently frightened and confused, the cub hefted itself onto its rear limbs. The boy's eyes widened. His child was taller and broader than any man he had ever known! Swaying on its feet and visibly groggy and sluggish from its long winter sleep, Bear Brother was looking at him as though at a stranger. And, incredible as it seemed to the boy, the cub was lifting its snout and lips to show him its teeth in a display that was clearly meant to warn him away.

Not understanding how this could be, Warakan strode forward, explaining his intent. "I will take the bone trigger pin from your paw. What is the matter with you? How can you not know your Boy Mother of Bear after all the long moons that we have spent together, traveled together, with you sucking my fingers as though they were your mother's teats and—"

"Warakan!" Jhadel's cry was a plea. His voice was quavering with fear and very weak.

But not as weak as Warakan's knees when his enormous yearling child humped its neck, swung its head, clacked its jaws at him in deadly menace, then charged.

The boy screamed.

The bear screamed back at him and, turning away only at the very last instant, loped off into the trees on three legs, dragging the snare lines after it.

Stunned, breathless with terror, Warakan stared after the bear. He could not believe what had just happened until, slowly, it occurred to him that Jhadel's outcries must have frightened and confused the wounded cub; surely his child had not been hostile before the old man had come. As anger replaced the terror within him he turned. The old man was standing close by, very still and noticeably flushed of face despite his tattooing. One gnarled, ungloved hand was pressed to his forehead; the other was steadying his quaking old bones against a tree.

"You should not have followed me! My child would not have brought harm to—"

"Your 'child' *is* a bear, Warakan! Now, before I perish from what it has done to me—and might well have done to you—help me back to what that animal has left us of our lodge."

It was in that moment that Warakan saw blood oozing from between Jhadel's fingers. He frowned. The Old One's face was not flushed from the exertion of his run through the trees; it too was wet with blood.

Jhadel smiled with grim amusement and raised his hand from his head. "On its way from the lodge, your child that can do no harm did this."

Now Warakan needed a tree to steady himself. Jhadel's scalp had been laid open from the top of his left eyebrow all the way across the peak of his skull nearly to the nape of his neck.

It was somewhere on the way back through the woods that Warakan decided he hated Mah-ree. He knew she was known as Medicine Woman, and her reputation as a healer had been acknowledged in the Land of Grass villages of Shateh even though she was from the despised tribes of the Red World. Again and again he called to her, shouted for her to come and offer assistance so that he could get Jhadel back to the lodge before the Old One bled to death—and also before he was forced to admit to himself that he was still only a small boy who was barely up to the task of bringing one scrawny old man safely home across the snow.

"How could she have let you come after me with a wound like this?" he raged at Jhadel.

"I was off after you before she could see the extent of my injury, before even I was aware of just how . . . But this is of no importance now. She will help us when we return. She will . . ." Jhadel's words trailed off.

Warakan felt sick with despair and exhaustion. He could not move fast enough, and the old man was failing.

Then, at last, they were at the lodge. It lay in ruins as they had left it. There was no sign of Mah-ree.

"She has gone . . . and taken the sacred stone with her, no doubt!" Warakan was in a fury of frustration and anger. The stone! He had forgotten all about it. Was she using its powers against them?

"Warakan . . ." Jhadel sighed the boy's name as he slumped against one of the few lodgepoles still standing. "Come. I must look to you for suturing."

"But I—I have never . . . I do not know how to—"

"Find my medicine bag and parfleche, boy. Quickly. It must be done before my thoughts flow from my head along with the last of my blood."

Warakan obeyed instantly, but try as he might, he could not find the Old One's medicine bag or parfleche amidst the tangled ruins of the lodge. He emerged distraught. "After all we have done for her, she has stolen your medicine bag and run off in hope of returning to her band with the sacred stone, or of following her shaman over the edge of the world with it. Either way, I regret the day we found her! And I hope she dies of cold or starvation, or that some animal will eat her before—"

"No, Warakan! Do not wish it." The old man had

gone rigid with sudden dread. "If she has taken the talisman, you must go after her, find her, and take back the sacred stone before it is lost and all that I have dreamed and hoped for are lost with it."

Warakan was aghast; Jhadel appeared to be dying. "I will not leave you!"

"Nor will I."

The boy whirled around at the sound of a familiar and unexpected voice. Mah-ree was standing behind him. Dressed for traveling in garments appropriated from the lodge, with her arms folded around the old man's painted rawhide parfleche and with his medicine bag dangling from her shoulder, she came forward shyly and repentantly.

"You would both be better off without this Bad-Luck-Bringing Woman, who has failed to work true healing magic for anyone," she said quietly. "I ran away because I had no wish for you to suffer misfortune because of me. Yet what you have just said of me, boy, is true. Selfishly, I took the sacred stone and the Old One's things and thought, perhaps, I might find my way through the forest and bring them to my band. But when I heard you calling, I could not keep on my way. My people and my shaman are long gone from this place; even with the sacred stone, such an unworthy woman as I has little hope of finding them. And you have both cared for me. I cannot do less for you. Suturing a scalp wound is not beyond my skills." She knelt before Jhadel. "Here, now, let me see the worst of it. Boy, stand away, out of the sun."

"Yes, Warakan," sighed Jhadel. "Allow Medicine Woman to see to her work."

Warakan was all at once relieved, insulted, and embarrassed. She called him Boy, dismissed him as a child; he would not stand away. "Wise One has asked me to—"

"No, Warakan," interrupted Jhadel. "Now that Medicine Woman has returned, there is no need of your assistance. Move aside."

Warakan's pride was deeply stung. "Give me the sacred stone!" he demanded of the young woman. "The magic of the talisman will show me the way to heal my shaman."

"It is not for you," she told him sternly. "Ever!"

Warakan was burned by righteous indignation. Mah-ree had driven off and caused injury to his cub. Her incoherently aggressive behavior within the lodge had resulted in Jhadel's wound. When he had called for her help, she had refrained from giving it until she herself determined the proper time and place. Indeed, when the boy thought about it, he realized that if Jhadel were to succumb to his injury, it would be Mah-ree's fault. Completely her fault. Yet now as he watched in complete amazement he saw the old man yielding to her probing touch, smiling through his pain, looking up at her gaunt, girlish face as though she were some sort of beautiful, benevolent spirit from the world beyond. Warakan was shaken by resentment and by a much deeper and less familiar emotion: jealousy.

"If I am not needed, I will seek my child!" he declared in a huff. "Because of this woman Bear Brother also has suffered a wounding this day. My cub has need of healing skills. But not those of a woman. With or without the sacred stone, I must find him. He, at least, has need of Warakan!"

"No, please stay." Mah-ree looked up. There was worry in her eyes, and more than that—a deep, heart-rending pleading. "Your brother is a bear, and this woman grieves for any pain she may have caused him, but his wound *must* wait. This Wise One, however, is a man; his wound will *not* wait. You may not have need of this woman's meager assistance when you journey bravely forth to heal your brother's wounds, Warakan, but now, in this place, under this rising sun, this woman has great need of you."

Warakan stayed.

His heart was hers in that moment. *Forever.* He knew it, swore it, but could not, of course, bring himself to speak words of love; it would not have been fitting for a future warrior. Instead, he did Mah-ree's bidding, eagerly and without question or complaint. He forgave her everything. No dog eager to please a new hunting master could have been more agreeable; if he had possessed a tail, Warakan would have wagged it.

At Mah-ree's command, he raced to bring water from the ruined lodge while she applied pressure to the old man's wound.

At Mah-ree's command, he held the bladder flask to Jhadel's lips while she encouraged the Old One to drink deeply, explaining that the women of the Red World had taught her that water made new blood in those who were wounded. When the old man mumbled that this was also said among the elders of the People of the Watching Star, Warakan would have echoed "So also among the People of the Land of Grass," but somehow, as he looked at Mah-ree, he found that he could not speak at all.

At Mah-ree's command, he took her place beside Jhadel and learned how to apply pressure to stanch the flow of wound blood while she brought forth from the Old One's parfleche a dried, prepared poultice, designed to absorb blood and eat away at the spirits of pain and possible infection. Weak as he was, Jhadel voiced his appreciation of the young woman's knowledge when she chose what he deemed to be the right bundle from among many.

"Willow and lichen are always good bad-spirit eaters; and lichen is always thirsty for all that is wet," she replied.

"Good baby swaddling, too," observed the old man.

Mah-ree smiled, appreciating his attempt at levity under trying circumstances.

Warakan, frowning a little, had nothing to contribute to their conversation and knew it. He listened intently as they spoke of the benefits of oak root, chewed or stewed as a preventive to hemorrhage, as opposed to a blend of artemisia flowers simmered with the inner bark of hemlock and then placed directly on the wound.

Warakan resolved to learn from what they were saying so that he might please them both with his own knowledge in the future. As he held the poultice to Jhadel's wound, he noticed that while Mah-ree laid out the suturing kit and threaded a length of horsehair through a bone needle, she was deliberately distracting her patient with light and easy talk of various green growing things that the old women of the Red World had taught her to use as healing aids. Jhadel, taken by her manner as much as by her words, did not seem to notice when she waved Warakan to one side; and the old man barely winced as she deftly began to stitch his wound.

Warakan winced for him.

Mah-ree noticed the boy's reaction, briefly looked up at him with a smile of approval, then turned back to her work. "This woman finds herself puzzled by Warakan's relationship with his Bear Brother and has wondered how a shaman who wears the tattooing of the People of the Watching Star has come to be in the company of an adopted son of Shateh of the Land of Grass. Even though I am sure you have explained all this to me while I lay quite useless in your care, I cannot imagine

how both have come to reside together in this far land
at the edge of the world."

Jhadel, his earlier lethargy piqued by pain,
breathily began to tell the tale of renewed war and betrayal that brought him together with Warakan. Although Mah-ree was obviously stunned by the Old
One's revelations, the boy was too impatient to sit still
for all of them.

"Warakan slew a great she-bear on his first hunt as
a man of the Land of Grass!" he interrupted with eager
boastfulness. "The robe Warakan wears, and the staves
he uses on the hunt, these he made with his own hands
from the bones and skin of the great bear. And now,
because he is a proven hunter, Warakan is also both
Mother and Brother to the great she-bear's cub!"

Again Mah-ree looked up at him, this time from
beneath a furrowed brow that revealed her displeasure.
"Then, truly, Boy, although you interrupt a shaman, you
*must* be a man."

Warakan frowned. She had called him Boy again!
He could not be sure from her expression whether to be
flattered or insulted by her words. Suspecting the latter,
he said defensively, "This boy is Warakan, son of
Masau, Mystic Warrior and shaman of the People of the
Watching Star, and grandson of Shateh, war chief and
shaman of the People of the Land of Grass! They have
both died, but their spirits live in me, so females must
be wary of how they speak to Warakan!"

Mah-ree was so startled by the boy's audaciously
framed disclosure that her needle stabbed Jhadel.

"Yah!" The old man sat bolt upright against the
lodgepole as the startled young woman dropped the
needle; attached to the bloodied length of horsehair, it
hung before his face as he told her, "Be at ease, Medicine Maker. This man is shaman, but he has lost much
blood and cannot hold steady for such hurtful sticking!"

"I . . . I . . . Forgive these unsteady hands," stammered Mah-ree. "But surely what this boy has just said cannot be true!"

Warakan's frown became a glower. He was beginning to wonder if he still loved her.

Jhadel resettled himself against the post. With the needle still hanging before his face, he closed his eyes, drew in a deep, steadying breath, then exhaled it slowly before saying, "The boy has spoken truth. The blood of the two tribes flows in him. Someday he will be a great chief, a great shaman, but there are many who would hunt him to prevent this, kill him to prevent this, even though I know that for this he has been born." He looked at the young woman, and although his voice betrayed his weariness and pain, there was also a hope so transcendent that his entire being seemed lightened by it. "And so it is that I, Jhadel, shaman of the People of the Watching Star, have turned my back upon my people and taken this boy of the two tribes ahead of his enemies to a place of safety. Someday, strong in the power of the sacred stone, he will hunt the totem and claim its power for the purpose I have foreseen for him. Then, when he is a man, and a shaman, we will go back into the land of the ancestors! *Yes!* Then my people will see—all the People of the ever-battling two tribes will see—that Jhadel was right when he named Tsana and his new Spirit Woman false! And—"

"There are three tribes, Old One, not two! And the sacred stone is not for Warakan, not for any of his people—or yours!" So aghast was Mah-ree that she brazenly interrupted the shaman, completely forgetting her earlier admonishment of Warakan.

"Nor is it for the disbelievers of your Red World band who have turned their backs to the totem, spurned their own shaman, and abandoned you and the sacred stone to the whims of the Four Winds!"

"What do you know of my band?" she demanded, astonished by the old man's amazing perceptiveness.

"Jhadel is shaman!" Warakan informed her loftily. "He knows *everything*!"

The old man exhaled a surprised guffaw at this unexpected vote of confidence from his most constant challenger, but his eyes remained on Mah-ree as he said, "Do not gape, woman of the Red World. Mah-ree, Medicine Maker, Lawbreaker, Bad-Luck-Bringing Woman . . . by whatever name you call yourself, as far as this shaman has seen, you have proved to be Talking Bear—or perhaps, simply, Talks a Lot! You have babbled your entire story to us. Now, finish with this man's wound so that he may rest awhile. His spirit is weary."

The sun was high by the time it was done.

Mah-ree was satisfied. It was a nasty wound, and the old man had lost far too much blood, but she knew from experience that blood would cleanse the gash, the poultices would feed upon pain and fever spirits, and the stitches—as neatly made as any in the seam of the most fastidiously sewn garment—would hold fast until the time came to remove them. She sighed; Cha-kwena would be proud of her workmanship. If only he were here to see it!

"I must seek my child now," declared Warakan, casting a relieved but worried eye on Jhadel, who slept against the lodgepole, mouth agape, brow furrowed against exhaustion and continuing pain.

"You will not go!" Mah-ree countered. She was tired. Her labors over Jhadel had tapped deeply into her already limited reserves of energy. Even though she wore the sacred stone talisman of the Ancient Ones secreted beneath her furs, she was exhausted; the stone, attached to its meticulously mended braided thong, shared nothing of itself with her—it never had. "You must help this woman to reassemble the lodge so that the Old One will have shelter against the cold of the coming night. You must bring meat and fat from the storage pits. You must make fire and gather and heat cooking stones. You must raise posts for the boiling bag, melt snow for water. You must—"

"And what will Talks a Lot be doing while I do *everything*?"

Mah-ree was not surprised to hear annoyance and resentment in the boy's voice. He was a moody child, one moment smiling and panting at her side like one of her lost dogs, the next scowling and arrogant. She cocked her head as she looked at him, remembering him well from her stay among the people of Shateh. The runaway foundling from the war camp of their enemies. The chieftain's adopted son. The boy whom other youths mocked and demeaned behind Shateh's back, against whom the women whispered, and for whom the men swore there would never be a place within the tribe once Shateh made a son of his own blood. Warakan had never complained, never told Shateh how poorly he was treated. Mah-ree had sometimes seen him alone, perched like a young eagle in a tree, lost to his thoughts and dreams—as she had often seen her beloved Chakwena when he was a boy—and her heart had gone out to Warakan.

As it did now. Seeing the golden eagle feather braided into his forelock, she found herself asking, "Did Shateh not name Eagle his brother? And are you, truly then, a son in his line? And also of Masau's . . . a boy born to two tribes? I do not understand how this can be when Shateh himself did not know of it in the days when my people shared his villages."

The boy's long obsidian eyes narrowed, his scarred mouth tightening over his teeth. "Masau was a son of Shateh's youth. In starving times he was abandoned by

Shateh—a chieftain's sacrifice for the good of his people. Masau was found by others, who raised him. In the
hunting grounds of his new tribe, Masau grew to become a warrior and a shaman. It is said that he came
into many women, but only with my mother was there a
child, and since she was not his woman, not even her
man knew that I was his. And so I stand before you,
Warakan, son of Masau, grandson of Shateh . . . offspring of two tribes and outcast from all! Yes, Shateh
named Eagle his brother. On the day he died, he sent
this feather to Warakan upon the wind, so that his spirit
could live in me forever!"

Mah-ree heard his voice break, saw him turn his
eyes down and away lest she see tears in them; again
her heart went out to him. He too had lost all he loved.
She extended a hand to him. "Come. This woman will
help Warakan to do all that must be done, not for her
sake or for his, but for the good of the Old One . . .
for the good of this band."

# 2

Warakan's heart was Mah-ree's again.

They worked together, and although the young woman's abandonment in the forest had left her gaunt and in need of periodic rest, the boy found that Mah-ree—now that she was able to think clearly at last—was stronger and more resilient than he would have believed possible. Soon the lodgepoles were up, the hides back in place, and the anchor pins secured again. By the time darkness fell, the boy and the young woman were snugly ensconced inside with the old man.

"It is better now," said Mah-ree, using two sticks to draw from the central fire pit a heated stone, which she deftly plopped into a hide bag suspended above the coals from a bone tripod.

Warakan listened to the hiss and bubble of the melting snow inside the boiling bag. Soon Mah-ree would begin to add jerked meat and dried fat to her broth of snow. His stomach growled to remind him that he was hungry. Nevertheless, he announced, "Bear Brother has been too long away. I must go in search of my child. Medicine Woman will give me the sacred stone. It will keep me safe as I journey through the dark forest."

Mah-ree looked up from her work and said apologetically, "This woman cannot entrust the sacred stone to you, Warakan."

"Nor will this man allow you to go alone into the forest at night," added Jhadel, his head swathed in fresh poultices, his body bundled in his old furs as he leaned against his backrest. "Warakan must eat and rest and wait for the light of dawn. Besides, Bear Brother will return to his mother when he is ready, or seek his way among his own kind."

Warakan was stunned. "I am Mother and Brother to him!"

The old man ignored the boy and directed his next words to Mah-ree. "When Medicine Woman from the Red World said that it is better, what did she mean?"

"That the lodge no longer smells of soiled feet and moldy things. And it is orderly now," she replied. "No more stone fragments on the floor, or bits of bone and cast-off pieces of old meat and rancid fat under the mattresses. You have had need of a woman to care for you, Jhadel of the Watching Star, and you, too, Warakan of the Two Tribes!"

"He should have returned by now." The boy was worried; the last thing on his mind was lodge keeping. "*We* are his kind. Bear Brother knows no other!"

Jhadel observed the twosome before him. "One kind, not three. One band, not many. So it must have been in time beyond beginning. How has it come to pass that of all the shamans in all of the fragmented bands of the world, this man is the only man who has not forgotten that in time beyond beginning the People were one —a single family living together in peace and harmony beneath the ever constant eye of the Watching Star?"

Mah-ree dolefully replied, "The time beyond beginning was long ago. In this time, the ever constant eye of the Watching Star brings war and death to the world below, and the battling Twin Brothers of the Sky set the tribes one against the other as each seeks the power of the stone for its own purpose—to win domination over all others. That is why the spirits of the Ancient Ones have placed the sacred stone in the care of my people and of my shaman, Cha-kwena, who has brought it— and the totem—out of the reach of the warring chieftains of your tribes."

Warakan looked at her; his concerns about his cub had scattered and refocused. "We will find Yellow Wolf and the totem!" he promised. "The sacred stone will show us the way. And then—"

"Enough!" interrupted Jhadel, raising a hand in admonition of the thoughts of vengeance that he saw shining in Warakan's eyes. "Once there were many stones, all fragments of the bones of First Man and First Woman, each in the care of a shaman of the many scattered bands among the three great tribes. Now there is only one." His gaze moved to Mah-ree.

The young woman set down the wooden fire prods. Her right hand went to her throat, where the talisman hung from its mended thong, hidden beneath her roughly made shirt of bearskin. "The sacred stone was left in my care by my shaman, for my band, for—"

"No!" The old man was emphatic. "It is the purpose of the sacred stone to unite the People forever in the knowledge that all tribes are one with First Man, First Woman, and the great white mammoth totem, Life Giver! Since long before the days of Ysuna, the People of the Watching Star have known this!"

"Ysuna . . ." Mah-ree whispered the name and shivered.

Jhadel was lost in reverie. "Ah . . . when she was first brought to me by the elders, the first woman singled out to learn the wisdom of the Ancient Ones, I thought, perhaps, in her innate wisdom and beauty and gift of Seeing, this first high priestess of the People of the Watching Star would be the one to unite the tribes." He stared bleakly into the fire. "It was not to be. It was Ysuna who shattered the traditions of the ancestors. It was Ysuna who, in times of endless winter and diminishing game, heard the voice of Thunder in the Sky, and followed that dark spirit's command to invade the hunting grounds of others, to steal the daughters of other tribes for the purpose of sacrifice, and to go forth across the land in endless search of Life Giver." Sadness twisted the tattooed face. "I warned her that was not the purpose of the totem or the stone. I told her that was not why, in the days of her youth, the white bear came out of the storm and allowed itself to die so that she, who had been abandoned by her people, might return to her band and lead her starving tribe to live again and be strong through its meat! For so it had been with me in my own youth! Bear chose me to be shaman, on my first hunt, as it was with Warakan and—" He paused, looked hard at the bearskin-clad young woman who knelt across the fire from him, and was obviously shaken by the parallel.

Mah-ree was also shaken. Her eyes were enormous. "You are the one I heard spoken of in the villages and encampments of Shateh—Great Teacher, Wise One, Spirit Master of the People of the Watching Star! It was said that you knew all the healing secrets of the earth and could make magic to cause people to live forever, and to make men put babies into their women even when those women—"

"We are all immortal through our children, woman of the Red World," interrupted Jhadel. "And I have known few men in my time who needed any of my 'magic' when it came to putting life into their women."

Mah-ree stared dejectedly into the fire and confided, "My shaman has put no life in me."

Jhadel raised an eyebrow, then, grimacing against the resultant pain, told her kindly, "This is often the way with those who walk the path of dreams. To be shaman, a man must be more than a man, and a woman more than—"

Mah-ree seemed amazed by where his words were leading. "In the Red World it is forbidden for women to be shaman!"

Warakan was uncomfortable with the way the fire talk was progressing. He cared nothing for baby-making magic or for dream paths or for living forever, unless it was through the blood and flesh of the totem, and in the way of a fighting man invincible in war against his enemies. Besides, he sensed an unexpected and growing communion between the old man and young woman, and he did not like it. Feeling left out, he said with more than a little snappish petulance, "If all that Talks a Lot is going to cook is snow, then I will go now and find my child. You two do not need this boy to make talk of babies and magic!"

"No!" Jhadel snapped back. "Boy Mother of Bear will stay where he is. And he will not again insult Talking Bear. There is great meaning in this moment . . . and in this night there *is* magic! Listen!"

Warakan, puzzled and irritated, settled himself back on his haunches. As the old man began to speak, the boy felt the power of his magic in the age-old tale that he recounted now. . . .

"In time beyond beginning, in the days when the animals and People were of one clan, Bear came forth to be First Shaman. Both male and female was Bear in those days. Wise was Bear, maker of knowledge, eater of meat and grass, of fungi and fruit and bark and all green growing things. Never did the belly of Bear go empty, nor was the head of Bear ever empty of thought.

Seeker of warmth and all good things for the animals
and People was Bear.

"Then, in a daydream, Sun commanded Bear to
warn the People and animals that White Giant Winter
had been born out of the Watching Star. In a great,
freezing hunger to feed upon the living warmth of the
world below, White Giant Winter was falling to earth
from northern skies along with his Cold Sisters, Snow
and Ice and the Great Nagger, Howling Wind. Bear listened. Bear was obedient.

"In the way of Bear's dream, Bear gave warning to
the People and animals that they must prepare for the
coming of White Giant Winter and the Cold Sisters.
Bear ate until Bear could eat no more; Bear dug a den
in the soft, warm flesh of Mother Below; Bear went
away into the ground to sleep away the time during
which White Giant Winter and the Cold Sisters would
feast upon all warm, living things that did not defend
against their great hunger.

"The People heeded Bear. The animals heeded
Bear. Even green growing things heeded Bear and en-
trusted the warmth of their living spirits to seeds and
spores that they sent burrowing into the ground or away
to safety upon the Four Winds. And Sun smiled, drew
on a robe of cloud, and retreated to a warm, far place in
the blue land of Sky.

"And not until White Giant Winter and the Cold
Sisters had fed upon the living warmth of the world and
gone away did Sun take off the robe of cloud and come
close to the earth again. And only then did Bear venture from within the warm skin of Mother Below to tell
the People and animals and green growing things that
they too could emerge from their cold-time lodges.

"But Bear was no longer alone. Deep inside the
den of winter sleep, Great Bear Shaman had given birth
to First Man Shaman and First Woman Shaman. This

was Bear's gift to the People so that they, like the animals, would also hear the voice of Sun.

"And so it is that when a man or woman is called to walk with Bear and welcome daydreams in the hidden places of the earth and seek the healing secrets of green growing things, that man or woman is called to be Shaman . . . Bearwalker . . . Dream Seeker . . . Goer into the Earth . . . Forest Forager . . . Bringer of Renewal of life to the People and animals and all green growing things."

There was dead silence in the lodge. Both Warakan and Mah-ree were transfixed, then stunned to incredulity by Jhadel's next declaration.

"Now, at last, I see where the path has been leading! Jhadel of the Watching Star will teach Mah-ree of the Red World and Warakan of the Land of Grass all he knows, for in this far and lonely land that lies in the path of the rising sun beyond the edge of the world, behold, the three tribes are united! In this land of no people, Warakan of the Land of Grass will be more than Boy Mother of Bear, and Mah-ree of the Red World, although she is indeed Talks a Lot, will be more than Talking Bear. They are First Man and First Woman reborn through Bear, *both* shaman, male and female together, each destined to become stronger in the power of the sacred stone than any man or woman who has ever lived before."

Jhadel paused, breathless, overcome by fatigue, pain, blood loss, and the euphoria of revelation. "The stone is yours, First Woman, and yours, First Man. Here in this place you will grow strong together in the knowledge and power of the Ancient Ones until the shaman returns from the forest with totem reborn . . . and we may walk forth together in its shadow, not to bring death and vengeance to our enemies, but to bring the gift of peace and unity to the world of the People. Until that day . . . until . . . until . . ." His words trailed off, his eyes rolled up, his lids quivered and closed.

Certain that Jhadel had just died, Mah-ree gasped. She fairly flew around the fire to kneel at his side, with Warakan breathless beside her.

"His spirit . . . it . . . it is still inside him?" the boy asked.

Mah-ree's fingertips touched the Old One's throat, seeking the pulse of life, but not boldly, for she was afraid to discover that it was no longer there.

A sudden burst of snores from Jhadel put an end to her fears.

She withdrew her hand and, exhaling a sigh of relief, heard the same sound come from Warakan as he knelt back on his haunches. She looked at the boy, and he looked at her. For a long time it seemed as though the words of Jhadel hung before them in the smoke above the fire.

*"First Man and First Woman reborn through Bear,* both *shaman, male and female together, each destined to become stronger in the power of the sacred stone than any man or woman who has ever lived before."*

Mah-ree's heartbeat had quickened. The idea of a future mating with the boy who knelt beside her seemed not only ridiculous but impossible; he was a mere child, and she was, after all, Cha-kwena's woman, now and forever. Yet when the old man had spoken, all of the hopes and dreams of her girlhood had been reawakened. She had yearned then to set herself upon the pathway of shamanic knowledge in the way of First Woman. Was it possible, she wondered, that after the passage of so many seasons the Four Winds had heard and answered the secret prayers of her youth? Surely, she thought, it must be so! The old man who had rescued her in the woods was not merely a shaman, he was

*Jhadel*! He was the one whom the women of the Land of Grass had spoken of with such reverence and fear. He was Spirit Master, Wise One, Great Teacher! Through his wisdom had Ysuna come to power and brought the tribes to war! Yet he spoke now to her and Warakan of unity and peaceful coexistence between the tribes. And of much more.

Mah-ree's hands pressed against her heart to still its pounding. She felt the texture of her crude bearskin garments and again recalled the old man's words: *"And so it is that when a man or woman is called to walk with Bear and welcome daydreams in the hidden places of the earth and seek the healing secrets of green growing things, that man or woman is called to be Shaman . . . Bearwalker . . . Dream Seeker . . . Goer into the Earth . . . Forest Forager."*

Mah-ree closed her eyes, remembering other things. Bear had called her into the forest. Bear had given his life so that hers might continue. Upon the meat of Bear had Mah-ree survived. And in the warm skin of Bear had Mah-ree sought the green growing things of the forest that her body needed as additional sustenance when White Giant Winter prowled through the forest.

In the den of Bear—a deep, dark hollow beneath the roots of a great tree—had Mah-ree made a den for herself, a hidden place from which she emerged only now and then to tend Gah-ti's bones or journey to the cold, misted heights of the gorge from which she could look across the land in all directions and wail on the wind in loneliness, crying for her people to forgive her for denying them the sacred stone and begging Cha-kwena to return to his lost and lonely little girl-of-a-woman before she perished from missing him so much. But then, had it not been her intent to die?

There were tears in Mah-ree's eyes when she

opened them, and a great, hot lump in her throat that she found nearly impossible to swallow down. Could it be that when Cha-kwena finally returned to his people with the totem, she would dare face him and them again . . . no longer Bad-Luck-Bringing Woman but Medicine Woman, a true healer and, like First Woman, a shaman in her own right? She trembled. It seemed too much to hope for.

And yet, as Mah-ree's gaze moved around the lodge, took in the now neatly ordered assembly of the old shaman's and the boy's belongings, then strayed back to the shaman himself, fast asleep in his robe of bearskin, it was obvious to her that the spirit of Bear had touched all three of their lives.

Each had killed a bear, and each wore the skin of that bear. Each was an outcast. And each had been swept by the Four Winds to this dark, cold forest at the edge of the world.

Mah-ree closed her eyes again. Although she tried very hard, she could think of no reason why she, the old shaman, and the young boy were here together now unless it was, as the old one believed, for some wondrous purpose.

And then, suddenly, she understood. Her eyes batted open. Tears were flowing freely as she spoke her thoughts aloud. "The old one is Shaman Past—Teacher, Spirit Master; I am Shaman Present, a woman grown and, in my own small way, Medicine Woman, shaman of healing ways; and the boy, this son of Masau and grandson of Shateh, he is Shaman Future!" It all made perfect sense until she asked herself: "But where, then, in all of this past, present, and future, is *my* shaman . . . my *man* . . . my Cha-kwena?"

"Do not cry, Talks a Lot. Warakan will be your man!" the boy proclaimed.

Mah-ree blinked, startled. She cleared her throat,

wiped her tears, and said quietly, so as not to disturb the sleeping old man, and kindly, so as not to hurt the feelings of the youth, "This woman already has a man . . . an always-and-forever man."

Warakan's face tightened. "Your man is a yellow wolf! Your man is Trickster, Brother of Coyote! Your man has stolen the power of the totem and fled with it beyond the edge of the world! But now, through you, the spirits of the Ancient Ones have brought the sacred stone to me! Strong in its power, I will hunt the totem! I will find it! I will kill it and take the magic of its blood and flesh into myself. Then *I* will be totem! And, before I return to the land of my ancestors to make war upon all those who killed my father and grandfather and sister, I will take the skin of Yellow Wolf and dance in it, and you *will* be my woman!"

Mah-ree's eyes were enormous again. The boy had spoken in a whisper, but if he had struck her, she could not have been more stunned. "And have you shared these ambitions with the Old One, who sees a place for you in his dreams of peace and unity, son of People of the Watching Star?"

Warakan's face twisted with contempt. "Jhadel says that Warakan will not be a warrior. Jhadel is wrong! Someday the People of the Watching Star will share the fate of the yellow wolf and—"

"Beware of what you say, Boy!" Mah-ree interrupted, speaking low but as nastily as she knew how. "The spirits of the wind hear all things, and the forces of Creation can turn words back onto the tongue of a careless speaker like the teeth of a dog biting its own tail."

Warakan's face went blank, but fear showed in his eyes.

Mah-ree was gratified. He was no stranger to the warning, and she knew it. She shook her head and made the moment her own. "Twig of a Boy, beware, for when my shaman at last comes back to this place, intent upon returning with the totem to his people, may the forces of Creation grant that I am near enough to see you stand in his way. By then the Twig of a Boy will have become Stick of a Man, and my shaman will break you in two and throw you away into the face of the sun!" This said, she picked up one of the fire prongs, snapped it in half, and tossed both halves into the fire. "Like this!"

"And then there will be two of me instead of one," the boy responded in a flash that was quicker, brighter, and hotter than the reaction of the flames in the cooking pit to the wood the woman had just fed to them. "Hardened by fire like a well-made spear or stave, I will fly to the hunt to make an end to the yellow wolf, but first I will look forward to seeing his coyote face when he sees you here, Lawbreaker! Will he rejoice when he hears the excuses that spill from Talks a Lot as she tries to make him understand why his band has left this place to travel homeward across the hunting grounds of his enemies without the protection of the sacred stone that you were commanded to return to them?"

Mah-ree's heart sank. In a single moment he had dashed all of her hopes and dreams. She could not believe that one so young could be so perceptive, and so cruel; he had seen straight into the heart of her deepest fear and twisted it as though he were twisting one of his bone lances into a wound.

Warakan smiled at her displeasure. But then, in the darkness beyond the sanctuary, the screeching cries of a fang-toothed cat raked through the forest. The boy stiffened. "My child, my cub . . . Bear Brother is alone and wounded in the night . . . without his mother!"

Before she knew it, Warakan had taken up his lances, made a grab for his winter robe and snow walkers, and was on his way out of the lodge. The boy was as quick on his feet as he was with his tongue, Mah-ree saw, and as set in his love and loyalty to an animal as Cha-kwena to the totem.

"Boy!" Mah-ree called. "It is dark. Moon is not yet risen. Fang-Toothed Cat is in the forest! *Return!*"

"I am not Boy!" he shouted back to her over his shoulder just as the weather baffle closed behind him. "I am Mother and Brother of Bear. I will not return without my cub. And I am Warakan, grandson of Shateh, son of Masau, Mystic Warrior! Leaping Cat should be afraid of me!"

Mah-ree could not believe the audaciousness of the boy. For an instant she almost wished that he would be eaten! Then her maternal instinct roused, and she thought of the brave, albeit unpleasant child running off alone through the dark, carnivore-infested forest and nearly came to tears. Moving hurriedly to the door flap, she looked out, called again, stared into darkness, and saw . . . snow and trees, and the starlit tracks of a boy leading off into darkness.

"You must follow!"

Mah-ree turned. Jhadel was sitting up, squinting at her reproachfully. "Do you still doubt that the sacred stone is for you, Daughter of the Red World . . . and for him? Have the spirits of the ancestors not been with you through the power of the talisman until this moment? Go, I say, take your spear and bring Boy Mother of Bear back to me . . . with or without his child. Go, I say, before my fledgling runs afoul of the trap of his own hotheaded pride. Walk warily and wisely, First Woman, and you will have no need to be afraid. The spirits of the Ancient Ones are with you. You *are* Shaman."

\* \* \*

Warakan was afraid.

He was also angry and confused—angry with Mahree for behaving toward him as though he were a child and confused by the way his heart responded to her. One moment he was entranced, tongue-tied, yet feeling all grown to manhood and as sweet-tempered as a happy song; the next he was infuriated by being made to feel small and childish by one who refused to see him as he was.

*And just what are you?*

Pricked by his own unspoken question, Warakan scowled as he went deeper into the night in search of his wounded child. "I am Warakan!" he shouted to the wind and stars. "I am son of Masau, Mystic Warrior of the People of the Watching Star! I am grandson of Shateh, shaman and hunt chief of the People of the Land of Grass! I am Bear Slayer and Brother and Mother of Bear all in one!"

Warakan had long ago found that boastful words emboldened his spirit; his last shouted statements proved no exception. Nevertheless, when the screech of the fang-toothed cat again raked the forest, his gut churned with fear, and his left hand tightened on his staves. "Bear Brother, where are you?" he called, intending a loud, brave shout. He was startled by the frightened squeak that left his mouth.

Concern for the cub kept Warakan on his way and strengthened his resolve. He was not sure when he heard Mah-ree calling after him; quite suddenly, the rising voice of the wind brought her cries to him. And there was something else—a growling, but not from the wind. Not from any animal. But from the earth itself!

Warakan caught his breath. Was the snow-covered skin of Mother Below shivering beneath his feet? *Impossible!* Yet he was inexplicably dizzy. For the first time since leaving the lodge, he realized with no small start of terror that the forest was in motion all around him. *How can this be?* With arms extended, reaching for balance, he looked to his right and left, then turned his gaze to the canopy of wind-riled trees. Although the ground seemed steady once more, he was again dizzied, this time by the swaying of massive trunks and branches. *They are going to fall!* Overcome by panic, Warakan broke into a mad, mindless run.

He felt something—perhaps a root or a winter-dried vine—an instant before he tripped over it and went sprawling. With the breath knocked out of him, Warakan lay still, waiting for the forest to fall on him. It did not happen, and after a few moments, when he felt no movement in the earth and heard only the natural singing of the wind in the forest, he commanded his heart to stop racing.

He looked up. The trees were still rooted to the ground. Above the moving, sighing canopy of the forest, stars seemed to be swarming like gnats over a marsh on a summer day. Beneath such vast magnificence, Warakan knew that, like it or not, he *was* only a boy, a mere twig, as Mah-ree had called him, a vulnerable sapling deluding himself into thinking that he was already a great tree capable of offering shade and support to any woman, even the woman of shaman.

*And yet, must not even a sapling reach for the sun or die?* he asked himself. *And given time, do not even the tenderest of saplings mature into great trees such as those that surround me now?*

"Boy! Warakan! Ah . . . at last! Did you feel the earth tremble? It has not moved so since the moons of last summer when it shook so terribly that the trees at the base of the far gorge fell to crush the lodges of my people. I saw you run. I saw you fall. Are you unbroken?"

He blinked. Mah-ree was bending over him, free-

ing his ensnared ankle as he had, not so long ago, freed
hers. His emotions were overwhelming, too many, too
intensely concentrated, confounding him as he pulled
himself to a seated position and then stood erect. "You
did this! With the powers of the sacred stone, you
caused the skin of Mother Below to twitch and growl!
You tried to make Warakan afraid. But Warakan is *not*
afraid. He may be a twig in your eyes, but he is not so
easily broken!"

She was on her feet beside him, holding up what
appeared to be one end of a long slender length of . . .

"My snare line!" Warakan exclaimed, reached for
it, gave a yank, and found to his inestimable joy, and
then regret, that a wounded bear was on the other end
of it.

Ensnared in heavy shrubbery, the animal was
standing on three limbs, head down from exhaustion,
slobbering from pain, and staring at them as though at a
pair of antagonistic strangers.

Warakan was heartsick. "My child no longer knows
his mother!"

"Your child is a cub no longer. Pain has made him
seek solitude; but solitude will not heal him, any more
than it healed me. He needs you, Warakan. Your
brother has not forgotten you."

Warakan swallowed hard. In the cold glint of starlight, the size and power of his child was apparent to
him for the first time. He remembered the night of the
burning sky, when the weight of the animal had pressed
him to the ground, stunning him into helpless immobil-
ity as stabbing teeth twice the length of his thumbs had
slipped along his jawline. Bear Brother had leaped
upon him in a display of joy that night, and he could still
feel the lingering bruises from its overly enthusiastic
embrace.

Again the boy swallowed, gulping down rising fear as he recalled Jhadel's wound. Was the cub capable of scalping him as it had half-scalped the old man, if he dared venture near? But what else could he do? It was his snare line and bone trigger pin that were disabling the creature. "I must go to him," he said.

"No. Wait. He will come to you, if you speak your heart to him . . . like this."

As the boy stood beside the young woman, he bore witness to that rare quality of her nature that few, save Cha-kwena, had ever seen. Although she wore the sacred stone, Mah-ree did not draw it forth; instead she dropped to one knee and, laying her spear on the ground beside her, looked into the eyes of the bear and spoke as though the animal were human and fully capable of understanding every word she said.

"This woman offers apology to Bear Brother of Warakan. Bad spirits were in her head when she threatened him. He was right to show anger toward her. But now the bad spirits have left her head, and Mah-ree of the Red World asks forgiveness and trust of Bear Brother."

The cub cocked its head, made low, grumbling sounds of distress and confusion.

"Yes, Mah-ree understands your hesitance, but she sees that you understand what she says." Mah-ree went to both knees and began to move slowly forward, well away from her weapon, until the warning *whoof* of the bear brought her to an immediate pause.

"He warns you back and away!"

"Yes, it is so, for the moment," she conceded, but her eyes remained focused on the bear as she spoke to it in a voice as light and sweet as the first warm breath of a summer dawn. "Mah-ree does not fault you for not trusting her, Bear Brother. May she call you this? Ah, well, yes, Mah-ree understands if you are still angry with her, but she thanks you for considering her request. As you see, this woman has set aside her spear. Without it she has no claw with which to defend herself against your might. You must believe her when she tells you that her teeth are not worthy for such as you even to blink at in the way of a threat from her."

Warakan winced as the bear *whoof*ed several times in quick succession, swaying now, back and forth, as though the earth were shaking once again, but it was not; it was indecision that was rocking the bear on its feet. And something else. The boy saw his child extend and raise its head to sniff and slobber at the air, and then his eyes widened in amazement when he saw that Mah-ree was blowing into the air as though attempting to kindle an invisible fire within it. When she raised her hands and began to fan her breath forward, Warakan was certain that the spirits of madness that had been with her for so long had returned as suddenly as they had left. Until, sensing his thoughts, she spoke again to him and the bear:

"This woman sends her life essence upon the wind to Bear as a sharing and revealing of her inner self. Breathe deeply of the breath of Mah-ree and know that there is neither fear nor hostility nor duplicity in her heart as she speaks to Bear. . . . For this woman is Shaman's Woman, and her man is Cha-kwena, Guardian of the Totem and Brother of All Animals. With her breath and words this woman has spoken to many a wild creature of this world, and once, long ago, in a gentler place, she touched Life Giver, Grandfather of All Mammoth, with these healing hands that she now extends to Bear."

Warakan was astounded. "Truly?" he gasped.

Mah-ree did not look at him or deign to respond as she continued to speak to the bear, holding out her hands, palms up, fingers spread wide. "Behold these hands! They have no power themselves to heal the truly sick. But there is sympathy in these hands, and concern in these hands, and now, with careful, gentle fingers, these hands offer to pluck the 'thorn' from Bear's paw even as Bear's Brother, Warakan, would free Bear's limb of the snare line that confounds it."

Warakan was instantly alert to the danger of the situation to which Mah-ree had just committed him; nevertheless, he knew that even if she had not spoken, he would have committed himself to the same cause. It was why he had come into the night in the first place! Because of his carelessness, his child was injured and hostile toward him; because of his thoughtlessness, his cub might never trust him or any of his kind again.

The animal was standing still now, head down again, but there was a change in its stance, a visible diminishment of tension.

"Come, Boy. Put aside your staves. Kneel beside me," invited Mah-ree. "Show your brother that you mean him no harm."

Warakan obeyed.

And slowly—so slowly that Warakan could sense the gradual shifting positions of the stars above his head —the bear came forward. It limped on three limbs, holding out its injured forepaw as it dragged the snare line behind it, along with a good portion of the scrub growth within which it had been entangled. At last it paused before them, scented them, and as Mah-ree exhaled softly into its huge, quivering nostrils, the animal drew in her breath and, sensing a friend, uttered a long, shivering moan that clearly told her of its pain and unhappiness.

"I know," she said and kissed his nose. "We are here to help you, your brother and I."

In the next moment the bear laid a sloppy lick across her face, turned slightly, and went with a great sigh onto Warakan's lap.

The boy went over backward and came up somewhere under a hairy armpit, exclaiming with delight as he threw himself into a wild embrace with his wounded child, fondling the beloved head, caressing the great neck, and working his fingers into the soft, thick fur under its ears and throat. "Ah, Bear Brother, I feared that you had turned your heart against me forever!"

"It was you who ceased to see him as your brother, Warakan," accused Mah-ree, albeit not unkindly as she too ran her hands over the body of the great cub. "He did not look at you with enmity. It was your own fear that you saw reflected back to you out of his eyes. It is the cruelest hurt of all, you know—to see distrust in the eyes of one to whom you have given your heart forever."

The boy knew the truth of her words; they cut him to the quick. Once, and not so long ago, in a land drowned by a great, mad river, Shateh had looked at him like that. On that day the chieftain had driven Warakan from the tribe to die because the lies of others had set the entire band against him. He would never forget that day, or that look on Shateh's face, or those ambitious men among the People of the Land of Grass who had so maliciously manipulated his grandfather for purposes that led to his death. *Ranamal. Teikan. Ynau.*

"Warakan . . . distract your brother."

Mah-ree's command brought the boy gratefully from the past. With a start he saw that she was holding his child's injured paw in both hands, commiserating with Bear Brother over the unfortunate wound. Warakan's eyes went wide. She was spitting on the perforated pad, blowing on it, preparing to take hold of the bone pin. "Bear Brother!" cried Warakan. "Look this way!"

The bear's head swung around, and an instant later Mah-ree had the bone trigger pin out of the animal's paw and in her hand. "There!" she exclaimed in happy triumph. "The thorn will no longer trouble the brother of Warakan!"

Warakan felt sick. He waited for his brother to re-act instinctively to pain by either swatting or biting off the offending woman's head. It did not happen. Without so much as a hostile growl, Bear Brother was examining and licking his paw. The boy was incredulous.

"I would not have had the courage to do that!" He half swooned and immediately regretted his admission.

Mah-ree was on her feet, smiling down at him in the starlight. "Yes, you would. If I had not been here."

He stared up at her. "The sacred stone gave you the power."

"All creatures understand the language of kind intent, Warakan. And this bear, he says that you have been a very good mother to one who, for all his newly acquired size, is, after all, only a yearling with much yet to learn about the world, and about himself."

Warakan was not at all sure if she was speaking seriously or not. Having long been the butt of cruel jokes made by the boys of Shatch's tribe, he was quick to suspect mockery and careful not to allow himself to be led into a position from which he might later be derided. He eyed her suspiciously. "He *said* this to you? I did not hear him speak the words."

"He needed no words. His is a language communicated through other senses." Mah-ree paused. Far off in the wind-stirred forest, a fang-toothed cat was screaming. She shuddered. "That one claims this part of the forest as its own. It is not alone. Do you hear? It calls to its mate. It has found meat. And it will not be the only kind of predator hunting beneath the stars this night. Come. We should return to the lodge."

Warakan knew that she was right. It took him a few moments to free the snare line from the leg of the bear, and then he was on his feet. "We will go!" he said.

Mah-ree looked to the bear. "You must come, too. Do not worry about the Old One. He is not angry with the Brother of Warakan. Jhadel is shaman, you know! He will have seen into the heart of Bear and learned that you intended him no harm. So come, Bear! The night is cold and dark. A warm fire burns in the lodge, and there, in its light, the hands of this woman will soothe your paw with healing salves that will eat your pain. So come to this woman, Bear, and walk once more beside your brother, Warakan."

Her words made the boy smile, and the sight of Bear Brother following through the trees lightened his heart until, after a short while, Mah-ree paused and, leaning on her fine, black-and-white spear as though it were a staff, looked back with a troubled sigh.

"What is it?" he asked, gripping his bear-bone staves. "There is nothing there. Only the wind. And the hunters of the night. Warakan will protect you."

Mah-ree's right hand was at her throat, pressing the talisman that lay hidden beneath her furs as her gaze held westward. "Yes. Warakan is brave. Brother of Bear would not allow harm to come to his cub, or to this Medicine Woman. And it may well be that the powers of the sacred stone are with us in this dark forest. But what of my people, my band? How will they be safe from our enemies without it?"

Warakan gave a careless shrug. "They are far away. No one told them to go their way without their Medicine Maker, their shaman, their totem, or the sacred stone of their ancestors. Whatever happens to them, it can have nothing to do with us now."

# 3

"We will hunt!"

Tsana's declaration brought Kosar-eh from dreamless sleep. Propping himself on an elbow, he looked around the stronghold of the People of the Watching Star and saw that everyone was awake. How many days and nights had passed since he had slain and mutilated a woman in this place? He had no idea. Time was passing in a sullen blur. He spent it alone, brooding, staring across the valley, sending away or ignoring the slaves whom Tsana sent to serve his needs; he had no needs, save the need to mourn, and this they had allowed him. Until now.

"Up, Spits in the Face of Enemies! You have grieved long enough. Now you must eat. Now you must be a man among men again."

Kosar-eh frowned. The cave smelled of smoke and burning sage and boiling meat as the women and girls were hurriedly preparing the meal of first light. The men, already dressed, were selecting and assembling their spears, spear hurlers, and hunting bags. The children were busily greasing the sinew netting of snow walkers, and the older boys were readying some of the dogs and laying out sections of unassembled sleds.

"Come!" invited Tsana from his own fire circle, standing tall while a pair of slaves deferentially placed his robe around his shoulders.

"Yes! Join us, Woman Slayer!"

Kosar-eh, stung by Indeh's deliberate slur, raised an eyebrow. His killing and subsequent mutilation of Cheelapat had won him the admiration and acceptance of the warriors and women of the People of the Watching Star, but his memories of the event did not sit easily with him, and Indeh knew it. He met the man's contemptuous stare and glared back at him, thinking, *Someday, Loose Tongue, you will regret the barbs with which you sharpen your words when you send them toward me!* Drawing his sleeping fur with him, Kosar-eh rose and continued to glower at the man.

Indeh, gratified by his success in riling the newcomer, made a show of mimicking Kosar-eh's expression before turning away, tittering.

The big man was hard-pressed not to go after him and wring his neck, but in the short time he had been with his captors, Kosar-eh had learned that the meaty-faced warrior from the Land of Grass was a respected fighter within his adopted tribe even though he enjoyed playing the clown at the expense of anyone vulnerable to ridicule. It was common knowledge, shared by Tsana only last night, that when Shateh and his right-hand man, Teikan, had been lured to their deaths in the hidden depths of this very cave, Indeh had found great amusement in dressing as a woman and brazenly leading a handful of similarly attired male "hostages" into the encampment of the enemy Land of Grass warriors. There, at a critical moment, they had been joined by strategically placed ranks of Watching Star fighters and had boldly fallen upon Shateh's unsuspecting warriors, slaughtering many a man before forcing their enemies to break and run for their lives.

Kosar-eh's already grim mood darkened. He had to concede courage to the man as he wished that Indeh and his "women" had been more successful against their enemies that night. If only they had killed them all! His band would be intact, his woman and children still alive. And he would not be here now, a captive with his two sons, a blind daughter, and the hateful little sister of the shaman, Cha-kwena.

He saw that Joh-nee was watching him now from that little space that she had made her own close to the mammoth-bone sleeping platform of Spirit Woman, no doubt so that she could maintain her constant watch on Doh-teyah. As if the blind child needed watching! Ban-ya had taken the suckling to breast as though the toddler were born of her own flesh. Even now the woman lay blissfully on her side, nursing and cooing to the little one.

His brow furrowed. Doh-teyah seemed content. But since the episode with Cheelapat, Joh-nee had not spoken a word to anyone, nor had he seen her smile, even when Tsana had gone out of his way to bring the girl special portions of meat and a fine new sleeping fur of fox skins.

The chieftain was approaching him now. "Xanahay has returned from the valley," he said, dark eyes shining. "We sent him to scout that part of the land where autumn grass grows high and a small herd of hoofed ones with high, dark humps, great, wide horns, and shaggy beards has chosen to pass the winter." He paused, looked closely at Kosar-eh to see if the man understood that he meant bison; there was not a man of any tribe who would name prey before a hunt lest the spirits of the wind overhear and alert the chosen animal.

Seeing that Kosar-eh understood, Tsana nodded and continued, "There are several small herds of bearded ones wintering in various places across the valley. This ready supply of fresh meat has been a gift to the People of the Watching Star from the forces of Creation. And now, once again, snow conditions favor a hunt. So eat! Strengthen your body! And take up your fine spear and your bag of extra projectile points and knapping tools. We will provide our new brother with all else that is necessary for him to be Hunter this day. Come! For the pride of your sons, daughter, and for New Sister, you must hunt at Tsana's right hand this day . . . and show Indeh, onetime man from the Land of Grass, what a man of the Red World, now Spits in the Face of Enemies, can do!"

It was an invitation and a challenge that Kosar-eh could not refuse.

They went across the frozen valley in winter shirts and leggings, on snowshoes of bent willow, dragging bone sledges that carried their provisions. Later, if the spirits of their prey and the forces of Creation consented to their kills, they would drag home on the sledges the meat of a successful hunt.

It was familiar country to Kosar-eh: the broad hills bending down to the flat, ice-whitened lake, the dark woodlands fingering deeply into snowy basins that would be sage flats and grassland when—and if—White Giant Winter at last stormed northward with the Cold Sisters.

The morning wore on under clear skies. Soon the sun shone brightly enough to make the hunters sweat within their heavy garments, and the angle of the eye of Father Above confirmed their belief that spring should long since have come to the land. But the wind remained cold, hard out of the mountains; its subfreezing breath veneered the snowy ground with a thin layer of ice so that it was difficult to proceed without breaking through and sinking into the soft snow beneath it. Had it not been for snowshoes, travel would have been impossible. The dogs rode on the sledges now, or across the shoulders of the hunters. A combination of fragmented ice and subsurface snow kept clogging the sinew netting and packing around the frames of the snowshoes, so that at any given moment someone could be found lagging behind to kick his snow walkers free of the considerable weight of this annoying and exhausting impediment.

Kosar-eh found himself puzzling over how these miserable conditions could make for good hunting. On what seemed yet another interminable stop to knock snow from his snow walkers, he looked up to see himself being observed by an amused Isana.

"As it is with men, so will it be for the ones we hunt," the chieftain explained as he slung a big, tawny, wolf-eared dog from his shoulders. Placing the animal on its feet, he said to Kosar-eh, "Let us walk together. As we do, observe this dog, and you will understand the wisdom of the hunters of the Watching Star."

Kosar-eh removed the last of the offending snow from his snowshoes and fell into step beside the chieftain. It was a while before he realized what was happening to the dog. At first the animal trotted friskily across the ice, happy to be free and able to stride beside its master. Now and then a forepaw or hind limb broke through the ice; the dog fought to be free, found solid footing again, shook itself, and trotted on. With each such occurrence, however, small bits of snow and ice adhered to the warm, shaggy hair of the animal's chest, loins, and underbelly. Soon there were frozen fringes dangling from its undersides, and after a while the fringes became knots; those grew into clumps, and before long the dog was dragging along the ground a solid, tumorlike mass. Extending like an enormous snowball from its genitals to its chest, the growth exhausted the animal and impeded its progress so much that, after numerous unsuccessful attempts to roll free, it collapsed onto its side and lay still.

"Easy prey, yes?" Tsana opened his robe, withdrew his skinning dagger from its sheath, knelt, and chipped away the snow mass that had brought the healthy, powerful dog to a state of collapse in less time than it had taken the sun to move two handspans across the sky. "So it will be with the high-humped bearded ones we seek. Come! We are nearly to the place of high summer grass, where the great horned givers of much meat have found winter browse and, on days such as this, answer the prayers of hungry men, women, and children. We will praise the Watching Star and thank the Great Tusked Spirit, Thunder in the Sky, for the gift of life in this land that others—not in favor with the spirits of the Ancient Ones—have so mistakenly named the Valley of the Dead!"

The sun was high, the snow hurtfully bright, and ravens, teratorns, and hawks were circling overhead when the travelers sighted the herd of some twenty bison immobilized and waiting to be meat. Kosar-eh was dazzled.

The hunting band had followed Xanahay into a broken range of intervalley hills, and now, from the crest of a low hogback ridge, they looked down on the river and a narrow, snow-covered span of grassland. There the wintering nurse herd of bison cows, calves, and adolescents had chosen to pass the time of storms. Kosar-eh knew that it was the way of the great herds to come together en masse for the summer rut, then gradually to disband, bulls drifting off in small groups to seek their own blustering way beneath the autumn skies while the cows and calves dispersed with the adolescents in larger, individual nursing units.

"There are several small herds wintering in different places within the valley," explained Tsana. "Look . . . do you see? There . . . the small calf with the yellow hide, a newborn. Snow *does* lie late on the land. And this herd that follows the broken-horned old cow, do you see the error of its ways?"

Kosar-eh observed the narrow stretch of land below. The matriarch of this herd had surely chosen the grazing land between the hills for sound reasons in the last, lingering days of autumn heat. It was apparent from the appearance of the herd that the animals must have been browsing with ease, maintaining their fat, until the last spate of storms. He imagined how it must have been for them—endless days and nights of snow falling straight down, burying the grasses, forcing them to forage through chest-high wallows of frozen whiteness. The old cow would then have led the herd to seek sustenance on scrub growth until that too was buried, and all that was left to eat was the bark of trees in groves along the river's edge; but there, where the river took a sharp bend through the hills and exposed itself to the impetuosities of wind, the snow conditions were exactly those that Kosar-eh had seen mire the dog.

He stared at the bison; the entire herd was mired. Young, old, the newborn, those in their prime—it made no difference. All were immobilized and helpless, vulnerable to the carrion-eating birds that circled in the sky, to the human hunters who stood ready to make meat of them, and to the pair of wolves that even now was feeding on the cow with crooked horns. Still alive, bulging-eyed and slobbering with shock and pain, the old bison trembled and twitched as she was disemboweled, her body upright, supported by the monstrous accumulation of snow that had packed between her limbs.

"As Yellow Wolf led to blood and death those who trusted him, so it will it be for this herd that has so foolishly placed its trust in one unfit to lead."

Kosar-eh frowned at the chieftain's observation.

Tsana nodded with grim intent. "So it will be for Yellow Wolf when you lead us to his hiding place beyond the edge of the world and, remembering his betrayal of your band, you finish him as we will now finish this herd!" The chieftain raised his arms and, uttering a ferocious ululation, signaled his followers to the kill.

The men swarmed down the hillside as one, waving spears and shouting maniacally until the startled wolves fled, leaving the slaughter of bison to carnivores much more efficient and deadly than they.

The hunters killed until the snow was red and melting with the hot blood of slaughter. Not once did a man have cause to look to his own safety. There was no danger in the hunt until Tsana rushed in for a first thrust on one of the larger cows and was surprised when the animal somehow levered up and charged him.

It happened in an instant and was over nearly as quickly. The snow would not support the tonnage of the massive animal. Almost as suddenly as the bison's forelimbs and hooves found enough purchase on the thick, rough surface ice to enable it to rise and start forward, the encrustation cracked, and the animal, with all of its power concentrated in forward motion, collapsed headfirst into the snow. Its six-foot lateral spread of horns and fatty, meat-rich hump took it down with such force that its comparatively slender hindquarters were propelled over its shoulders. Kosar-eh heard the animal's spine snap in the same moment that instinct sent him flying toward Tsana. Casting his spear away, he shoved the chieftain out of the path of the somersaulting bison with such force that the impact with the other man stunned him. The two of them landed in a heap of tangled arms and limbs and broken snowshoes. Moments later, when they emerged shaking their heads and spitting snow, it was to the accolades of all—except a scowling Indeh.

"There is not a man here who would not have done the same, had he been as close to our chieftain as the Red World man," he snapped. He looked to where the bison lay heaving in the snow, its back broken as surely as Tsana would have been broken if the weight of the huge animal had fallen on him.

"Nevertheless, the black-and-white warrior risked his life to save a man of the Watching Star!" exclaimed Hrak, openly impressed. "Now he must *truly* be considered one of us!"

"The horns and prime portions of that cow are yours, Spits in the Face of Enemies," stated the chieftain, untying his broken snow walkers. He rose unsteadily, working his shoulders and arms to free them of knots as he looked down at the man who had just saved his life. "From this moment, Tsana owes a life debt to the black-and-white warrior."

Kosar-eh stared up at the chieftain. Tsana's face was strained. Was he smiling or suppressing a snarl? It was impossible for Kosar-eh to tell, but there was a sharpness in the man's eyes that made him wonder if Tsana was grimacing against pain or chafing against having to acknowledge a life debt to a man of the Red World. Frowning into the setting sun, Kosar-eh found the question troubling until Tsana smiled and extended a hand.

"Come, Brother!" the chieftain said. "We have made much meat. Now, in the way of the hunters of the People of the Watching Star, let us butcher it and feast together!"

\*        \*        \*

They worked until the dark came down.

Feasting on bison brains and livers, on tongues and eyes and tender nose gristle, they cut their way through the slain cows and calves, tossing unwanted portions to the dogs. The best skins they set aside, along with any fetuses that were found, for all knew that the latter yielded the tenderest and mildest meat of all. Afterwards, although more than half of the bison carcasses remained incompletely butchered, they sought a level place out of the wind and, upon the thickest of the newly taken skins, made a fire of deadwood dragged from the grove. Around this they spread other freshly taken skins, placing the fleshed sides against the snow, and seated themselves around the flames to rest and warm their bodies.

Now was the time for talk, low and relaxed—the talk of hunters after a successful kill. They praised the bison that had died this day. They complimented one another for the thoroughness of the slaughter. They told of acts of daring, such as Tsana's bold charge and Kosar-eh's leap across the path of death to save him. While they spoke, they tossed marrow bones into the fire and spitted favored cuts of meat, roasting them until the juices ran. When the hunters had eaten their fill, three cross-skewered udders were brought forth and held outward over the fire until the milk within was bubbling hot. The udders were passed, and all took suck. Even Kosar-eh was amused when Indeh, fondling an udder as though it were the breast of a woman, said that it was a pity that all females did not have "breasts as big as bison's."

Kosar-eh thought of Ban-ya's great "udders" and might have made a responding comment, but in that moment Indeh began to squeeze a teat aggressively and squirt streams of hot milk at everyone. Shouts of startled merriment erupted, and suddenly all three udders became armament. The "battle of the teats" lasted until the udders were wrung dry and the men were wet with milk and laughing so hard that tears smarted from their eyes. Many collapsed back onto the skins and howled with pure glee.

Kosar-eh was no exception. Not since the careless, happy days of his boyhood had he enjoyed such joyful revelry; he was among friends and he knew it. It was a good moment, the first completely happy moment he had known in longer then he could remember. He lay back, pleasantly fatigued. His eyes traced the vast, arching span of the Sky River. Slowly his thoughts drifted among the stars until—free of regret over the past and concern for the future—his consciousness followed the shimmering pathway across infinity into the welcoming realm of sleep.

He dreamed of bison—of enormous herds of bison pounding across the sky—and of himself, one man among many, eagerly pursuing them. Under the curving star body of the Great Snake, Tsana ran ahead of him.

"Brother!" Kosar-eh cried and, lengthening his stride, soon matched Tsana step for step as they raced on together, hunting bison across the sky—until somewhere in the night a mammoth trumpeted.

"The white mammoth!" proclaimed Tsana.

"We will hunt it!" affirmed Kosar-eh.

They hurried on. Under the fixed and steady gaze of the Watching Star, they loped like wolves until . . .

"Kosar-eh! Man of My Heart! *Kosar-eh!*"

He did not pause at the unwelcome cry of his woman's voice. Ta-maya was dead. And he was no longer Kosar-eh. He was Spits in the Face of Enemies, the Black and White Warrior of the Watching Star. For the first time since leading his band out of the dark forest, he was unafraid. He ran as a wolf among wolves, a man among men, a big-game-hunting warrior of the plains! Was this not what he had always wanted?

"Yes!" he cried. Consenting to the conditions of his dream, he ran on without looking back.

"Xohkantakeh! Zakeh says you must come! Axwahtal and the others prepare to move on again, higher and deeper into the mountains."

Ta-maya opened her eyes as the woman's whisper trespassed into the cold darkness of the snow-covered shelter, where she lay warm beside the sleeping giant. She recognized the voice; it belonged to Neeracheela, one of Zakeh's two women. Her jaw tightened. It was Neeracheela and Shan who had tended her when she was first carried into the pathetic little cluster of shelters that the surviving warriors of Shateh euphemistically referred to as their "winter village." The twosome had worked together to reset her arm and suture the torn flesh of her ravaged woman parts; and all the while that Xohkantakeh had held her down and open to their ministrations, they had not spoken a single word of kindness to her, nor had they apologized for the agony they caused. Loathing filled her—for the two women and for the giant who now slept with his great bare back curled against her own.

"Xohkantakeh!"

Ta-maya winced. She could feel the tension of wakefulness move through the giant's body. A moment later he sat up, grumbling, pulled on his moccasins, reached for his knee-length winter shirt, and crawled from the shelter without so much as a word to her.

Ta-maya sighed, grateful for his absence, which was rare. Xohkantakeh usually kept her close, watching her and studying her as though she were some never-before-seen creature whose form impelled his eyes and touch. Each day he came to her, drew the furs from her body, and after exploring and invading her with his eyes, lay his hands upon her, applying healing salves and poultices that in any other encampment would have been administered only by women. And every night, alone with her within the hollow arch of hides that passed as his lodge, he stripped himself naked and drew her close, stroked her, massaged her until she cringed and sobbed in fear of him, certain that it was only a matter of time before impatience with her injuries prompted him to use her for the purpose he had taken her.

Now, with a start, she overheard Neeracheela's continued whispering coming from outside the hut.

"How long will you insist on carrying the useless one? The others mock you. You will never be able to make it through the high pass with the burden of all you possess *and* the injured woman on your back!"

"Soon Broken Wing will be strong enough to walk," he growled.

"Today? Tomorrow? Sometime *before* we reach the land of our ancestors?"

"Do not prod me with insults, Zakeh's woman. Xohkantakch will keep that which he has made his own."

Neerachcela issued a deprecating hiss. "You and every other man in the band . . . and how many others before them, eh?"

Ta-maya was angered by the unfairness of the woman's disparaging remark. Clenching her teeth, she readied herself to deal with pain in her broken arm and woman parts as she sat up. Staring into darkness, she breathed deeply, allowing her pain to subside. Soon Xohkantakeh would return; the raiders would have eaten together and completed the predawn council that had preceded every move since Ta-maya had been with them.

She had hoped that they would stay in one place awhile, now that they were once again ensconced with their women and little ones. But clear weather had made Axwahtal restless to return to the Land of Grass. And early yesterday Ynau and several others had returned from a reconnaissance of the high country with an unexpected bounty in meat—three big-horned sheep —and also with news of having sighted across the range to greening land that lay below and beyond. Ta-maya knew that with fresh meat to sustain them and the lowlands in sight at last, the final trek over the mountains would soon begin.

She closed her eyes, imagining the tortuous distances of rock and ice that still had to be crossed before they reached the west-facing hills, much less set themselves to journey across the Land of Grass toward the hunting grounds of their ancestors. If she survived the trek, she would live and die there, a captive in the homeland of her enemies, her spirit forever parted from her people and her beloved Kosar-eh. The prospect chilled her to her very soul.

Ta-maya trembled as her good hand moved to her feathered hairpin. Carefully, she withdrew the little clip. Her fingers pressed the delicately carved bone, caressed the smooth contours of the attached silken magpie feather, and as always happened when she willed it so, memories of Kosar-eh brought comfort to her despite pain and darkness and despair.

Ta-maya smiled at recollections of her beloved's gentle touch, of his wide, white smile, of his strong hands proffering the cherished gift of adornment that was now, along with Klah-neh, her only tangible link with him and all that made life worth living—love of her man and his children and band; hope in a future within which sons and daughters born of her body would someday gentle her old age with the laughter and love of children of their own while Kosar-eh, powerful and loving grandfather, gathered their family close and told the ancient tales that had filled the little ones of her tribe with wonder since time beyond beginning.

Again Ta-maya trembled. Her fingers curled around the feather. She imagined her beloved beside her, speaking long-remembered words: *"For the Woman of My Heart, this small gift . . . a sign of this man's love . . . always and forever."*

Tears smarted beneath Ta-maya's closed lids. Her eyes opened in cold darkness. He was not here! Kosar-eh and the little band were far away, in another world, it seemed. She and little Klah-neh were alone among enemies, and she was enslaved to a mauling, predaceous giant in whose embrace she would remain powerless until the ending of her days unless the man of her heart found and rescued her soon.

*If he has not done so by now, then surely Xohkantakeh must be right,* she thought. *Kosar-eh is dead.*

"No!" The premise was too devastating to be considered. "I will not believe it!" Ta-maya's fingers tightened into a fist. She felt the hard, unyielding lines of the bone hairpin pressing into her palm before she realized with a startled cry that she had stressed the attached ornamental feather to the breaking point. She opened her hand too late. Darkness nearly blinded her, but a seeking fingertip discovered the truth: The shaft of the feather had cracked in two places.

Ta-maya trembled yet again. Violently. The broken feather was a terrible omen, a sure sign of the finality of her severed union with her beloved. She felt sick. "No . . . no . . ." she whispered as gently but fervently she pressed the feather flat upon her palm. Straightening the shaft, she wondered if it could be mended with glue and binding and thus made as good as new. But movement had roused pain in her broken arm, and frowning, Ta-maya knew that once something was broken it could never be as good as new again.

Her heart sank.

And then, quite suddenly, it occurred to her that she had no cause to remain alone in the darkness waiting for Xohkantakeh to return, or for Kosar-eh to rescue her. She was *not* powerless! She had yielded to her fate in fear of harm coming to little Klah-neh if she failed to obey her abductors' every whim. But since she and the boy had entered the winter "village," every female in camp doted on him and lavished praises upon their men for bringing such a fine, sturdy little prize to their band.

Ta-maya smiled. Klah-neh was safe at last; she was certain of this. Regardless of anything she did or failed to do, the boy would be raised to become a big-game-hunting warrior of the People of the Land of Grass. The bitter irony of the situation tightened her mouth and turned her smile upside down. Was this not what Kosar-eh had so long desired for his sons? *Yes! But not like this!* She flinched at memories of the raid upon her man's encampment. So silent. So deadly. So devastating. *If only he had been there, they would not have been so bold! Indeed, they might not have come at all! Ah, Kosar-eh, Man of My Heart, what kept you so long away? And where are you now? Why have you not come for me?*

Ta-maya's brow furrowed. She did not want an answer to the last question; she would not concede to his death, *ever,* nor would she passively yield to the dark, life-twisting forces that had swept her from her loved ones to dwell as a captive among her enemies. And so, with the intensity of purely focused resolve, she whispered to the confines of the benighted lodge, "The daughter of Tlana-quah, chieftain of the village by the Lake of Many Singing Birds, once woman of Masau,

Mystic Warrior of the Watching Star, and of Shateh, high chieftain of the People of the Land of Grass, and now the woman of Kosar-eh, will *not* be a slave! This woman will seek the man of her heart. Ta-maya will walk with him in this world, or she will spend her last breath seeking him."

She found that her mouth had gone dry as, with her heart racing and her spirit singing with newfound purpose, she fumbled in the darkness for her moccasins, found them, and pulled them on. After inserting her hairpin deep into the protection of her boot, she crouched over the stone tallow lamp, impatiently fingering up fat and slathering it over her skin to help insulate her from the cold. Pulling her sleeping fur around her shoulders and clutching it tightly with her good hand, she hurried into the night.

The surface snowpack was hard and granular beneath Ta-maya's feet. She moved cautiously, silently, until at last the village was well behind her. Giddy with a sense of freedom and sighing with longing for reunion with her beloved, she quickened her pace.

Kosar-eh was out there somewhere! With her band! With the children! Ta-maya nearly wept to think of it. Onward she hurried, trying desperately to remember the way she had come and, succeeding, finding it difficult to keep herself from singing out with satisfaction when familiar landmarks loomed ahead, and then fell behind.

Familiar stars lighted her way as she concentrated on the journey ahead, back across the way the raiding band had come, back toward that far country in which she had lost her heart and all that she had ever loved beneath the wings of circling ravens.

It was cold, brutally so. The soles of her winter moccasins—formed from laterally joined strips of twisted rawhide—maintained a relatively solid grip, but now and then she slipped. Always, despite her broken arm and weakened condition, she rose again, more determined to continue than before. Hope kept her going. She would find Kosar-eh, or she would die; either alternative was preferable to the life she had left behind in the lodge of the giant. She hurried on until, shivering, her teeth chattering and her face and ungloved hands growing numb, exhaustion brought her to her knees.

Ta-maya looked up. The night was fading. Soon it would be dawn. The stars appeared to be looking down at her like little eyes. Were they watching her effort? Were they mocking her for it? Or were they merely dispassionately observing? She exhaled a sigh of acquiescence; she knew that the stars did not care whether she failed or succeeded in her attempt to find her man, and she knew that they were not eyes. Her father once told her that stars were the campfires of the dead, and she must not grieve over the loss of loved ones, for they would always be with her, there, above her in the night sky, sitting close to their fires, warming their spirit bodies, waiting to embrace her with their love if she would only look up and smile in memory of them.

Ta-maya could not smile. There were too many stars, too many memories of beloved dead. Was Kosar-eh with them now? And U-wa and old Kahm-ree and the children? *No! It cannot be! I will not think it!* A sudden emptiness opened within her spirit, dark and cold. She recognized it as despair.

Ta-maya forced herself to rise. She had come far, but not far enough. Suddenly, from out of the darkness behind her, she heard . . .

"You will not fly from Xohkantakeh, Broken Wing!"

She whirled around, too late to cry out, too late to run as she felt one of the giant's hands encircle her waist and pull her back, just as his other hand came down across her mouth to stifle any scream she might utter.

"And you will not cry out to alert our enemies to your presence or that of your new band!"

Stunned, Ta-maya felt herself lifted into his arms. Finding her mouth free, she stared into the massive face of her captor and said simply, "Then you must break both of my wings, for *you* are my enemy, and your band will never be mine! This woman will return to her man. In this world or in the world beyond this world . . . Ta-maya is his, always and forever!"

Someone laughed.

Ta-maya flinched. The raiders and a few of their women and dogs had followed Xohkantakeh.

"She is trouble, that one," said Ynau, then added mockingly, "Break her other 'wing' and give her the death she asks for, Xohkantakeh. Or have the wheedlings of a Red World woman sapped the courage of a Land of Grass man?"

"You will not tell this man what to do with his woman!" snapped Xohkantakeh angrily.

Ta-maya sensed anger and embarrassment in the giant.

"The lame woman *is* trouble!" Axwahtal's confirmation of Ynau's statement was as sharp as the head of his spear. "Xohkantakeh will leave the captive here. It is what she wants, to be free of us, to seek her man in the world of spirits. Her death will be a good thing for the band."

Ta-maya felt the giant's arms tighten around her as, his way barred by Axwahtal's spear, he growled menacingly at the headman.

"Xohkantakeh will return to the village with his woman," the giant said stubbornly. "She will be no trouble."

"Leave her." Axwahtal's command allowed no debate. "We have a long journey ahead of us this day. She will only slow us down."

The tension in the air was thick, threatening. Tamaya was afraid to breathe.

"This man repeats what he said in council before the dawn: It is not a good thing for our people to move across the mountains now. It is too soon. The meat of a few sheep will not feed us all if the weather closes again. Green grass may be showing on distant lowlands beyond the mountains, but that country is far, and the way to it is precipitous. Ynau has boasted that he and his hunting companions found little hardship crossing the snowfields of the great pass, but what of their women and little ones—will they find the way as easy? I say no! They will not. There is still too much risk of weather. White Giant Winter is still on this land. Until Warm Moon rises and ice leaves the rivers, this man says that we should stay in our winter village rather than risk starvation or freezing while attempting to return across the mountains to the Land of Grass."

"Xohkantakeh is afraid!" accused Ynau.

"Xohkantakeh is cautious!" countered the giant. "We have been surviving on this side of the mountains for many moons. Why not wait until the pass is free of snow and ice before—"

"We have waited long enough!" interrupted Axwahtal. "Perhaps the time of endless dark and cold that our grandfathers have spoken of in the ancient tales has returned! Perhaps this winter will never end! And who among you has forgotten the drums we heard sounding in the Valley of the Dead? Our enemies dwell there. Close, too close. And so I say that while there is meat and blood and fat and marrow to be shared among my people, we will return to the land of our ancestors. The ice fields that lie across the great pass may be crossed safely if we walk with caution."

"You cannot be sure of that," said Xohkantakeh.

Ta-maya was as shocked as everyone else. The giant had openly challenged the elder.

"But we can all be sure of *this* . . ." Ynau left his statement unfinished as he fixed raptorial eyes on Ta-maya. "Am I the only one to see how it has been among us since *she* came? Enmity. Arguments. Disagreement in council. The Red World people are bad-luck-bringing people. It has always been so. Yellow Wolf, shaman of this broken woman's band, has stolen our luck along with the totem and sacred stone of our ancestors. Now Shateh and many a fighting man from the Land of Grass lie dead, and although Trickster has fled beyond the edge of the world, his powers work against us still . . . through this female! It is because of her guile that White Giant Winter holds us captive in this land, bringing hunger to our women and children."

"No!" Ta-maya could bear to hear no more from the hateful Ynau. Righteous indignation impelled her into a furious lurch that forced the startled Xohkantakeh to loose his hold on her. A moment later she was on her feet, advancing toward her accuser, rage flaming in her eyes. "It was you and your raiders who stole me away from my band! I do not remember asking to be brought here, to be beaten and mauled and humiliated before being left to die! And when my life was saved by one who thinks that he will own me, I did not ask his 'mercy,' nor am I grateful for it!"

Ta-maya paused before Ynau. She knew from his expression that her unexpected display of audacity had stunned him. She was glad. The others, too, were silent; she could feel them around her, a sullen human circle focusing its disapproval through hostile eyes. The hackles rose on her back; it was as though the others were touching her, invading her body with their glares, attempting to break her spirit with their unspoken reproach. She would not allow it! She was Ta-maya, daughter of a chieftain and woman of warriors, and now she willed herself to stand proud as she glared up at Ynau and proclaimed contemptuously, "If you and Shateh and the fighting men from the Land of Grass had not set yourselves to mindless pursuit of Chakwena, you would not have blundered into the hunting grounds of the People of the Watching Star and found yourself here, on the wrong side of the mountains, with your women and children vulnerable to the whims of weather and the war bands of those whom you once thought vanquished! And do you truly imagine that—if this woman were capable of working the will of her shaman—she would not have used the power of Yellow Wolf to save herself from you?"

Ta-maya's question hung in the air. Her heartbeat quickened when she saw the man's hand tighten around the haft of his spear, his knuckles white. If she said the wrong thing now, he would kill her. "Despite all that has passed between us, warrior of the Land of Grass, this woman cares not what you do. Stay on this side of the mountains or cross the great pass . . . return to your village or to the land of your ancestors . . . and leave Ta-maya of the Red World to find her way back to—"

"So that you can continue to work your shaman's magic against us?"

Ta-maya heard Ynau's accusing query in the same moment that, with a forward jab of his spear, he pushed her back and down. She fell hard, sickened by the blow to her midsection, certain that only the thickness of her robe prevented the stone head of the spear from piercing through to her flesh. As she fell, a blur of form and fur hurdled over her to tackle Ynau and send him crashing backward, spear still in hand. Ynau cried out in pain and anger.

"Enough!" Axwahtal's shout was a roar.

Cringing, Ta-maya saw the massive form of Xohkantakeh move like a great cloud over the prostrate body of Ynau, then pull away, leaving the other man where he lay, growling and cursing and vowing to make the giant regret his decision to attack a band brother for the sake of a captive.

"That captive is mine!" Xohkantakeh reminded him. "Ynau may do as he wills with his own females, but this woman is—"

"Dead."

Again Ta-maya cringed, this time at Axwahtal's coldly spoken dictate. She looked up at him. His wide face was set, implacable, and when he met her gaze, she knew that he saw not a woman but an owned "thing," to dispose of as he saw fit.

A low murmuring rose from the others now; there was something dangerous in the sound, hungry somehow, like the low, eager purr that resonated from the throats of large felines when they prepared to feed. Ynau was on his feet, snarling as usual. Xohkantakeh, however, stood hunched, head down, obviously repentant; his posture made Ta-maya think of an aged, oversized dog that she had once seen brought to submission by a master of the pack that was half its size.

Axwahtal moved his gaze to the giant, but he was pointing at Ta-maya as he said, "This captive *is* trouble. Her presence among my people is not a good thing. She is weak and unfit to do a woman's work or to continue through the mountains into the country of our ancestors, but not so weak that she cannot run away and cause the men of my band to follow and clash over her like stags in rut. No longer will she be Xohkantakeh's woman. In the Land of Grass he will find females of his own tribe to spread themselves for him. The Red World woman will die. Now."

Kosar-eh awoke with a start, flat on his back, staring at the sky. The Sky River had faded with the full light of morning. He sat up before a cold fire, surprised and grateful to find that someone had thrown a traveling robe over him; the morning was bitter with cold, and a disconcerting restlessness chilled his spirit. Just before dawn he had bolted upright from deep sleep, his senses afire with certainty that Ta-maya was coming toward him, calling his name, but all had been silent in the hunting camp. When he looked around, he had seen only the starlit forms of sleeping dogs and snoring hunters. It had occurred to him in that moment that if he were to rise, take up his spear, and walk away, no one would see him go, and he would soon be a free man. Then a terrible loneliness had touched him. Free to do what? Seek those who had slain his woman and stolen his son? Ta-maya was dead. Klah-neh was probably safe enough among the many warriors who would surely slay his father if Kosar-eh blundered into their encampment alone. Despondent, he had lain down again, turning his back to freedom and retreating once more into sleep. He had no doubt that he had done the right thing, for he had learned the hard way that revenge was the reward of patient men.

"Here . . . take this! Crack open a marrow bone with it. Eat! There is plenty for all!"

Kosar-eh reached forward as Hrak tossed a palm-sized stone his way. A moment later he was on his knees, fingering a charred bone from the ruined fire and pulverizing its jointed end with the stone. After pulling a large splinter from the smashed femur, he began to scoop and then spoon into his mouth precious marrow from the bone.

"It is good! Marrow is the strength of life!" stated Tsana, coming close. "My brother has rested long and well. This too is good. The sledges are loaded. We will return now to our people with this gift of much meat!"

"And on the journey back to the cave, may these snow walkers once again serve the Black and White Warrior who has risked himself for a brother," said Hrak, anxiously joining Tsana and handing the snowshoes down to Kosar-eh.

Kosar-eh, marrowbone still in hand, accepted and stared at the footwear, amazed to see that the snow walkers had been exquisitely mended.

Hrak was beaming with pride. "This man has taken it upon himself to bind the cracked frames with bison blood, hoof glue, and new sinew. They have been kept close to the fire all night so they would dry, but slowly, so the bond between old and new would be well made. This man says that—with the consent of the spirit of the bison whose strength will walk now with the Black and White Warrior—these snow walkers will serve the new brother of our band more strongly than before."

"May the bond be as strong between *us,* my brother!" exclaimed Tsana to Kosar-eh.

Hrak nodded. "May it be so, for—and you must not take this as boastfulness—it has been said that a bond made by Hrak is one that can never be broken!"

"He speaks the truth," affirmed Tsana. "Most of the women of our tribe look to Hrak when they want a good joining between the wood and stone portions of their hand tools. And the young boys seek him out when they want to learn the way of spear-making. His hands are strong in the knowledge of these things."

Hrak was visibly pleased by the chieftain's compliment. "It is a skill that chooses the man," he explained modestly. "It has a spirit of its own. This spirit enters the man in his youth, and when he first learns the skill of working stone and bone and wood, it speaks through his hands. The stone yields, the bone breaks, the wood bends to the will of the spirit that lives in his hands. But the skill is not his own. It is a gift from the forces of Creation, not to him, but to his tribe." Hrak, his face rapt, directed his words to Kosar-eh. "All who have shared this spirit gift among the People of the Watching Star are dead now, slain in war. Only Hrak is left to instruct our boys, to be alert for those among them whose hands show the promise of someday lodging the spirit gift, to teach them that a good bond must be a mating of stone to wood or bone, that until the death of one or the other it must endure, as it once was with the marriage of a man to a woman, and as it is now with a warrior to his tribe." He paused and added haltingly with open awe, "This man has seen the spear of the Black and White Warrior. Truly, Spits in the Face of Enemies, the spirit lives in your hands more strongly than it does in mine! It has been long since this man has seen so perfect a mating of stone to shaft, or a stone so finely shaped."

"It is a skill I learned in the Land of Grass, among those who are now my enemies."

"*Our* enemies," corrected Tsana.

Others had come near.

"The Black and White Warrior brings with him the favor of the spirits," said Xanahay, his wide, ruddy face greasy from his morning meal. "He will share his stone-working skill with our youth. And the meat we have taken will make us strong for the time when he leads us on the pathway of the shaman Yellow Wolf and to the power of the sacred stone and of the totem!"

"It will be soon," said Unai. "Each night the stars shift westward across the sky. Their changing places promise the rising of the Warm Moon. Soon White Giant Winter will return to the north. The great passes through the mountains to the west will be open to the Land of Grass once more, and the way east into the face of the rising sun will lie open to the People of the Watching Star."

Kosar-eh trembled as a sudden wave of need swept through him. "Our enemies will seek safety in the west with the first melting winter snows. If we do not pursue them, we may never—"

"When we are invincible in the power of the totem and sacred stone, we will follow them into that country to reclaim the hunting grounds of our ancestors!" interrupted Tsana, then added further assurance. "All who stand against us will walk the wind forever!"

"And the Black and White Warrior will find those who raided his camp and make them regret the day they brought death to his women and children!" promised Hrak. "With the many fine spears we will have made by then, surely this will be so!"

Kosar-eh rose and appraised his fellow hunters. "Who is to say that you are not invincible now?" he asked them.

Tsana eyed him thoughtfully, then gestured to the loaded sledges. "The forces of Creation have brought us to much meat. Spits in the Face of Enemies has dipped the head of his spear many times in the blood and flesh of bison. Would he dishonor the lives of those animals whose spirits he has sent to the world beyond this world by abandoning his kills? Would he deny his children the pride that will rightly be theirs when their father returns to them, proven on the hunt, a warrior who has risked his life to save his chieftain?"

Kosar-eh eyed the sledges, then the kill site. "So much meat to be carried back . . . and so much to be left behind. Is this not a dishonoring of our kills?"

"Come!" Hrak extended a friendly hand. "We cannot carry it all. We have far to go! Those bison were as good as dead in the snow before we came. And even though we will leave much meat for wolves and foxes, we will still have much meat to carry. Our children and women will rejoice to see us come!"

"I have no woman," Kosar-eh reminded him darkly.

Tsana shook his head. "You are a warrior of the Watching Star. You have saved the life of your chieftain. Tonight you will have a woman! A gift from one who owes a life debt to a brother. You have mourned enough."

"There is no room in this man's heart for any woman except the one he has lost forever," Kosar-eh responded stiffly.

The men exchanged looks.

Kosar-eh could not tell what they were thinking, but he would not believe that they did not understand the way of his heart.

Xanahay looked longer than the others at Tsana, as though waiting for permission to speak.

But Tsana, with a frown and an impatient wave of his hand, dismissed him, then exhaled through his teeth as he shook his head and slung a brotherly arm around Kosar-eh's shoulders. "This man was not thinking of his brother's heart but of another part of his body," he said.

And the others laughed to a man.

# 4

Joh-nee felt sick.

Again the cave stank of blood and meat.

She knelt at the foot of the throne of Spirit Woman and told herself that this time it was all right. This time it was not human meat or human blood she saw or smelled. *No.* The produce of that night of terror had been fed to the dogs and fire. Yet the little girl could still see it, smell it. She closed her eyes and told herself that she must stop thinking about it. When she opened her eyes, the memory of the slaying of Cheelapat would be gone!

Joh-nee stared ahead toward the ceremonial fire pit; she was a strong-willed child, and for the moment, at least, she felt a little better.

Men and youths were crouched close to the flames, searing skewers of fatty hump steaks; the scent was good, soothing until she saw the bison fetuses singeing on racks of bone, the sight and smell of which were as revolting to her as the great ropes of intestines looped around roasting spits held at each end by slaves. Disgusted, the girl looked away from the main fire, scanned her surroundings, and saw that beside every individual family cooking circle were assorted slabs of butchered bison flesh and piles of bones, horns, hooves, paunches, various organs, and rolled, uncured skins and loops of sinew.

"There will be woman work for many days," observed Oan, coming to stand before Spirit Woman. "But not for tonight."

Spirit Woman was crooning to Doh-teyah, who was fussing at her breast. She said nothing to the scar-faced matron.

"I will look after Sees the Wind if you wish to join the others," offered Oan. "The hunters will now settle around the main fire to tell of the hunt. They will dance for their women and sons and make a great show for us!"

Spirit Woman ignored her. She was completely engrossed in Doh-teyah, smiling at the child, pursing her lips and clucking her tongue in loving admonition as she told the toddler to look around and see what a fortunate little girl she was to have found such a wondrous new home and mother.

Joh-nee watched the priestess, wondering just what kind of "spirit" woman could not see that the toddler was blind. *One who is no spirit woman at all! One who is really Ban-ya of the Red World! Clever, lying-always-to-serve-herself Ban-ya! This girl remembers you. This girl knows who you are. This girl has seen what you commanded others to do. And she will not trust Doh-teyah to your care!* "Let this girl hold the little sister of her band." She spoke before thinking, then went on in an earnest rush, "Doh-teyah fusses because you try to feed her all the time and will not let her off your lap to walk about to stretch her legs or—"

"What do you know of mothering?"

Joh-nee winced and drew back. The voice the woman had used to her was not the same voice she used to the child. It was deep, scraping, so imperious and hostile that Joh-nee felt clawed by it. Her eyes went round. Her skin crawled. She remembered the night of terror, the night when she had lost faith in everyone and everything except herself and the baby in this woman's arms.

Again Joh-nee felt sick. Suddenly shaking uncontrollably, she lowered her head and placed her hands over her face. Tsana was right! Spirit Woman *was* truly a spirit living in the body of one who had been abandoned to die, for not even in her worst moments could Ban-ya have been as hateful as the woman who sat before her now with Doh-teyah in her arms.

"Ah, little sister of the Watching Star, Spirit Woman has frightened you. It must not be!" The woman's words had softened; there was no hostility in them now.

Nevertheless, Joh-nee cringed. Spirit Woman was touching her head, stroking her hair with long, gentle movements meant to placate and soothe; instead they made her want to scream. She shivered, reached with one hand for Tla-nee's doll, drew it from her lap to her breast, and held it tight. The spirit in the doll gave her courage. *I must be brave, for Doh-teyah's sake, until Chakwena comes . . . or until Kosar-eh remembers that he is a man of the Red World and finds a way to lead us safely away from this Valley of the Dead!*

Kosar-eh was aware of the little girl staring at him as he knelt with the other men and youths, enjoying the male prerogative of roasting the first hump steaks and sharing them with his sons while the women prepared the bulk of the feast to come. Spirit Woman also looked on. It had been explained to him that when the priestess rose and came to the fire, her attendants would follow with her chair, and the hunters would respectfully give her small portions of the best cuts from their kills; only then would the celebration of the successful hunt begin. Kosar-eh did not relish the thought of offering anything to the woman, but since he had no choice, he comforted himself by thinking how much Joh-nee would benefit from fresh red meat.

His brow came down as he looked at her sitting stiffly in the shadow of the priestess, keeping perpetual, distrustful vigil over Doh-teyah. Ever since the night of Cheelapat's death she had been sullen and withdrawn, picking at her food, disdaining all attempts at friendship from the women and girls, refusing to speak to Tsana, and avoiding Kosar-eh's glance whenever he looked her way. Yet now she was looking straight at him, her eyes steady in her wan little face. He wondered what she was thinking and could only hope that she was beginning to understand and forgive what she had seen him do in this cave to the woman of Shateh.

Now, however, was not a time to concern himself with the little sister of Yellow Wolf, whose lies and deceptions had led him to this moment. Kiu-neh and Kho-neh were eating hungrily at his side; now and then the boys looked up to exchange friendly glances with other youths. This pleased Kosar-eh. His sons appeared to have been fully accepted into the ranks of the Watching Star boys. When he had returned to the cave with the other hunters who had lauded him as savior of their chieftain, he had seen pride of their sire brimming in the eyes of his sons for the first time in all too long. It had been enough to erase his memories of the savagery of the first night in the cave, enough to make his heart quicken with pleasure as he realized that perhaps all was not lost to him after all.

Spirit Woman was rising. Kosar-eh watched her come forward, slowly, regally, deliberately drawing the eyes of every man, woman, and child. Barefooted, she approached the fire with Doh-teyah hefted on one hip.

Kosar-eh wondered if his blind child was going to lose
the use of her limbs as well as her eyes, for Ban-ya
seemed determined to keep the baby always in her
arms. His little daughter was going to mature into a fat
woman if she was not only allowed but encouraged to
suckle constantly at those elephantine breasts. Focusing
on them, Kosar-eh recalled the previous night's "battle
of the teats" and was suddenly hard-pressed to con-
strain a smile.

The high priestess's attendants dragged the throne
forward to the place of honor opposite Tsana, who gestured to Kosar-eh. Skewers of chunked hump steak in
hand, Kosar-eh went to assume this prestigious position, but first, as with every man there, he passed before
Spirit Woman, placing an offering of meat on the
planked piece of carved wood at her feet.

"Koshray!" Doh-teyah spoke her father's name
and reached out to him.

He looked up, startled; how had the child recognized him?

"Truly, Sees the Wind, daughter of the Black and
White Warrior, is blessed by the forces of Creation!"
exclaimed Tsana, pointing across the fire. "She sees
through eyes that cannot see . . . with the senses of
one who will be shaman! Truly, Spirit Woman, *this* child
is worthy of your breast!"

Kosar-eh rose and was surprised when Doh-teyah
launched herself from Spirit Woman's arms into his.
The baby said his name again, touched his face, and
smiled. Despite his mixed emotions toward her, he
smiled back and found himself kissing the little one's
questing hand, touched by her unexpected desire to be
close to him again until suddenly Ban-ya reached out
and snatched the girl from his grasp.

"Mine!" shrieked the woman in the way of a pos-
sessive child with a favored plaything. Doh-teyah

pouted and pushed to be free, but Ban-ya drew her
closer, staring at Kosar-eh with eyes as wide and wild as
a heart-struck doe's.

Kosar-eh was startled by what he saw in the
woman's face. Torment? Fear? Love? Those emotions
seemed incompatible with the brazenly manipulative
woman he remembered from the Red World and the
encampments of Shateh, and certainly ill suited the
wolf-robed visage that stood before him now. Yet
Kosar-eh was sure he saw all three emotions in Ban-ya's
eyes—the torment of a woman who had suffered a loss
for which she could not be consoled, the fear of a
woman who knew she could not face the specter of such
a loss again, and the love of a mother for a child who
had become the single focus of her own existence. He
frowned, recalled Tsana informing him that Spirit
Woman had borne two babies in this cave—one for
meat, the other for bait. He cringed; perhaps those acts
of infanticide had not come easily even to such a self-
serving creature as Ban-ya of the Red World. She obviously still grieved over the suffering she had brought to
others, as well as over the death of every child she had
ever birthed.

She must have found at last, in the affection of a
Red World child, some small measure of solace. Could
he, of all men, begrudge her this? After all, when everything was said and done, he—whose love and concern
for the welfare of one woman had led to his abandonment of his band and the deaths of two women, a little
girl, and his eldest son—could do no less than em-
pathize with Ban-ya. Pity moved him, but only briefly. If
he could not justify or forgive his own actions, how
could he abide hers? And why should he allow himself
to be unduly moved by the affection of his blind child?
Until the previous moment, Doh-teyah had been happy

enough to be coddled and nursed by any stranger willing to change her swaddling and hand her a teat.

Spirit Woman was doing the latter. She was calmer now, cooing to the child. Doh-teyah, her little face puckered into a scowl, said, "No!" and spoke her father's name again.

At this, Ban-ya looked at Kosar-eh out of eyes that had lost their momentary expression of vulnerability. They were open and steady but devoid of emotion, as cold and impenetrable as ice-sheathed pools on a sunless day. "Black and White Warrior, it is not fitting for a man of the People of the Watching Star to take a suckling to the male side of the feast fire," she said, her voice flat, as cold as her eyes.

"Unless, of course, as a man of the Red World, he is somehow *not* a man," suggested Indeh. "Who knows? Perhaps he can spurt mother's milk from his nipples just as true men send the milk of life surging into their women through their man bones!"

A roar of laughter went up from the assembly.

Kosar-eh felt his face flame at the outrageousness of the slur. "Five sons has Kosar-eh made on his women. Five! It may be that only three are left to me and one of these is captive among enemies, but no one can say that this man has failed to *be* a man! Where are the sons of Indeh? I have seen no boys step forward to name that man Father. Perhaps that was why he left his own tribe—because he was not man enough to make sons to hunt at his side!"

Indeh's face showed anger and annoyance. His brows expanded, and he made a snort of derision. "Bah! I have made sons. They were not worth keeping! And not even the great Shateh was able to put male life into his women in those last days in the land cursed by Yellow Wolf. The People of the Land of Grass had no power! That is why this warrior took his woman-pleaser and joined with the People of the Watching Star—so that it could rise to the challenge of making life on women better than his own!"

Tsana guffawed.

Kosar-eh, despite his anger toward Indeh, was impressed by the extent of his clever audaciousness as he saw and heard an immediate ripple of pleased murmuring stir the women of the tribe.

A good-looking young woman patted her distended belly and said, "By the rising of the next moon we will see just what results from the milk of that one's man bone, for until she became as you see, he was on this woman as much as he now is on Eyah!"

Another young woman looked at Indeh and giggled through raised fingertips.

Tsana stood and raised a hand. "Enough! There is meat in this cave!" He stated the reminder loudly, and not without irritation. "There is fire in this cave! There is reason to feast in this cave! Let there be no more words of enmity between band brothers. As in time beyond beginning, this people *will* be one. Like *this*!" He made a fist of his right hand and held it high. "In *this* will be our strength, each man like a finger bent to serve the will of the hand, the strength of each combining to create the strength of all! In this will reside our power when together we go forth from this stronghold to take the sacred stone and totem and send our enemies to walk the wind in blood forever!"

Kosar-eh was stunned by the ferocious intensity of the man's words and presence. It was as though an invisible force had swept through the cave, a thing of fire and strength that seared and shook every man, woman, and child until, with fists and voices raised, they affirmed the chieftain's intent with resounding ululations. Soon even the dogs were howling.

"Yes!" Tsana cried and, with both arms high and

his hands held open, smiled a wide, white smile until gradually his people and dogs fell silent. The chieftain's eyes found Kosar-eh again. "Leave Sees the Wind to the milk of Spirit Woman and seek the man side of the circle, Black and White Warrior. Tonight we will honor the life spirits of the bison whose meat and blood and bones will give strength to the tribe. Tonight we will honor the hunters who have brought this meat. Tonight we will honor the man who risked the horns of a charging bison to save the life of another! Now . . . let the feasting begin!"

They ate until they could eat no more, and all the while the women, children, and men who had not been on the hunt listened, transfixed, to the low, relaxed talk of the hunters. They spoke of the long, cold trek across the land to the place where the bison were waiting to die. They told of the hunt and of Kosar-eh's unprecedented bravery. And they spoke of all that they had endured to bring meat and bones and blood and hides to their families.

"Show us!" cried a boy.

Wearing hides and horns, Xanahay and Unai came forward. They circled the fire, weaving in and out of those assembled, prancing and pawing and huffing in the way of bison. The women "aahed" and "oohed," and the children exclaimed with delight at the antics of the dancers, who were singing the traditional song that honored the seasonal coming and going of the great herds across the land.

"Once it was so with mammoth!" Tsana said to Kosar-eh with an accompanying nudge from his elbow as he and all the others clapped the rhythm of the dance. "So many mammoth! Now all have vanished from the land, with only bones and tusks left to make the hunters of the Watching Star remember that those

of other tribes failed to honor the mammoth kind . . .
as we honor them still, though bison have become the
meat and blood and bone of our children, save for
scrapings from the bones of the great white mammoth
totem."

The dancers whirled on, but Kosar-eh was distracted by what Tsana had just said. *Scrapings from the
bones of the totem?* Had he partaken of such forbidden
food since coming here? He would have asked this
question of the chieftain, but two spear-carrying hunters
had joined the dance, and Kosar-eh was surprised to see
that one had assumed his battle colors, black and white,
while the other had donned a bison-bone facsimile of
Tsana's trophy collar.

The crowd grew breathless with awe as the dancers
began an intricate and totally captivating reenactment
of Tsana's bold feint toward the great bison cow, the
animal's valiant charge, and Kosar-eh's own wild and
daring leap into the path of potentially man-skewering
horns.

"Aiee!" the women exclaimed in wonder of such
unprecedented bravery.

"A true brother of the Watching Star!" The men
nodded and shouted the acclamation.

Kosar-eh was not quite sure how to react until he
saw the radiantly proud faces of his sons beaming at
him from where they stood among the other boys. His
heart quickened with joy for the moment.

The dancers were moving to a new rhythm now,
and another twosome of hunters was weaving among
the crowd, passing out small lap drums to the women
and rattles to the men. Kosar-eh looked at the long-
stemmed, bulbous-tipped music maker that had been
placed in his hand.

Tsana, already shaking a new rhythm with the rattle
he had been given, explained to Kosar-eh, "The woman

drums are made from the life-generating female parts of cow bison taken on past hunts. The man shakers are the life sacks taken from between the thighs of the great bulls, then filled with seeds before being sewn and hardened to shape in the sun. With these things we make the music of life. As the great herds pound that rhythm on the summer plains, so we beat it now, in hope of new life in them . . . and in us."

The women rose for the first time to join the dance. Striking their little drums and mimicking the bison, they cavorted lightly, bending as though to browse, pretending to lick their sisters in the way of mothers grooming calves, all the while followed by the two male bison dancers who, scenting like bulls in rut, nudged them from behind.

Kosar-eh was not the only man to laugh aloud as the nudging became more vigorous and some of the "cows" began to lift their skirts to allow the "bulls" a sniff. At this the boys hooted, and the younger children and girls giggled and covered their faces before they were escorted from the circle by the pregnant cows, snorting in feigned irritation.

Kosar-eh was suddenly aware that Spirit Woman was staring fixedly at him through the broken circle of the dancers from her place across the fire. She still held Doh-teyah on her lap, and Joh-nee was in her usual place at her feet. His brow furrowed. He did not like the way Ban-ya was looking at him; there was something expectant and avaricious about her expression that set him on edge until the dancers closed ranks again and he could no longer see her.

Kosar-eh was grateful. The dancers were moving to a new rhythm. He was not sure if they were setting it or responding to it. It was slow, sensual, and somehow imperative. As he found himself joining the other men in sustaining the emphasis of every beat with a low, bison-like exhalation, he stared, rapt, at the circling dancers.

The cows were slipping from the sheathing of their human clothes, casting away the garments, and with slow, provocative hand movements greasing their bare bodies with bits of fat they had evidently carried to the dance for this purpose. Naked and glistening in the fire-light, they joined hands and stood back as two of the youngest among them began to circle the two bulls. When, with knees bent and limbs spread wide, these two leaned forward, swung their breasts, and shook their backsides in invitation to be mated, Kosar-eh caught his breath and experienced a purely reactionary flow of heat to his loins.

To the cheers of all, the rhythm of the dance became strident, faster, more imperative than before as Unai and Xanahay displayed their impressive state of readiness to answer the invitation of the two women. They made a dance of their intent. Circling the cows with bold symbolic thrustings of their hips, they came close, then danced away, only to return. They nudged. They scented deeply between parted thighs. They "gored" with engorged "horns." And then, to the goads of all and a rhythm that could not be denied, each bull came up hard behind a cow, curled his body forward over hers, reached around to grip her breasts and pull her back, and with a single violent thrust penetrated her from behind. A communal sigh rose from the crowd as each bull now brought his dance to ferocious completion with loud and furious ejaculations into his cow.

"Choose a woman . . . any woman," Tsana encouraged Kosar-eh. "All are assembled here except those who are already filled with new life, or those who pass their time of blood in the woman's place at the far side of the cave. Now that the bison bulls have honored their kind in the ancient way of our ancestors, custom allows this man first choice from among the rest of the women. Tsana gives this honor to the Black and White Warrior as reward for risking his life to save the life of this man."

Kosar-eh was no less startled by Tsana's invitation than by the realization that the women of the tribe were indeed coming toward him—all naked, all moving in ways that made him know that they were eager and ready for him. Already aroused, he reminded himself and the chieftain that "This man has told Tsana that he mourns the woman of his heart and will have no other."

"And Tsana has told the Black and White Warrior that he is not concerned about his heart!" The chieftain was openly irked. "One man and one woman always together, this is not a good thing! Too much does this bring heart pain. I know! This pain I too have suffered! And so now, among Tsana's People of the Watching Star, war and death and the diminishment of the tribe have taught the necessity of a new way. These women, these men . . . they and the People are one! The need of a man to join with a woman to make life must never be restrained. All are free to mate with all. What does it matter if one time that man comes into that woman, and another time that woman opens herself to another man? What *does* matter is that our women swell with new life so that there will always be warriors to replace those slain in battle, and new life bearers to replace those too weak to survive the ordeal of bearing of life. In this way the harsh words that were exchanged between you and Indeh need never be exchanged again. For soon, among this people, no man will know which sons or daughters have been spawned from the milk of his passion. He will have pleasured himself many times on many women. In this new way each man will have many sons, many daughters, all belonging to the tribe, and not one bringing more heart pain than another when Spirit Sucker summons his or her spirit to walk the wind forever."

Tsana paused.

Except for the sound of the fire, the cave was deathly silent. The chieftain looked straight at Kosar-eh as he continued, "Your woman is dead, Black and White Warrior! Grieve for her as you will, but even as you rightfully yearn for the day on which you and your new brothers among the People of the Watching Star *will* avenge her death in the blood of those who have dishonored her, you must take another woman. And another. You must make new sons on the life bearers of the People of the Watching Star . . . strong, brave sons such as those you have brought with you to this stronghold . . . sons to replace those slain or taken by our enemies. The spirit of your slain woman would expect this of you, for all females know that the force of Creation that impels a male to rut is not given for pleasure, or as a way to express heart love. It is for the making of new life that the great bulls seek their cows as stallions seek their mares and men dance the dance of life on their women. It is to be done for the continuation of the herd and the tribe . . . for the good not of the one but of the many!"

Tsana's logic struck Kosar-eh like a cold wind beating ahead of a storm; somehow he sensed entrapment in it and could not understand why. Mating for its own sake, no emotional commitment to the recipient of need? A man moving as a bull or stallion amidst his herd, rutting for the pure sake of rutting? The premise hardened his man bone; it defined a long unsated need. Never had he missed the loving embrace of Ta-maya more than in this moment, but his thoughts were far from love as Tsana gestured a small, tight-bellied, full-breasted young woman forward. She knelt before him, eyes down, limbs wide, hands cupping and offering her breasts, her body so close that he could smell the warmth of her breath and skin and the moist, musky readiness between her thighs.

"This woman, Eyah, has been Indeh's favorite of late," explained Tsana. "And this man can say that she knows how to dance on a man. Take her as your first choice . . . use her, and as you fill her with the heat of life show the warrior from the Land of Grass that he is as unwise to form an attachment to one female as he is to insult the Black and White Warrior before the chieftain who has named him Brother!"

Several men laughed, and a pair of women cat-called.

Hrak shouted good-naturedly, "Make your choice, Spits in the Face of Enemies, so we may get on with ours!"

Perhaps, had Kosar-eh not scanned past Eyah's shoulder to see Indeh glowering at him, he might have refused the woman. As it was, seeing the Land of Grass man standing livid with indignation and frustration while others mocked him, Kosar-eh was swept by a wave of satisfaction that made him smile. His hand strayed to his mouth to encounter the lingering pain of the injury that Indeh had given him with the butt end of his spear when he had returned to his gutted encampment. Then suddenly he was aware of Eyah drawing his other hand forward, guiding it between her thighs as she positioned herself over the rattle. Looking at him boldly, she began to work her hips, making low, moaning sounds of pleasure as she moved on the rattle as though it were the hard, upright, seeking bone of a man, and all the while the tip of her tongue moved in and out between her pursed lips in a telling parody of that which she would have from him.

"Ay yah!" one of the hunters cried.

"Join the dance, Black and White Warrior, or let someone else fill that woman as you choose another!"

Kosar-eh did not hear. He was looking straight at Indeh as, still smiling, he stood and exposed to the sight of all that part of his body that would serve the "dancing" woman much more effectively than the rattle upon which she was pleasuring herself.

Men and women acknowledged the impressiveness of his state of readiness.

Still smiling, Kosar-eh pulled Eyah to her feet, snatched the rattle from her hand, and tossed it to a startled Indeh, who with a snarl cast it aside. Kosar-eh laughed, curled his big hands around the woman's narrow waist, then lifted her high. Lowering her slowly, he felt her legs part to enfold his hips. He penetrated her with a single thrust and, still looking straight at Indeh, joined her in the dance of life.

All night it went on.

Joh-nee did not think it would ever stop. She crouched on her mattress of soft furs at the foot of Spirit Woman's dais, close to Doh-teyah, who had long since fallen fast asleep in the priestess's embrace. The Spirit Woman sat and stared ahead, a creature of stone, like a lizard on a rock, sleeping with its eyes open.

Joh-nee pulled her bed furs over her head and tried not to hear the high, happy laughter of men and women at sexual sport with one another, and the deeper sounds—the harsher, harder huffs, groans, and occasional shrieks of more violent matings. Now and then she dozed. Dreams woke her. She peered from beneath her fears and wondered what was worse—her nightmares or reality.

Kiu-neh came close. He had an odd look in his eyes. Dropping to his knees, he displayed himself and whispered low, "Come away from this place where 'she' sees everything. Let me do to you as the others do . . . look, see how big I am!"

Appalled, Joh-nee stared at his sweated, ready young boy's body and whispered back, "Put your worm away or I will bite it off!"

He scowled at her unexpected insult. "I am Third Son of Black and White Warrior!" he hissed. "My father has saved the life of the chieftain and will lead us to the totem and the sacred stone. Three girls with breasts have let me prick them this night! You will—"

"Shaman's Sister will remain unbloodied by the bone of any boy or man until she is given to the one who has been chosen for her!" Spirit Woman's interruption rasped from her throat and was followed by a chuckle. "If the other girls refuse you, Boastful Boy, come, dip your hard little bone in this woman, or are you as afraid of me as of the girls you claim to have bloodied?"

Kiu-neh answered her question in the most forthright manner possible; he turned and ran.

Joh-nee heard the low, twisted laugh of the woman on the dais and looked up at her. Rarely did she speak to the woman, but she spoke now, with audible trepidation. "*Who* has been chosen for me?"

"Ah . . . in time you will know, Shaman's Sister, in time. In blood it will be done."

"Blood!"

"Is it not always the way of a woman? Blood . . . pain . . . death . . . and rebirth . . . as with this child, this dear and lovely child?"

"Doh-teyah?"

"A Red World name! It cannot be, not here. Not in this place. No! This child is Sees the Wind! A worthy child for Spirit Woman! Mine . . . at last a child Tsana will let me keep . . . *mine*!" She looked down at Joh-nee, her expression one of pure ferocity. And then suddenly it changed, softened as she whispered, "In your band there was an old woman and a small boy . . . grandmother and son of the woman Ban-ya. Are they safe beyond the edge of the world with Cha-kwena and—"

Joh-nee was startled; the woman *was* Ban-ya. "Your old grandmother Kahm-ree was killed by Shateh's raiders, and your firstborn boy, Piku-neh, was sent to walk the wind forever by fever spirits that dwell in the great forest beyond the edge of the world."

A moan went out of Spirit Woman. Indeed, as she closed her eyes and sagged against her backrest, it seemed as though her very soul had been pierced and made to bleed by the news she had just heard. Then, with a sigh, she opened her eyes, stared into the firelit cave, and said without emotion, "As you see, Tsana eases his need on others now. He has made no life on me . . . none of them have made life on me . . . I have shown them that I *am* life!"

Joh-nee knew that her eyes had gone round with dread. The strange, fixed ferocity that she saw so often in the eyes of Spirit Woman was back, and somehow the girl knew that it was the stare of madness—and that it was dangerous to her and to all whom she loved. She clutched her doll. "This g-girl will hold Doh-teyah if Spirit Woman wishes to sleep. She is not too heavy for me and—"

"Spirit Woman does not sleep! If Spirit Woman sleeps, they will take her babies! They will eat her babies as they will someday eat the totem!"

"Tsana does not eat babies."

Spirit Woman laughed. It was a low, malevolent chortle, the sort of sound one might hear coming from the bloodied beak of a condor or teratorn as it perched on the bones of its prey. "Run away, foolish child . . . before that carnivore eats *you*!"

\*     \*     \*

"We must go!"

The girl's words only partially roused Kosar-eh from heavy sleep. How long had it been since he had come to the outer cornice of the cave and, bundled against the cold night air in his sleeping furs, sent the last of the women with whom he had coupled to find her pleasure elsewhere? He had no idea. After the hunt and the long trek across the frozen land, how much could they expect of any man? Too much.

He smiled, drifted back to sleep, allowed his tired body to relax and rest again as he yielded to dreams of how it had been—first Eyah yielding to his rough, all-too-quick release, then others coming forth, kneeling before him, asking with subdued reverence to be mated by the one who dared place himself before the horns of death to save the life of another, so that any sons made on them this night would be as bold and strong and incomparably brave as the Black and White Warrior. Tsana had laughed and encouraged him to take any who could sustain the drive of his need.

As the chieftain and men of the tribe had turned away to pursue their own pleasure, Kosar-eh experienced sensations like nothing he had ever known or imagined—women touching him, fondling and handling him, mouthing him in ways that he would never have allowed his beautiful beloved. It was different with the women of the People of the Watching Star. They were strangers. They did not matter to him. He allowed and encouraged their advances and excesses as they invited his—languorous, invasive tonguing and fingering, soft suckings that made him moan with pleasure until, half mad with ecstasy, he would position the most eager of them and demand that she dance, joined to him, moving on him, taking him deep until he was overcome by the driving heat of an elemental passion that was purely male, purely sensory, without affection or concern for anything save to intensify and prolong the almost unbearable pleasure of the moment. At last, drained and shaken by the overwhelming sexual satisfaction that he had found with females not remotely like the one woman he had sworn to love forever, he sent them all away and sought sleep at the edge of the cave.

But now, it seemed, he was no longer alone. Another female had come to join him. She stood looking down at him, a very small, worried-looking little girl clutching a battered buckskin doll. "Joh-nee." He spoke her name. "Go away, child. It is late. This man needs his rest."

She stood very still; it was a moment before she spoke. "Kiu-neh and Kho-neh are proud of you again. They will follow you now. Wake them. Look . . . everyone is asleep. Even Spirit Woman is dozing at last. Go to her. Break her neck as you broke Cheelapat's! Then, while everyone is lost to dreams, we can run away at last! By sunrise we will have made a great distance. When the others wake, there will be great upset, but—"

"These people have taken us into their tribe, Johnee. Our future lies with them now. Has not Tsana named me Brother, and you Sister?"

Beyond the cave, springtime stars swirled across the black robe of the night, and wolves were singing in the Valley of the Dead. Stars shone in Joh-nee's eyes and in the tears that streaked her cheeks as she looked at the sky and across the valley. Listening to the wolves, she shivered. "Soon the Warm Moon will rise. White Giant Winter will go away with the Cold Sisters. Then it will be the time of Green Grass Showing and Ducks Coming Home, and they will make you lead them back across the badlands and through the great forest that lies beyond the edge of the world. They will hunt my brother and the sacred stone and the totem. And when they find these things, they will do to us what they have done to Shateh and you have done to Shateh's woman."

"No." Kosar-eh shook his head.

"Spirit Woman has said that they will take Doh-teyah away to eat her!"

Again he shook his head. "It is no secret that, to survive alone in the Valley of the Dead, that woman fed upon her own infants. Guilt and regret make her believe that others did this. Spirit Woman is all that is left of Ban-ya of the Red World, girl, and Tsana has taken pity on her because his tribesmen believe that the power of long-dead shamans lives on in her body. But this man's eyes have seen that it is Tsana who holds the power in this place. And the milk of Spirit Woman gives life to my blind child. You must learn to trust again, little one. It is your brother, Cha-kwena, who has betrayed us. And now, at last, Tsana has made me see that I must do as he would have me do, for the sake of my children and—"

"*I* am not your child! I am Joh-nee, sister of Cha-kwena, daughter of the Red World, of U-wa and Tlanaquah, chieftain of the People of the Lake of Many Singing Birds!" With quivering chin, she choked back a sob. "It would have been better for all of us to have died than for even one of us to lead those who would slaughter the totem onto the path Cha-kwena has taken with the mammoth and sacred stone. For when the white mammoth dies, so too will the People die forever, all of the bands—Red World people, Land of Grass, *all*! But you no longer believe this. You have become one of *them*."

"Joh-nee, I—"

"It is a good thing that Ta-maya walks the wind forever, for she would weep to see how quickly you have forgotten her! I am glad that my brother has followed the mammoth into the face of the rising sun where you and the other warriors of the People of the Watching Star will never find them!"

Cha-kwena strode across the lengthening day with an implacability of will that was almost, but not quite, unshakable. The vast, frozen lake lay all around and beneath him. The western forest into which the star had fallen still lay ahead, a long wall of dark trees rising beyond a shoreline that had only just become visible. For two days and a night the shaman had been on the ice. And now, when he turned and scanned back across the miles, he saw that he was no longer alone. Two of the mammoth were following. He frowned. With the sun well risen behind them, the shadows of the great cow and little white calf fell long upon the world and upon the man in the owl-skin headdress who walked before them.

Cha-kwena paused. The wind was out of the east, cold and dry, a low, hollow rasp that seemed to scrape from the throat of some invisible giant. And that giant was mocking him. The strangest sensation of emptiness came over the shaman. His hand went to his throat; he knew that the sacred stone was not there, but for the first time since the talisman had come into his possession, he felt absolutely devoid of even the smallest vestige of its power. Since setting himself upon his homeward trek, he had experienced no dreams, no visions, only a deep, all-pervasive hope and longing to be reunited with his people . . . with his band . . . with his little girl-of-a-woman.

"Mah-ree." Cha-kwena spoke her name aloud, the name of his first woman, the name of his only love, and knew at last that his life had no meaning without her. A smile touched his lips as his eyes held on the slowly approaching mammoths. Perhaps Mah-ree might yet realize her dream of riding high upon the twin-domed head of their totem.

Yet as he watched the mammoths plodding toward him across the ice, a terrible sinking feeling of impending doom churned in the shaman's belly. How long would the ice support their weight? And if the totem were to break through and drown, what then would be the fate of his people, and of his beloved?

"Go back!" Cha-kwena demanded of the mammoths.

The great tuskers kept coming on.

And in that moment the young shaman heard what he most feared—a crack like that of a lightning bolt, a single long, sharp, jolt of a sound. It did not come from the sky. It came from beneath his feet, and as Cha-kwena continued to look across the ice toward the mammoths, he saw a fissure opening between him and them. The ice shook, shifted, rose on one side of the break and fell on the other. He saw the mammoths stagger even as he fought to maintain his own balance. Understanding dawned like an explosion as, in an instant, he saw the cow go down and into the breach that her awesome weight had opened beneath her. Gray water frothed around her shoulders as her great limbs worked desperately for purchase that was not there. With her tusks upraised, she screamed like a frightened woman while the calf—still on solid ice—screamed back in terror.

Cha-kwena ran, impelled by instinct. He knew no fear for himself. Hurling his body into a slide that brought him quickly to the very edge of the breach, he used his spear as a brake, then caught hold of the tail of the calf and, scrambling to his feet, yanked back hard.

"Come away! Away!" he gasped.

It was no use; the little white mammoth pulled free of him and trunked outward for its mother.

The ice was shifting, breaking into broad segments that rode roughly upon the frigid deeps. Later Cha-kwena would wonder how the great cow managed to keep her head above water as long as she did. In that last moment before the ice slid over her, the drowning mammoth gave one great upward heave with her limbs and, lifting her head and shoulders out of the water for the last time, rammed forward with her tusks to shove the calf hard away from the edge of the ice. It slid, slipped, fell splay-legged, and was bawling in hurt dismay when Cha-kwena came to its side.

The great cow was gone. The little white calf took the shaman's hand into its mouth and sucked hard as it swayed and squeaked to itself in confusion. The ice lurched and groaned beneath them.

"Come!" commanded Cha-kwena, and this time, having no mother except the man, the totem followed.

# PART IV

# SOUTH WIND

"There is no changing . . . All is glaring light
. . . I beg of you, create something to warm
me and soften the blazing light."

—Creation of the Universe
*Lakota Myth* by James R. Walker

White Giant Winter went from the land as it had come
—cloaked in rain and mist, and howling like a gut-
wounded dire wolf.

From inside the lodge Warakan listened. He knelt
by the weather baffle, holding it slightly parted as he
stared out and waited for Bear Brother to return.

"Come back to the fire, Boy!" Mah-ree commanded with the easy authority of a matron twice her
years. "You are allowing Wind and Rain to enter!
Would you chill our Wise One? Would you turn my
newly made entry mat into a bog beneath your knees as
my woven moss drinks up Rain?"

Warakan turned to glare at her and would have
spoken had she given him the chance.

"Do not stare, Boy!" she ordered sharply. "Come
in out of the damp, I say! Our Bear Brother will return
to his lodge when he has finished snouting and clawing
through mud and melting snow for mice and voles and
squirrels, and then you will clean up the mess he makes,
for it is growing more and more difficult for me not to
take my broom to him! A bear cannot be expected to
dwell within a lodge forever, Warakan."

Warakan deliberately remained as he was. Mah-ree

sounded more like a meddling mother every day. *Come here! Go there! Do this! Tend that!* And yet, despite himself, his heart lurched as he beheld the young woman. She was such a small, pretty thing, sitting cross-legged beside the fire pit opposite Jhadel. Nevertheless, he scowled as he watched her pluck feathers from the songbirds he had netted before that morning's rain. Had she thanked him for his offering? He could not remember. And since when had she taken to calling him Boy again, as though the word were his name?

Irked, Warakan snapped at her, "What makes you imagine that I am looking into the rain waiting for Bear Brother's return? Perhaps I am in need of air, of a chance to breathe free of all your fussing! My cub will return when the clouds settle down and bring new snow. He always seeks the lodge in snow, to sleep."

"Bear Brother is no longer a cub," she said. "You must learn to accept that. Soon he will go into the forest and will not come back. It is the way of his kind—to live most of his days alone, far from the lodges of Man."

"He is my brother, my child. We will always be together."

Mah-ree's head swung from side to side. "Now that the time of snow is over, he could be seeking one of his own kind, a woman bear, to walk briefly at his side through the forest. The Mud Moon has risen at last. Soon the land will grow green and warm, and all creatures will seek to make new life and—"

"It is a good thing," interrupted Jhadel enthusiastically. The old shaman shivered within his furs, closed his tattooed eyelids, and whispered in the tone of one remembering, "This man had begun to fear that the ancient time beyond beginning had come again. It was in that endless winter that mountains of ice walked upon the world and rivers ran no more. It was a time without trees or green growing things, a time when wind spirits took life within storms and prowled the land as beasts. Long was the sleep of Great Paws in those days when First Man and First Woman joined together to make the future generations of the People. Long did White Giant and the Cold Sisters feed upon the land and upon the bones of old men until—"

"Rain has driven that family away on the back of North Wind for now," assured Mah-ree, looking at Jhadel with kindness and concern. "Now is the season of South Wind. I have scented her breath in the mists and rain. In the Red World of my forefathers it is said that South Wind brings the time of Green Dawn, of Earth Waking Up, of Birds Flying Home in clear, dry skies that take the aches from the bones of old men and make their spirits young once more."

"Ah . . . may it be so, may it be so," sighed the old man.

Warakan was on his feet, glowering. Mah-ree's opinion that Bear Brother might one day fail to return from his wanderings had shaken him, and he was jealous at the way Jhadel was managing to smile with blissful approval of the young woman's every word, even while wincing against the hurtful pull of the new scar that parted his scalp like the zigzagging track of a purple lightning bolt. Jhadel never smiled at him as he smiled at Mah-ree. Indeed, all too often of late, there was a closeness between the old man and young woman that made Warakan feel an outsider in his own lodge— not alone or unwelcome, just unnecessary and, worse than that, irrelevant. His emotions burst into turmoil as he declared, "I will go into the rain! I will seek my cub and brother and friend. We, at least, understand each other. Red World woman stories! Old man's tales! Warriors do not care about these things."

Mah-ree replied coolly, "I see no warrior in this

lodge. I see only a rude boy who has yet to learn from his elders—or to respect them!"

"It is so!" affirmed Jhadel. "To live in the world as one People we must learn, through the old tales, to understand the way of the long trail upon which the People have journeyed through time to become separate tribes that are strangers and enemies to one another."

Warakan was appalled. "I have no desire to understand the ways of lizard eaters or of those who killed my father and grandfather, skinned my sister as though she were a beast taken in a hunt, and sent me fleeing for my life beyond the edge of the world! I want to *end* their ways, forever!"

Jhadel huffed annoyance with the boy. "Warakan, you wear the feather of Eagle, who is brother to Moon and Sun and alone among all birds is welcome in the upper reaches of the sky. It was Eagle who, conspiring with the Four Winds, carried the slain spirits of Shateh and Masau to live in you and brought you into the care of this shaman so that you might be taught to see and know all things, even as Eagle sees and knows all things. How is it, then, after all this time with me in this forest beyond the edge of the world, that you remain as blind as Bat within the black cave of hatred that holds your spirit captive?"

Warakan's upper lip rose and quivered. The old man's words had bitten deeply into his pride. Humiliated before Mah-ree and hurt to the quick by Jhadel's insult, he turned, snatched up his robe and staves, and stormed from the lodge.

Bear Brother was easy to follow. On the cub's frequent comings and goings from the lodge, it had settled into a pattern of repeatedly stepping into its own footprints and had thus made permanent depressions in the rapidly vanishing snowpack and broad, muddy swatches of recently exposed earth. Warakan followed, doing his best to keep between or to one side of the footprints lest he find himself sloshing calf-deep in the little lakes of rainwater that filled each paw print. After some time, soaking wet and still mumbling against Mah-ree and Jhadel, he came to a fork in Bear Brother's trail.

Warakan was deep in the forest now. It was no longer raining. The wind had been down for some time, and with the sun shining through the dripping canopy of trees, a thick ground fog was streaming across the forest floor. He frowned as he watched the tracks of the bear disappear under the mists. "Now which way will I go?"

A squirrel called; another squirrel answered.

Warakan looked up and around, then uttered a call of his own. "Bear Brother! Where are you? Warakan would walk with you awhile!"

His cry went into the trees, into the shining wetness of hardwoods and conifers upon which sunlight was now striking uncountable water droplets, dazzling him. Somewhere ahead, something big bolted from a thicket. Warakan caught his breath, heard a great crashing, then glimpsed a high brown shoulder, the dull sheen of velvet on newly sprouted antler, the downward curve of a pendulous muzzle, a quivering dewlap, and the backward look of a round, startled eye.

"Moose!" Warakan exclaimed as the creature vanished into the depths of the forest. He cocked his head, wondering if the huge, hook-nosed deer would be trotting down a trail recently taken by a bear.

The squirrels answered his unspoken question. They were scolding madly from the treetops well ahead. Cocking his head again, he wondered if something was threatening their movement to and fro among the treetops, for as he listened to their raucous chatterings, he heard in the sharp, repetitive sounds a mix of anger, frustration, and fear. In his mind's eye, he saw them

poised high on branches, tails twitching and whiskers up
as their front paws beat a furious rhythm while they
scolded down at . . .

"Bear Brother!"

A languid sigh of sun-warmed air brought the unmistakable scent of pine resin to Warakan's nostrils; the
aroma was confirmation of his exclamation. He hurried
forward, wading through mist, sloshing in and out of
unseen pools of rainwater trapped in the footprints of
his child. Clambering over roots and newly extended
vines, pushing his way through shrubbery, he soon
paused amidst a tangle of just-budding currant bushes.
And there was Bear Brother, halfway up a young fir.
The body of the tree was bent almost completely in half
as the bear—wrapped around the upper trunk like some
huge furry bole—blissfully peeled bark with its incisors
and loudly slurped sap from the resultant wounds in the
flesh of the tree.

Warakan did not hear the sounds that the conifer
was making under its extraordinary burden. The position of the tree and the bear's alignment with it should
have alerted him to the inevitable. He was, however, so
happy to have found his child that he stood smiling
dumbly until the tree split in two with an explosive snap.

The boy screamed.

The bear bawled.

Warakan hurled himself out of the way as over two
hundred pounds of cub came hurtling toward him out
of the treetops.

Seconds later both landed, boy and bear together,
side by side between the currant bushes on the muddy
earth. Stunned and shaken, each rubbed his buttocks,
the boy with his left hand, the bear with his right forepaw. The boy moaned. The bear groaned.

Remembering boyhood dreams of flight and the
last time he had launched himself into thin air to avoid

catastrophe in this forest, Warakan found humor in the moment. "We do not fly very well, you and I," he said to the bear, not certain which was preferable as a landing site—boy-eating snowdrifts or buttocks-bruising solid ground.

"Mraaw," complained the bear in a self-pitying exhalation as it sagged across Warakan's lap, rooting unashamedly for a reassuring pat. It nearly buried the boy in muscle and fur.

Warakan readjusted his position so that he could breathe. Wriggling his fingers deep into the thick pelage, he massaged the warm skin behind the cub's closest ear and was comforted by the bear's sighs of contentment. "We *are* brothers, you and I!" he said to the animal. "Someday we will be warriors together. Someday, when we are both grown, our enemies will tremble before us when we come to them bringing Death—you standing upright like a man as you threaten with your great claws and teeth, and me striding boldly beside you with my spears and spear hurler, strong in the power of the sacred stone and as dangerous as any bear!"

The boy sighed. He could see it all in his imagination; the future shone like delectable fruit ripening toward perfection in a part of the forest that he was certain to discover in time. He snuggled closer to the bear. "In the meantime, Bear Brother, we need no one, especially women—bear women or human women—to walk the woods with us, or tell us what to do."

"Warakan!"

The boy stiffened. Jhadel was calling his name. The frail voice sounded worried and very far away. Warakan smiled. *So he does care!* he thought, pleased and gratified until . . .

"Boy!"

Warakan's smile vanished. Mah-ree's voice was as

strong and angry with impatience as Jhadel's was frail and strained with concern.

"Where are you, Boy?" she called again.

He scowled. *Boy.* Warakan, son of Masau and grandson of Shateh, would not answer to that name even if she continued to call until her voice grew as faint as the old man's. And this she did. Warakan listened, nursed his injured pride, and steadfastly refused to respond.

"Let them both stew in the juices of regret over the way they have banded together to insult this boy and count Bear Brother's life as a thing of no value!" he declared and, after thanking the woodland mists for concealing their trail, followed the cub deeper into the forest.

Day turned to dusk, and dusk mellowed into evening.

Beneath the canopy of the forest, Warakan stubbornly kept company with his brother as the cub rambled on, following its nose, tirelessly snouting up moist duff in search of larvae, moldering nuts, and shriveled fruit. Now and then in the gathering darkness Bear Brother paused to paw up stumps and turn over rocks, bending low to sniff out and slurp up whatever dwelled beneath. It was at best meager fare for the bear and would have been unpalatable, barely digestible food for the boy if the animal had not greedily consumed it all immediately upon discovery.

"We will never become warriors on such food as this," said Warakan, shivering a little in his damp clothes as he spoke, choosing to ignore his brother's heretofore unnoticed selfishness. "When we stop to rest, I will set snares before taking up my staves to hunt for myself and my brother. Together we will soon share *real* meat!"

Bear Brother, however, showed no interest in stopping to rest so that the one who had raised him could hunt and provide for him now. The animal's instinctive ability to eke out a meal for itself was as undeniable as it was impressive. With wide nostrils snuffing and snorting and defining scents that eluded Warakan's human nose, the cub ambled from snack to snack, from thicket to thicket, from grove to grove, across small clearings, then back into the trees again. At last, belching contentedly after plundering a maze of rodent runs exposed to predation by melted snow, the bear sat back on its haunches, cut wind, and settled in to lick its bloodied paws.

Warakan, hungry and tired to the marrow of his bones, stared at the animal as though betrayed. "You do not offer to hunt for your brother as he has offered to hunt for you!" he accused, then looked down as a tiny, disoriented, long-tailed survivor of Bear Brother's raid darted toward him from beneath the sprawl of the cub's extended limbs. As the skittering blur of soft gray streaked between the boy's moccasins on its mad dash for the forest, Warakan looked at the bear again. "One mouse! Is this all that you would share with a brother?" He hunkered down on his heels, leaning on his staves, glowering. "No matter! Mouse is not fit food for Warakan, son of Masau and grandson of Shateh! I will rest now. It is better for a warrior to eat nothing than to eat such food as that which satisfies Bear. I will hunt for myself tomorrow. Maybe, if Mouse Eater provokes my wrath, Warakan will hunt *him*!"

The cub stiffened, stared, eyes fixed as though appraising a threatening stranger.

Warakan was stunned, as much by his own words as by the bear's reaction to them. Where had he seen that expression on the animal's face before? In the woods not far from the lodge when he had pursued his child

after it had half scalped Jhadel. The hackles rose along
the boy's neck. Had Bear Brother's eyes always been set
so far apart, or was it only that the cub's head had
grown as wide as a tree trunk? He gulped. If his child
was so large now, at the beginning of its second summer, how big would it be when White Giant Winter
returned with the Cold Sisters to send it, strong-boned
and summer-fat, from the autumn forest in search of
winter sleep? The prospect was sobering. Warakan swallowed; his mouth had gone dry. He licked his lips and
immediately cursed himself as a fool.

The bear responded instantly. It rose, laid back its
ears, clacked its jaws, and extended a long wet tongue
along the periphery of its mouth.

Warakan saw the animal's canines flash long and
white in the gloom of impending night. He nearly
retched. Bear Brother's cutting teeth were the length of
a grown man's thumbs! Slowly the boy unfolded his
limbs and shakily got to his feet. He remembered old
Lahontay, eldest of Shateh's hunters, saying that when
Bear laid back its ears, clacked its jaws, and licked its
lips, a man must be ready for attack. Lahontay should
have listened to his own advice; the mother of this bear
had killed him. A small voice at the back of Warakan's
head mocked him: *And you are not a man, you are Boy!
Is it not time to leave this bear to walk the forest with its
own kind?*

The bear's head was moving. Its nose worked the
air, pulling in the scent of the boy until, finding fear in
it, it huffed, indignant, and shook its head back and
forth in a fury.

Warakan was shaking, too. He wanted to run. He
wanted to turn and flee into the forest. He wanted to
race, screaming, for the lodge, but somehow he made
himself stand his ground. This bear was not *any* bear.
This bear was *his* bear, his cub since the first time it had

sucked the milk of its dead mother from his fingers and elected to follow him across the land, accepting food and love from him as though their flesh were of one and the same source—not bear and boy, but brothers sharing life and love between them, always. Warakan cast his staves aside.

"B-brother? Do you n-not know m-me?" The boy fought for every stammering word. What was it Mahree had said? Something about being able to see fear reflected in the eyes of another? And distrust . . . yes! *The cruelest hurt of all . . . distrust in the eyes of one to whom you have given your heart forever.*

"Forgive me, brother." Warakan spoke forthrightly now, repentant. "The day has been long. We have come far. If we have different tastes in food, so also it is with many brothers. I did not mean to snarl. And if there were no food to be had in this world, or the world beyond, Warakan would still not hunt his brother."

The ears of the bear fanned forward. It huffed again, then dropped to all fours, still staring at the boy, still measuring until, grumbling a little, it yawned prodigiously, then turned and ambled into a stand of mixed evergreens and hardwoods, where it pawed pine needles and leaf mast into a sizable mound between the trees. When all was to its satisfaction, it waded into the wood and settled on the mound, facing the boy, staring at him.

Warakan stared back.

It was dark now, a dank, heavy dark that made him shiver to his bones. Long moments passed. The darkness thickened. Soon, although he could hear the bear breathing in the deep, slow, rhythmic pulls and exhalations of deep sleep, he could no longer see the animal as he advanced toward it into the black.

And there, within the trees, Warakan lay down beside his child. Cautiously, he snuggled close. After a moment he was drawn into an ursine hug that warmed his body and reassured him that Bear Brother had forgiven him and was content and happy to have him near.

He lay awake for a long time, staring up through furry forelimbs into the treetops and the thick, humid darkness above. Somehow it robbed the stars of light; if they were there above the forest, the boy could not see them. He closed his eyes. The wind was very low, from the south, a heavy, turgid thing. Now and then it turned, gusted briefly from the north to bring cool air into the forest, and in these moments Warakan heard voices in the wind. He listened. Far away, their calls disembodied by distance, Jhadel and Mah-ree were still searching for him.

*Truly they do care,* he thought as his eyes batted open and he heard the old man call his name. Then the woman named him Boy. His jaw tightened; he would not answer.

*Let them search! Let them worry! Let them fear that Warakan is meat in the belly of a beast this night!*

He closed his eyes again. Gradually, the voices fell away. Drifting into sleep, he heard a pair of owls conversing with each other in the treetops while distant wolves sang to the accompaniment of a barking fox. Sometime later, a feline screech permeated the shallows of his dreams and caused him to remember that Fang-Toothed Cat still stalked the forest. The boy sighed, willed himself back to sleep, and, safe in the arms of his brother, was not afraid to dream on.

He awoke with the dawn. Somewhere far away a jay was scolding. Warakan propped himself on his elbows. Even before the sound abated, he knew that no bird would be calling "Boy! Boy!" through the trees.

"When you call out to me using my true name, Mah-ree of the Red World, perhaps then I will return to the lodge. In the meantime, search for me as you will, but you had best start looking to the power of the sacred stone if you want to find me, because from the sound of your voice, you are going the wrong way!"

The declaration brought a smile to Warakan's face as he looked around, rejoicing in the certainty of rebellion accomplished, in the warmth of the new day, and in the absence of rain. Clear skies showed above the canopy of the trees, and South Wind was rising with the morning.

Warakan rose with it. In lengthening shafts of morning sunlight he clambered from the mattress that Bear Brother had made. His moccasins and furs were still damp, but the fur of the bear had absorbed most of the moisture, and he felt no chill as he relieved himself and shouted happily at the cub to get up and greet the sun. The bear obliged. It rose and stretched and languorously rubbed itself against the nearest tree. The previous night's enmity forgotten, it approached Warakan for a hug and a pat and, after an affectionate wrestling match, was off with a *whoof* into the trees, following its nose again.

Warakan laughed with pleasure as he took up his staves and clomped off after his brother, wading through ground mists, sloshing across streams, and slipping now and then in mud and snow. What a fine, free morning it was with no one to tell him where to go or what to do when he got there. Deep into the morning he ran on, pausing to eat when the bear ate of buds and fern roots and tender corms. When they happened upon stream-fed pools, he managed to impale fish upon his stave while Bear Brother slapped them from the shallows and speared them with his claws.

And still Bear Brother ambled on, snouting his way from one munching spot to another as he had done before. Warakan followed, his hunger satisfied, his curiosity piqued by new surroundings. The songs of unfamiliar birds and the constant hum of insects filled his ears. The forest murmured and sighed in every springtime breeze. While crossing broken sections of rapidly vanishing snowpack, he could hear the snow whispering to itself as it seeped away into the skin of the earth. Warakan smiled as understanding dawned; snow, transformed into water, lived on in the uncountable streams, freshets, and shallow spans of mist-shrouded pools over and across which he vaulted and splashed alongside Bear Brother, reckless in his gladness to be on the far side of winter.

"Yah!" Warakan gave a shout of appreciation to the morning, to the new season, to the sweet warmth of the heavy spring air. "Yah yah, hay!" The words were no words at all; they were an articulation of pure joy summoned from memories of brief days and nights during which he dwelled in the hunting camps of his grandfather at the base of high mountains whose passes opened into the Land of Grass. "Hay, yah yah!" It was the cry of the hunter when much game was taken and the day was done with no man hurt. "Yah yah, hay!" It was the cry of the chieftain signaling the feast to begin when night came down and the People gathered around the fire to sing songs of praise to the hunters and spirits of the game that had died on the spears of men that day.

Warakan stopped. A lump had formed in his throat; it was all at once hurtfully bitter and soothingly sweet as his hand rose to touch the eagle feather braided into his forelock—Shateh's feather, his dying grandfather's parting gift to him. He whispered the slain chieftain's name, and at that moment sunlight struck through the trees at a long, oblique angle, bathing the boy in light and warmth. High above the trees a golden eagle wheeled before the eye of noon and called, *kya, kya, kya!*

He turned his gaze upward and saw the dark, broad-winged raptor bank sharply, the sheen of gold at its neck sparking sunlight just before it turned and disappeared.

"Golden Eagle, spirit of my grandfather!" The words ripped from the boy's throat. "Warakan has not forgotten Shateh. Behold! Warakan walks the forest unafraid with Bear. Behold! Soon Warakan will be a man and a warrior and, strong in the power of the totem and the sacred stone, will make our enemies tremble when he comes forth to them with Bear bringing vengeance in your name!"

His words seemed to hang in the air, enmeshed in light like images seen in windswept clouds, until soon they were no more.

Silence filled the forest.

Warakan held his breath, waiting, though for what he could not have said. The eagle was gone. In the lingering shaft of sunlight, no bird, animal, or insect could be heard. It was as though the entire world was holding its breath along with him, until a woman's call invaded the moment.

"Boy . . . where are you? *Boy!*"

Warakan reacted as though to a slap. Mah-ree still called him Boy! The voice seemed much closer than it had at dawn. A trick of the forest, of the heavy air, the golden noon? Puzzled, he frowned, but his heart gave a leap. Had the old man and young woman left the safety of the lodge and clearing that surrounded it to follow him into the unknown depths of this great and dangerous woodland? Had they, out of concern for his safety, put themselves at risk for him? The premise pleased him so much that his eyes smarted with tears. *Surely, then, they are worrying about me! They do care! They . . .*

His eyes fastened on his surroundings. He was *not* in an unknown part of the forest. He knew exactly where he was! Amidst sentinel spruce and pine, greening foliage had softened the winter-stark angularity of familiar stands of hardwoods. Boulders—gray in the depth of winter—rose from the mists like monolithic mushrooms furred with moss and lichens. Mouth agape, Warakan spun around on his heels and, placing his own position relative to that of the sun, realized that Bear Brother must have been circling back toward the lodge since dawn!

The boy was furious. Mah-ree and Jhadel had not risked themselves; Bear Brother was leading him back to them! He was not ready to return to the bullying of the young woman who insisted upon treating him as a child, or to the old man who had fallen under her spell and sided with her against him.

Again the boy looked around in puzzlement. Why would the cub want to return to the lodge if he, Warakan, was not in it? Just where *was* Bear Brother?

He cocked his head. The sound of slurping pulled him forward through heavy undergrowth where his child was sitting belly-deep in ground fog beside an upturned, hollow-ended tree stump. Warakan stared, disbelieving, as he observed the animal's latest snacking technique: holding a paw in the broken end of the stump long enough for resident ants to swarm over the invading member, then raising the paw and nonchalantly, but with noisy enthusiasm, licking it clean.

Warakan was indignant. Forgetting the bear's reaction to his angry words of the previous night, he shouted, "Ants! Mice! Grubs! Beetles! The bark of trees and the buds and roots of green growing things! This is not fitting food for warriors! But Mah-ree of the Red World would be proud of you. Her lizard-eating people also eat ants and grubs and all foul things that

crawl as low upon the earth as their own miserable ancestors. And look at what such meat has done for them!
It has turned them into outcasts, despised and hunted
across the edge of the world and—"

The bear looked up. "Mah-ree of the Red World
has the sacred stone of the ancestors. Cha-kwena of the
Red World walks with the totem beyond the edge of the
world. She is Medicine Woman! He is Coyote, Trickster,
Yellow Wolf, *Shaman,* and the warrior who has bested
*all* men of all tribes! What are you, Boy who disdains
the ways of the bear kind and runs away from the wisdom spoken by Wise One and Shaman's Woman?"

Warakan's mouth fell open. Had Bear Brother actually spoken to him? He met the gaze of the animal. It
rose, huffed, then turned and began to walk away—
straight toward the spear-carrying young woman coming
through the trees.

"Mah-ree!" exclaimed Warakan, shocked by his
failure to notice her presence before now and feeling
foolish, too, because he realized that it was the woman,
not the bear, who had spoken. His heart gave its usual
*thunk* when he looked at her. Bear Brother had paused
before her. He saw her lay a hand on the animal's head
in greeting, but there was ice in her eyes as she looked
at him. She had overheard his disparaging words about
her people. His face burned with embarrassment. "I, uh
. . . uh—"

"Do not speak!" Mah-ree was openly angry. "Fang-
Toothed Cat laid its tracks close to the lodge last night.
Is it possible that you did not hear its cries, or that you
gave no thought to the safety, if not of this woman, then
of Jhadel, who risked his life for you in the darkness of
this cursed forest? Come! Or perhaps you do not care
that Death has come to the forest because of your self-
ish, unthinking arrogance!"

"Jhadel?" Warakan gasped the name of the old

man but could not bring himself to ask the question. He felt sick. As he scanned his surroundings, he realized that it was here, in this very place, that he had called back the death wish he had spoken against the old man on that long-gone night when, in defiance of the Wise One, he had raced into the bloodred glow of the Northern Dancers in search of the wind spirit that warned of approaching enemies. Now, as he stared into the coldness of Mah-ree's eyes, he wondered if she might not be the enemy he feared, a spirit after all, a creature not of flesh but of mists, a ghostly guardian of the sacred stone who bewitched the minds of men, beasts, and foolish boys who failed to heed the warnings that came from her own mouth.

*"Beware of what you say, Boy! The spirits of the wind hear all things, and the forces of Creation can turn words back onto the tongue of a careless speaker like the teeth of a dog biting its own tail."*

Warakan felt himself shrink within his own skin. Had she overheard his death wish for Jhadel? Had she taken his words into herself and nurtured them until a moment when he was not looking, and then—to mock and spite him—contrived with Fang-Toothed Cat to set the life spirit of Jhadel free upon the wind? "No!" he cried, all at once terrified and enraged. "I called back my words against the wise one! I *did*! Surely the forces of Creation would listen to me!"

"Would they?" pressed the woman with withering reproach. "Go to the lodge, then, and see . . . *Boy.*"

## 2

Mah-ree laughed.

The sound pleased her; too long had laughter been a stranger to her spirit. She smiled, warmed by a sense of well-being as she stood beside the bear and watched the terrified boy disappear into the trees.

"Perhaps now he will learn to control his temper," she said.

Moments passed. Mah-ree waited patiently, listening to the splash of youthful feet pounding across pools and freshets, to the slur and snap of branches being parted as the boy's body forced its way forward through them. She heard the complaints of startled birds taking wing, and then, "Aiee!"

Mah-ree did not flinch at Warakan's cry; she had expected it. "And so!" she exclaimed with quiet satisfaction. As the bear moved forward in obvious alarm, she followed on its heels.

Suppressing laughter, she willed herself to appear unamused as she came to the edge of the clearing and scanned across the stream and up the stony embankment, where the boy stood. He was staring toward the lodge, frozen in shock.

Mah-ree's head went high with satisfaction. All was

exactly as she knew it would be: the boy, stunned and staring; the bloody skin of Fang-Toothed Cat stretched wide on an upright frame of cross-braced branches, its head still attached, gape-jawed mouth hanging wide and terrible teeth showing in all their devastating splendor as its dead eyes looked down upon . . .

"Jhadel!" Warakan cried. With the bear beside him now, he raced forward to fall upon his knees beside the freshly arrayed corpse of the old wise man.

Mah-ree's free hand flew to her mouth; laughter bubbled between her fingers as, using her spear as a staff, she hurried to the lodge.

"Wise One!" Warakan was bereft. "Spirit Master! Teacher! This boy did not mean to . . . to—"

"To *what*?" The question snapped from the tattooed mouth of the "corpse" as Jhadel, crowned in his ceremonial headband of raven's feathers, sat bolt upright on his funeral mattress of freshly cut spruce branches and stuck a bony finger hard into the boy's chest. "To run off in a temper as you always do when anyone disagrees with you? To cause others to risk themselves in concern for your welfare? To—"

"You are alive!" the boy interrupted, half swooning with relief.

"Of course I am alive!" Jhadel boomed. "I am talking to you, am I not? Or did you expect to be having this conversation with the corpse I would have been had Mah-ree not slain Fang-Toothed Cat when he leaped out at me while both of us risked our lives to search for you in the dark of the forest night?"

Mah-ree saw Warakan blink. He turned to look at her. Then he turned again, setting his eyes upward to appraise the skin of the animal she had killed. She had to admit that it was impressive. Her hand tightened on the haft of her spear. Last night the weapon had flown from her grasp as though it were not an inanimate tool of wood and stone but a living extension of her body and will. One moment she had been walking behind Jhadel, searching for Warakan, treading cautiously in the sputtering glow that emanated from the oil-impregnated strips of hide that formed the head of the old man's foul-smelling torch. In the next moment she had been brought up short by something sparkling in the darkness ahead. And then suddenly—with the light of Jhadel's torch reflecting in its eyes—the leaping cat had charged from the trees. Without so much as a breath of indecision Mah-ree had levered back and, with all her strength, sent her spear flying to bury its stone head in the thorax of the great cat.

Her hand pressed against the sacred talisman that lay against her throat. She knew that the forces of Creation had been with her last night. Her eyes moved over the remains of Fang-Toothed Cat. It was the largest of its kind she had ever seen. Indeed, for one small woman to have killed it with a single spear thrust was nothing short of astounding, unless that woman was, as Wise One insisted, a shaman in her own right and perhaps First Woman reborn. It was a heady thought, one that made her breathless with yearning for her man.

*Ah, Cha-kwena, when will you return to your First Woman? Now, at last, I think you would not be ashamed to call Mah-ree of the Red World yours. And in the days and nights to come this woman will make from the skin of the great cat a gift of welcome for her man, a cloak to make her shaman proud, not a thing of rabbit skins, but a cloak that will make him know Jhadel is right when he says that the spirits of the ancestors have brought Mah-ree of the Red World to this place, to this spear, to this . . .*

Her thought stopped short in a panic. Bear was reconnoitering her prize, sniffing and licking at the bloodied tissue on the inside of the pelt left by her fleshing dagger. "Stop!" she demanded, realizing that the bear also saw potential in the uncured skin—not as a future cloak but as an immediate meal. With a sigh of frustration and alarm, she regretted conceding to Jhadel's scheme to use the skin of the great cat as a ploy to frighten the intractable Warakan into future obedience. She could hear the old man's words now: *"Hmm. I think we will skin this cat, and by the manner in which we display its pelt, we will skin the boy, too. Yes! He will learn from the death of this cat! Later you may do as you will with it. Now we will raise its pelt in the way of my people when an animal has killed a hunter and has then been hunted to its own death. I will lie out beneath the skin. On freshly cut boughs I will lie like a corpse! And when the boy at last returns, he will take one look and be sure that the cat has killed me, and that you have killed the cat. Before he sees the trick, you will make him certain that all that has happened is his fault. Perhaps the next time he thinks of running wild into the wood, he will think again and remember what his actions could well have brought had it not been for Daughter of the Red World's skill with a spear, and the power of the sacred stone to protect us all!"*

She shook her head; how could she have forgotten Bear's potential as a threat to her plan for transforming the raw pelt into a finely worked fur garment? "Away, Bear, away!" she commanded.

But Bear, like its brother, did not respond well to commands he had no wish to obey. The animal did not move away from the pelt but stood upright like a man, took hold of one of the forepaws of the slain cat, and, with a solid shake of its head, jerked downward, pulling the skin to the ground along with the frame that had held the great cat upright.

"Stop!" Mah-ree cried again.

Bear did not stop. He ambled off a few paces, lay

down on top of the raw side of the pelt, and settled in to lick and nip the skin free of residual meat.

Mah-ree's eyes widened. The bear would perforate and ruin the skin in a matter of moments if not stopped. Brandishing her spear, she burst into a run, shouting furiously as she clambered across the stream and up the embankment toward the animal.

Warakan leaped to his feet and moved to block her progress.

Mah-ree pushed the boy aside.

Jhadel ordered her to stop.

Mah-ree did not stop.

The bear raised its head and glared.

Mah-ree paused and glared back at the animal. "That pelt is for my shaman, not for you! Leave it, or this woman who has mended your paw and soothed your wounds will see to it that you are soon nursing new wounds inflicted by this spear!"

What happened next shocked her, in more ways than one. Perhaps it was the taste of raw meat coupled with the stink of the flayed skin of a dead animal that turned the mood of the bear. Mah-ree would never be sure. Even though her temper was high, it was not her intent to do more than bluff and bluster the animal into a retreat that would allow her to retrieve the pelt of the fang-toothed cat before the teeth of the cub reduced it to shredded ruins. Nevertheless, she failed to hold the gaze of the bear long enough to judge its mood. When the animal snarled, Mah-ree's eyes were on the pelt, assessing it for damage. Despairing at several rips in the cat skin, she looked up in anger, snarled back at the bear, and made a menacing forward feint with her spear. It was in this moment of eye contact with the animal that she suffered the first shock.

The bear's eyes were dilated with outrage, fixed and unblinking. Yellow eyes like twin suns, so searing in

their hateful focus that Mah-ree was burned by the realization that she had blundered onto dangerous and unfamiliar ground. Truly, Warakan's cub *was* no longer a
cub, nor was it Friend or Brother or member of their
little band. The creature was all that she had known it
must someday be—an animal, a great short-faced bear
on the brink of maturity, larger by a third than its most
fearsome cousin, the grizzly, and, like all of its kind who
shared its gender, unmanageably male and instinctively,
indisputably territorial.

The bear rose in a single, fluid movement that
brought it to its full height, head out, lips working, stabbing teeth in full display.

Terrified, Mah-ree caught her breath as the long,
wide shadow of the beast fell upon her. She knew she
should move back, slowly, one step at a time. She knew
she should lower her spear and begin to speak in conciliatory tones that would concede the contested skin to
the animal. But she wanted that pelt, wanted it so badly
she could not bring herself to abandon it.

"Bear Brother, do not be so angry!" Warakan's
command was unnaturally high and taut. "It is only the
skin of a dead cat! Back away, my brother!"

The bear did not back away.

"Woman . . . if you value your head, it is you who
must back away!" Jhadel's statement was heavy with
warning. "Or would you test the power of the sacred
stone against that which stands before you now?"

Mah-ree held her ground, thinking: *Has this bear
not stood to challenge this woman before? Yes, and turned
from this woman's spear in fear! And has this bear not
come to this woman at her command, and cried like a
baby in her arms, and licked her face with gratitude as she
tended his wounded paw? Yes!*

Mah-ree was breathing again as she slowly moved

her gaze from the face of the animal to the pelt that lay between them. *Ah! It is too fine a skin to be fed to a bear!* she thought when she saw that the bear had not only nipped several small holes in the main body of the pelt but had also lacerated a portion of the head. Her brow furrowed as she remembered how Jhadel had been half-scalped by a single swipe of the bear's great paw. She swallowed, unnerved, but only momentarily.

Again she looked up at the beast. Boldly, in self-righteous indignation, she made another forward poke with her spear. And in that moment, once again, terror robbed her of breath. Every hair on the high, humping curve of the animal's shoulders was standing erect. The yellow eyes were burning into hers, and as clearly as though the animal were speaking, she knew that although she had killed the fang-toothed cat, Bear had put the mark of his teeth and scent of his saliva on its pelt; now Bear would keep that which he had made his own, despite the audacious, disrespectful aggressions of a lesser creature.

And now came the second shock. A great paw shot forward and down. A claw snagged the tip of Mah-ree's extended spear, then pulled back, hard. Did someone scream at that moment? Jhadel or Warakan? Or had Mah-ree heard her own outcry of terror? She was not sure. With a startled gasp, she felt herself jerked forward as the spear was yanked from her grasp with such force that she was pulled against the bear. Panic-stricken, she lurched back, attempted to turn and run, but slipped on the raw skin of the pelt and fell hard on her side. Fighting dizziness, she could smell the sweet scent of blood. The blood of the uncured pelt or her own blood? Her right shoulder ached terribly, and for one horrifying moment she was certain that, along with her spear, her arm had been ripped from her body.

Gasping, aware of the bear moving and growling savagely close by, she heard the wooden shaft of her spear being crunched in its massive jaws, the stone point flung against a rock. She fought her way onto her hands and knees and, with a sob of gladness to find her right arm still connected to her body, desperately attempted to crawl away under a pounding rain of spear fragments that the enraged bear was hurling down at her. Then, like a storm cloud, the bear came down upon her.

Mah-ree screamed as the lightning of terror flashed within her. She was certain that, like her spear, she was about to be torn to pieces. Jhadel was too old and frail to help her, and Warakan, even if he had been able to command the bear, would not raise a hand against his brother. Her life was over. Now, when she had finally rediscovered hope in the future and longed to be reunited with her man, she knew that when Cha-kwena at last returned to the forest with the totem, there would be no woman to greet him with a fine new cloak or to place the sacred stone of the ancestors once more in his care.

"The stone!" Hope reigniting within her, Mah-ree pulled herself into a ball, tucked her head between her hands, and wished with all her might on the power of the Ancient Ones to save her.

And then the third shock came.

"Bear Brother, you will *not* eat that woman!" shouted Warakan.

A quiver went through the bear.

Mah-ree heard the animal bawl as though it had been struck a mortal blow. Then, suddenly, she felt its suffocating weight lift from her as it rose and bolted for the trees.

She sat up in time to see the animal disappear into the forest.

"Well done, Warakan," said Jhadel, breathless with relief.

Mah-ree turned to look up at the boy. He was pale. His features bore a stunned and stricken expression, and the stave in his left hand was wet with the blood of his brother.

**3**

Warakan did not follow after the bear.

For many days and nights after it had disappeared into the forest, he went to the edge of the clearing and called into the trees, but memories of yellow eyes and slavering jaws held him back. He was afraid. And, in fear of his brother, Warakan returned to the clearing, ashamed.

He kept to himself after that, most often perched atop a boulder at the edge of the clearing, staring into the forest, waiting for Bear Brother to return even though he knew in his heart this would not happen. A terrible sadness was on him. The wound he had inflicted upon the bear had been no more than a superficial piercing; he was certain that it would heal in time. But what of the animal's trust? Warakan knew he had broken it as surely as Bear Brother had destroyed Mahree's spear.

He brooded.

He watched the young woman from his perch as she worked on the cursed cat skin, ignoring the bruising she had suffered during the bear's brief attack. She patched the lacerations on the skin with sinew taken from the cat. She finished fleshing the pelt, then set

herself to alternately smoking it, softening it in warm
water, and letting it dry as best it could in the meager
forest sunlight. Now it was staked on the ground, well
away from the lodge, and she passed the days on her
knees before it, rubbing the flesh side with a tanning
mash of pulverized cat brains and kidneys, bleaching
the skin, working out the smallest imperfections. At
night she dragged her backrest from the lodge and
posted herself close to the skin, a pair of sharpened
staves made from the cat's leg bones across her lap.

Warakan hated her, and he hated the skin of the
fang-toothed cat. It was all he could do to keep himself
from leaping upon the pelt and finishing what the bear
had started. He knew that Mah-ree's efforts were all for
Yellow Wolf, for the shaman Cha-kwena, who had
abandoned her in this miserable forest within which he,
Warakan, had betrayed his brother to save her life.
Truly, he thought as he watched her sitting in benighted
mists or pale forest sunlight, she *was* Bad-Luck-Bringing Woman, and he cursed the night he found her
snared in his trapline.

Day after long, dank, misted day and night after
ever-shortening cloud-veiled night, Warakan kept to his
perch or lay scowling upon his bed skins. He would not
answer when Jhadel spoke to him. He remained dis-
dainfully silent with Mah-ree, even though she tried to
show her gratitude by taking special care with his food,
keeping his bed furs aired, and cutting fragrant green
boughs for his mattress until she saw him cast these
from the lodge with a sneer. They reminded him of the
Wise One's funeral mat and of the cruel trick she and
the old man had conspired to play on him. He would
never forgive them for that. And he would never forgive
himself for turning on his brother—or for being afraid
to follow the wounded animal into the trees.

"How many times must this man say that Boy

Mother and Brother of Bear could not allow his cub to eat his future woman?" Jhadel asked with a grunt and grumble of impatience as he came with Mah-ree to stand at the base of Warakan's boulder.

"This woman *has* a man, Wise One, a *shaman,*" Mah-ree reminded him gently.

"Hmm." The old man refused to concede the point to the young woman. He kept his conversation directed upward to the boy on the rock. "Bear Brother's own true bear mother would have driven him from her lodge in his second year. It was time for Bear to walk the forest alone in the way of his own kind. You must not brood over his absence, for he was a danger to us all. We are well rid of him."

Warakan smarted at the old man's words and was glad to see him turn his back and walk away.

Mah-ree offered up a basket of roasted meat. "Here. The flesh of Fang-Toothed Cat will soon be gone. It is good. You must eat. And you must know, Warakan, although Wise One's words are harsh, he is right about your cub. Your brother has outgrown our lodge and our company. You have raised that bear. Because of you, he is tall and strong and able to make his own way in the forest. Soon he will find a woman bear, and together they will make cubs of their own. Then, long before she goes to den with the return of White Giant Winter, she will drive off your brother, for she will know what you refuse to admit—that it is the way of the great boar bears of the forest to walk alone. They have no need of their own kind, much less Man kind in their lives." She smiled encouragingly. "Truly, all will be well for him in the forest, and when snow lies deep upon the land and the Cold Sisters sing with North Wind once more, he will den alone, but he will dream of Warakan, son of Masau and grandson of Shateh, and twitch his paws with pleasure, remembering the days when you and he were cubs together. And this woman tells you now that she too will never forget that Warakan saved her life . . . even though his bravery on her behalf forever alienated a brother."

Warakan was shaken by her words. He wanted to tell her that she was wrong, that Bear Brother would always need him and was probably bawling in confused loneliness out amidst the trees, but he remembered the animal's successful foraging in the woods and the two yellow eyes spaced a tree-trunk's distance apart above stabbing teeth the length of a grown man's thumbs, and he knew that she was right. He scowled, ignored the food she offered, and knew in his heart that it was he who needed Bear, a brother, a fellow hunter, a friend in a world of enemies and old men and bad-luck-bringing women!

Warakan cocked his head. As he glowered down at Mah-ree's upturned face, his heart gave its usual *thunk*. She looked so much like a tawny young forest doe that he was struck dumb by her beauty and the amazing realization that, although she had just spoken his name four times, not once had she called him Boy.

That evening Warakan came down from his rock and shared a meal with Jhadel and Mah-ree for the first time since Bear Brother had run away. He did not speak, but he did not glower, either. As darkness settled upon the forest and the old man sought sleep within the lodge, Warakan did not go back to his perch, nor did he seek rest upon his bed furs. He kept watch with Mah-ree beside the skin of Great Fang-Toothed Cat.

"It is a good thing that Bear did not eat you."

She looked at him, startled by the sound of his voice and by his concession.

"Warakan will make Mah-ree a new spear," he told her.

Mah-ree shook her head. "That spear was Gah-ti's, made by his father, Kosar-eh of the Red World, in the fashion of the warriors of the Land of Grass. Only Kosar-eh could make such a fine spear! It was not meant for Mah-ree. It was only a temporary gift to her from the spirit of Gah-ti, for whom Kosar-eh left it so that his firstborn son might journey proudly in the world beyond this one." She sighed. "That spear cannot be replaced."

"Warakan will replace it!"

Mah-ree was touched by his eagerness to please. "Then this woman will thank you," she said kindly. Although she knew him well enough to be certain that it was useless to attempt to dissuade him from any new intent, she could not keep herself from adding, "But, truly, these staves made from the leg bones of Fang-Toothed Cat will serve well enough and will honor the memory of the one whose skin lies before us now."

"Sharpened cat bones!" The boy was openly disdainful.

"Hardened in fire, like your own bear-bone lances."

Now it was Warakan who shook his head as he leaned close to confide proudly, "It was said that Masau, Mystic Warrior and father of Warakan, could speak to the stones of the earth and cut them into spearheads with his eyes! The men of the Watching Star sent their sons to Masau so that they might learn this magic from him. And it was said that when Masau was a boy living among his true people, he learned how to work stone from his father—Shateh, grandfather of this boy, who *will* make a new spear for his woman!"

At that moment, high in the windless black canopy of the trees, a pair of owls called to each other in the language of the hunting raptors of the night. Mah-ree looked up. Her mind swam back across time to a night of wind and starlight when she had stood beside Cha-kwena in the high gorge and listened to Owl, helping animal spirit of the holy men of their tribe, *oo-oo*ing in the trees.

"Cha-kwena!" Mah-ree sighed the name of her man, unaware of the boy's scowling reaction to it. It was as though her shaman were beside her now, strong and handsome in his owl-skin headdress, his face upturned to the night alongside her own as they watched the wings of Owl shadow the moon while a great star fell from the sky and mammoth trumpeted beyond the edge of the world. Mah-ree caught her breath as her hands rose and folded across the sacred stone that lay against her throat within her furs.

"My man will return to me, Warakan! With the totem he will come! And then all that Jhadel hopes for us will come to pass. You will see. Why else would this woman be here now, alive, sitting beside Warakan of the Two Tribes instead of dead meat in the belly of a bear, unless there were a purpose, a—"

"Mah-ree is here now because Warakan saved her life!"

"Yes! For *him*! Soon Cha-kwena will come. With the sacred mammoth, Life Giver, he *will* come. And then we will go forth, back across the edge of the world, back into the country of the three tribes to be reunited with your people and with my band—with Ta-maya and Kosar-eh and his children, with U-wa and old Kahm-ree and Tla-nee—to live together in peace!"

Warakan was on his feet. "Never!" he proclaimed and with a snarl stalked back to his perch on the boulder to await the return of his brother.

Mah-ree watched him go off into darkness, straight-backed as one of his staves, head high, hands curled into fists. She was unsure of just how she had

angered him and found her head swaying in befuddlement. What a difficult youth he was, with moods like
moonlight on water when an intermittent wind blew
clouds across the night—sparkling one moment, shadowed the next, and always unpredictable. Could he truly
imagine that she would be his woman someday, or that
the bear would return?

She rose, followed the boy across the clearing,
paused before his boulder, and looked up at him. His
shoulders were thrown back, his chin thrust out, his
long, narrow eyes as black as his mood as he glared
straight ahead, his face strong and good to look upon
despite his scars. "You have saved this woman's life,
Warakan. Until the ending of her days, Mah-ree will call
you Brother and keep in her heart a special place for
you."

"Warakan's sister is dead!" he blurted, angrier than
before. "He needs no other!"

"Then let it be between us as a mother and son, as
it was between you and your cub when—"

"Warakan's mother is also dead! A warrior can
only have one mother in his life. And you are a woman,
not a cub who turns into a bear and runs off from the
one who has nurtured him."

"This woman will not change the way of her heart
toward the warrior who saved her life," she interrupted
in kindly earnest, believing that she understood the way
of his heart at last. "Nor will she turn her back and
leave him to go her way without him."

He bristled. "As her man has turned his back and
gone his way without her?"

Mah-ree would not allow herself to be shaken. "My
shaman will come back for me, Warakan." With her
hand now curled around the sacred stone, her voice was
as clear and sure as a freshet running toward sunlight
through a glade. "The totem will be with him. And

then, together with the sacred stone, Cha-kwena will return with us. We will join once more with our band and—"

"Cha-kwena! Yellow Wolf! Trickster! Thief! Betrayer of Women and Bringer of Death to Shateh and all who ever trusted him! Your band has walked into the land of your enemies with no shaman or totem or even the sacred stone of the ancestors to protect them. By now your band is no more."

"You are wrong," she told him.

"No! Warakan is *not* wrong! And if Yellow Wolf comes here, Warakan will use the power of the sacred stone to kill that shaman and slaughter the totem. Then the blood and flesh of Life Giver will be for Warakan, as it should have been for his father and grandfather before him! And on that day the woman of Yellow Wolf will be for Warakan!"

The night was still and warm, but Mah-ree shivered. Now it was her turn to proclaim, "Never!" as she turned and strode toward the lodge with the sacred stone pressed so tightly in her hand that she could feel her heart beating like a trapped and dying bird within her fist.

They did not speak for many days and nights after that. South Wind gusted through the canopy of the forest, a warm, moist breath sighing through the treetops, singing wordless springtime promises of summer soon to come. On the forest floor, however, the air lay heavy and still, mother of mists and mold, and of great humming warrior bands of insects that attacked and fed upon all creatures that dwelled below.

Bear Brother did not return to the lodge, nor was his sign seen in the forest.

Game was scarce.

And the meat of Fang-Toothed Cat was no more.

Jhadel commanded Warakan and Mah-ree to slather their faces and all exposed skin with a thin coating of mud whenever they left the lodge to fish along the stream or set snares or check their traps for whatever the forces of Creation saw fit to send their way—birds in the main, and small mammals whose flesh tasted of the amphibians and insects that formed the bulk of their diet. Mah-ree kept a smudge fire burning constantly within their shelter; smoke, it seemed, not only carried invocations to the spirit world but kept biting gnats and flies out of the lodge as well.

Warakan was miserable. Without Bear Brother at his side, he found no pleasure in the forest. And, try as he might, he failed to make Mah-ree forgive him for the things he had said in anger against her shaman and her band.

Now, as he moved through thick undergrowth, he searched for an outcropping of suitable stone from which to fashion a projectile point for the fine new shaft of virtually knot-free second-growth ash that he had already prepared for final adornment.

"There is no workable stone to be found in all this forest!" he proclaimed loudly, at the same time looking around to see if Mah-ree and Jhadel had heard him. They were nearby, as always, busily poking around the woodland floor for familiar roots, bark, fungi, and green growing things that would serve as food and medicine for their little band of three. When he saw Mah-ree look sternly his way, Warakan smiled at her. She did not smile back.

He sighed wistfully when Mah-ree returned to her work. She barely spoke to him these days. If she was ever going to smile his way again, he had to keep his vow to make a spear for her—the most beautiful, most wonderful of all spears—to replace the one Bear Brother had destroyed. This was disturbing to one who had learned in childhood that he had a keen eye when it came to selecting workable stone, for he had also learned that choosing the right stone and cutting usable flakes from it were totally different talents. He sighed again, this time with remorse, as he wondered what mindless spirit of malicious intent had taken over his tongue when he had promised to make the spear. He could duplicate the shaft, more or less, but unless the ghosts of his slain father and grandfather were to return from the world beyond this world to offer guidance, he had no hope of matching the artistry that had gone into the creation of the exquisite projectile point fashioned by the warrior and master stoneworker Kosar-eh of the Red World.

Mud-saturated perspiration dripping from his brow, Warakan turned toward Jhadel, who was again sagging against his staff. The boy frowned with concern. Spirit Master had yet to recover his full strength after his unfortunate wounding by Bear. The damp, heavy air of the forest was weighing too heavily on the old man. His breath was labored; he ate little and slept too much. Yet, since the incident with Fang-Toothed Cat and Mah-ree's near mauling, he had refused to allow Warakan or Mah-ree to venture far from the lodge alone.

*As though his frail old bones could protect us!* thought Warakan when he saw that the old man, although standing upright, was sound asleep.

Mah-ree had also noticed this. She straightened, hefted onto her hip one edge of the wide, flat, nearly empty gathering basket she had woven of green vines, and went to the old man's side. "Wise One?"

Jhadel gave no response.

Warakan cocked his head. How gently Mah-ree touched the old shaman's shoulder. How compassionately she spoke one of his many names. When had she last spoken to him like that? *On the night when she came to you with food and kind words and you answered with shouts and threats against the one she loves.* The boy's mouth tightened. *She will love me. Someday. When Yellow Wolf is dead.*

"Jhadel, can you not hear me? Teacher?" The old man raised a hand and combed back a strand of hair from his muddy brow. "How is this woman to learn new sources of healing magic, or to find the magic flower you seek as medicine to quicken your heart and restore strength to your blood, unless you in your wisdom teach her how to recognize these things?"

Jhadel slept on.

"Magic flower?" Warakan pressed. Curious and feeling left out as usual, he strode forward through the undergrowth.

Mah-ree deigned to reply but kept her eyes fixed worriedly on the old man's face as she did. "Wise One searches for a tall green growing thing, with many blossoms the color of purple sunset growing like stars on a single spike. I do not know this flower." She shook her head and rubbed Jhadel's shoulder. "Wise One, my mother and the grandmothers of the Red World—even the old women of the Land of Grass—have shared much of their healing wisdom with me. But this forest names me Stranger, and even if it did not, there is so much I do not know. So much that my mother had yet to teach me before her spirit walked the wind forever."

Jhadel was responding to her touch, his eyes working beneath his closed lids as her words penetrated his state of sleep. Then, suddenly, he stiffened, blinked, shook himself awake, and stared at the young woman in obvious embarrassment.

"Hrm!" He cleared his throat. "Just resting these old eyes. Just resting."

"Yes, Wise One, of course," she agreed, granting him his pride.

Jhadel nodded with dignity as he placed a gnarled, trembling, mud-caked hand upon Mah-ree's cheek in a gesture of love and reassurance. "Your mother lives! In *you*! As do all of the grandmothers of the People since time beyond beginning. Yes! Someday you will join them. Someday you will dance and sing happy songs with the ancestors in the Blue Land of Sky. Until then, are you not First Woman reborn? Have you not walked in the shadow of the great white mammoth totem? Do you not wear the sacred stone? Yes! You have only to open your heart, Shaman Woman, and the spirits of the ancestors will speak from within you in the spirit voice that you name Instinct."

"But this forest is unlike any place that this woman's mother or grandmothers ever knew," she told him. "How can they share the healing secrets of trees and green growing things that were strangers to them in their time? If I am to learn, you must teach me, Wise One."

Jhadel began to speak. A cough took him. He tottered against his staff and would have collapsed had the young woman not moved to support him.

Warakan leaped forward and, with Mah-ree, eased the old man into a seated position upon the ground. There, steadying himself with his hands knotted around his staff, Jhadel sat wheezing and hacking and gasping for breath.

Warakan felt the blood rush from his face. The old man was dying. And the woman with the sacred stone was doing nothing to prevent it.

"*Do* something!" the boy raged at Mah-ree. "Are you not Medicine Woman? Shaman's Woman? Healer? Use the powers of the stone . . . or give the talisman to me!" He made an upward lunge, intending to snatch the sacred stone from around her neck, but the staff of Jhadel stopped him.

"Back, boy, and down!" the old man demanded.

Warakan's face flushed again as he crouched beside Wise One, who had spoken to him as though he were a dog to be brought to heel.

Jhadel "tsked" mockingly, then wheezed, "It is not this shaman's time to dance with the ancestors in the Blue Land of Sky, Warakan. There is much that you must yet learn from me . . . and . . ." He paused, did successful battle with another cough, and after a moment of rest said weakly, "We must seek the green growing things that will cure this cough, and the root of the flower that will make this man strong again."

Mah-ree was openly distraught. "But so many of the green growing things of this forest are strangers to me, Wise One!"

"And to me," he conceded.

Warakan saw the color drain from Mah-ree's features.

She raised a hand to her throat and rested it over the sacred talisman as she knelt down and said to the old man, "You must believe this woman when she says that she means no disrespect when she tells you that the first lesson her mother taught about the use of green growing medicine things was *never* to use the unknown thing!"

"And where would we be if we all listened to such advice?" Jhadel raised an eyebrow, then gestured Mah-ree close and rasped, "The medicine spirits to cure all the ills of the People are in this world, hiding in roots and mushrooms, in spores and bark, in the horns and organs and blood of living beasts, and in green growing things. It is up to the Medicine Maker to find them and catch them and make them obey. Since time beyond it has been so! I will teach you the way of this. Soon, strong in the knowledge of the three worlds of the People, this man will be strong again—and there will be no

Medicine Maker to equal this Shaman Woman who stands before him now!"

"The root of the flower you seek will not come walking into the forest from the grasslands that lie on the far side of the great gorge," Warakan said flatly, again feeling left out.

Stunned, Mah-ree looked at him as he stood up. "You know this medicine flower? You know where it grows?"

"Not here," Warakan informed her. "It is a flower of grassland and meadow, of sunlight and sand, in which its root grows fat and strong with medicine. When I was a boy among the People of the Watching Star, many times my band followed herds of the strongest and fleetest horses to the places where they fed upon that flower when it opened under the Moon of Yellow Grass, when the bison bulls come to . . ." The boy paused; until this moment he had no idea how much he missed the wide plains and open skies and sunstruck mountain meadows.

"Our enemies are there," Jhadel reminded him. "Someday we will return into that land. Now it is too dangerous. No. We will find the medicine we need here, in this dark and misted forest. If we look hard enough, we will find the root of the flower . . . the right green growing things." He closed his eyes and was asleep.

Mah-ree touched the old man's brow, then looked up at Warakan. "There are willow trees in this forest. The medicine spirits that dwell within its stalks and leaves will eat our Wise One's fever, but he is so old, so weak, that I fear for him. I have asked the powers within the stone uncounted times to make him well and strong. Perhaps it has been speaking to me through the voice of Instinct. I cannot be sure, but, although this woman's knowledge of healing is a poor thing compared to that of Jhadel, I would say that it is sun he needs, and clean, sweet, dry wind, and the healing scent of sage smoke in his nostrils, and antelope and hare and grouse on roasting spits under an open sky. For in truth, here in this dark, misted forest at the edge of the world, it is clear to me that not even Jhadel can call forth the spirits to heal himself."

Warakan trembled and to his surprise saw that Mah-ree trembled, too. For the first time in all too long, they were on common ground: In their shared concern for the welfare of the old man, they must return to the sunstruck, game-rich land on the south-facing slopes of the great gorge through which they had both traveled to reach the forest. His heart quickened. It was not an easy decision for either of them, and he knew it. Someday he would venture eastward in search of Yellow Wolf in order to steal the living power of the totem for the purpose of turning that power to vengeance, but now that day was even farther in the future than before. As for Mah-ree, who yearned for the return of her shaman so that, strong in the power of the totem, he could reclaim the sacred stone and walk once more at her side, she would have to turn her back on her man and carry the stone away from him to find the flower that would heal Wise One.

"We will leave the stone in the lodge for my shaman," she said.

"No," Warakan objected. "We will need its power in the land of our enemies."

"Together we will be strong. Together we will be wary. Together we will make our Wise One well again. Then, together, we will return. And if my shaman comes out of the face of the rising sun while we are gone, he will know where to find us, for we will make a pathway through the forest for him to follow!"

Warakan made no reply; he knew by the set of her jaw and steady glow of her eyes that she would not be dissuaded.

Together they carried Jhadel to the lodge.

Together they gathered their belongings and contrived a travois for the old man.

Together they made an altar of wood within the lodge and placed the sacred stone upon it. Over this Mah-ree draped the fine new cloak she had made for her shaman, setting the head of the great cat upright, mouth open, its dagger teeth pointing down on either side of the stone so that the slain animal appeared to be guarding the talisman, ready to spring to life and attack any interloper.

"Spirit of Fang-Toothed Cat, this woman who has slain you honors you above all others. Wait here for Mah-ree and Warakan and Jhadel to return. Guard the sacred stone of our ancestors. And if Cha-kwena returns before us, embrace him in your warm arms and lie softly upon his skin. Tell him that Mah-ree is still his woman . . . always and forever!"

Together they set off through the woods, traveling in solemn silence, helping each other with Jhadel, taking turns using a stone ax to mark the way of their passage in the trunks of trees. At last, when night came down upon the world, they prepared to rest until dawn —until they heard the deep, reverberating meows of a fang-toothed cat.

Mah-ree shuddered as she reached for the comfort of a talisman that was no longer hers to hold. "Fang-Toothed Cat cries for her lost mate. May his spirit ease her solitude, and may she choose to hunt in another part of the forest this night!"

"She is not the only beast we need fear," said the

old man. "Twice since leaving the lodge have we crossed the trail of a bear."

"Yes, it *is* so!" Warakan's emotions were a sudden mix of gladness and apprehension. "My brother walks ahead of us!"

"Hmm. Perhaps," conceded Jhadel. "The sign was old, and we cannot be sure if it was his."

Mah-ree looked around and crossed her arms over her chest, hugging herself not for warmth but for courage. "I doubt that Warakan's cub is the only bear in this forest."

"Without the sacred stone to speak to us, there is no way to know," Warakan reminded her sourly.

The old man went rigid on the furs of his travois. "The stone . . . what have you done with the sacred stone?"

Mah-ree told him. She spoke simply, with no attempt at apology. "It will be safer there, hidden in the dark deeps of the forest. Until we return to reclaim it or until my shaman comes to us strong in its power, Instinct and the wisdom that has been passed down to us from the ancestors will tell us what to do!"

And so they raised a smoky fire to keep four-legged ground-hunting carnivores and six-legged winged predators at bay. They shared meager traveling rations, drank deeply of water from a nearby creek, and talked softly of where they were going, how long it would take them to get there, and how they would survive so close to known enemy hunting grounds without the talisman of the ancestors to grant them protection. The old man, exhausted by worry and frailty, was asleep long before the last words were spoken. And Mah-ree soon gave herself to troubled dreams.

Warakan lay awake. He wondered where his brother slept this night and if the bear had found the company of his own kind; the tracks and trail sign he

had lost amidst the brambles had been those of a solitary animal, and somehow this pleased him. *Ah, Brother,
will we ever meet again? And if we do, how shall it be
between us?* The latter question was not one he wished
to consider. Not now. Not when the strained, fitful
breathing of the old man reminded him of the purpose
to which he was committed.

South Wind rose. Moon slowly showed her profile
above the shifting canopy of the trees. Pale, silver light
filtered to the forest floor, seeming both affirmation and
invitation to the boy. He rose, looked at the sleeping
forms of the young woman and frail old man, and knew
what he must do.

Taking up his staves, Warakan left in hurried silence. He went boldly into the night, back the way he
had come, telling himself he could no longer yield to
the luxury of fear. Moon lighted his way. South Wind
parted the trees as on and on he ran until, at last, he
crossed the stream, clambered up the embankment,
strode through the clearing, and flung aside the weather
baffle of the lodge.

Moonlight illuminated the interior, where Fang-
Toothed Cat was waiting.

Warakan stared at the silvered beast Mah-ree had
slain and prepared as a gift for the shaman whose
twisted powers still controlled her heart. "I am not
afraid of you, Ghost Cat, or of him!" He crossed to the
altar and reached boldly between the dagger teeth of
the slain cat.

Taking the sacred stone into his left hand, he said
to the talisman, "Before Mah-ree came into our lives,
Wise One said you were for me! Now it shall be so!" He
slipped over his head the thong to which it was attached, opened his robe, and pushed the stone beneath
his shirt. "Warakan, son of Masau and grandson of

Shateh, will not leave the sacred stone of the Ancient
Ones behind for Yellow Wolf!" he declared, and after
slashing and mutilating the head and pelt of the fang-
toothed cat, he turned and raced back along the way he
had come.

# 4

"They come!"

The voice of the blind child sang in the air. On any other morning the People of the Watching Star might have heard despair in that high, tremulous little shout, but not on this sunstruck day. For today the stone hunters and their women were returning across the valley under vast clouds of wild fowl winging out of the southern sky.

"They come!" the little one cried again, gesturing outward with open hands.

Ban-ya smiled as she held the child, savoring the feel of the strong little limbs gripped tightly around her hips. Doh-teyah had been restless all night. Long before dawn, Spirit Woman had risen and gone to sit with the child at the edge of the cave. She had been aware of Joh-nee following and then hunching watchfully nearby, but Ban-ya had ignored her; the girl had become like a second shadow. With the toddler on her lap and South Wind sweet in her face, Spirit Woman had awaited the dawn. Under the glinting eye of the Watching Star and in the glow of a curving moon, the toddler had slept in her embrace, waking at first light to reach outward as though to touch the warmth of the rising sun.

"They come!" cried the child.

And slowly, as Ban-ya watched the valley below transformed by the growing light of the new day, she heard what the toddler had already heard: a faint thrumming on the air, a wind that was not wind. She frowned, squinted across the distance, then caught her breath as she saw long, undulating, black skeins of cloud coming toward her. A few moments passed before she was able to hear the distant honking and the beat of multitudinous wings. The clouds were not clouds. They were great tides of birds!

Ban-ya leaped to her feet in excitement as she became aware of the distant voices of men raised in song and knew that those who had left the cave to journey to the stone quarry Kosar-eh had told them about were returning. Somehow the blind child in her arms had looked sightlessly into the dawn and known they were there.

"Behold!" Spirit Woman announced joyfully to awaken her people. "Truly, Sees the Wind has shaman eyes! She is sightless in this world but is first to see the returning hunters! She is first to see the birds coming from the world beyond this world to be food for us! Truly, Black and White Warrior and his children are good-luck people! Praise the wisdom of Tsana for bringing them to us, for with them has come the meat of many bison, the return of South Wind, and the end of White Giant Winter!"

Joh-nee stood in silence. Clutching her doll, she stared at the priestess. Since when had Spirit Woman decided to speak favorably of Red World people? Joh-nee did not trust her, would *never* trust her. All too often the girl had caught the priestess observing her as though she were some sort of little prey animal to be pitied before it was consumed. And how many times had she seen the woman's weasel eyes covertly watching Tsana in the way of a captive wolf, measuring the man who had ensnared it? Joh-nee's mouth tightened. Tsana deserved better from one whom he honored above all, and to whom he always brought the prime portions of his kills.

The girl's eyes narrowed as she watched Spirit Woman facing into the wind. There was something ominously otherworldly about her—the way she stood stiff-backed as a spear, as though poised to fly away upon the wind; the way her long hair blew back from her tattooed features like so many braided strands of graying sinew; the way she held her wolfskin robe open in order to bare her great breasts to the rising sun, and to the returning hunters. And all the while she held Doh-teyah ever captive in her arms. The girl pulled in a quick, tight breath of frustration. If only Spirit Woman would trust Doh-teyah to her care, *she* would be the one to fly away upon the wind, far, far away from this cave in which Kosar-eh and his sons had become strangers to her.

"Aside, girl, aside!"

Joh-nee looked up at Oan's impatient but kindly command. A throng pressed her now as the People of the Watching Star, summoned by Spirit Woman, came forward along with their dogs to vie for the best positions from which to view the returning hunters and waterfowl. She took a step back, right into Kiu-neh, who was advancing to the edge of the cave with several other youths his age. Elbowing past her, he managed a hurtful tweak at her bottom.

"Ah!" she cried out in surprise, slapping hard at Kiu-neh as he chortled until one of the youths gave him a withering glance.

"Eh! What is the matter with you?" the boy demanded of Kiu-neh. "She is Shaman's Sister. And she has named Tsana Brother. You must show respect!"

Kiu-neh shrugged and went his way.

Joh-nee was grateful. She did not know the name of the other boy, but he was no less a stranger to her than Kiu-neh had become. Although they had lived their entire lives together as members of the same band, she no longer knew Third Son of Kosar-eh. Indeed, since coming to the cave, she did not even like him.

"You are always too sad, Joh-nee."

The girl looked up to see that Kho-neh had paused before her. His hair was growing long, and like his older brother he had filled out. His face was well oiled. Despite the rigors of the past winter and all they had endured at the hands of raiders, she had to admit that he had been well cared for. Frost Spirits no longer fed upon his feet. Indeed, he appeared to be thriving.

Joh-nee was glad for the child, but as her eyes scanned past him into the interior of the cave, her heart grew heavy. She appraised the vast, arching space, saw mammoth bones and sleeping mattresses, drying frames and painted hides, fringed hunt banners of feathers and animal skins, and the great black star that sprawled like a spider across the darkened ceiling of the cave. She shuddered, remembering nights of feast fires and dancing, and death. "Do you not long for your own band, Fourth Son of Kosar-eh?" she asked him.

"My people are *this* people now," Kho-neh replied without hesitation. "And no one calls my father by his old-life name. My father is Black and White Warrior! My father is Spits in the Face of Enemies! Kosar-eh— that name is as dead as our band."

The words stung. Joh-nee pressed her doll close to her chest as she watched Kho-neh tromp off to join the others. Her band dead? *Yes!* She had seen the leavings of Spirit Sucker. Yet had Tsana not echoed the teachings of her own tribe when he promised that her loved ones would be with her as long as she kept them alive in her heart? *Yes!* And so Joh-nee closed her eyes tight. She wished her mother and sister alive. She asked them to come from the world beyond this world and be with her once again.

For a little while the magic of wishful thinking made it so. Until barking dogs and the welcoming shouts of men, women, and children brought her from reverie, she was certain for one wondrous moment that Cha-kwena had come back from the edge of the world at last, riding upon the totem, with Mah-ree at his side.

Kosar-eh entered the cave smiling. A deep, warm glow of self-satisfaction was upon him until, coming happily through the welcoming throng, he was brought up short by the expression of utter disappointment on Joh-nee's face. Irritated, he stalked past her. He was tired of the girl's morose behavior and saw no reason to encourage it by showing her the least concern.

The past few days spent out of the cave had been good days. In the company of a small party of stone hunters and their favorite women, Kosar-eh had led Tsana to the old quarry site he had discovered many a long moon ago when dwelling in this valley with Cha-kwena before the last war. It was over a half-day's strenuous walk from the cave, but no one complained when he brought them to stop beneath pale, ragged, creek-side cliffs banded with some of the most promising brown flint they had ever seen. While Eyah and the other women set up camp among the greening hardwoods, the men gathered small, palm-sized stones from the creek and attacked the cliffs, hammering and chopping until chunks and splinters of the desired flint went flying. Soon they stood amidst growing piles of debris, singing as they worked, stopping now and then to bend and examine particularly promising nodules of broken rock.

"Good stone! Good stone! Yes, yes! Good stone!"

Kosar-eh could still hear Hrak's delighted exclamations.

Later, with only the best, most solid and finely grained selections of flint transported to camp in leather bags, the hunters were fed and praised by their women as each man took up a hammer stone and set to flaking individual nodules into smaller, more easily transportable sizes.

Each day, for as many days as a man could count with the fingers of one hand, passed in the same manner. And now, with both male and female members of the hunting party carrying two, sometimes three leather waist bags laden with precious stone cores, Tsana raised his arms and announced to all, "Black and White Warrior has led us to the best stone this man has seen in more moons than he cares to remember."

A surge of pride swelled Kosar-eh's chest. His sons had come to stand before him. He saw pride in their eyes, and in Eyah's as she pressed close to run a proprietary hand around his waist, then ease her fingers provocatively downward across his belly, and beyond. The big man raised an eyebrow as he looked down at her. She was a pretty thing, no beauty, but exciting, like a warm, furless little animal that could not have enough of his strokings and was always moist and ready to receive his need. Eyah seemed to know his thoughts. She smiled up at him. Kosar-eh wondered if there was affection for him somewhere behind the brazenly sexual invitation he saw in her eyes. He doubted it. And did not care. The young woman's appetite for the pleasures of the flesh gratified his own.

Seeing Indeh glowering jealously at him from a distance, Kosar-eh smiled and drew Eyah into a rough one-armed hug that made her giggle as it took her briefly off her feet. When he saw Indeh shiver with suppressed anger, Kosar-eh felt no pity for the man. Only days ago, the boastful woman whom Indeh had favored before Eyah had given birth to a daughter. It was no secret that Indeh had been so disgusted with the outcome of his ruttings that, had it not been for Tsana's intervention, he would have strangled the newborn and thrown it from the cave. And so Indeh stood apart now, penalized by the chieftain, who had been so irritated at the man's callous disregard for life that he had not included him in the hunting party.

Watching Kosar-eh with his favorite woman, Indeh's eyes narrowed in his ugly, meaty face. Kosar-eh saw hatred in them. Sooner or later, if the man could not free himself of his obsession with the deliciously venal Eyah, they would clash "horns." The tip of his tongue moved to trace the rough edge of the eyetooth that had been chipped by the butt end of Indeh's spear. He owed the man and looked forward to the day when he would teach Indeh why he had earned the battle name of Man Who Spits in the Face of Enemies.

The returning stone hunters slung off their heavy bags and unloaded their treasures onto the floor of the cave to the appreciative "oohs" and "aahs" of their people. Kosar-eh's attention was drawn from Indeh as he heard his name praised again and again. Xanahay and Unai came close to give him a brotherly slap on the shoulder as they extolled the virtues of his skilled eye.

"When it comes to knowing where to hunt the best stone, the eyes of Black and White Warrior are like the eyes of a soaring hawk seeking earthly prey from the clouds above!" proclaimed Xanahay.

"It is so!" agreed Unai.

And all around the cave, children looked with awe

at Kosar-eh, men and youths lauded him with their eyes, and women and girls looked at Eyah with envy.

His boys standing proudly nearby and his new woman clinging to his side, Kosar-eh raised his head high. Never had he been so certain that he had been right on that firelit night of epiphany—when he had stood in this very spot and realized that beneath the veneer of varying tribal customs, men were essentially the same and that these men, although long his enemies, were now his brothers.

"Now, Black and White Warrior, you will show us all your skill, eh?" urged Hrak, rising from his knees with a cylindrical core of dark stone in his upraised hands. "This is good rock, yes? Solid, even grain. No inner flaw that eye can see or ear can hear, yes?"

Kosar-eh eyed the man's selection. "If Hrak says it is so, then it must be so!"

The man flushed with pleasure. With utmost deference, he held the stone to Kosar-eh. "Our sons must see the way the hands of Black and White Warrior seduced the stone at our campfire. Our sons must hear the way those hands made the stone sing out again and again. Ah! When those hands struck flake after flake from the body of the stone, it was like hearing the repeated cry of a woman at the moment of life coming into her from a man! You must show our sons these flakes that your hands have brought forth from the stone, my brother."

Kosar-eh slung the smallest of three leather bags from his waist belt, then knelt and carefully withdrew and held flat upon his palm three long, slender, sharp-edged stone flakes he had pressure-cut with a hammerstone from a core far too heavy to be transported back to the cave. "These are the best of many. They are still newborn from the rock, unformed as yet," he said. "Later I will shape them."

A communal intake of breath hissed through the

cave at the sight of such obvious mastery of stone by mere flesh and bone.

The big man was pleased, flattered, humbled, and more than a little embarrassed by the extent of their admiration. "Hrak has told me that the spirits of the stone choose the hands of the man to whom they will yield. If they have chosen this man, they have done so only because the stone masters among the People of the Land of Grass taught me the language through which I could communicate with them through these hands."

Tsana's face was tight. "The spear you carried into the Valley of the Dead and used in war against my people proclaimed that truth for you."

Kosar-eh was startled. He looked at the chieftain. The man's face was bitter, hostile, closed to his seeking eyes. "You do not see the irony in this?"

Hrak seemed oblivious to the tension that Tsana had introduced into the moment, but he apparently did see the irony in it. He was smiling, eagerly holding his chunk of stone to Kosar-eh. "And now Black and White Warrior will teach this language to the sons of the People of the Watching Star, who have lost their own best stone talkers in war with the People of the Land of Grass!"

Kosar-eh nodded. "Yes. As we make new weapons together and prepare for war, I *will* teach them. When we have made many fine spears together, we will go forth against our enemies. And then those who have slaughtered my woman and children—as they have slaughtered the women and children of Tsana—will receive the gift of Death from spears that could not be made had they not foolishly given this man the gift that I now bring to you . . . in these hands!"

A murmur of appreciation went through the throng.

Tsana nodded, darkly amused.

"And if our bodies fall in battle and our spirits walk the wind forever, the sons of the warriors of the Watching Star will remember the language of the stones that a warrior from the Land of Grass has taught them!" vowed Hrak, euphoric.

"Is war and killing to go on forever?" Joh-nee had come through the crowd to stand accusingly over Kosar-eh. "Are we to fight and die until there are no people left in all this world?"

Xanahay uttered a bleak snicker. "Until we are the *only* people left in this world!"

Joh-nee's lower lip and chin were quivering. "It is a good thing that my brother took the sacred stone and followed the totem—"

"To where?" Tsana's interruption was as smooth and slippery on his tongue as warm fat.

The girl looked at him out of sad eyes. "To a safe place where his enemies will never find him, or the sacred stone, or the white mammoth!" The declaration made, she turned on her heels and hurried away.

Tsana's eyes half closed as he watched Joh-nee disappear into the gathering. "Oan, see to the girl. I do not want New Sister unhappy."

The scar-faced woman obeyed.

Kosar-eh nearly blurted his annoyance at both headman and child. He could not understand how a warrior of Tsana's merit could trouble his mind and burden his people with superstitions passed on to him by dead old men. And he had lost patience with Joh-nee's stubborn loyalty to a brother who had abandoned her and, through his deceptions, brought death to her band. Weary with talk of totems, shamans, and the magic power of talismanic stones, Kosar-eh took the chunk of flint from Hrak and rose to his feet. His eyes scanned the faces of the men around him—Tsana, Unai, Xanahay, Hrak, and all of the others with whom he had hunted and shared meat and laughter and women since being brought to this place as a captive. He saw his sons, Kiu-neh and Kho-neh, standing strong and forthright among the sons of onetime enemies—and in this moment Kosar-eh's sense of brotherhood with his new people was as strong as his feelings of loss for the old.

"The bones of the great white mammoth lie in this cave!" he proclaimed. "The shaman Cha-kwena killed that mammoth. If it is the will of the People of the Watching Star to hunt Yellow Wolf, this man will lead his brothers to the kill. But now I say that the power of the totem is still here, not only in the bones and tusks of the great white mammoth, but in the blood and sweat and will of the warriors and women of the Watching Star to do vengeance against their enemies!"

"Eh yah!" the gathering exclaimed as one.

And the big man—who was Kosar-eh to the Red World, Spits in the Face of Enemies to the People of the Land of Grass, and now Black and White Warrior among the People of the Watching Star—held up the stone that Hrak had given him. "Come! Now will your brother share with you the language of stone!"

They shared. They learned. They laughed with pleasure as Kosar-eh sat in a circle of boys and youths, the warriors of the Watching Star gathered around, approving and affirming old techniques while observing new ones. The women and girls peeked into the circle, watching with great interest as blade after blade was "called forth from the stone" and transformed by pressure flaking with a hammerstone into projectile points of infinite beauty, balance, and deadliness. Now and then a woman would speak out of specific needs, and Kosar-eh would listen as she handed him a piece of flint that her man had brought from the quarry and asked if it was possible for "the one who speaks to stone" to bring from the rock a special sort of burin or awl, or a perforator or scraper for her own use. Although Kosar-eh would sometimes hand back the stone as unsuitable, he would then choose a stone from his own collection, and always the woman received the object of her request and with shining eyes would praise "the master of the stone." In one way or another every challenge was met.

Tsana nodded, infinitely pleased. "Yes. It is good! Observe the way Black and White Warrior uses the tools he has made to help his hands speak to the stone," he urged his fellow tribesmen. "The hammerstone . . . the antler punch and driver . . . the small pressure flaker . . . the rawhide palm pads that allow him to work close to the cutting edge. Observe! Learn!"

The men pressed closer. The teacher worked on. The youths and boys frowned and grumbled at their mistakes, then sighed and shook their heads with hopeful acquiescence when the big man good-naturedly assured them that he had once made the same errors.

"Many stones will be broken, fractured, chipped wrongly and reduced to ruin," Kosar-eh told them. "And many a stoneworker's thigh and hand will be bruised and sliced and made to grease the stone with blood. You must not be discouraged. Only by trying again and again, by learning to sense the protests of the stone when you attempt to force your will against the grain of the rock, will you begin to *feel* the language of the stone and learn the subtleties of its being. Only by looking around the corners of your mistakes will you make it yield to your command."

"It is the same with women!" laughed Hrak.

"Learn well, boys!" Oan chortled.

And from sunrise to blue-shadowed evening of that day the cave rang with the sound of singing stone and contented, enthusiastic people. Kosar-eh's hammerstone struck again and again, and the men and women and children of the Watching Star lauded his efforts with exclamations and songs of praise. Now and then he rested, contentedly watching the other men work and the youths and boys follow his example with their own hammerstones and pressure tools. Eyah came with food for him and more, and when his appetites were sated upon both meat and woman, he slept.

He awoke long before dawn. Tsana was standing over him. Behind the chieftain, the Sky River ran brightly against the night, and beside him stood a naked young woman. Tsana put a hand on her shoulder and guided her forward, then pointed downward to Eyah, indicating his desire for an exchange of sleeping partners. Kosar-eh eyed the chieftain's offering. In the darkness he was not sure who she was, but in silhouette against the stars her form was shapely and taut with youth, a good trade.

He nudged Eyah. "Go," he told her, and although she pouted and made little mewings of discontent, she rose quickly and went to the chieftain without complaint. As Tsana pulled her close, handled her briefly, then drew her impatiently away, Kosar-eh could hear her whispering hot, eager assent to the chieftain. He smiled; he felt no jealousy. Like Eyah, he had no complaint.

The young woman who stood naked above him was awaiting welcome. Kosar-eh gestured her down. She came with a sigh. Although in the darkness he was not sure who she was, she immediately knew how to please him, and he was therefore certain that he had lain with her before. Her name did not matter. She was not Ta-maya. None of them would ever be Ta-maya. She was merely Woman—breasts and thighs and warm, moist depths—faceless in the black night with his manhood thrusting deep inside her. It was enough.

He closed his eyes, worked until release came—savage, violent, woman-bruising release. When she cried out—in pain or pleasure or perhaps some strange female mix of both—Kosar-eh smothered her mouth with his own and did not care. She was not Ta-maya. Here, in this cave, in this Valley of the Dead to which the Four Winds and forces of Creation had swept him, she and others like her were all that would ever be for him. Their joining had nothing to do with affection. It was mating. It was life making. And when, gasping, she threw her arms around his neck and begged for more, he gave her what she would have of him.

It *was* enough. In a world without Ta-maya it was everything.

"Aiee . . . this man is impressed! Black and White Warrior also knows the language to seduce the 'stone' in his own 'blade' so that he can keep it hard all the night! My second girl, she says it is better with you than with Tsana—but do not repeat that, eh."

Kosar-eh opened his eyes. It was just past dawn. The cave was quiet. The people and dogs were still asleep. Hrak, however, was kneeling close to him. The big man blinked, frowned, then sat bolt upright on his furs.

"Your girl? Your *daughter*? I—" He felt himself blanch as he looked around; the faceless receptacle of last night's pleasure was also kneeling near him, her eyes downcast. She was clothed now; her upper lip was puffed and bruised. In one hand she held a bone fire prod to rouse life from the coals in his fire pit as deftly as she had roused flames in his loins the previous night.

Hrak chuckled at Kosar-eh's obvious consternation and said in a voice kept low lest it disturb others, "Black and White Warrior is still not a man of the Watching Star when it comes to women. It is good you maybe make life on my daughter. It is not the first time, eh? She dances a good dance under a man. Tsana himself has said so. Hrak, he teaches his children well!"

Kosar-eh stared. "You . . . have taught—"

Hrak made a fist with one hand and jammed it soundlessly into the palm of the other. "Like this!" he whispered. "Yes! Many times! But only after Tsana took first blood."

"You have lain with your own child?" The big man was incredulous.

Hrak shrugged. "It is an old saying among the People—in new times, men must make new ways!"

The girl tittered quietly and added, "New ways into many women!"

"Hmmph! Go!" commanded Hrak, his voice still no more than a whisper. "Your father would talk with Black and White Warrior."

Kosar-eh watched the young woman rise and walk away, slowly and, he thought, insolently.

Hrak said deferentially, "This man brings a gift to Black and White Warrior, a special gift for a man who speaks the language of stone. Before last night's sleep Tsana came to Hrak and said that it was time for him to bring it forth to you."

Curious, Kosar-eh watched Hrak unfold a rawhide parfleche and slowly bring into the light of morning four large, irregular chunks of rare white chalcedony. The big man caught his breath. "Where did you find this? There is no rock of this kind in the Valley of the Dead. There is none like it in any quarry that I have ever seen!"

"It was a gift from the forces of Creation, stolen by Hrak from a traitorous whelp this man took captive many moons ago. He was by the lake, talking to the bones of the totem as if he expected them to answer him! He had a bear cub with him. Can you imagine, a boy walking with a bear, and carrying such rare and wondrous rocks in his traveling pack? But then, even when Warakan lived among us, no one could ever predict what he—"

"Warakan? He was Shateh's foundling. I remember him from the days I dwelled among the People of the Land of Grass. I thought him drowned."

"May it be so! Surely he would have seen the end of his days at Tsana's hand had he not shown the good sense to run away with Jhadel, who was Spirit Master of our tribe before Spirit Woman came. May the forces of Creation wither that old man into dust wherever he is!"

Kosar-eh's eyes held on the white quartz exposed by the opened flap of the parfleche. The quality of the stone was magnificent. He had seen such perfection only once before, long ago, though that quartz had not been in its raw state. It had been cut into the most exquisite projectile points he had ever seen, and they had been hafted to the spears of Masau, Mystic Warrior, a shaman sworn to slay the great white mammoth with them. Instead it had been Masau who was slain, and when the white chalcedony had been reddened by the blood of that most infamous and feared of warriors, the forces of Creation had somehow brought the spearheads into Cha-kwena's care. Kosar-eh's face tightened. Cha-kwena had sworn to protect the totem with those spearheads, but he had not; he had slain the great white mammoth with them, then hurled them into the deepest part of the lake in the Valley of the Dead, where no man could ever hope to find them.

Hrak was looking at him introspectively. "Do you know what is said by my people about such white rock as this? That only spearheads called forth from it will seek and find the living heart of the great white mammoth totem, and that the man who slays the totem and takes into himself the blood and flesh of Life Giver, he and all who follow him will live forever."

"The totem is dead, Hrak. The bones of the great white mammoth lie all around you. The shaman Cha-kwena killed it with spearheads cut from such rock as this, yet, although Cha-kwena lives on, nearly all who followed him are dead, and the spearheads that took the life of the totem lie beyond the reach of any man."

"Yes. It is so. And now Cha-kwena is totem. A *bad* totem. And so my people seek him, and when we find him, we will kill him. With this gift that Hrak now brings to you, we will take back the power he has stolen to use against us." He leaned closer. "Many times Tsana has asked when Hrak will call forth spearheads from the white stone. Hrak has waited. Many times this man's hands have said to his head, 'Bring us the white stone! Give us the tools for breaking and shaping and let us call forth from the core of the white rock all it is waiting to become!' Yet this man's head told his hands that they were not yet worthy of the white rock, that they must wait until they became more skilled. But when this man's eyes saw the spear of Kosar-eh, they told his head they had found the hands to work the white rock. Those hands are your hands, Black and White Warrior, not mine! So take this gift of death that the forces of Creation have brought to me for you. Only through your hands will the People of the Watching Star find the power to hunt down and destroy those who have slain your woman and children and band."

# 5

Ta-maya did not understand them, any of them. For how many days and nights was the giant going to keep vigil outside his lean-to, staring toward the mountains, waiting for Axwahtal and the others to return? And for how many days and nights would the stubborn little hunter Zakeh stay at his hunt brother's side, forcing his family to suffer because Xohkantakeh had foolishly broken with their people in order to save the life of a captive?

"They will not come back for us!" grumbled Neeracheela.

"We must follow them soon," added Shan, emerging into the light of morning dragging bed furs from her lodge. "Already there must be so much distance between us that we may have to trek all the way into the Land of Grass before we see the smoke of their fires again. And with each new dawn, I fear that our enemies may yet discover this camp. Too long have we lingered here!"

"Game is getting scarce," said Zakeh, not looking up as he gutted his latest kill: a scrawny female wolf.

"They will come back," Xohkantakeh rumbled.

"For what? Two aged hunters, less than a hand

count of girl children, and a pair of women foolish not to have wrung the neck of a useless captive when they had the chance?" Neeracheela, hands on hips, snorted the insults like a riled mare as she moved her gaze from Xohkantakeh and glared at Zakeh. "Do you hear your hunt brother, Zakeh? Since Axwahtal led the others into the mountains, the Mud Moon has risen to look at us and then turned her face away. South Wind has come to eat the snow from the ground and set rivers running free of ice in the land below. Now the Moon of Ducks Coming Back rises out of the east. And still your hunt brother waits for the others to return!"

"White Giant Winter is still on the high peaks." Xohkantakeh was adamant. "They *will* come back."

The morning sun was warm on Ta-maya's face, but as she knelt and combed snarls from her loosened hair with her good hand, she was sorry she had come out of the hut to greet the new day. She looked at the scowling giant. It was always the same. The man had about as much flexibility as the ironwood trees of her distant homeland—none at all. And Neerachecla's wrangling with him and her own man went on and on until, this morning, as on so many others before it, Zakeh reached the end of his patience and threw something at her. Yesterday it had been a pit-roasted squirrel he had been about to enjoy for his midday meal. The day before, with nothing in hand when the critical moment came, he had knelt, scooped up a fistful of muddy earth, and lobbed that. This morning it was wolf guts.

Neeracheela ducked. Shan, snapping bed furs to freshen them in the morning air, did not. Standing just behind the smaller woman, she anticipated Zakeh's release of temper a second too late. The wolf intestines hit the fur she was holding, set up a bloody purple spray as they roped around one of her wrists, and slapped her in the face. Shan's reflexes were quick; an instant later the wolf guts were flying straight back at Zakeh.

Ta-maya's jaw dropped as the two kept flinging the slimy, sloppy missile back and forth until it burst, its foul-smelling contents splattering as it fell on the ground at her knees. She heard Neeracheela burst out laughing at her expense as she scooted back, wiping the offending matter from her face and hair.

"This must stop!" the giant roared, suddenly furious.

"People stay too long in one camp, people fight like dogs," said Neeracheela with a smirk.

"Not that we have been left any dogs with which to make comparison," Shan reminded her.

Zakeh shrugged. "Dogs would make too much noise; they might draw the attention of our enemies."

"No more than these children when they fuss or cry!" exclaimed Shan, her face strained, bordering on hostile as she indicated the little ones with a snap of her head.

Ta-maya frowned. The children sat nearby in a circle, dirty-faced as always, sharing whatever it was that Shan or Neeracheela had served them for breakfast. There were three scrawny little girls—Xree, Lana, and Ika. Each girl appeared to be somewhere between four and seven winters old. She did not know their exact ages, or to which woman each child belonged; they were similarly scolded and begrudgingly fed by both. Their greasy fingers in their mouths, they had stopped eating to stare at Shan out of frightened eyes. Ta-maya felt pity for them. "They are good children! If the women of Zakeh would show a little more affection, perhaps they would not have cause to fuss or cry!"

"You tend them, then," Shan hissed.

"Yes!" Neeracheela sneered as she voiced approval of her hearth sister's challenge to the captive. "You with your limp and your 'broken wing,' it is time you did something useful in this place of little meat and much mud. Instead you lie on your back with your limbs spread wide and your woman parts bared for the penetration of your man . . . but then, it is obvious that you have yet to do even that much for him, or he would not be growling around this camp like a storm cloud incapable of releasing rain!"

Ta-maya's face flamed with shame, anger, and frustration. "Xohkantakeh does with me as he will! And whether he comes into me or not, I tell you, Neeracheela, as I tell him—he will *never* be my man! I am sworn to another . . . always and forever!"

The giant's face contorted with sudden rage. He turned to look once more toward the high, snow-clad mountains. It was obvious from his twisted, tortured expression that he had just resigned himself to what the others had been insisting all along: Axwahtal and his fellow hunters and their women were not coming back. "May the White Giant have consumed them all, for this man sees now that four-legged dogs are not the only dogs to run with their pack! Only out of fear do men turn their backs on their brothers and abandon women and children. Come! Xohkantakeh has waited long enough for them to prove what they are. Now we will turn our backs to the dogs of the Land of Grass. We will leave these high hills and return to the land across which we have come. The hunting was good to the east —and there we will at least know who our enemies are!"

Ta-maya caught her breath. Return across the land over which they had come? *Kosar-eh is there! My band is there! U-wa! Tla-nee! Joh-nee and—*

"You are Xohkantakeh's woman!" he interrupted, somehow knowing her thoughts. "And in the land to which we will now journey, if by some chance this 'always and forever' man has survived to abandon you and go there, if I see this man, I will kill him!"

Shan was more distraught than Ta-maya. "But our people dwell across the mountains. Tell him, Zakeh, that we must follow our tribe if we are to find protection from—"

"From this day," the giant growled, "Xohkantakeh and his woman will be tribe enough for him. If this is not what you would have, then go with your man and follow Axwahtal over the mountains. Xohkantakeh has not forced Zakeh to stay with him."

Zakeh's weather-shrunken features expanded as, with a shrug, he said, "Since Zakeh and Xohkantakeh were boys, we have been hunt brothers together among Shateh's people. Keepers of the sacred flame and smoke were we in the sweat lodges of Shateh's band. Now Shateh is dead. Axwahtal was not our hunt chief before the last war. Why should he be so now? Besides, Zakeh says that not to have a chief to tell him what to do is good for a change. It is good to do as he pleases. And now it pleases him to walk with his hunt brother. So let there be no more talk from women! Now let us break down our huts and prepare to move on."

It was done.

No one spoke. Xohkantakeh made Ta-maya stand aside as the others worked. Now and then she felt the eyes of Zakeh's women burning her, and once Neeracheela whispered venomously that Ta-maya was indeed blessed by the forces of Creation to have such a forgiving man in Xohkantakeh.

"If this woman were as useless as Ta-maya, no man in this world or the world beyond would insist on keeping me at his side. Your face is ruined. You walk like an old and broken thing. If you would die, Xohkantakeh would not miss you for long."

Ta-maya allowed the slur to pass, but Xohkantakeh, who overheard it, did not. He silenced the woman with a backhanded strike that sent her sprawling. When Neeracheela looked up, her mouth bloodied, Ta-maya knew that she had made yet another enemy in a world in which she had already survived far too many —and in which she no longer had any wish to survive at all.

"Do not cry, Broken Wing."

Ta-maya wiped tears from her cheeks as Ika, oldest of the little girls, came close and looked up at her out of troubled eyes.

"Broken Wing is a good woman, like Ika is a good child, yes?" The little girl smiled, displaying a missing front tooth. "Ika will take care of Broken Wing. And Xokeekokee, too!"

Despite her sadness, Ta-maya found herself smiling at the child's unsuccessful attempt to pronounce Xohkantakeh's name.

"Xokeekokee is big and growls much, but he is good, like Zakeh, who growls only a little and throws many things but sometimes brings children presents. Here. Ika will share her present with Broken Wing, but not with Xree and Lana; they are too small."

Ta-maya watched the little girl look about surreptitiously. Only when the child was certain that no one was looking did she open her robe and bring forth by the scruffs of their necks two tiny wolf pups. "Zakeh found these in the den of Mother Wolf. Mother will be meat and fur for us. Pups will be like dogs and pull our winter sledges—when they grow up, of course!"

"Wolves cannot behave as dogs and walk tamely in the camps of men, Ika."

The little girl kissed the pups. "Xokeekokee says men can be as dogs. Zakeh says wolves can be like dogs. Ika says these pups are better than both!"

The little girl's display of affection for wild creatures swept Ta-maya back to the days when she and Mah-ree were children and her little sister was always following Cha-kwena, the two of them forever playing at finding Life Giver, the great white mammoth, and calling upon its power to help them heal some wounded creature or another. The memory was so sweet that she wept to think of all that she had lost and would never see again.

"Broken Wing cries too much!" admonished Ika. "Here. Take this pup. Love this pup. You have no baby, no child. This pup needs a new mother! For him you must be strong!"

As the wolf pup licked her face and the child tittered appreciatively, Ta-maya closed her eyes. South Wind was rising with the new day. The morning air was sweet with the scent of the awakening land. With the sun warm on her face and the pup and the child close, the strangest and most wonderful of sensations moved through her, even though she could hear Xohkantakeh and Zakeh roughly commanding Neeracheela and Shan to the tasks necessary to abandon camp.

Ta-maya's eyes opened again. Kosar-eh was out there somewhere! He was *not* dead! She felt his living presence in every fiber of her being. Someday he would find her, and on that day Xohkantakeh would die, for somewhere ahead, far to the east beyond the very edge of the world, Cha-kwena and Mah-ree walked strong in the power of the sacred stone and the totem. It was their loving thoughts that had saved her life and were even now bringing her toward reunion with her band and the one man she had ever loved, *would* ever love.

"Broken Wing smiles again!" observed Ika.

"Yes, little one," Ta-maya said. "This woman smiles again."

\*      \*      \*

Kosar-eh did not smile. He was as one possessed. He sat alone all the long morning, facing into the rising sun, his knapping tools arrayed before him. Balanced on his extended palms were the pieces of white chalcedony. His arms ached from keeping them raised to the sun.

He did not speak. He did not eat or drink. He stared at the rocks. Hrak went from his fire circle, and when the man's nameless daughter came with meat, Kosar-eh sent her away with a perfunctory grunt. After that no one disturbed him. Only at the height of noon did he set the crystals down. And then, for the remainder of the day, he lifted one rock and then another, examining each again and again, turning it, holding it to his ear, flicking it with his thumb and index finger.

In a low voice Hrak explained to the curious that Black and White Warrior was finding the heart of each piece of quartz, determining the position of veins and arteries that ran through the body of the rock. Fascinated, many came close to watch, but most sensed the change in Kosar-eh, and his darkly focused intensity sent them whispering away.

At last the sun slipped behind the western ranges. The valley went blue, and shadows filled the cave. Kosar-eh set the white rocks down, rose, relieved himself, then returned to sit alone before the four chunks of perfect white quartz. *One for each of the Four Winds,* he thought. *And if the rock is generous to my questing hands, a spearhead for each dead member of my band!* The premise was as comforting as the descending night.

He pulled his sleeping robe about his shoulders and, sitting upright, made a litany of the beloved names until sleep claimed him and he drifted among the stars, hunting a white mammoth across the Sky River with spears of white crystal in his hand and the pelt of a dead coyote bleeding down his back.

"You will not kill my brother with the spears you would make of this rock!"

Kosar-eh opened his eyes. Joh-nee had crept across the cave. Now, in the light of dawn, she stood before him with all four pieces of white chalcedony clutched in her slender arms. One look at the fury in her eyes and he knew her intent; she was going to hurl the stones from the cave in a mad attempt to shatter them. He reached up toward her and said, "Joh-nee . . ."

She stepped back. "Yes. *Joh-nee,* who is sister of Cha-kwena. You may have forgotten this, but I have not. Did you think I would let you or anyone else hurt my brother?" She whirled and started for the edge of the cave.

Kosar-eh flung himself forward, grabbed her by an ankle, and pulled her back and down. She fell hard. The rocks scattered but did not break. He heard the breath go out of the girl, followed by a muffled little sob of pain. "Forgive me, child, but here . . . let me help you."

She uttered a violent little yelp of reproach as she slapped his hand away and staggered to her feet. "This girl is not a child! And this girl wants nothing from you! This girl wishes you dead!"

Kosar-eh was saddened by the curse. How brave she was, how loyal, and how totally, annoyingly impractical. He had no doubt that she would have run away long before now were it not for her love for Doh-teyah. As though Joh-nee could survive alone! And as though Doh-teyah, even now sound asleep at Ban-ya's breasts, would not survive without her. "Joh-nee, our lives have changed. You must learn to accept this. You must—"

"It is Kosar-eh who has changed!"

He nodded his head in grim assent. "Kosar-eh died beyond the Valley of the Dead with his son and his woman, Ta-maya, and brave U-wa and old Kahm-ree and little Tla-nee, on the day that his youngest son was taken from him." He paused, frowned as he saw a dark and unmistakable form winging against the pale horizon. "Look, there in the sky, do you see the teratorn? If you would seek Kosar-eh, look for him there. His life spirit rides the wind on the wings of the bird that tried to warn him of what was to come. But that was long ago. Yes, Kosar-eh *is* dead. Faith in your lying shaman brother killed him."

Tears welled in Joh-nee's eyes. "If Kosar-eh is dead, it is because he would not listen to Cha-kwena. My brother does *not* lie. The power of the sacred stone *is* true power! The totem *is* reborn! And you are not dead! You only say this to make excuses for your new women and your killing ways. Have you forgotten the blood of Cheelapat on your hands? This girl has not! Once, in the night, I heard the wind blowing from beyond this Valley of the Dead, and it seemed to be Tamaya's spirit crying out for Kosar-eh, but surely it could not have been, for if her spirit could see her man now, she would die of shame forever!"

"It is to avenge her shame that I will work this stone. Then she will know that those who sent her spirit to the world beyond have met with the stone-white wrath of—"

"Woman Slayer!" Joh-nee sobbed, then ran off to that small portion of the cave she had made her own, close to the mammoth-tooth throne of Ban-ya, where Doh-teyah slept within the embrace of Spirit Woman.

Tsana stood hidden behind the mammoth tusk closest to where Kosar-eh sat brooding. The girl's movement had awakened the chieftain, and he had not needed the instinct of a shaman to guess her intent; he had anticipated her action long before now. Head up, he smirked as he observed Kosar-eh's pained reaction

to the little girl's accusations. Slowly, so as not to be
seen by the grieving Black and White Warrior, Tsana
turned and moved across the cave, silently stepping
around dogs and slipping past screened areas of sleeping people. He did not want to be seen as he made his
way to the entrance of the sacred cavern. Yet in the
thin, shadowy light of dawn he felt as though he was
being watched. He paused, squinting over his shoulders.
All was serene; no one was awake except the brooding
man and the girl, who could not see him from where she
had disappeared to stifle her misery beneath the sleeping furs at the base of Spirit Woman's throne.

Tsana ducked quickly inside the low arch that
opened into a series of labyrinthine hollows leading
deep into the hill. The sacred cavern lay at the end of
the second tunnel. He kept a stone tallow lamp hidden
inside the entrance, along with flints, kindling, extra
wicks, and fat with which to light his way. No one any
longer went into that cold, vaulted place into which he
and his warriors had lured Shateh to his death—except
Tsana himself. It was where he found his strength.

Tsana made light. He picked up the lamp and the
makings for sustained fire and went into the darkness,
bending low to avoid hitting his head on the damp,
rough-textured ceiling. On and on he went into the cold
belly of the world, holding the lamp in one hand, sheltering the wick in the curled fingers of the other. He
knew the way; he had marked it with lines painted in
ochre and chalk. Now and then he paused, distracted by
a thin ghostly whispering in the darkness behind him; he
listened, then went on, resolved not to be disconcerted
by the all-too-familiar drafts of cold air that moved mysteriously but constantly through these subterranean cor-
ridors.

And then at last Tsana reached his destination. He
held his lamp forward. The wick shivered. The flame

gorged itself on sudden quantities of air. Light flowed into the high, wide-vaulted space ahead.

"Ah!" Tsana exhaled as he always did at the sheer wonder of the size of the sacred cavern. And, as always, he remembered how the shaman Jhadel had often sought mystic inspiration within this "womb of Mother Below," like an old bear going to ground. Tsana shook his head. He hoped the old shaman was dead, along with that irritating scrap of a boy who seemed to think he was Shateh's grandson. What good had either of them been to Tsana? Mad Ban-ya had proved shaman enough for him and his people.

His mouth tightened. The cavern was alive with memories. The wailing of the woman Ban-ya had called him into the earth to discover her entombed within this cavern. He would never understand how she had survived as long as she did after Shateh abandoned her. Mad after feeding on one of her twin infants, she had claimed to be Spirit Woman, the ghost of the mountain. Jhadel had not believed her; neither had Tsana, but he had seen in her a chance to be rid of the old shaman, who refused to do the chieftain's will. And so he had brought Ban-ya forth to the band as Cannibal Woman, Spirit Mother of the Mountain, and his people, always gullible when it came to swallowing a good tale whole, had accepted her on his word.

Tsana smiled at the memory. In her desire to keep her surviving twin alive and at her breast, Ban-ya had been as easy to manipulate as warm fat until, in a moment of temper and bad judgment, he had killed the sickly child. The death of the baby had shattered her; blank-eyed, speaking only when spoken to, she had been all but useless to him. And then, in a flash of pure inspiration, Tsana had put the blind daughter of Kosar-eh to her breast! From the moment the toddler's mouth took hold of her nipple, Ban-ya had been his again; she would obey Tsana—or see the brains of another baby bashed against the cave walls.

Immensely pleased with himself, Tsana moved forward through the cavern. He reached the far wall, and there the true wonder of the inner cave shone forth in all its glory. Long before the last war brought the People of the Watching Star to the Valley of the Dead, the band of the Red World shaman Cha-kwena had occupied the outer cave. And here, on the innermost wall of that sacred cavern, the painting Cha-kwena had created during his band's occupation of the upper cave blazed dull gold and red in the light of the lamp.

"Ah!" Again Tsana exhaled in awe as his eyes took in the savage beauty and truth of it. It was all there. The coming of First Man and First Woman from the misted realm of ice spirits into the world of living beings. Life Giver, the great white mammoth totem, leading them and their children on vast migrations across endless lands, to success in many hunts until, at last, under the ever constant eye of the Watching Star, the People fragmented and spread across the world, strangers who were at constant war with one another.

Tsana advanced slowly, his eyes fixed on the portion of the painting that held his spirit captive—the depiction of a great white mammoth rising, bloodied, from a lake, entering the belly of the matriarch of a small herd of tuskers, and emerging transformed into a little white calf that led a small band of red-painted people eastward into the face of the rising sun.

He placed his hand on the depiction of the resurrected totem and on the image that seemed to dance ahead of it—the image of a dancing shaman with the head of a coyote, wearing around his neck a talisman that could only be the sacred stone of the Ancient Ones.

"Yes . . . I know you are alive, Cha-kwena! Even

now Kosar-eh sets himself to fashion the spear that will kill you. He will lead me to the place where you have gone into the sun with the sacred stone and the totem. Yes . . . I feel the power of the newborn mammoth growing in this world. When you are dead, Cha-kwena, it will be mine, and with its flesh and blood in me I will be totem, soon and forever!"

Trembling with resolve, Tsana allowed himself to vent a laugh. He moved closer to the wall and, with his hand moving on the painted image of the shaman, confided in a whisper, "What would your Red World warrior say if he knew that on the day I left him and his captive children to the care of my war band, so that I could hunt alone, the game I sought was Man, not meat? And what would he say if I were to tell him that fresh footprints in the drifts led me to a high, north-facing hill, from which I saw the ones we sought? Too many men for my small band to attack without incurring major losses, and much too far away to follow across so much snow."

Tsana smiled obliquely. "And what do you imagine his reaction would be if I were to reveal that among the tracks of the marauders on that hill were the smaller tracks of a limping woman . . . Kosar-eh's woman. Do you think she is still alive, Yellow Wolf? Perhaps. Do you think I should tell your Red World warrior all this? No. If Kosar-eh thought there was a chance his woman lived, he would cease to be manageable. And if Tsana is to lead his people to ultimate victory over the forces of the People of the Land of Grass, as he has vowed, he needs Kosar-eh to lead him on the pathway you have taken beyond the edge of the world, Yellow Wolf, so that Tsana may take for himself and his people the ultimate power of the sacred stone and the totem."

He stood back from the wall and nodded, assuring himself that before that day arrived, the Red World captives would die—the foolish boys Kiu-neh and Kho-neh, who believed that they would always be accepted as sons of the Watching Star; and Kosar-eh, who would, by then, have outlived his usefulness, not only as a guide but as a teacher of the art of stone working; and Ban-ya. Yes, Tsana decided that he was tired of Spirit Woman. He would groom the child Sees the Wind to be shaman in her place. Why not? His people had a long tradition of female shamans, and he would have all the time he needed to make her trust and love him and accept her place under his control. By the time Doh-teyah became a woman, she would have forgotten all about the Red World family with which she had been brought as a captive to this cave—for long before that time of celebration, the one major obstacle to her forgetfulness would have been removed.

A gust of wind caused the flame on Tsana's lamp to shiver. He turned—and saw the major obstacle standing at the entrance to the cavern with a lamp of her own.

"It is true. . . . My brother did not lie." Joh-nee's eyes were huge with amazement as they stared at the portion of the sacred painting showing a little white mammoth calf leading the People into the face of the rising sun. "Why have you not brought Kosar-eh here? If he saw this, he would know that Cha-kwena did not lie! He would know that it is his lack of faith in my brother and the totem that has brought death to our band."

Tsana stared at the troublesome, distrustful little sister of the shaman. Had she heard his words about Ta-maya? His voice had been low, meant for the image on the wall and barely discernible to his own ears. Nevertheless, the sooner she was brought to the fate he had chosen for her, the better it would be for all. But it could not be now, not until after Kosar-eh led Tsana onto the path of the Red World shaman. On that day, when he led his warriors out of the cave, then, to assure victory over the power of Yellow Wolf, Joh-nee—the living flesh and blood of Cha-kwena—would be sacrificed to Thunder in the Sky. Ban-ya would make the offering; she had performed the ritual before without flinching from it. He would leave trusted men and women behind to see to it that after the sacrifice the girl's heart and flesh were shared by all, her body correctly flayed, and her skin fashioned into a cloak, which, upon his return, he would wear until the eventual ordination of a new high priestess of the Watching Star.

Tsana was careful to keep his eyes half closed as he approached the child and knelt before her. How small and vulnerable she looked, standing wan and shaken, her pathetic rag of a doll clutched close to her flat little breast with one hand, a stone lamp trembling in the other. As on the day he took Joh-nee's hand amidst the ruin of her band's encampment, he reached for her hand now and stroked her fingers in the way of a caring friend. "It is a matter of faith, girl. A matter of trust. As you have followed this light to me. You want to see your brother again, do you not?"

Suspicious, Joh-nee nodded a hesitant affirmation.

"If Kosar-eh sees this painting, he will know that all you have just said is true," said Tsana, thinking fast as he spoke. "Then, instead of leading us to find the sacred stone and the totem and the good shaman Cha-kwena, Kosar-eh's heart will crack with grief. He will die of the knowledge that the blame for all that has befallen his band must be heaped upon his own back."

Still suspicious, Joh-nee shook her head. "You want to kill the totem. You want to eat its flesh and drink its blood, so that you will have the power to kill your enemies. This girl heard you say it!"

"When?"

"In the cave. When we first came. Long ago. Joh-nee remembers!"

"Ah." So she had not overheard his most recent pronouncements. "The words were for poor Kosar-eh's ears! To put the barb of vengeance under the weight of his grief. Vengeance is what drives most men, New Sister. As for Tsana, yes, he seeks the totem. And the sacred stone. He is a man who has been victorious in war but who heads a tribe whose true shaman has abandoned us. Poor Spirit Woman. Even so young a girl as Joh-nee can see that we have taken pity on that sad woman whose mind had flown her body until little Sees the Wind brought happiness to her once again. Even so, my people are heartened to think that perhaps, in her, they at least have some kind of a shaman! And Joh-nee must also see that Tsana has allowed Kosar-eh to assuage his grief in ways that are distasteful to me and to my people. We need Kosar-eh to lead us to Cha-kwena. Tsana would council with your shaman brother. He is strong in the power of the totem and sacred stone of our ancestors. Tsana would seek peace in that power."

Joh-nee stared at him. She was very young, yet the man had spoken to her as to an adult and with an earnestness that was unsettling; she did not know how to react. "Why should this girl believe Tsana when he admits that he has filled his mouth with lies?"

"Little sister of Yellow Wolf, why would Tsana lie to one whom he has taken to himself as though she were his own sister?"

She frowned. Tsana could be a charming man; he was charming now, but Joh-nee had seen ugly things since coming to live within his stronghold. She was more suspicious than ever. "This girl does not know. But she thinks you are."

Tsana measured the moment carefully. At last he said gently, "Then tell Kosar-eh what you have seen.

Call out his name. Summon him here. The cavern will carry your voice to the outer cave. He will hear. All will hear. They will come. Kosar-eh will come. But if that good man dies of the agony brought on by what he sees, the fault will be yours, New Sister, not Tsana's."

Joh-nee bit her lip. She thought long and hard. She did not call.

Beyond the edge of the world, Cha-kwena dreamed of wolves and leaping cats, of a great bear coming from the earth beneath falling stars, of phantoms rising out of red mists to become painted warriors, and of a spear-carrying young woman standing high within a dark gorge, her body clad in a bearskin, her firelit face staring toward him through time.

"Mah-ree!" Cha-kwena called her name as he sat upright, startled to see that while the little white mammoth was happily trunking down tender new leaves from a streamside stand of willow trees, a coyote was looking at him from the far side of the ring of stones that he had made to shelter last night's cooking fire.

"Ah, Cha-kwena . . . I see that you are still wandering the forest with your back to the rising sun. It is good that you have set yourself on this return journey into the world of men. And it is good that you have brought the totem with you. Ah, yes. It *is* a good thing," said Coyote, licking its mouth as though in anticipation of a meal.

"Not wise, Cha-kwena. Not wise, not wise, not wise! Do not listen to Trickster!"

The young shaman looked up, startled again, this time by the chortling run of words that had come from the beak of a molting owl perched high amidst the willows.

"Go back over the edge of the world, stupid man!" rasped the bird.

And then a gust of morning wind rose suddenly from the south, blowing a fine, gritty alluvial dust through the forest and into Cha-kwena's eyes. He closed them tight, cursed the wind, and allowed moisture to rise beneath his lids to wash away the minuscule particles of decomposing glacial rubble. The process took a few moments. His eyes were still smarting when, at last, he opened them and saw that both the owl and coyote were gone. He fingered residual moisture and dust from the corners of his eyes, rubbed them, then looked again. The absence of the furred and feathered twosome confirmed his suspicion that he had dreamed them. He sighed, rose, stretched, and looked around for more tangible signs of mystic portent, but if there were any, he could not recognize them.

Cha-kwena scanned the surrounding forest. Since turning his back to the lake and setting himself and the little white mammoth into the forest, he had been lost for at least ten sleeps and knew it. If he was at last seeing the conflicting ghosts of Coyote and old grandfather Hoyeh-tay's helping animal spirit, Owl, in his dreams, he was certain that these conjurings had more to do with wishful thinking than true Vision. After all, without the sacred stone to guide him, shaman though he was, he still had only his instincts and experiences as a hunter and tracker to rely upon.

And yet he *had* been seeing ghosts of late—the ghosts of the departing White Giant Winter, wind-blasted trees and north-facing patches of discolored snow, still whispering as they died away into greening earth; and the ghosts of his own longing to be back under cold, windy skies, to be walking in the great canyon at the edge of the world, to be exploring its vast, stony outwash plain, crossing its never-melting snowfields.

Cha-kwena's heart quickened. He found it strange

that he, a man born to a distant Red World of towering buttes and dry, pinyon-shadowed hills, should have been at such ease in that land of cold barrens beyond the edge of the world. He had been lonely there, and his spirit had bled for want of his woman and band. But it was as though some unknown part of himself had dwelled under those cold skies before, hunted and lived as brother to animals he had never seen but had only heard of in the tales from time beyond beginning, told by the shamans of his tribe on the sacred blue mesas. Magic tales! Stories that struck fire to young, unformed minds like sunlight striking color into clear ice! Tales of First Man and First Woman dwelling in a land of snow at the edge of a frozen sea, hunting hook-nosed antelope and stag moose, caribou and musk ox, until the ever-battling Brothers of the Sky fell to earth out of the Watching Star to bring war and death to the world below, and Life Giver, the great white mammoth, was born to lead the People to safety and immortality in the face of the rising sun.

Cha-kwena looked up, watched the little white mammoth stripping leaves from the trees, and found himself smiling. This green maze of a forest might well be confounding his efforts to return to his band, but he was confident that, using the movement of sun and moon to guide him, he would find his way back to them in time.

Soon he would hold his little girl-of-a-woman in his arms again and, for the first time in his life, tell her how much he loved and needed her. "It will be so!"

Soon he would hear the sweet laughter of children and hold his sister, Joh-nee, on his knee as he shared stories of his adventures while Kosar-eh's boys and old Kahm-ree listened, rapt, and his mother, U-wa, allowed pride in a long lost son to shine in her eyes once more. "It will be so!"

Soon, with the little white mammoth calf at his side, he would face Kosar-eh again, and see faith and hope in the promises of the Ancient Ones rekindled within that good man's heart forever. "It will be so!"

And then he would lead his band through the forest and beyond the edge of the world to a new life in the cold barrens, where the game of their ancestors was plentiful and the warring tribes of Man would never find them. "It *must* be so!"

A deep and all-pervasive sense of well-being expanded within Cha-kwena. The next time he lay with his little girl-of-a-woman, truly she *would* become a woman in his arms, for never again would he have cause to refrain from yielding to her the outpouring gift of his maleness for fear that pregnancy would make her vulnerable in a land where the warriors of People of the Watching Star and the People of the Land of Grass hunted the members of his band like ravening wolves. He smiled. He and Mah-ree *would* make new life together! His mother, U-wa, would rejoice in the grandchildren she so yearned to have! And the children of Kosar-eh and Cha-kwena would grow up and grow old together in a land where war was an unwelcome stranger and their People would live forever.

The young shaman's smile broadened. He had so much to look forward to! Until then, he would not allow himself to be discontent. There was good hunting for him and rich browse for the calf in this forest, and in the pale, shaggy body of the future tusker, the spirit of the totem and the hope of his People lived on under his care.

"For how long?" The question came on a gust of wind and struck the shaman's heart like an invisible spear hurled by the shadowing wings of the owl that flew from the trees above him.

Cha-kwena looked up, frowning; there was nothing

to see—only the green canopy of wind-stirred forest, only dark branches reaching for a sky that he could barely see.

"Come, Cha-kwena! Come walking into the light."

He snapped to his feet. Coyote was back on the other side of his fire circle. "You!" he exclaimed but, somehow, was not surprised.

"We have always been brothers, you and I!" Coyote reminded him. "Come, I say! Your little girl-of-a-woman *is* waiting for you. Follow this Yellow Wolf, and soon Shaman will be amazed by all that he will see!"

# PART V

# FOUR WINDS

"You are not on this earth, you are within this stone. No wind may reach you; no iceberg may crush you, for it will break in pieces against the edge of the stone. . . ."

—Chukchi incantation
*Peoples of the Earth* by Douglas Botting

## 1

Mah-ree was elated.

The forest lay behind them. They had reached the heights of the gorge at last. "Come!" she cried to Jhadel and Warakan, turning her back on the dark land of trees where so much sadness had come to her people. A world of light and open space lay ahead, and beyond that—dared she even think it—a land called Home! Would she ever see it again . . . with her man at her side? Perhaps it was too much to hope for.

"Our enemies dwell beyond this gorge," Jhadel mumbled, swinging himself from his travois and, using his staff as a balancing rod, fighting his way to his feet. "Our enemies hunt and make war and slaughter captives in the land below this gorge!"

Mah-ree was weary of the Old One's objections. She did not reply. As she scrambled up and over familiar lichen-clad boulders upon which she and Cha-kwena had spent many a long, starlit night together, she found herself breathless with excitement. She willed herself to remember only good things as she faced into the west wind and at last stared across lands over which she and her band had followed her shaman and the sacred herd of mammoth many a long moon ago.

"Ah!" she exclaimed, pointing down as happy memories set her heart pounding and brought tears to her eyes. "I can see the river! And there is the cottonwood grove where we made our last camp and feasted on the sweet meat of elk before coming here. And look! As before, there is game . . . so much game!"

It was all as Mah-ree remembered: the broad, shallow river cutting endless silver loops across a high, undulating plateau, with islands of tall, sheltering stands of trees here and there. Far beyond the plain, distant ranges eternally whitened by snow rose along the horizon. And between those far peaks and the plateau, dropping away into a vast, tawny sink to the west, were the badlands over which her people had fled for their lives ahead of Shateh's warriors.

Her brow furrowed. How far had they come, those tall, painted men with their war dogs and their unjust anger against her shaman? And what of Kosar-eh and her sisters and her band? Not once during the passage of all the long, cold winter moons had Mah-ree glimpsed the orange glimmer of firelight in the storm-clouded lands below.

"Perhaps by now," she hoped aloud, wanting West Wind to carry her words to the forces of Creation, "they have returned across the badlands and through the mountains—Kosar-eh leading my band southwest toward the Red World of our ancestors, and our enemies journeying into the northern grasslands of the two tribes, where they can live and fight together forever—where they will be no threat to us!"

Jhadel, panting and wheezing, emerged onto the level ground beside her. With his staff wobbling in one shaking hand and Warakan gripping him by the crook of an elbow, the old man oozed against a boulder to steady himself. He sucked air a moment before he squinted off, then observed grimly, and not without apparent surprise, "White Giant Winter still lives on the high mountains!"

"White Giant *always* lives there," Mah-ree stated, then with a wistful smile confided, "When I was a small girl, the wise men among my people in the faraway Red World, on the far side of that range, used to say that sometimes—even on the hottest summer day if the Four Winds held their breath and the air was very still and clear—a shaman's eye could fly with Golden Eagle and see to the edge of the world, where White Giant lay sleeping on the mountains that held up the sky. Cha-kwena saw White Giant. And afterward my shaman promised us all that one day he would travel to the great mountains and with his spear pick snow and ice from the snaggly teeth of White Giant Winter and send it running away into the sun, where it would surely melt forever!"

"Ha!" Warakan was neither amused nor impressed when Mah-ree spoke of Cha-kwena.

Jhadel eyed the sun, fixed in his mind its position relative to time and season, then looked away, shaking his head. "There is too much snow for now. Do you see? It lies not only on the peaks but on the shoulders of the range and well below the tree line, deep in the canyons and passes."

"May White Giant sleep long and deeply on those mountains, for as long as he is there, if our enemies have returned to the land of their ancestors, they may not be able to come back!" Mah-ree's mouth tightened with satisfaction.

"Hmm." Jhadel was still shaking his head. "And if our enemies wintered on *this* side of the range, they may still be here."

Warakan hunkered on his heels and, with his left hand pressed to his throat, stared ahead from slitted eyes. "If our enemies *are* out there, we will see their fires from the gorge by night and may even be able to catch wind of them by day. We will know where they are."

"And where to avoid them!" Mah-ree turned and stared hotly into the boy's long dark eyes. They were steady and cutting sharp, full of the roiling, self-focused passions she believed she knew all too well. Yet somehow they were closed to her. "You will not make war on them yet, Warakan. We have come here out of concern for Jhadel, and you will not put him at risk. Until we can return for the sacred stone, or my shaman comes from the forest with it and the totem, this woman will do nothing to provoke the forces of Creation in this land!"

Warakan looked up and said evenly, "Warakan will protect his woman."

Mah-ree's brows rose. The youth was impossible! "With what? The fine new spear you have yet to make for me? This woman is beginning to think that Warakan will never find stone of a quality to suit his 'skill,' because if he does, this woman will see that he has no skill at all!"

The boy's eyes held steady on her face. "Warakan has found a stone that suits him," he replied obliquely, then turned away to stare into the west, his thoughts his own.

They rested only a little while. With Jhadel dozing happily in the revitalizing light of the sun, it did not take long for the boy and young woman to heft and drag their belongings from the forest floor. Working together, they soon raised a lean-to among a gathering of boulders and then stood together, facing into the setting sun, watching long, tender shadows of purple and blue fill the hollows in distant hills and ranges.

"My brother is down there somewhere, hunting in the tall grass," Warakan said.

"Yes. I too have seen his tracks and sign. For a while I feared we might catch up with him . . . or he with us." Mah-ree crossed her arms over her chest and ran her hands up and down the thick dark fur of her bearskin. "This woman would not want to kill another of the bear kind."

The boy eyed her with resentment. "This hunter would not let you."

She looked at him from under a speculatively raised brow. "And perhaps, then, it is out of fear for your brother's life that you have failed to make a spear for me?"

Warakan's chin went up; he took the opportunity she gave him. "It is!" he lied, and squatted, resting his forearms across his thighs as he gazed at the world below. "Look . . . game comes to the river to drink."

"And birds settle onto every pool and shallow. Listen! You can hear them! Cranes and herons, and swans, too! And geese and ducks and fat crested grebes, and look . . . there. Do you see where the water seems overrun with black ants? Red-eyed coots!"

Warakan was amazed by her enthusiasm. He did not care about birds; among his people any feathered creature short of an eagle had always been considered meat fit only for women.

"There were many fat fish in that river when my people camped there under the Dry Grass Moon. Perhaps now, under the Moon of Ducks Coming Back, it will be the same," she declared hopefully.

Warakan made a face. Fish was famine food, fit only for starving times—or, he conceded a little sheepishly, for hungry boys following bears through unfamiliar parts of a forest.

"Do you see where the river widens and grows

shallow, where it allows its flow to be slowed and gentled by reeds?" Mah-ree was holding her hand out, gesturing wide. "There will be snakes there, long and meaty and sweet of flesh! And tender cattail shoots! And frogs and salamanders and many eggs left by mothering birds, and—"

"Eggs? Frogs? Salamanders?" Jhadel had come from his nap. As he paused beside the two young people, it was apparent that rest, warmth, and the dry west wind had visibly refreshed him. Nevertheless, his face showed revulsion as he asked with undisguised incredulity, "Did I hear this woman say that she would eat frogs and salamanders and the eggs of birds?"

Mah-ree nodded. "And fish and snake eggs, too. And the nut-sweet grubs that can be found under the old, peeling bark of cottonwoods. It is good food! Red World food."

"Like lizards?" blasted the old man.

"Yes," she affirmed, head high, making no apology. "Like lizards."

"Blucch!" Warakan's exclamation was a gargle of pure disgust.

Mah-ree appraised him thoughtfully. A space of several breaths passed before she said quietly, and without even a hint of disdain, "Wise One has said that Mah-ree of the Red World and Warakan of the Two Tribes are First Man and First Woman reborn through Bear. Warakan, who has mothered a bear and names him Brother, has made it quite clear to this woman that he believes Wise One is right! And so this woman says that Warakan should not make rude noises at one who eats as Bear eats—of the flesh of all green growing things, of seeds and spores and black-gilled fungi, and of all creatures that yield themselves in every form to be food for her mouth!"

"Eat as you will, you are *not* a bear!" he scoffed.

"Believe as you will," she retorted. "But once you were not so certain of just what this woman was. Perhaps you should not be so certain now. Perhaps one day, in response to your arrogance, she will rise up and *become* a bear—an angry bear that will swipe out at you even as your brother raised his paw against Jhadel!"

Warakan's mouth dropped open. He was astounded. Never could he have imagined Mah-ree capable of such a threat against him.

Jhadel chuckled. Impressed by the young woman's show of temper and amused by the boy's stunned reaction to it, he shook his head and "tsked" a gentle reproach. "Warakan has met his match in this Talking Bear! It seems that not all Red World people are passive grub eaters who speak a bloodless tongue."

Now it was Mah-ree who "tsked" a reproach. "In the faraway land of this woman's ancestors, war was even more of a stranger to us than rain. Yet Life Giver, the great white mammoth totem, walked in our land. The sacred stone of the Ancient Ones was in the care of our Red World shamans. Until the warriors of the two tribes came, seeking captives and making war upon us to steal these things for themselves. They told us how we must eat and how we must live, until there was nothing left for us except to run away and hide from them, or fight and die for what the forces of Creation had seen fit to put in our care in the first place."

Jhadel's face sagged around the high hump of his tattooed nose. "The mammoth had vanished from our land. Lest our people be forced to turn to lesser meat, we sought the totem and the stone."

"Among those unfit to possess them!" Warakan injected in as superior a tone as he could muster.

"You should not mock or denigrate that which you do not know or understand," the young woman replied coolly. "In the Red World of this woman's ancestors

there is little grass and less water to sustain big meat
animals. Yet the forces of Creation have spoken to my
people as they have spoken to the people of Warakan
and Jhadel. They have shown us the way that we must
live—in the Red World, on whatever the Four Winds
send into the snares and winnowing baskets of our
women, and onto the throwing sticks of our men; in the
Land of Grass, on the long-horned bison that once
passed across your hunting grounds as plentifully as the
coots now settle on the river below; and in the land that
lies beneath the Watching Star, on the meat of mammoth taken in such numbers that now the great tuskers
have nearly vanished."

She paused again, then rushed on angrily. "No!
This woman has seen the hunting ways of the two tribes.
The forces of Creation could *not* have taught your ancestors to hunt like that! It is an offense against Father
Above and Mother Below to take all of a herd, to kill
and kill until there is not one animal left alive, and then
to glut yourselves on only the best meat, leaving the rest
for wolves and foxes and the meat-eating birds of the
sky! If the mammoth and long-horned bison have all
but vanished from the hunting grounds of your people,
it is no surprise to this woman, who has seen your hunters offend life itself by singling out pregnant animals to
be speared, so that they might gorge themselves on the
flesh of an unborn calf or foal or—"

"It is the tenderest meat!" exclaimed Warakan; he
was becoming very annoyed with her. "Everyone knows
this! Except Red World people. And how is eating unborn meat more offensive to the forces of Creation than
sucking unborn birds out of their shells, or popping the
grubs of unborn insects between your teeth?"

Mah-ree stared, brought short by his last question;
it was obvious from her expression that she had never
considered either to be "living" in the full sense of the

word, nor was she ready to do so now. "It is not the same!"

"Of course it is the same." Jhadel corrected her matter-of-factly. "But this is of no importance. The bird, the fish, the limbless and many-legged thing, the beasts of paw and hoof and claw, the fungi in the excrement beside a bison wallow, the green growing things . . . even lichen on rock. Life must eat life to sustain and make new life! Since time beyond beginning, it has been so. This is the great Circle of Wisdom, the great Joy and the great Sadness, the great and unchangeable Teaching that all must learn and abide."

Mah-ree shivered.

Warakan frowned up at the old man. "Rock is not alive—unless it is the sacred stone of the ancestors, in which the spirits of First Man and First Woman reside."

"Tell that to the lichen that eats rock, and to the big-antlered deer that eats only lichen, and to the biting fly that fattens on blood drawn from that deer, and to the bird that eats that fly, and to the fang-toothed cat that eats that bird, and to this man and young woman who stand before Warakan now! Are we not strong with life because we have eaten the meat of the fang-toothed cat that has eaten the bird that has eaten the fly that has eaten of the deer that has eaten lichen that eats rock?" The run of words left Jhadel breathless. In the rising wind of impending sunset, he was quaking like an aspen as he held fast to his staff and added breathily, "The sacred stone of the ancestors is a fragment of the bones of First Man and First Woman. It is a stone like no other. It has power like no other. But all rock is alive. Any man who makes his own stone weapons and tools for his women will tell you that the spirits of each individual rock sing in his hands to guide him to the forms they will or will not take as his hammerstone releases them into new lives and purposes."

"Kosar-eh has spoken these words to this woman," Mah-ree affirmed.

Jhadel nodded, pleased by her revelation. "It is a knowing passed down from First Man to the males of all tribes, a sharing that comes to us from the time beyond beginning and proves to this man's mind that in that long-gone time of eternal winter, the People *were* indeed of one band."

Warakan ignored the old man's statement as he scowled with disbelief of the young woman. "Males do not speak about such things to females!"

"Kosar-eh of the Red World has spoken so to *this* female!" Mah-ree insisted with her nose at a tilt. "And if Warakan believes that rock has no living spirit, then Jhadel is wrong to believe that the sacred stone of the Ancient Ones could ever be for him, and it is obvious to this woman why Warakan has yet to make a spearhead to replace the one his brother shattered—his hands cannot communicate his will to rock, for his ears must always have been closed to those wise men among his people who have attempted to teach him such knowledge!"

Warakan bristled against a partial truth and would have defended himself by spouting off about his days and nights in the encampments of Shateh, when he had tried so hard to win the favor of the great war chief by learning those things he had failed to master among his native tribe, but Jhadel put an end to this intent.

The old man was still nodding; if he had heard the combative exchange between the two young people, he gave no sign of it as he continued to articulate his previous thoughts. "When a man takes rock into his hand, he is touching the skin of Mother Below. In time beyond beginning, lightning—which is the silver, many-forked woman-pleaser of Father Above—penetrated deep into Mother Below's flesh of stone. And with this mating of earth and sky, life came forth from living rock, a thing of spirit and also of flesh, a thing that must eternally feed upon itself in order to re-create itself again and again . . . always and forever!"

"And so the tribes *must* make war upon one another!" exclaimed Warakan, taking the Old One's rambling to what seemed not only a logical conclusion but a teaching that he could warm to. "It is wrong for Jhadel to dream of peace in a world where all things war upon one another to survive."

Again Mah-ree shivered. "No. It is wrong for one kind to feed upon its own. Wolves feed upon deer, not upon other wolves. In the land of this woman's ancestors, the stone heads of our hunters' lances were for antelope, not for other men."

"Until the People of the Watching Star came and taught you better," Warakan reminded her, smirking.

She glared at him. "Ah, you are beyond reason, a true son of the Watching Star! Look at what war has brought to the tribes. Sorrow! Endless mourning! Is this what feeds your spirit, Warakan? Has your spirit not been saddened by the sight of bereaved people going hungry in once-rich hunting grounds, where the foolish, greedy hunters of the two tribes have killed and killed until the last beast in every herd of bison and mammoth is no more? And does your heart not weep along with those who mourn their dead as the men of the two tribes endlessly war upon their brothers and sisters in a world where Death will come to us all soon enough?"

Warakan was suddenly both irked and edgy; as far as he was concerned, the conversation was going in circles, and no matter where he found himself in the loop of words, he was on the down side of criticism and sobering implications that soured his mood. Impatient and ill-at-ease with questions he would just as soon not answer, he rose and pointed off across glorious sunset

vistas of open land and sky, attempting to guide the
day-end talk from gloom toward optimism. "The sun
disappears beyond the distant peaks! When was the last
time any of us saw a sunset that was not furred by trees?
Ah! This is fine. This is a good thing, a beautiful thing.
Feel the west wind! Smell the open plain, the grass and
the river and the game below—"

"The wind grows chill," Jhadel interrupted, turning
away from the sun and tottering back toward the lean-
to. "This day must now die so that a new night may be
born, but with tomorrow's dawn, the coming darkness
will give up its life so that the sun may be born again."

"Always and forever," assured Mah-ree.

"Aiee! Enough of such talk!" snapped the boy,
rolling his eyes in despair of them as he watched Mah-
ree slip an arm around the old man's waist so that she
might steady his faltering step as together they moved
toward the shelter within the boulders.

"With the birth of tomorrow's sun, this woman and
Warakan will seek the magic flower that will make our
Wise One strong again, will we not, Warakan?"

He glowered at Mah-ree. She was looking at him
over her shoulder. Her face was beautiful in the glow of
sunset, but her eyes were filled with worry and her statement had not been a question; it had been a command.

"Warakan *knows* where that flower grows!" he informed her loftily, his nerves prickling with resentment
at the way she constantly reverted to the misbegotten
idea that the number of her years gave her the right to
claim authority over him. "Warakan does not need a
talking bear from the Red World to help him find it.
Talking Bear is old. Talking Bear must stay here and rest
with 'her' Wise One. Together they can talk about the
days of their youth . . . if they can remember back so
far!"

Mah-ree's eyes narrowed, but it was obvious that

she deemed his insult below consideration. With a toss
of her head, she turned away and guided Jhadel into the
lean-to.

Warakan found himself alone in the fading red
glow of sunset. He did not like it. He could hear low
talk coming from inside the shelter—the old man's
voice thin and wraithlike, whispering imperatively of future unity and of a lasting peace among the three tribes;
the young woman's voice low and conciliatory, soothing
as a healing salve. Once again the boy felt excluded.
And then he was angry. Why did Mah-ree never speak
to him in that special tone of affection and respect that
she reserved for Jhadel?

Warakan pivoted on his heels and stepped boldly to
the rim of the gorge. He looked down upon the world,
and suddenly he smiled. This was how Golden Eagle
must see the land of men . . . from the top of the
mountains, from above all but the sun and stars. His
hand moved to touch the eagle feather braided into his
hair, and as his fingers strayed along the sleek shaft of
the plume, he felt a shock of kinship with the raptor. It
was a good feeling, a heady feeling, almost as nourish-
ing as red meat taken hot from a kill. Emboldened by it,
he reminded himself that he was Warakan, grandson of
the great war chief Shateh! Let women and old men
speak "wisdom" that emasculated the spirit and whined
for peace in a world at constant war. Warakan would
not acknowledge such wisdom! Not when those who
had betrayed and slain his grandfather still lived and
laughed and, by their very existence, mocked him in the
world below.

"Life eats life!" he snarled to them, allowing West
Wind to take his words, to carry them away to those
upon whom he had sworn vengeance. "Someday
Warakan *will* eat his enemies!"

The words were sweet, more satisfying than meat.

Yet as dusk yielded to darkness it occurred to him that he was hungry. Under intensifying starlight he waited for Mah-ree to summon him to the lean-to or come out offering an apology and, even better, something to eat.

Mah-ree did not call. She did not come. Within the lean-to, she was singing a slow, dulcet song, no doubt to ease the old man into untroubled dreams.

"Mah-ree does not care about Warakan," the boy said with self-pitying recalcitrance. "Talking Bear will be Warakan's woman someday, but now she cares only for Jhadel and her cursed Yellow Wolf."

Growling to himself, he sat down, crossed his legs, and resolved to pass the night alone. He could not bring himself to go to the lodge and ask for food when it was Mah-ree's duty to bring it to him! Warakan was of warrior stock; he had fasted before and would not starve. The stars would keep him company—and *they* would not argue with him.

The boy looked up, pivoted on his buttocks to take in the vast, glimmering sweep of the Sky River. So many stars! They were like old friends looking down at him out of the night—the sparkling, multicolored little cluster of eternally gossiping Many Old Women; the ever-battling Twin Brothers of the Sky; the curving body of the Great Snake; and, close to the head of that star beast, the glinting, constant eye of the Watcher.

A coldness expanded within Warakan. He did not want to look at that star, not yet. He turned away from the north, and his gaze followed the outreaching star paws of the Great Bear to where Little Bear walked close beside its larger brother.

"Ah!" sighed the boy, suddenly lonely for his cub. "Bear Brother, we are both alone this night. But we will meet again soon. And all will be as it was between us!"

The words were comforting until, far away within the forest behind him, a fang-toothed cat raised its voice in screeching ululation. Warakan listened. He wondered if the animal cried because it was the last of its kind in the world. Recalling his unsettling conversation with Mah-ree and Jhadel, he said, "Impossible!" and turned from the stars to look at the world below.

The land was submerged in darkness. If the campfires of wandering tribes burned on the plain or in the hollows of distant ranges, Warakan could not see them. For now, at least, he was glad. He knew that one who could not yet fashion a decent spearhead for a woman could not hope to fight and win against men— yet.

"The powers of the sacred stone will teach me," he said as, holding his face into the wind, he breathed in the sweet scent of the land. He could hear animals grazing far below. "So many!" he exclaimed, but would not speak aloud the names of the varying species lest the wind take his words, alert potential prey to the presence of a hunter, and send the herds scattering across the plain before he had a chance to reach them. With an exhalation of longing, his left hand went burrowing under his tunic. Holding the sacred stone tightly, he willed his thoughts across the miles.

*Forces of Creation, hear the prayer of this hunter!*
*Pronghorn!*
*Elk!*
*Camel!*
*Horse!*
*And bison, too!*
*May the forces of Creation keep you where you are this night, animal brothers and sisters of this world! Drink deeply of cool water and browse on sweet green grass through the time of stars and moon. Fill your bellies. Rub noses together and talk the talk, and then dream the dreams of your kind. In the morning this boy will come to you! In the morning you will decide among you which of*

*you will be meat for Warakan, Jhadel, and Mah-ree when the sun goes down tomorrow! For by the powers of the sacred stone of the Ancient Ones, who have set this boy upon the trail of Bear Brother and revealed to him the way that his cub has gone, one of you—or more—will die upon the bear-bone staves of Warakan! And then, on the rich red meat and blood of your kind, Jhadel will grow strong again. Not on magic flowers. Not on fish or birds or other woman meat. But on the food of warriors!*

**2**

He went before dawn, while Mah-ree and Jhadel were still fast asleep. With his bear-bone staves in one hand, the sacred stone around his neck, and his body warm in his bearskin robe, Warakan descended from the heights down a long slope of precipitous scree. He moved cautiously in the dark, trying to make as little sound as possible. This was no easy task. Now and then, despite his best efforts to prevent it, his moccasins slipped on the steep, pebble-strewn slope, causing earth and rocks to avalanche.

The boy looked back up the gorge, half expecting to see Mah-ree or Jhadel silhouetted against the stars. He knew that one of them would call him back. Neither would approve of his hunting alone. He remembered the night of the death of the fang-toothed cat and cringed. Then resolve hardened his heart. This time he had not gone off alone in anger—or for any reason other than to serve his band. He was hunting for them, for his woman and Wise One! They would need meat in the days ahead, and he would fulfill their need and be back to boast of his success. In the meantime, with the lean-to set among the protective boulders, they would not be at risk from predators while he was away.

Warakan went on. Twice a sudden sound made him pause: the snap of a dried branch somewhere in a broken stand of trees up ahead, and then the clatter and chink of sliding stones loosed by feet other than his own. He tensed, hefted a stave, held his breath, and listened. Moments passed, and still he waited, expecting the mate of the fang-toothed cat Mah-ree had killed to come hurtling at him from the darkness. Far below, a horse whinnied somewhere along the river, but Warakan heard no fear in it. The gorge was silent.

The boy swallowed hard and hurried on his way. The snappings and slidings had most likely been caused by creatures whose comings and goings did not concern him—night-feeding rabbits or mice, a pack rat scurrying in or out of its nest of sticks, or a mountain sheep skittering across the scree. But then larger predators came to mind—until he was back to the fearful image of the great fang-toothed cat. Dry-mouthed with dread, he cut a wide half-circle around the trees and kept to open ground as best he could. The horse might be grazing undisturbed by the river, and Mah-ree and Jhadel were no doubt sleeping securely within the lean-to on the heights, but Warakan—despite his proud lineage and the comfort afforded by the sacred stone—was vulnerable to predators and knew it.

He was not sure when he first noticed that the slope beneath his feet was leveling, but it was growing light, and he was grateful. Able to see, he no longer felt so open to attack, especially since the land across which he walked was now familiar. It was across these high plains that he, Jhadel, and the cub had followed old mammoth sign, nicks in trees, and piles of charred stones, which told them that others—the followers of Yellow Wolf—had passed this way before. Reappraising these signs of passage, Warakan's reaction was the same as it had been when he first saw them: Had Yellow Wolf wanted his enemies to follow him? Or had the cursed Red World shaman and his band been confident that no one would ever dog their trail beyond the edge of the world?

The latter question caused the boy to smile.

*Perhaps, until the newborn totem grows once more into the mature power of the great white mammoth, Trickster does not always make the right decisions. Perhaps he is not invincible.* With his free hand touching the talisman at his throat, Warakan laughed aloud as he realized that his thoughts must indeed be true. "The sacred stone of the ancestors is no longer Cha-kwena's! Thanks to his disobedient Red World woman, it is Warakan's, as she will be Warakan's! Do you hear, Yellow Wolf? Do you hear, spirits of Shateh and Masau? Yah hay! Warakan walks strong in the power of the Ancient Ones! Behold all that Warakan shall do this day!"

The wind took his proclamation and carried it across the miles, making him suddenly feel a little less omnipotent. He heard the whinnying of the horse again, and this time he did hear fear in the sound. Dust rose from several places upon the plain and along the river. Warakan shook his head. He was glad that Mah-ree was not beside him, for surely she would have spoken out—justly—to name him Fool.

The boy waited. Slowly the dust settled on the plain, and just as slowly morning light spread across the land. Warakan noticed that the lush green of spring grass was already fading toward gold; the color spoke to him of the lack of rain on this side of the gorge. Staring west and north, he slitted his eyes against invasive brightness as sunlight sparkled on distant ice-mantled summits. Jhadel was right. The White Giant sprawled low and heavy upon the mountains. How many bright springtime mornings would come and go before winter would retreat?

Gazing at the frozen wastes of glacier-weighted mountains, he recalled Jhadel's tales of the time beyond beginning in which First Man and First Woman fought to survive against eternal winter in a land of ice. Was it possible, since Wise One insisted that Warakan and Mah-ree were First Man and First Woman reborn, that those times of cold were about to return? The question was disturbing. After just coming through the longest, coldest, most miserable winter he could remember, Warakan had no wish to consider it.

A cool, dry wind was rising at his back. It felt good, healing, and almost as soothing to his spirit as the sound of Mah-ree's voice when she sang her low, quiet Red World songs to pass the time. Warakan cocked his head. Since when was he soothed by the songs of Talking Bear? They were always gifts to Jhadel, not to him!

With a new day growing all around him, Warakan's heart softened toward Mah-ree. He could not fault her for being concerned about Wise One. The old man was failing; they both knew it. The boy was glad she had pressed him into leaving the forest and seeking the sun for Jhadel's sake. He was certain that beyond the gorge, all was still dark and damp. He was so grateful to be on the far side of that dark woodland that he almost shouted with joy, but this time he held his tongue. He looked behind to the heights of the gorge; it would be midmorning before the disk of the sun showed above the summit. In the meantime, in the cool of morning, Warakan would hunt! And tonight, if the forces of Creation looked with favor upon his intent, Mah-ree would smile at him for a change and forget all of the harsh and hostile words.

He moved forward to a stony overhang that gave him a good view of the plain. Immediately he spotted the prey he would seek—a badly lamed doe within a small herd of pronghorn grazing in deep grass at the base of a riverside bluff. The small, buff and cream antelopelike animals were the fastest creatures on foot, among the tastiest, and if startled, impossible to run down. Warakan's eyes narrowed. Even from his great distance, he could see that the doe favored her right forelimb to the extent that was she was not using it at all. With care and patience he would work his way onto the bluff, upwind of the animals, so they would neither hear nor scent his presence before he could hurl his staves their way. Even if he failed to make a killing strike, the doe would be further incapacitated, and he could trail her until she dropped. What a prize this would be!

Losing his scent in the wind, Warakan went down onto the plain. The tickling grasses were shoulder high and sweet with the unfurling faces of flowers usually not seen until late in the summer, their petals gilded with colors stolen from Rainbow. The boy was giddy with pleasure in the beauty of his surroundings. Slowly he moved forward, rousing no more sound than the wind itself.

Soon he was on the bluff, moving with ease through some sort of wide, channeled depression in the grasses until, with a start, he was brought short by the strong scent of fresh animal droppings. His nose led him forward to a dark, semiliquid mound. He stopped, stared down, and knew exactly what kind of animal had moved through the grass ahead of him.

Meat eater?

*Yes!*

Chewer of fiber and flowers, too?

*Yes!*

Eater of fish and insects?

*Yes!*

Bear Brother?

*Yes! But then again, perhaps another bear, not my*

*brother at all . . . a mature boar, or a sow with cubs . . .*

His suppositions bled away into a sick, sinking feeling in his gut. Warakan did not need Mah-ree to name him Fool. In all of the hunting grounds across which he had traveled, first with the People of the Watching Star and later with the People of the Land of Grass, he had never come across game-rich land that did not have its share of bears in it. And was it any wonder that he had come upon bear leavings when he had been mindlessly walking along a path that the animal had cleared for itself? Such carelessness was inexcusable.

He gulped, hefted a stave, and began a slow retreat through the grass until a sudden noise up ahead brought him to pause. Something big had just gone crashing through the grasses and was now charging down the bluff. Warakan heard earth flying and hooves pounding and then water ferociously splashing. He tensed, heard the high, unmistakable *nyik-nyik* of a terrified antelope, and then . . . silence.

The choice was his: retreat or advance. Whatever had just happened along the river must surely have sent all game in the vicinity stampeding beyond any hope of hunting on this day. On the other hand, whatever had charged to the river was no longer on the bluff. Since Warakan was certain from its droppings that it was a bear, he had to know if it was his bear. He went forward cautiously, telling himself that he was safe in the protective power of the sacred stone.

Soon enough he was through the grasses and at the edge of the bluff. All around, the bear had been digging, feeding on stalks and flowers and some sort of root. His gaze moved up from the ground and out to the river, and there he saw the bear, *his* bear, standing in the shallows, looking fit and powerful and even larger than when he had last seen it. Head extended, it was staring at the far shore to which the lame doe had swum; the doe was now managing a three-legged hop to freedom. Warakan dropped to his knees. It seemed that neither he nor his brother, nor Mah-ree nor Jhadel, would feast on pronghorn this day.

He sighed, shook his head, and, wondering if the power of the stolen talisman was not all that the Ancient Ones had promised, absently picked up a torn stalk and began to chew on it. The flavor was familiar— green and very raw, very much like . . .

Warakan stared down with a start. The plant was not yet flowering, but he recognized the shape and texture of the leaves. He gasped as he realized what he was sitting in. "The medicine flower that will make Jhadel strong again!" He had no idea that any of its kind grew so close to the base of the gorge. "Aiee! May the spirits of the sacred stone forgive Warakan for ever having doubted them!" The proclamation made, he uttered yet another hoot of happiness, then bent and proceeded to uproot as many medicine flowers as he could see—until the sound of an animal charging up the bluff caused him to remember the bear in the river.

The boy looked up.

The bear was on him.

Warakan screamed. The bear "mraawed" and collapsed into a heap beside him, pulling him into an embrace, smothering him in happy licks of ecstatic reunion.

And Warakan was laughing and crying all at once. The bear had become his brother again, his cub, his friend! They rolled in the grasses and medicine flowers, healing the wounds of enmity that had separated them.

At length they sat up together, and the boy looked up at the bear and said, "It seems as though your backside has healed without any help from me or Wise One or Medicine Woman. And what is this that Warakan sees in your mouth? A chipped front tooth? Hah! That is what you get for crunching spears!" He made a face of admonition, then confided, "Your brother did not want to raise his hand to you, you know? But the woman, she makes us both so angry. Still, Warakan must tell his brother—it would not be a good thing if you were to eat that woman. Pronghorn are better . . . if you can catch them."

The bear sighed as though in mutual befuddlement with the opposite gender, then began to root around the grasses, energetically nipping up greens. Warakan watched him, then lay across his great back, savoring the feeling of the animal moving beneath him, close again, Brother again. At last he moved off a few paces and busily set to pulling up his own medicine plants, stuffing them into his tunic until he bulged at the seams.

"Come now, my brother! The sun is high. Warakan must return to the top of the gorge. They will be angry with him until they see how fat he has become! Then they will be curious as well as angry. They will wonder just what he could have eaten to have become so bulky so quickly. And then Warakan will show them what he has brought them, what the sacred stone and Bear Brother together have led him to find . . . for them! And then, Warakan thinks, they will not be angry with him anymore. So, come! Too long have you been away from your band!"

The bear followed, but only for a little way. Sometime before Warakan reached the stony overhang, the animal disappeared into the grasses. Warakan waited. He called. But it was Mah-ree who answered, shouting down from the gorge, sounding like a mother again.

"Boy! Where *have* you been!"

Warakan boldly told her about everything except the sacred stone and his fear of the unseen predators of the night.

Mah-ree stared at him, hard-eyed, reproachful; she looked tired, gaunt with worry. "Wise One is so weak. This woman dared not leave him alone! What if you had been killed, or injured? And if your cub follows you here . . . ah! You *must* let him go his way, Warakan. Can you not see how dangerous he is? If you turn your back to that bear, he will seek unity with his own kind, as you must seek knowledge and wisdom through the teaching of Jhadel. And you and I . . ."

She paused; her tone softened, and gently she implored, "We *must* make peace between us, Warakan, if not to please ourselves, then to please Wise One. He broods over us. He wants so much for us. And he has so much to teach us that we cannot learn if we remain at one another's throats."

Warakan was shocked by her words of reconciliation. He frowned, suspicious, instantly on the defensive. "Jhadel's words have not been for Warakan since Mahree has come to share our lives."

"Only because Warakan does not listen."

"Warakan listens!"

"But Warakan does not try to understand what he hears."

"No?"

"No!" Again she paused. Now she frowned. "You have been gone so long. And you have brought no meat. Yet you have become so fat, Warakan! How—"

"Warakan brings better than meat!" he declared, and a moment later his heart gave more than its usual *thunk* when, in the rain of medicine flowers that he tossed high into the air, Mah-ree cried out with pleasure and kissed him square on the mouth.

# 3

In the cave within the Valley of the Dead, the spear-heads of white chalcedony had long been complete.

Kosar-eh kept his gaze on them as he sat cross-legged and stiff-shouldered before his fire pit, stoically ignoring the painful pricks of the female tattoo artists who worked on either side of his face with styluses of sharpened bone dipped in a colorant of fat and ash. Head high, the big man held his eyes on the spearheads; they were no longer his, but focusing on them kept his mind away from pain.

His long eyelids narrowed as he willed himself to remember how he had been instructed to carry the fin-ished projectile points—displayed flat on the parfleche that had once held the four white stones—around the cave to be touched by every man, woman, and child of the People of the Watching Star. He could still see the expressions of wonder on their faces and hear the heavy hush of awe that had accompanied his slow circuit of the cave. Then, after being bathed in sacred smoke and the collected blood of the tribe, the spearheads had been hafted lovingly by Hrak onto long, fire-hardened shafts of specially selected hardwood, as yet unpainted or incised, and brought forth to Tsana as a gift to the tribe. After a night of rousing celebration that had feted Black and White Warrior as Master of the Stone and Hrak as Master Joiner, the new spearheads were again bathed in smoke before being wrapped by Spirit Woman in strips of rare, age-softened mammoth hide. Now, positioned upright on either side of the high priestess's dais, the spears would remain in this place of honor to enable the spirits within the newly fashioned projectile points to rest and grow strong until they were called into service in the final hunt for the great white mammoth. On that day, the chieftain would speak to the individual spirits that dwelled within each spearhead and be advised as to which man should carry each weapon.

Kosar-eh smiled. All knew that the best weapons would go to Tsana, chieftain of the tribe, to Hrak, Master Joiner, whose skill had mated the spearheads to the shafts that would propel them to their task, and to Black and White Warrior, whose hands had called the spearheads forth from the stone.

Still gazing at the wrapped heads of the sacred spears, the big man was able to see in his mind's eye through the shaggy mammoth-skin binding to the exquisitely fluted spearheads within. Long, wide at the base, and tapering to a point, they were like willow leaves rendered in stone. Held to the sun, they were nearly transparent and so sharp that he had sometimes wondered if he could be cut merely by sliding his glance along the lanceolate double edges. Never had he done such fine work! Indeed, Kosar-eh had to concede that, although he had long since lost faith in spirits or forces beyond the grasp of mortal men, it had been as though something outside of himself had guided his hands when he had brought these spearheads to a perfection that he had heretofore thought impossible. Now, knowing to what purpose they would soon be put, they were the pride and focus of his existence.

More than his sons.

More than his blind daughter.

And certainly more than any of the four females, including Hrak's daughter, who had not shed moon blood since he had chosen to pump the wet heat of a man's release into them.

"One new life for each of the Four Winds that have brought Black and White Warrior to dwell with his new tribe! It is a good thing!" Tsana had proclaimed.

Kosar-eh, however, was not certain that he had been the one to put life into any of the newly impregnated women—nor did he care. He had lain with them all, and his chances of being the father of any or all of the eventual outpouring of life that would come from between their thighs were good; but in a tribe with such sexual habits as this one, no man could be sure of the results of his spent passions. The big man was glad. He wanted no more of the emotional bonding that went with the siring of children and had long since conceded that Tsana was right when he said that his people's ways in the matter of mating were the best ways—all free to mate with all; the children of one, the children of all.

The supposition stirred him. He reached back with one hand, caught the wrist of the female closest to him, and pulled her around to face him. She was Bhandi, a captive, one of Shateh's youngest wives, a tall, slim-hipped young woman, daughter of the giant Xohkantakeh of the People of the Land of Grass. Kosar-eh's eyes narrowed. The giant had been among the raiders who savaged and slew his woman. Now the man's daughter was his to take and humiliate whenever the mood moved him, which was often. His eyes bespoke his need. As a slave, Bhandi could not refuse him; free women of the tribe could do so, unless the chieftain commanded otherwise. But no woman had yet looked away from the needs of Black and White Warrior, Master of Stone.

Pushing aside his loin covering, Kosar-eh displayed his readiness. She stared. He smiled. He was too big for her and knew it. Roughly and impatiently, he positioned her for pleasure. She was not ready for him; her eyes went wide, begged for kindness from him. There was no kindness left in him. He rammed deep, felt dry, tense muscles tear. His smile broadened; his penis would be bloodied from this mating. Her brave attempt to show no pain moved him to give her so much that she could not keep from crying out—as his beloved must have cried out, again and again before this woman's father and tribesmen wearied of their sport and made an end of her. And so he held the daughter of Xohkantakeh fast, and worked her until she sobbed, as he took her in the way of his new tribe. No need to withdraw to a place of privacy unless such was desired. No need for explanations or excuses. Simply done and enjoyed in whatever manner the moment dictated, and then over, finished, with no regret.

"We will have to move against our enemies soon, or all of our females will be swollen with the outflow of that man's life and useless for the needs of the rest of us!" slurred Indeh.

"I keep the captives clean of new life for the pleasure of all, never fear," Oan assured him.

Indeh was not appeased. "They take no pleasure in it after he has been at them."

"And since when has the pleasure of captives mattered to men of the Watching Star?" Tsana reminded him.

As the mated young woman moved to rejoin her tribe sister, Kosar-eh backhanded them both impatiently away. He would not let either of them touch him

with their styluses for a while. He looked to the far side
of the cave where Indeh was crouching by his own fire
circle, redefining the chipped head of a spear damaged
on a recent hunt. *Someday,* Kosar-eh thought. *Someday
soon, this man will give Indeh the gift of a new spear,
straight through his insolent mouth!*

Tsana was smiling drolly as he stood at the lip of
the cave, eating a wedge of bison fat and surveying the
growing day. "Black and White Warrior is still new to
our ways. He is to be encouraged, not faulted, if he rises
often to the opportunities presented to him!"

Kosar-eh refrained from commenting that, when
not off hunting or eating or busy with the various enter-
prises associated with keeping their hunting tools and
weapons in top form, there was not a man of the tribe
who was not on one woman or another. Indeed, in this
place, among these people, mating was the most popu-
lar pastime. Even the youths and boys were encouraged
to experiment with their sexuality, and often, as now, he
would look across the cave and see his Kiu-neh pounding one of the older girls—a plump, unpretty child who
made faces during what was obviously an ordeal for her.

The big man shook his head. He neither approved
nor disapproved of the boy's rutting. His concern for his
sons and daughter had vanished with the ripening
spring. They no longer needed him. They were not his
children; they were the children of the Watching Star.
Never had he seen his boys happier or more physically
fit, and never in his wildest dreams had he dared hope
that his blind daughter would be given such extraordinary care by those whom he had too long named Enemies, and by one whom he had long thought dead.

Spirit Woman was staring at him now. Kosar-eh's
smile vanished as he saw her rise and stand before her
dais. Ban-ya of the Red World, high priestess of the
Watching Star—whoever or whatever the mindless crea-

ture was, he had not felt pity for her since the night of the celebration after the bison hunt. His flesh crawled whenever he looked at her tattooed skin and braided hair and necklace of human hair and finger bones, and at the daughter of his flesh clamped to her breast. Why did she stare at him? What did she want of him, she of the hollow eyes and weasel face and—

"Black and White Warrior!" Tsana called his name. Kosar-eh was grateful to be distracted.

"Come!" invited the chieftain. "The day grows toward noon! There is game in the valley. Unai, Xanahay, Hrak . . . take up your spears! Join this man and the Black and White Warrior! Tsana feels the need to kill something this day!"

They went into the sun, across the valley and around the lake, making a game of sending rafts of waterfowl screeching skyward, panicked by stones hurled and skipped across the water in their direction.

"You do not eat of winged meat?" Kosar-eh asked, frowning when well-thrown stones hit a mark and a bird came tumbling from the sky only to be ignored and left behind.

"In starving times," conceded Unai. "But we are not hungry now."

Kosar-eh almost said, *Then why kill a thing if you do not intend to take its life force into yourself as sustenance?* But he had not forgotten the wanton slaughter of the bison, and now, as then, he accepted the ways of the men with whom he traveled. Besides, he thought, with his flesh tattooed and his spirit transformed by his need to take vengeance against the killers of his beloved woman, was he not one of them?

"Ay yah!" Kosar-eh shouted. Inexplicably angry— at them, at himself, at the birds, and at the sky itself—

he gathered up a fistful of small stones and hurled them
one by one into the blue light of day.

"The birds are now out of range, Black and White
Warrior," remarked Tsana. "At what do you throw your
stones?"

"At the Four Winds," he replied and, with Ta-
maya's feathered bone hairpin braided into his forelock
and blown across his face by the afternoon breeze,
added, "lest they forget the need of this man to taste
the blood of those who have slain his woman and children."

Tsana smiled. "They have not forgotten. Nor have
we. Come," he invited, lengthening his stride and turning toward the hills through which they had brought
Kosar-eh and the children as captives into the valley.
"Black and White Warrior told us that he killed one of
them on the night of the raid against his encampment.
Let us go to that place. Let us hunt the corpse that you
made."

Kosar-eh stopped dead. "And the body of my
woman?" The world seemed to have lurched beneath
his feet.

Hrak was frowning. "White Giant Winter has been
gone from that land long enough for meat eaters to
have found those bodies. There will be nothing. It is
better for my brother who talks to the spirits of stones
to let those other spirits go."

Tsana was still moving forward. "Let the Four
Winds answer to the Black and White Warrior!" he
called over his shoulder. He gestured the others on.

With no children to slow their pace, they loped like
wolves across the land. Soon the Valley of the Dead lay
below, and all too quickly darkness came down upon
them.

"We should have told our people that there was a
chance we might be long away." Hrak intoned the after-

thought as though obliged to do so; if there was genuine regret over the oversight in his voice, Kosar-eh could not hear it.

"Spirit Woman will know and understand what we are about this night, and in the days to come," replied Tsana.

Because of the possibility that enemies from the Land of Grass might be nearby, Tsana instructed the others to make a cold camp at the height of the pass. They settled in to rest and share a light meal of jerked bison meat, and as they ate, Kosar-eh stared back across the world in which his woman had been raped and slain, in which his children and band had been taken and slaughtered.

"Stone Talker must eat," said Hrak, coming close to offer food. Kosar-eh had no appetite. He waved away the offering, and the man who brought it, briefly wondering why they had bothered to pack food when, as far as any of them had told him, they had left the cave intending to return before sundown. It seemed unimportant, only one more thing to learn about his new brothers who wisely prepared for all contingencies whenever leaving the stronghold.

All night long Kosar-eh sat alone in the dark. Once, for a few moments, he thought he saw the glow of a campfire in the distant hills; it was soon gone, and he decided that it had not been a fire at all, but only the light of a bright star shimmering briefly on some distant lake or river. He looked up, marked the passage of late spring stars that, by their very familiarity, seemed to ridicule him. His entire world had changed since he had last looked upon those stars, and nearly everyone he loved had been cruelly slain, yet the stars moved on, untouched, undisturbed in their seasonal migration across the sky. And there, near the apex of the north-

ernmost portion of the sky, the Watching Star glinted
palely.

He stared up at it with hatred. It seemed to cast a
long, black, invisible shadow on the world to mock the
very humanity of his soul. He shivered.

"Yah!" Kosar-eh shouted in anguish and, after
fumbling in the darkness to gather loose stones once
again, leaped to his feet and pitched them at the star.

The others awoke to stare at what seemed to be a
man possessed by spirits. Only Tsana understood and
smiled.

"Do not try to kill that star, Black and White Warrior. It shines for you now."

The well-remembered avenue of corpses lay behind. Kosar-eh did not look back. Reeking in the
springtime air, the staked heads and bodies of the slain
warriors from the Land of Grass and their chieftain,
Shateh, had not been a pretty sight. Nevertheless, it had
pleased Kosar-eh to see his enemies' remains so displayed, and images of them stayed in his mind, giving
strength to his steps and hardening his sense of purpose.

Without the cover of snow, the land did not look
the same as he remembered it. Yet soon he and the
others sighted familiar outcrops of stone and stands of
trees. Moving quickly, they traveled out of their way to
avoid the place where they had put U-wa's body to look
upon the sky forever; Kosar-eh had no wish to set eyes
upon her bier again, and his fellow travelers preferred
not to disturb her spirit. Then suddenly, it seemed, they
were there, in that land of wide hills where Kosar-eh
had seen a teratorn fly with ravens on that long-gone
day on which he had died along with his people.

Hrak was speaking to him.

Kosar-eh did not hear. He moved in a daze now,

overwhelmed by recollections of events that scalded his senses. Had a full day passed, or two? Had he spent another night staring at the stars? He did not know. He did not care. With Tsana and the others at his side, he searched for the body of his beloved and did not know whether to rage against despair or weep with relief when they found nothing.

"Hrak is right," said Xanahay. "The meat eaters of earth and sky will have left nothing of the tender flesh and marrow-rich bones of a young woman sent naked into the night to die."

"It is so," affirmed Unai.

Kosar-eh flinched. The words of his fellow hunters pierced like stone lancets—as did the eyes of Tsana, who spoke guardedly but not unkindly to him.

"Truly, Black and White Warrior, did you still dare to believe that with all the forces of the shaman Yellow Wolf allied against your band, your woman could have survived? Or that her body would not have been as cruelly sundered by beasts as your lives were sundered by those whom Yellow Wolf set against you?"

"Look! By this fallen tree . . . There is not much left, but what is here was the underpinnings of a man . . . once."

Hrak's words came like a slap. Kosar-eh stiffened and fairly ran to the place where the man was standing. Even before he fully focused on the site, he knew that it was here that he had killed Ranamal.

"There . . . do you see?" Hrak said. "All but hidden under the tree!"

Kosar-eh saw. The winter snowpack had lain heavily on the corpse and the fallen tree against which Ranamal had breathed his last. Several heavy branches had been broken by the weight of the snow and now lay like massive, protective arms over all that remained of what had once been a man.

"Ranamal." The name seeped out of Kosar-eh as the dead man's last words rose to haunt him. *"The days and nights spent in this world of the living are short for all men, eh? Ah, yes. It is so. The spirits of the dead of your camp, and of your woman, Ta-maya, will wait for you on the wind! I will soon be with them. And I will enjoy her body there, in the world beyond this world, as I enjoyed it in the land of the living until you come. . . ."*

"I have come back," he said, shivering with new-found purpose. Although small predators and decay had stripped the corpse of most of its skin and meat, the skull still wore a remnant of its cap of hair, and the skeleton remained more or less intact. "Too long have you been separated from your tribesmen, Ranamal!"

The others watched while Kosar-eh, with a strength born of righteous wrath, placed his hands first upon one branch, then another, pushing and pulling until each was cracked and broken away from the skeleton. Without a word, the big man glared at his prize. He could not believe his good fortune; in his haste to be away after mutilating the corpse, he had left the man his hair. Where there was hair, there was still spirit. And where there was spirit, there was life enough to be dishonored by enemies. For Kosar-eh's purpose, there was just enough desiccated tendon and moldering, albeit sun-dried, unmasticated skin for him to take hold of the hair on Ranamal's head and jerk the remains of the dead man upright.

The others stepped back as what was left of the corpse's scalp loosened in Kosar-eh's hand. From beneath the tearing skin, the stench of putrescence oozed to stagger them.

"In the country of his enemies, is there a stake of mammoth bone waiting for the head of this dead dog from the Land of Grass?" demanded Kosar-eh.

Tsana's head went high. "There is!" he exclaimed.

"And also for the Yellow Wolf who fled beyond the edge of the world with the totem and sacred stone of our ancestors, who used his shaman's powers to cause this dog of a Land of Grass man to slay your woman and band! Soon now, Black and White Warrior, we will leave our stronghold to hunt that Yellow Wolf. And you will lead us to the kill!"

Kosar-eh's blood was up. "Yes!" The assent felt good on his tongue, as good as the drag of Ranamal's corpse weighting his hand. Tsana was right. Chakwena's lies had brought his people to disaster. Why should he not hunt the shaman who had proved his undoing? Did it matter in which order revenge was served? Sooner or later, before the last days of his life were spent, Kosar-eh was determined that all who had participated in the raid upon his encampment and subsequent slaying of his woman would share the fate of Ranamal. Ta-maya was dead, her remains devoured, her spirit dead forever in the belly of beasts!

Outrage shook him. If Tsana and his warriors would not be turned from their need to possess the sacred stone, slay the shaman Yellow Wolf, and devour a totem mammoth, why should he dissuade them? Afterward they would stand with him in battle, and with their support his chances of ultimate victory over his enemies were virtually assured. Why should he continue to distrust them? Had they not proved to be his hunt brothers? Had they not shared their women with him and taken his children to be their own? Had they not placed into his hands the finest stones he had ever worked, and honored him by allowing him to be the one to fashion from them the spearheads they now deemed sacred? And even now, after sensing his unhappiness, had they not deferred a hunt and brought him across the land so that he might savor some small act of vengeance against those who had so wronged him, and them?

"Yes!" Kosar-eh said again, and with the name of his beautiful beloved on his lips, he knelt to take the head of Ranamal.

Joh-nee screamed when she saw him.

"Kosar-eh is theirs now!" Spirit Woman's sigh scraped through her vocal chords like that of a dehydrated snake. "As Tsana knew he would be if they led him back to the place where his woman died."

"Yah hay! Behold! We come bringing meat!" Hrak was strutting proudly with the other hunters who were returning to the cave after many days and nights away. "And we come telling all that Black and White Warrior has staked the head of an enemy beside that of Shateh! Behold, we return with a new and true warrior of the Watching Star!"

Joh-nee rose and backed away in horror, staring from behind the dais of mammoth bones as the tattooed stranger named Kosar-eh entered the cave beside Tsana. He strode boldly forward, displaying a new armband of distinctly human finger bones and a new fixed and savage smile that she had not seen on his face since the night Cheelapat had died at his hands. The girl's eyes widened, locked on the man's armband. She hugged her doll tight and whispered, "He wears the fingers of a man! Aiee! He has become like Spirit Woman!"

"No one can be like Spirit Woman," chortled the wolf-robed woman on the mammoth-bone throne, deliberately provoking Joh-nee by sending her own long fingers straying through the collar of human hair and finger bones that she wore around her neck. "Ah, so rare these bones, so fine." She smiled, encouraging the blind child on her lap to grasp the bones and clap them together. "Yes! Make pretty music with the bones of Spirit Woman! Yes, yes! Like that! Such a pretty sound!

There. No need for Sees the Wind to be frightened by the shouts of men returning or the outcries of a foolish girl!"

Joh-nee pressed a hand to her mouth and stifled a sob as Doh-teyah began to laugh and clap the bones of the collar in her small, pudgy hands. The older girl had not intended her remark to the doll to be overheard, and she hated to hear the little one happy in the madwoman's arms. "I am not a foolish girl!"

"You have not run away."

"I will not leave Doh-teyah."

"That baby is dead. Sees the Wind has taken her place in the arms of Spirit Woman. So run away, Shaman's Sister. There is no future here for you. Soon Morning Star will rise to show her beauty to the Watcher. The time of the eating will be soon. Look. Behold! The carnivore returns to the cave. He grows hungry now."

Joh-nee stared ahead. She knew that Spirit Woman was referring to Tsana, but it was Kosar-eh who was staring back at the high priestess of the People of the Watching Star, and Joh-nee could not bring herself to look away.

**4**

Xohkantakeh did not like the signs.

Ta-maya watched him as he eyed the sky. The weather had been clear and cool since the rising of the Duck Moon, but as the giant resolutely led his little band out of the country of their enemies, there had been no rain. This troubled Xohkantakeh; under the Duck Moon it always rained, she had heard him say, but although Zakeh and his women agreed, Ta-maya knew better.

"Perhaps in the hunting grounds of the ancestors of the People of the Land of Grass this is so, but this woman has encamped with her band before in these dry hills," she told them. "We are beyond the rain shadow of the mountains. Water is scarce. In places it is absent altogether. But there are springs and pools and tree-shaded rivers whose banks are green with reeds and where there is also much game."

Xohkantakeh disagreed. "Last year there was rain and a warm sun in the days of the Duck Moon. Much snow melted in the mountains. A great flood covered the land."

"You have led us along the rim of the floodplain of the great mad river," Ta-maya reminded him. "But with the air so dry and the sun so cool, this woman does not think that river will overflow its banks to drown the land as it did before."

The giant eyed her thoughtfully.

They all stared at her. The day was new, but the resentment in the eyes of Neeracheela was old.

"Xohkantakeh does not ask Broken Wing what she thinks!" snapped the woman with open annoyance.

Ta-maya made no reply. She knew that Neeracheela disliked her. The woman made no secret of her feelings, and nothing Ta-maya said or did had been able to change that. Yet, even so, she had not been abused by the woman of Zakeh, unless she counted the continuous lashings Neeracheela's abrasive tongue had given her. Since leaving the mountains, she had been treated with consideration, if not kindness, by Shan, who was relieved that Ta-maya had taken the three little girls under her one good wing. Ta-maya could not comprehend why a mother should dislike her own children so. As for the little ones, they had taken a genuine liking to Ta-maya. They looked to her for care and returned it in kind, for although her arm was beginning to heal, it was obvious the bones would never again be straight or the muscles as serviceable as they once were. Ta-maya could not do much for the children, but they responded to her genuine concern and affection.

They were seated on either side of her, Ika somewhat aloof from the younger two as she hand-fed the wolf pups the guts pulled from the rabbit she had just killed with her throwing stick.

"They take meat from the mouths of this band and would be better served if they were turned into meat themselves!" Neeracheela protested.

Ika bristled. "Zakeh, tell that woman to stop such talk!"

Zakeh eyed Neeracheela with strained patience.

"That Woman, stop such talk! The pups will grow to serve the band like dogs. Someday the meat we feed them will become brawn that will carry our loads on long trails from kill sites to butchering camps. You will thank this man for having the foresight to bring them into this family. In the meantime you will harness your tongue! Its sharpness grows tedious!"

Neeracheela's face was contorted. This time she was not going to wait for Zakeh to throw something at her; she looked around for something to hurl at him.

"No!" Xohkantakeh's angry command had enough implied threat in it to freeze the woman on the spot.

Neeracheela took a deep breath to steady her temper.

"Maybe this man should give Throws Everything to his hunt brother?" Zakeh tittered at her expense.

"It is Zakeh who throws things at Neeracheela!" she said. "Go ahead! Give this woman away!"

Zakeh shrugged. "Not this time, but it does seem to this man that when Xohkantakeh speaks, Neeracheela comes at his command like a good dog!"

Ta-maya frowned, uncertain if the man had intended the double meaning of his statement as an accusation against his woman.

Neeracheela's face flushed bright red. "What need has Xohkantakeh of this woman when he already has his Broken Wing?" Her tone dripped venom, and there was the fire of confrontation in her eyes. "Xohkantakeh is satisfied with the woman he has chosen for himself, a small and useless woman! But then, Neeracheela should not be surprised! Long ago her mother told her that the woman pleaser of the biggest man is always in opposite proportion to his size. Therefore, as big as he is, Xohkantakeh's man need is as small as that which he hides under his loin cover. Two women would be too much for him. And even if he had only one woman, it is best that he keeps the small and useless one, for Neer-acheela would surely be too much for him!"

Ta-maya was stunned.

So was Xohkantakeh.

Zakeh and Shan gaped in shock, along with the children, who were not quite sure what Neeracheela had just implied about the giant.

Ta-maya's heartbeat quickened. She had no love for the combative Neeracheela, but she had no wish to see the woman clouted by the giant again; Neeracheela's upper lip still bore a small, vertical purple scar from his last strike against her.

"Xokeekokee, what is a woman pleaser?" asked a puzzled Ika.

The adults exchanged startled looks.

Ika pouted, not understanding their reaction. "Show me!" she demanded.

And suddenly the giant laughed. It was a deep, good-natured rumble as he replied to Ika, "Someday, little one, when you are in the arms of your first man, he will please the woman in you. Then you will know and see and understand."

The little girl frowned, looked around the camp, then back at Xohkantakeh. "Who will be this girl's man in this land with no people?"

Silence followed the child's question, heavy and unsettling. Shan eyed the giant accusingly.

"Yes, Xohkantakeh," she said. "In the days and nights to come, when we are old and these children are grown and the pups in that girl's lap have become wolves, who will be Ika's man? Or have you thought that far ahead since the broken-winged woman of our enemies sucked the spirit from your head and made you blind to all but her needs?"

"My people dwell in this land," Ta-maya reminded her, determined to ignore the nastiness of the other two. "Perhaps they need not be your enemies . . . any more than you need be mine."

Xohkantakeh stared off across the land. "We have come far away from that place where you were taken captive, Broken Wing. This man and Zakeh, we would not disturb the spirits of the dead whom we know must have been put to 'look at the sky forever' in that place after we left it."

Zakeh shook his head. "It was not a good thing, the raid on that camp. To kill women, children, a boy . . . no, not a good·thing. It shames my honor as a warrior to think of it. When Ranamal and Ynau saw that the shaman was not there with the sacred stone and totem, there was no need for him to—"

"Perhaps the ghosts of those slain people are working together with their evil shaman," Shan interrupted him, "conspiring with this Red World woman to punish us for what Ranamal led the others to do that day. Perhaps it is she and they who keep rain from the land."

"Cha-kwena is not an evil shaman!" Ta-maya was angry; she had heard this infamy against him and her people voiced too often by those who had so heinously wronged them. "The forces of Creation were wise to have placed the sacred stone and the totem into his care. If only my man had chosen to stay at his side! And . . ." Her thoughts paused in midstream; this was the first time they had discussed the raid in her presence. Before, in the encampment of Axwahtal and the others, surely she must have overheard them speak of it, even taunt her with it, but she had been beyond comprehension. Now, looking at Zakeh, she remembered the death of Ka-neh, heard old Kahm-ree snoring in the shadows of the winter lodge, saw U-wa gathering up Doh-teyah and the children. If that good woman had not succeeded, then all she had yielded, all she had suffered, had saved only one life other than young Klah-neh's: her own. Her heart sank. She was light-headed as she asked, "Women? Children?"

"A boy. An old woman. And a young girl. There was much blood. And then fire. Ynau brought the burning lodge down upon them. The girl, she screamed long and could not escape. It was a bad thing."

Ta-maya stared. She saw nothing. She could not speak. Old Kahm-ree, dead? And her dear, ever-teasing little sister, Tla-nee . . . or had it been Joh-nee, so bright, so quick, and always eager to help with the baby? Ta-maya cleared her vision and managed to say, "There was a baby . . . and another woman and girl."

Zakeh's face was full of pity and regret. He gave an embarrassed shrug and made a sincere attempt to cheer the stricken woman. "Ranamal said three ran away and were not seen again. Perhaps they live and are safe with your man . . . I mean, with the headman of your band and those who were not in camp that day, eh?"

A shiver went through Ta-maya. The news struck her heart like wounds from a knife; she could feel herself bleeding as she realized that all her hopes and prayers for her people had gone unanswered. If the Four Winds had carried her invocations to the forces of Creation, they had refused to listen . . . or, much worse than that, simply failed to hear.

Shaken to her very spirit, Ta-maya closed her eyes and conceded a devastating truth—Kosar-eh was right to have lost faith in the ancient belief of the ancestors; prayers and spirit offerings made to intangible forces in the world beyond this world did not affect events here below. The Four Winds and the forces of Creation moved upon the lives of Man and beast alike with relentless transfiguration—ever generating, ever destroying, uncaring of outcome as they eternally wove the wondrous and terrible web of Creation; beyond this they moved in awesome unawareness, mindless and dispassionate, knowing neither joy nor pity, sadness nor regret.

Again Ta-maya shivered. Hers was a desolate epiphany in light of the ruinous decisions that her man had made for their band. She opened her eyes and, distracted by the honking of migrating geese, looked skyward to see the long skeins of birds winging northward. And there, ahead of all, flew the lead bird, the brave bird, guiding the others steadfastly across the skies, following the opening of the waters and greening of the grass in the way of his kind since time beyond beginning. What impelled him to take the lead? What assured him that the waters of ancestral nesting grounds would be open when he arrived, the grasses ripe with sustenance for all who followed?

*Hope in the future of his kind.*

And if his great wings failed him, or an eagle struck him down, or ice sheathed the waters of his destination and wolves were waiting in a land where there was no grass to feed his children? Another would take his place. Another would lead the followers. And under the blue, uncaring sky, and upon the unfeeling skin of the earth, some would survive. For those who did, life would be sweet and bright, bitter and dark—and all the more wonderful because of its poignancy and inherent risk.

Ta-maya started, her epiphany transformed in an instant. She could *not* blame her beloved Kosar-eh for the tragedies that had befallen their band any more than she could fault the geese for putting themselves and their young at risk in their eternal search for warmth, sustenance, and survival in the face of the rising sun! Snared in the great web of Creation, each individual must die, but while life flourished, all beings were compelled to nurture and sustain it in the way of their kind for the good of all. And in this world of violence and beauty, when all was said and done, was this not a gift from the forces of Creation after all?

"Always and forever," Ta-maya avowed, her eyes holding on the birds until they disappeared into the distance. "In the way of their kind." The words touched her with understanding. A strange, almost lyric sadness was on her as she looked at her captors and told them softly, "It may well be that someday the wrath of my man, Kosar-eh, will fall heavily upon those who have stolen his woman and son and slain the others of his band. But even on that day—unlike the raiders of the Land of Grass—Kosar-eh of the Red World will not bring death to innocent women and children with knives and spears or lay waste their encampment with fire. His heart is set to the good of the People in the way of our kind . . . always and forever."

"Your kind?" Xohkantakeh measured her thoughtfully. "Is your tribe so different from mine? Among my people did your man not become a warrior and earn the name Man Who Spits in the Face of Enemies?"

"Kosar-eh's enemies are not women and children," Ta-maya told him.

Grimly he responded, "Red World man or Land of Grass man . . . in war and battle all men do things that later lie heavy on the spirit."

Zakeh nodded. "When a man is of the tribe, he must do as his leaders say; unless he is chief or has a big voice in council, what else can he do?"

"He can leave the tribe and become his own chief," said Xohkantakeh. "This man has seen too many raids like the one Ranamal led on Broken Wing's camp, and few wars with merit in them." He stared at Ta-maya, then at the three girls. "Xohkantakeh does not regret breaking from the company of dogs like Axwahtal, who command the deaths of innocent women and abandon parentless female children only because their presence

among his people might slow them down as they run in
fear of enemies whom they have roused against themselves!"

Ta-maya's eyes widened. "Unwanted? Without parents?"

"These are not our daughters, Broken Wing," explained Shan. "Their mothers and fathers were slain by
the men of the Watching Star. They are trouble, like
you, but since Axwahtal ordered them abandoned, we
could not very well turn our backs to them, eh?"

Ta-maya was shocked, then overcome by a surge of
unexpected empathy when the hard-eyed Shan looked
at her and said, "Does Broken Wing think that she is
the only woman to have suffered and lost loved ones in
war? This woman and Neeracheela, we have both lost
sons! And this woman has seen her grown daughter
abandoned by her own people along with Xohkantakeh's last living daughter because they had been
chosen to be the new women of Shateh before that man
led us all to war and death! So our daughters were considered bad luck to the tribe! For the good of our people we turned our backs to them and left them in the
country of our enemies, where, if they have not been
taken as slaves, then, with White Giant Winter so long
upon the land, they must surely walk the wind forever!"

Ta-maya was shattered and ashamed. She remembered now—the giant's words, so long ago it seemed, a
rumbling whisper in the dark . . . revelations of
mourning, something about a slain woman and a daughter lost to the ravages of war. His words had not
touched her. He was Enemy then. He was Enemy now.
And those who chose to walk at his side were also Enemy. It had never occurred to her that any of them
could feel pain; even if it had, she had been too preoc-
cupied with her own suffering to care.

Shan buried her face in her hands, weeping, as

Neeracheela swept to her side to enfold her in a loving embrace of commiseration.

Zakeh's expression only barely contained the agony of his regret. "Sometimes it is not good to look back. And my Shan, she is sometimes hard toward these children because too much do they remind her of our own. To love a child, to lose a child . . . sometimes it is better not to give one's heart again."

Looking at him and at the weeping women, Ta-maya thought her own heart would break; instead, it went cold.

Now, on the rising wind of the new day, distant drums sounded in the mountains that the band had put far behind. Ta-maya cringed with dread. Was Kosar-eh there, a captive of the cannibal People of the Watching Star, and were the surviving children of her band at his side?

"Come."

Ta-maya looked up. Xohkantakeh was standing over her, extending a massive hand down.

"We must continue on," the giant said with great emphasis. "If the forces of Creation remain with us in the days to come, life will be better for us outside the shadow of warring tribes."

They broke camp and moved on. The days and nights that followed were much the same as those that had gone before. Yet for Ta-maya nothing was the same since that one moment of shattering self-realization. How easily she had put herself above all others, judged them through the eyes of her own pain and suffering, her own preconceptions, with no understanding of or concern for who they really were or how they had come to be in this desolate land.

Zakeh . . . no longer a murderous raider in her

eyes but an obedient tribesman with many regrets, a
fiercely loyal friend and mourning father.

Shan and Neeracheela . . . no longer cruel and
uncaring handmaidens but brave, faithful wives, grieving the deaths of sons and daughters of whom they had
not been able to bring themselves to speak, their na-
tures so bruised by pain that they feared to embrace
pleasure ever again.

Ika, Xree, and Lana . . . no longer dirty-faced
children neglected by their parents but parentless, sheltered and cared for by near strangers who would not
stand by and see them abandoned.

Xohkantakeh . . . no longer a purely predaceous
giant but a troubled, grieving man who had come to
loathe war and the violent whims of his tribesmen
enough to turn his back on them forever.

As the little band traveled from one increasingly
dry hunting camp to another, Ta-maya did not speak her
thoughts with words but tried to show by action what
was in her heart.

"It is time Ta-maya carried some of her own load,"
she told Xohkantakeh. "My arm is healing. I limp, but I
am not lame. Does Xohkantakeh think that Ta-maya is
the only woman to have suffered in this life? It is time
the one he calls Broken Wing did more than just look
to the children."

Shan and Neeracheela were openly amazed. They
did not offer thanks, but they did not offer argument,
either. And so the days were easier for all, and often in
the night, Ta-maya was doubly glad to have a day's work
behind her, for as she lay tense and fearing what must
inevitably come to her from the giant, she could now
beg the excuse of weariness.

"You still say that Xohkantakeh is not your man?"
he asked of her one night before sleep took them.

"My man is not in this camp."

"'This man could take you."

"This woman could not stop you, but she would say when you finished that her man is still not in this camp."

"And it will be so, as you say, 'always and forever'?"

"Always and forever . . . Ta-maya and Kosar-eh."

"Mmm. We will see. The day has been long. Sleep now."

And so it was with them for many nights until, early in the cool, blue light of one dawn Ta-maya awoke alone within her sleeping furs, as she often did; but this time she heard the low shivering gasps of a woman and the equally low rumblings of a man, coming from just outside the lean-to; clearly, the rumbling was coming from the giant, the gasps were Neeracheela's, and the combined sounds were of a mating.

Ta-maya sat up. Something stirred her. Jealousy? Impossible! Surprise? Yes! She lay back, wondering what Zakeh would throw at Neeracheela if he caught her at this.

At sunrise she found out.

"Zakeh says to all of this band that, with the rising of this sun, within hearing of the Four Winds and the forces of Creation, he gives his woman Neeracheela now to be Xohkantakeh's all-the-time woman. It is not a good thing in a band with only two hunters for one man to have two women, and the other . . . almost none."

Ta-maya waited for a reaction from the twosome in question. There was only a nod from each, a sidelong exchange of glances, and a hint of satisfaction in the corners of Neeracheela's mouth. There was no expression on the giant's face at all.

Nothing more was said. Later, trudging behind the others and falling into step beside Zakeh, Ta-maya could not help herself from whispering an embarrassed apology to him for a situation for which she knew she was in more than a small way to blame. "This woman is sorry that Zakeh has given away Neeracheela . . . but, in truth, soon enough Ta-maya will not be able to keep herself separate from Xohkantakeh. Your woman has taken pity on a band brother's need, and soon Xohkantakeh will have two women and—"

"Pity? Neeracheela and Broken Wing for Xohkantakeh?" Zakeh stopped walking. "No, Broken Wing," he corrected kindly, gesturing her closer so that he could speak in a lowered voice. "This has not been in Xohkantakeh's heart for you. Ever. Now, if these words will not bruise the pride of a brave woman, and if this brave woman will not speak of what I say to the brave man who would not seem weak in her eyes, Zakeh will tell the brave woman something. For all the time we have been together, Xohkantakeh looks for signs of Broken Wing's man, to give back into her own band the hurt and wrongly injured thing. If these people still live, if this 'always and forever' man still lives, to return the brave woman to them would be for Xohkantakeh a way to make peace with bad things done, to mend—if not the broken bone—at least the spirit of the wounded thing."

Ta-maya could not speak. Once again she was shattered by a devastating truth. Xohkantakeh—a man she had again and again wished dead at the hands of her beloved—had been willing to become an outcast, not because he was motivated by obsessive lust for a captive woman but because he was impelled by the noblest of human emotions: the compassion of one human being for another. Tears welled in her eyes.

Zakeh nodded, understanding. "Xohkantakeh is a good man. The best of men. Zakeh is proud to be his friend and hunt brother! And Zakeh is proud to have

shared his Neeracheela with him these many moons
since Xohkantakeh's woman walked the wind forever.
They have long wanted to be together. Now, because of
you, Broken Wing, we have all three found a way by
which it may be done with the blessings of the Four
Winds and the forces of Creation, which do not look
favorably upon broken promises. So do not apologize to
Zakeh. Instead, let Zakeh say 'thank you!' "

"I have misjudged you all."

He gave one of his offhanded little shrugs and went
on his way.

Ta-maya watched Zakeh stride off toward the others. The land over which they moved was unfamiliar,
but farther to the south and east were the badlands. It
was obvious that Xohkantakeh was avoiding that stark,
bitter country across which Cha-kwena had led Shateh
and his people toward better hunting grounds, and
upon which the People of the Land of Grass had lost
faith in the Red World shaman's ability to lead them to
anything but hunger and misery. They should not have
turned on Cha-kwena and set themselves to hunt the
sacred herd of mammoth, Ta-maya thought. They
should not have forced him to flee for his life with her
sister, Mah-ree, as he drove the mammoth ahead of him
into a rising snowstorm.

Her heart was pounding in response to her memories. There *were* good hunting grounds ahead beyond
the badlands. Shateh had never found them; he had
paused midway after his final confrontation with Cha-
kwena and led his people straight back into the heart-
land of his enemies, where he and many of his men
were later slain. But Kosar-eh and her band had fled
into the storm with Cha-kwena and found the golden
grassland rich with game at the base of a great, sunstruck gorge.

*Ah! What drew the mammoth on through the gorge*

*and into the dark forest beyond the edge of the world?
Perhaps they have returned to that sweet grassland with
Mah-ree and Cha-kwena, and perhaps my man has found
his way back to them with Kiu-neh and Kho-neh, with
U-wa and Doh-teyah and Tla-nee . . . or Joh-nee . . .
ah!*

"Broken Wing!"

Xohkantakeh's call brought Ta-maya sharply from
her reverie. He was striding toward her, a giant with a
little girl on each shoulder, another at his side skipping
along with a pair of wolf pups, and a happy Neeracheela
holding his hand. And in that moment Ta-maya realized
that she was happy, too. As her thoughts returned to
focus on the present, she hoped with all her heart that
her beloved Kosar-eh and the others were alive and
well. But, in the meantime, she had another band to
care for, a band of good people, caring people, loving
people! Suddenly Ta-maya knew that she loved them, all
of them, especially the great hulk of a man with his
growling voice, bearlike hands, gruff talk, and brooding
disposition.

"You have fallen too far behind your man, Broken
Wing!" the giant growled. "Have you not been taught
better by your Red World band and this always-and-
forever man you always whine of?"

"Broken Wing would not follow Neeracheela's man
over the rim of a north-setting range of hills, when he
should be heading to the east. There, beyond the badlands, there is water and good hunting. Ta-maya would
lead her people there—if Xohkantakeh and Zakeh will
swear on the power of the Four Winds that they will
never hunt mammoth again."

"I swear it!" Zakeh responded easily. "Why hunt
mammoth if there is easier meat to be had?"

"There is!" promised Ta-maya.

Xohkantakeh, however, was rumbling suspiciously.

"Your always-and-forever man will have gone to this hunting ground if his spirit still walks in this world."

"Perhaps," Ta-maya replied honestly and not without hope as her fingers drifted to the little feathered bone pin she had mended and wore again in her hair; somehow, just knowing it was there secured her beloved's life, kept him safe and near in her heart even though in some dark and unacknowledged place within her spirit she knew that if he lived, he would have come for her by now. "Kosar-eh may have returned to that country. When we left it, it was a land without people, without enemies, and Cha-kwena walked with the sacred stone, following the totem somewhere in deep forests beyond the edge of the world. If he has come back to the Land of Grass, and if you come to him walking at my side, Cha-kwena would name you Friend, and Kosar-eh would—"

"You have wished my death at that man's hands," Xohkantakeh interrupted. "When Ynau and Axwahtal and the others asked Broken Wing to tell them the whereabouts of the shaman, the stone, and the totem, Ta-maya faced Spirit Sucker and still would not speak the words they would hear. Why would Broken Wing lead Xohkantakeh to these things now?"

It was a moment before Ta-maya replied, "For the sake of hungry women and children, and for one who is no longer my enemy."

"If Kosar-eh is in this place, maybe Xohkantakeh will be *his* enemy, and maybe he will die at the hands of Broken Wing's new man!"

Ta-maya remembered Zakeh's words, but she would not betray her knowledge of them lest she bruise the pride of a brave warrior who would not want a woman to know of his kind heart lest she mistake compassion for weakness. And so she feigned fear of his threat, stammered a little, hung her head, and pretended to be speechless.

Xohkantakeh smiled and lifted her chin. "Broken Wing, you lead this man to a land of much meat and to a place without enemies where these children will grow fat and strong, and if your always-and-forever man is there, I will give back to him his Broken Wing—and gladly will I name him Brother!"

**5**

It occurred to Kosar-eh that he was not unhappy.

Time was passing quickly as the People of the Watching Star busied themselves with preparations for the eastward trek to the great gorge at the edge of the world and then into the forests beyond. Under clear, dry, windy skies hunting was good within the valley. All hands, save those of the youngest children, helped to carry meat and hides, bone and hooves, and precious sinew and fat to the cave. Drying and smoking frames were sagging with meat. Blackflies that hatched from spring-fed pools within the inner cave buzzed around people, dogs, and meat, while fat glistened on the pounding stones, and the women boasted of all the fine and useful things they were making for the men who would go on the journey.

By day Kosar-eh hunted with the men of the Watching Star and honed his fighting skills with them. Between these activities, he continued to instruct eager students in the intricacies of stoneworking. By night he enjoyed the meat of his kills and sat stoically for the ritual tattooing that was gradually transforming his face into an elaborate pattern of black and white striping. Oan did the work now, since Kosar-eh no longer trusted

the captives. He lay on them often, especially the
daughter of the giant Xohkantakeh, whose footprints
had been so conspicuous among those of the other raiders. He found a rare and exquisite pleasure in brutaliz-
ing her. "For Ta-maya!" he would say again and again
and leave her dazed and bruised and cringing in fear of
him. Often he found Tsana watching him, nodding,
smiling in approval. Sometimes, long after the cooking
fires burned down and the meat of sloth and antelope
and elk had been consumed, the headman and others
would come to him in the dark with females, and in the
way of the tribe they shared the gluttonous sexual pleasures of the night.

"Man Who Spits in the Face of Enemies is one of
us now," Hrak assured Kosar-eh.

"In the way of this people," added Unai.

"What would your Red World woman say if she
could see you now, Black and White Warrior?" The
goad of Xohkantakeh's daughter was intended to cut to
the bone.

It was the young woman who was cut. Poised for
penetration, Kosar-eh struck her face brutally with his
forehead. "My woman is dead! You are nothing! This is
nothing!" He was on her like a storm, punishing her
until she begged him to stop. While Hrak and the others urged him on, he burned Bhandi with his anger until
she screamed her contrition. His release came as savagely as lightning striking exposed flesh. Uncaring of
her feelings, he left her to further punishment by Hrak
and the others as Tsana moved beside him in the dark.

"Yes! It is good!" the chieftain whispered. "Never
forget! Until the day you take just vengeance in your
woman's name, let her memory sear your heart and all
that you do!"

Kosar-eh slept heavily. Even after Bhandi was
found dead, her wrists slashed, curled on her side in a

black pool of her own blood, he rarely dreamed. He did not blame himself for the young woman's death; her father had savaged his beloved, so why should his daughter live on in a world that Ta-maya would never see again? On most mornings, he awoke sated, usually rested but never refreshed, especially when he would sense Spirit Woman watching him from across the cave, her eyes blank and unblinking. Sometimes she would simply stare for a while and then close the furred and feathered streamers that gave privacy to her little dominion of mammoth bones; more than once she opened her wolfskin robe and held her engorged breasts out to him, mocking him with her eyes, daring him to react—with lust or revulsion. Instinct told him that he dared show neither. No man lay on the priestess. No man insulted her. All seemed afraid of her—except Tsana and Kosar-eh. He knew her for what she was—only poor, mad Ban-ya of the Red World. He had seen long ago that for all her ceremonial importance, it was Tsana who told her what to do and who held absolute power in the stronghold of the People of the Watching Star.

Ban-ya was looking at him now. Kosar-eh would have turned his back to her, but he was startled to see pity in her eyes. Pity? From Ban-ya? He tried to understand, but the woman was holding Doh-teyah to her breast, and he was distracted by memories that seared his consciousness. Of Ta-maya holding the baby, loving her, rocking her, kissing her brow, and singing in that sweet, tender voice. . . .

"Ah!" Kosar-eh could not bear to think of it. He closed his eyes tightly, willing himself to obliterate the past, to think only of what would be when at last he drowned his memories in blood. In a few moments the pain of recollection passed. He opened his eyes again and, with relief, saw that Spirit Woman had closed the blinds of her enclosure.

Joh-nee had seen that he was awake and had scooted forward to sit before Spirit Woman's dais.

Kosar-eh did not appreciate the girl's all-too-predictable glare of disapproval. What an insufferable child she continued to be! Pampered and spoiled as Tsana's favorite, given the best meat alongside Spirit Woman at every hunt fire, presented with gifts of fine clothes, feathers, and scented fat for her skin and hair! Gradually she was beginning to relax a little in the company of other girls and the many women who wished to mother her, but she still refused to allow Doh-teyah out of her sight. Oan had recently gone out of her way to surprise Joh-nee with a new doll. The little sister of Cha-kwena disdained the offering, preferring to cling instead to the old rag toy of stuffed buckskin, just as she clung to her refusal to yield to the ways of her new tribe.

Yet, of late, Kosar-eh had noticed a change in her demeanor toward Tsana. During the early part of each evening, the chieftain insisted upon taking her on his knee, stroking her hair, sharing his food, and whispering secret confidences to her as though she were, indeed, a beloved little sister. Now and then, the girl actually giggled at something the man said to her, and more than once Kosar-eh caught a hesitant expression of growing adoration on her upturned face. But never was there anything less than contempt for Kosar-eh in her eyes.

She sat now, as on every morning, glowering her disapproval of him. She looked like a large brown-eyed mushroom sprouting defiantly, staring at him as though all that he had dared to win in this new life for her and himself and his surviving sons counted for nothing!

Infinitely annoyed, Kosar-eh made a threatening face at her and gestured wildly with his hands. Joh-nee flinched and turned away. He laughed, then looked up, surprised to see Tsana standing above him, shaking his head.

The chieftain hunkered beside him. "Your manner toward the girl concerns me, Black and White Warrior."

"How so?"

"You know that I have told her we will soon go forth to bring her brother to her from beyond the edge of the world, to council with him, to gain and share his power."

"She has seen the spearheads of white crystal; it is no secret what the Ancient Ones have said of them, or to what purpose they will be put."

"I have explained that we must be ready to battle any enemies we encounter on the way, and that is why we prepare spears. I have assured her that the Red World shaman and the totem will come to no harm at your hands. Do you want her to hate us, and you, Black and White Warrior?"

"She hates me now."

"Your heart has grown cold."

"No. My heart has grown hot in its impatience to appease my spirit."

"Have you no compassion left, then, for a trusting child who has seen too much of death? There is no need for the girl to know the truth."

"She will know it soon enough when I return from the edge of the world with the hair of her lying, treacherous brother braided into my own, even as you wear the hair of Shateh. And she will know when she sees you wearing the sacred stone."

"And the others carrying the hide and meat and tusks of the great white mammoth!"

Kosar-eh fought back the impulse to roll his eyes in impatience with the chieftain's continuing faith in that which no longer existed. "If this is what you wish and believe, then may it be so!"

Tsana's eyes narrowed. "On that day Shaman's Sister will not care if the truth I would keep from her is palatable or not."

Kosar-eh raised a brow. "The killing of her brother and the eating of the totem, if there *is* a totem, will never be palatable to Joh-nee, Tsana."

The chieftain's long lids fluttered slightly but did not rise as he lowered his voice and said, "Black and White Warrior, very soon now you will lead Tsana's warriors over the edge of the world to the hunting grounds of Yellow Wolf. With your own hands you have made the spearheads that will slay him and the totem. This man has named you Friend. This man has named you Brother. This man has taken in your sons and blind daughter as children of the tribe. Nevertheless, although we hunt together by day and share meat and women in the night, you *must* remember that Tsana *is* chief. And in this matter, in the consideration of Shaman's Sister, you *will* obey him!"

Kosar-eh was taken aback. The man had not raised his voice, but there had been no mistaking the change from casual speech to formal usage. Had there been threat in the chieftain's tone, or only a deliberate distancing, an understated and, perhaps, necessary reminder of authority?

Kosar-eh could not be sure. Disturbed, he acknowledged, "This man has not forgotten that Tsana is chief, but he does not understand why the happiness of one stubborn little girl from the Red World should be so important to the People of the Watching Star. Whatever happens to Joh-nee, she will have to accept it in time, whether she likes it or not."

Tsana lay a brotherly hand on Kosar-eh's forearm. "Life is short for us all, Black and White Warrior. Soon you and I will leave this place and begin our hunt in those dark forests that you say lie beyond the edge of the world. On that day, Tsana would not wish to think that his new sister was unable to consent joyfully with open arms and heart to all that is to be for her among the People of the Watching Star."

"You have named her Sister, but I am sick of the girl. She carries the blood of one I despise, and she makes no accommodation to me because of it. Once we leave the stronghold, I will not look back in concern for her."

Tsana's eyes barely flickered. "Good," he said. "We will leave tomorrow, before the rising of the Morning Star. It will bode well for our journey."

All that day and into the night the final preparations were made. At dawn the main force of the warriors of the Watching Star and their dogs—plus a double hand count of women, more than half of them slaves—prepared to leave the cave. Drums sounded. Good-byes were made. Songs were sung. After Tsana had communed with the spirits of the white quartz spearheads, he ceremonially handed one weapon to each of the four men who were to be honored with them. The apportionment did not go contrary to Kosar-eh's expectation, except for the recipient of a single spear, a man he had requested that Tsana leave behind.

"Indeh?" Kosar-eh was incredulous. "How can the spirits of spearheads I have honed choose to honor one who has consistently chosen to dishonor me?"

"No man can say how the spirits will speak!" replied Tsana. His tone was apologetic to Kosar-eh, though his expression was encouraging to Indeh. "Come! Let there be no more words of hostility among us!"

There was no arguing with the chieftain's command. To flutes and whistles and pounding drums, the warriors went forth.

"Tell my brother that his sister waits for him here!" Joh-nee cried out to Tsana.

Kosar-eh was not sure, but he thought he felt a ripple of tension go through the gathering. So the girl still believed Tsana's well-meaning lies about the reason for this journey.

"And Kosar-eh!"

He turned back, surprised to hear Joh-nee call his name.

"When you see the white mammoth with your own eyes, then you will know! Then you—" Joh-nee's proclamation was cut short by Oan, who pulled the girl back to gain a better view of the departing warriors.

Kosar-eh felt an unexpected pang of sorrow for Joh-nee. What a gullible child she was, to still believe in the totem, to maintain faith in a brother who had led her band to destruction, and to believe Tsana's talk of peaceful intentions toward that brother when his warriors were fully outfitted for the kill. Ah, well, with luck on the part of the hunters, the girl would learn the truth in time, and then—despite his comments to Tsana to the contrary—Kosar-eh hoped the child would not be too badly shattered by it. But all that lay in the future.

Black and White Warrior raised his head and was about to turn away toward the new day and the journey ahead when he again saw pity in the eyes of Spirit Woman. She was holding Doh-teyah in her arms, and Joh-nee was standing faithfully beside the blind child, who began to cry.

"Bad things!" she wailed, pointing at Kosar-eh. "Bad things!"

No one spoke.

The child's cry seemed a bad omen—until Tsana shook his head and mocked his men for their foolishness. "Have none of you ever heard a little one protest the sound of our flutes and whistles and drums before?"

The question was well asked. Many children had been upset by the noisy clamor in the cave. The men relaxed.

Later, long into the day when dusk was coming down and they paused for rest, drumbeats could be heard again from the Valley of the Dead, imperative now, a deep, sonorous, distant booming. The chieftain smiled.

"The sound from the cave . . . it sounds like . . . no, no, I do not think I have ever heard the like," said Kosar-eh.

Tsana fought to keep the guarded expression locked on his face and was proud of his brothers of the Watching Star when they did the same. *Nor will you ever hear it again in your lifetime, Kosar-eh, for tonight my people prepare to greet the Morning Star in the way of our tribe . . . in the way that is most pleasing to the Four Winds . . . in blood and flesh . . . a gift to the forces of Creation . . . a gift to assure our victory against shamans and totems and the powers of the sacred stone!*

Cha-kwena caught his breath as though stabbed to the heart.

It was morning, and he was wide awake. Yet with his eyes wide open he dreamed the dream again—saw phantoms rising out of red mists to become painted warriors, saw the river of blood, the great bear, the spear-carrying woman—and then he heard his sister scream.

"Joh-nee!" he called out to her.

Sensing worry in his voice, the little white mammoth called out, too.

The sounds of shaman and totem came back to their starting place, snared in the heavy forest air, trembling in the way of vibrations set up by a dying insect shivering in the spider's net that holds it captive until the end.

If only he had the sacred stone! Somewhere, somehow, something was wrong in the world. He knew it, *felt* it. There *were* dangerous, shifting elements of change stirring in the very air he breathed, and deep within the marrow of his bones he knew that his people were in danger.

Cha-kwena hurried on. He had lost track of time. Save for deepest night and high noon, the light in the forest remained dull and diffused, as green as the trees. The air was stifling, neither warm nor cold but damp and heavy, and alive with insects. Coyote had disappeared several sleeps ago, but now and then Trickster's laughter came through the trees, and somehow, with Owl flying ahead, Cha-kwena sensed that the animals— or spirits—were leading him in the way he must go.

Twice before high sun each day, he climbed the tallest tree around and sighted as best he could across the canopy of the forest. At night, if the treetops afforded no view of the sky, he did the same. He had not forgotten the meteor that had burned his senses and seared its pathway against the night sky; now, remembering the fiery brand of its passage, he used the stars to point the way home.

# 6

Warakan awoke with a start. Mah-ree's arms were around him. He made a little jump, not toward her but away, bending his head, hiding his tears.

"It was only a bad dream," Mah-ree assured him.

"I do not need a mother to tell me that!" he snapped, but the very statement made him drop his forehead to his knees. Humiliated and shaken, he wrapped his arms around his head, snuffling up his tears lest she bear witness to any more of them.

"In this world of warring tribes, we all dream bad dreams, Warakan." Mah-ree's voice was gentle, consoling. "You have had more than your share of them of late, that is all. But things for us are good now. Jhadel is growing stronger. We have two fine camps, one here on the heights of the gorge and one in the cottonwoods below! Put bad dreams from your mind now and—"

"A shaman must open his mind to dreams as an eye opens to the light," Jhadel interrupted her. "Both visions are true visions. Share this dream that causes you to weep, Warakan."

Warakan did not want to speak of it. Things *had* been good of late for his little band. Long, warm days of constant sun beneath which he and Mah-ree hunted to-

gether with staves and slings; clear, cool nights ablaze
with stars, beneath which they sat and listened to the
endless wisdom tales of Jhadel. Indeed, Warakan was
even beginning to concede that the old man's words
were a rare and wonderful food; if digested properly, it
offered a nourishment that mysteriously transcended
that of meat. The Wise One told tales of the hunt, of
magic and reality, of a thousand disconnected yet inter-
connected things—tales that broadened the minds of
his listeners and sent them journeying off with him
upon the Four Winds to the time beyond beginning.
Sometimes Mah-ree and Warakan would be so lost in
his imagery that when Bear Brother occasionally came
snouting up the gorge to beg a meal, they hardly knew
the animal was there until its golden eyes would flash in
the firelight.

Yet Warakan had been having nightmares on and
off ever since coming from the forest. Surely, he
thought, his mind was only reacting to the open skies
and vistas, which set fire to fearsome memories of what
life had been like for him in the grasslands and mountains beyond the high plateau. But at least he had not
dreamed of Neea. Until now.

Warakan frowned within the cave he had made of
his arms. He had risen early, as he so often did, and
from the top of the gorge had scanned eastward across
the forest to observe the sunrise. This morning a star
had risen first, a bright star, the Morning Star. Hating
the memories it brought him, he had taken his first meal
of the day of cold leftover roasted rabbit and stalked off
across the heights, his back to the east, seeking other
views.

Briefly in the thin, translucent light of dawn he had
imagined a fire twinkling on the western edge of the
plateau. Then, the sun rising at his back, distant out-
croppings of crystalline rock glinted in the first light of

day, and Warakan grew certain that the fire had only been a trick of the morning light. He made no mention of it to Mah-ree or Jhadel, for he had come across fresh prints of Bear Brother and had followed them a ways, until he saw that the pup was headed toward the forest. Not wishing to follow his brother from sunlight into the dank, green mists, he had returned to the heights of the gorge.

Hours later, after a fine, lazy morning of watching Mah-ree fleshing small animal skins while talking animatedly with Jhadel about all the new and familiar medicine roots and flowers they were finding on the grassland below, he dozed . . . and then he dreamed the dream.

A dream of the Morning Star.

A dream of a distant stronghold filled with fire and color and sound—so much of each that his senses ached. He recognized the songs, the dances, the vibrant patterns of tattoos and body paint of the celebrants who circled him in the dream.

A dream of himself, frightened, so small, his body bound and helpless in cobwebs that meshed him tight to a painted wall.

And a dream of his sister, young, smiling, walking to a fire before which she was transformed.

Warakan shivered.

In his dream he had seen Neea as a bird, not a bird of feathers and grace but a winged thing, grotesquely flattened and flayed. It had shrieked around the cavernous interior of the stronghold as her eviscerated body spattered blood upon the tattooed woman who had gutted and skinned her and passed her flesh to all of the celebrants while a shaman in a browband of raven feathers leaned on a crooked staff and raised his hands to the Watching Star.

Warakan looked up. "You were in my dream, Jhadel."

The old man's face tightened. His tattooed lids quivered. He knew the boy's thoughts. He, too, was shaman and had risen before the dawn. "The Morning Star ascends. We cannot halt its passage across the sky. So look not to the past, Warakan. We have put it behind us forever. Unlike the stars, we are free to choose a new life . . . a new way . . . and it *will* be a good thing."

Mah-ree nodded. "I thought I heard a mammoth in the forest last night. I, too, must have been dreaming! It was a good dream . . . of my shaman and the totem coming toward us with Kosar-eh and Ta-maya and the children following close behind!"

At the edge of the grassland, high on the rim of the plateau, Xohkantakeh was upset with the children.

"You, Ika, take your pups and stop this at once! And you, Xree and Lana, why do you laugh to encourage that thoughtless and careless girl?"

"But Xokeekokee, I—"

"No, Ika! You are the oldest! No words from your mouth do I wish to hear! You will listen to Xohkantakeh! Look! The mother women have worked hard to lay this cooking fire to rest with earth and small stones. And what do you do, child, the moment they look away and try to attend to the work of packing up and moving on? Do you help? Do you pack a sack or parfleche? Do you offer to heft a pack? No! You run your wolf pups through the fire pit, rousing ashes that may hold sleeping embers!"

"The girl meant nothing, Xohkantakeh," Shan said.

Ta-maya's heart was warmed to see Zakeh's woman no longer unable to show affection for the little ones. "We will tend to the fire pit," she assured the giant.

He was not assured; he was even more upset. "No! Ika will do it. And never again will she play close to fire in this land of dry grass. Ah! The wildfires this man has seen in his time! When set by hunters to run the game, a wondrous thing; but if the wind turns, fire also turns and feeds upon the air and grass until it becomes alive, an eater of all that lies within its path!" He focused on the cringing Ika. "A girl-eating thing! A band-eating thing! A *pup*-eating thing! Is this what Ika would have this day?"

"Xohkantakeh, stop! You have made the little one cry!" Ta-maya pulled the child into a protective one-armed embrace.

He was not moved. His face was stern, unforgiving. "If we lose control of fire, a great beacon will burn across this plain. If our enemies are near, they will know *we* are near and will come for us. Never forget the beat of the war drums you heard coming from the distant Valley of the Dead before we put that cursed place behind us. A band as small as this must strive to remain unseen and always be alert for enemies!"

The cautionary words saddened Ta-maya; she remembered similar advice given to her own little band by Kosar-eh—to no avail. It had not been fire that had drawn the raiders. It had been ravens circling over snare meat. She sighed. They had been so careful. She had not imagined such a threat. Now she would never forget.

But the sun was high, the air was warm, and Ta-maya was soon cheered by the happy children and gamboling pups as the band moved on again.

By late in the day the badlands were completely behind them, and they were crossing the broad sage flats that she remembered so well. By evening they had reached the springs. They made another camp and ate another meal. The little ones were soon back at their games, this time under closer supervision as Zakeh and Xohkantakeh sat nearby reknapping hunt-damaged spearheads. Ta-maya had set herself to cleaning the bone meat skewers in the ashes of the fire pit when Neeracheela and Shan called her away.

"Clean up later!" Shan demanded.

"Yes! Come!" Neeracheela insisted. "See the gift that we have made for Ta-maya!"

"Gift? For me?" Ta-maya was overwhelmed and delighted to find herself suddenly surrounded. The girls were giggling. Neeracheela and Shan were beaming proudly. And Zakeh and Xohkantakeh were doing their best to appear composed, though their eyes were crinkling with smiles as each woman simultaneously pulled from behind her back a moccasin and handed it to Ta-maya.

"Here. For summer!" declared Neeracheela. "Your moccasins have a long time ago worn out!"

"It is time to put away the old for the new. New band, new shoes. From your new sisters!"

Ta-maya's eyes filled with tears as she accepted the unexpected offering. The moccasins were lovely, beautifully sewn out of mixed but good-quality small animal skins that the two women had somehow managed to acquire and prepare without her knowledge. Ta-maya knew that they had gone to much effort on her behalf. Yet, although she made a great show of gratitude and appreciation of the workmanship involved, it was not easy for her to smile. In truth, her heart was heavy when she took off the old moccasins that Kosar-eh had made for her; somehow the act seemed a final good-bye to a past life from which she had no desire to be parted.


"At last!"

Following neither Coyote nor Owl but the old mammoth sign he had once before followed in the opposite direction, Cha-kwena led the little white mammoth through the forest. He was not sure just when he picked up the tracks of a boy and a bear. Drawn by curiosity to see where they would lead, he soon came to an abandoned hovel. He went inside to find a barren altar and the savaged pelt of a great fang-toothed cat.

"Come," he said to the calf, feeling a sense of loneliness and devastation in the place. "There is nothing for us here."

Yet even as he crossed the stream and waded through mists to the far embankment, a strange sensation came over him, as though something had been here for him once, waiting, but had been withdrawn. His hand went to his throat. "Yes," he said. Somehow he knew that the barren altar had been for the sacred stone—and that somehow his little girl-of-a-woman had touched this place, been a part of it. Her scent was here, the feel of her presence and of her absence. "We are still far from the place where I left the talisman with Mah-ree and commanded her to go back to the village without me."

He did not understand. The hovel he had just left was not of familiar workmanship. Who had dwelled there these past moons? Why had they gone away? And who was the boy who walked with a bear in the forest? Surely Kosar-eh would never encourage his sons to such familiarity with animals; the man was hard-pressed to tolerate even pack dogs in his camps.

Cha-kwena's gut tightened. He paused in the mist. His surroundings and the ursine paw prints recalled his oft-seen vision—a boy, himself, moving through the forest with his ancient grandfather, and a great bear rising from the mists, standing upright in a river of blood under the shadow of circling ravens and teratorns, speaking to him in the voice of a woman, blocking his progress along the clouded path of Vision while lions and wolves advanced threateningly on either side.

The young shaman was not comfortable with the recollection. With one hand gripping his spear, he went on, moving slowly out of consideration for the calf, who was not faring well in the stifling, restrictive confines of the forest with no mother mammoth to instruct it what to eat. "When we find my band, we will return to the cool land of open sky beyond the edge of the world," Cha-kwena vowed, regretting ever having left it as the little white mammoth moved with its head down, its tail halfheartedly twitching at flies, its trunk perpetually wound about Cha-kwena's waist or wrist, or its mouth seeking a comforting suck on his hand. "If my Mah-ree were here, she would know what to feed you. In the days of your father, Life Giver, often she came through the forest to bring Grandfather of All Mammoth gifts of sweet grass and special food from the People."

Thinking of Mah-ree, Cha-kwena quickened his step until, at last, with the calf sagging and swaying against his side, he paused. He knew this place. It was a mossy copse of ancient conifers. Everywhere was mammoth sign, old, moldering, but heartening to both calf and man. "Yes!" exclaimed the shaman. "I remember this place!"

He watched the little white mammoth circle and sniff, bleat and growl as it trunked over old diggings and fecal matter, scenting places where shrubs and tree bark had yet to recover from the tusking of the mammoth herd that had chosen this for a temporary feeding ground in the last days of summer a year ago. It seemed to Cha-kwena that a lifetime had passed since then.

He breathed a sigh of relief when he saw the calf hungrily trunk down familiar leaves and needles. "Eat. Renew your strength! Soon we will reach the village of our band. And when Kosar-eh sees that you are real, that you are the totem, he will regain his faith in the forces of Creation, and all will be forgiven between us!"

The young shaman found hope and comfort in the thought. He rested, hunkering on his heels, and watched the night come down within the somnolent forest. He slept on his feet, balancing against his spear, knowing neither hunger nor thirst. Ahead lay the village of his people. The little white mammoth had good browse at last. Cha-kwena was content.

But the next day when he approached the village, he knew from the silence and the absence of smoke that it had been long abandoned. He called nonetheless. No one answered. He called again, more earnestly than before. The little mammoth raised its trunk and trumpeted as best it could, as though wanting to assist.

Silence was heavy, and all the more so upon Cha-kwena's heart. He stood in solemn disappointment where his people had once dwelled. He saw the collapsed abandoned lodges, the stone rings surrounding small scars of burned earth that had underlain cooking fires. For a brief moment he dared hope that he would find the sacred stone waiting for him within the little bough-covered sanctuary where he had once sought a shaman's retreat. Here he had raised his sacred smokes and incantations that filled the nights with the songs of the Ancient Ones. The bough-covered structure was more or less intact, but the boughs themselves had gone dry, and the sacred stone was not there.

It was the mammoth that found the open-ended structure of poles and branches. Recognizing a funeral bier, Cha-kwena cried out and waved the calf away; it obeyed, but only after upsetting the structure and making off with a neatly bound bundle of dried forest grasses that had been left as an offering to the spirit of the charred bones. The young shaman was stunned. The bier lay in ruins at his feet. He was afraid to lift the boughs lest his little girl-of-a-woman lie dead beneath. And yet he did—and gasped with relief and sadness when he saw the remains.

"Gah-ti," he said. The charred skeleton had fallen in disarray, but it possessed only one arm, and if this had not been enough to identify it, a slim black and white banner cut from the black-tipped tail of a lion marked the bones as those of Kosar-eh's eldest son. Cha-kwena was deeply saddened. Young Gah-ti had survived the attack of the lion that took his arm; he had been so sure that he would outlive the fever spirits that had come to him in the forest.

The mammoth was sidling close, trunking around for more grass. Cha-kwena started. The smell of sap rose from the boughs that had covered the bier. He lifted one; the needles were only beginning to dry, and the cut marks on the end of each branch still oozed sap.

"Someone has tended this no more than a moon or two ago!" he declared. Of the villages that his people had raised since coming over the edge of the world, two had been in the forest, and one had been on the flank of the great gorge that opened onto the western grasslands. Hope flared brightly in his heart. "They have gone to one of the other dwelling places. They will be waiting for us there!"

And so Cha-kwena hurried on.

How far was the original forest camp? A full day's walk and then some. He wished that he could fly! He and the mammoth had journeyed through part of the forest before, and the closer they came to the gorge, the stronger was Cha-kwena's sense of Vision; it was as though the sacred stone was near, guiding him to his band and the arms of his little girl-of-a-woman.

"Come, Cha-kwena, Brother of Animals, Yellow Wolf, Kindred of Coyote! Come!"

He flinched. Coyote was trotting through the trees

ahead, looking back with its wolf face and eyes. "Yellow Wolf, are you leading me . . . or baiting me?"

"Are you not also Trickster, my brother?" parried Coyote. "Are we not Yellow Wolf together? Can you not tell the working of your own mind? To have come so far upon a trail and still hesitate upon the path to which you have committed yourself . . . and the totem!"

"Beware of Trickster!"

Cha-kwena stopped, turned, looked all around. Yes! There was Owl, helping animal spirit of his grandfather, hovering high above the trees, its broad wings spread and working as though on the steadying updraft of a thermal—but there was no wind.

"And have I not become *your* helping spirit, you stupid boy!" shrieked the molting old bird. "Is that not my skin you wear upon your head? Are you not seeing with my eyes, and is my spirit not attempting to guide you as I—"

"I have not been a boy in all too many years!" Cha-kwena snapped. He raised a hand to touch the beaked and feathered headdress that he wore as he added, "Would that I were a boy again! The world would seem a much easier place."

"Bah! What seems and what is—never the same, never the same! And you cannot go backward in life, Shaman, for in this world and the world beyond, the stars and moon all move in one direction—forward—into the face of the rising sun! So why do you set your eyes to the west? The sun dies there, and West Wind rises to whisper of the ending of the world of Man and Beast alike!"

Cha-kwena caught his breath. "My people dwell to the west. I cannot live without them!"

Coyote yapped; somehow the sound articulated mockery—of the shaman and of the feathered vision above the trees. "Come, Cha-kwena! What you seek lies ahead!"

"Going ahead is going back!" warned Owl.

"Beware of West Wind, Cha-kwena! Always it speaks of ending!"

The voice had not come from Owl or from Coyote. Cha-kwena turned, stared eastward, and saw shrouded in the muted green shadows and mists of the forest day a diaphanous form, rising like blue smoke from an invisible fire. It was the ghostly figure of a man—blue-faced, bright-eyed, wrinkled as a tortoise, and wearing the tufted grass bonnet of a Red World shaman. "Grandfather Hoyeh-tay!"

"Yes. This dead shaman knows his name. But what of you? Are you no longer Cha-kwena, Brother of Animals, Guardian of the Sacred Stone and the Totem? Or have the mists of this forest blinded you to the calling of the Ancient Ones?"

"I seek the stone."

"It is for another . . . the heart of the tribes . . . forever."

Cha-kwena was stunned. "I—"

"Beware of West Wind, Cha-kwena!" exhorted the smoky figure of the Ancient One. "And remember to what purpose you have been called to be Shaman!"

The little white mammoth was butting nervously at Cha-kwena's side. He looked down. Did the calf see the visions? Or was it worrying over its human mother's tendency to talk aloud to himself and forget its needful presence? He patted the pale, wiry-haired head, roughed behind the twitching elephantine ears. The calf sighed and leaned into him, trunking his face so that he might know through its breath that it was comforted and grateful for his . . . *protection*.

"Yes!" proclaimed the ghost of the shaman Hoyeh-tay. "When the last mammoth is no more upon the land

. . . when the spirit of Life Giver is only a ghost in the memory of the People . . . then shall the People die forever! And then shall the sun be consumed by West Wind and never be reborn!"

In that instant the wind rose hard from the west, carrying the ghost of Hoyeh-tay and the owl away upon a blast of air that shook the trees and plucked the feathers from the ghost bird's back and the grasses from the spirit shaman's bonnet before it waned and blew on. The mammoth trumpeted nervously and sought Cha-kwena's hand. He gave it and stood for a moment in a rain of falling feathers and wisps of grass. But when he leaned his spear against his shoulder and reached with his free hand to catch them . . . they were not there.

"Come, Cha-kwena! Come, I say!"

He looked back to where Coyote stood, his yellow coat rippling in the wind like the grass on the golden, sunstruck plain that lay beyond the gorge.

"Why do you hesitate, Yellow Wolf?" goaded Coyote. "Your woman waits for you. Surely you remember the way through the dark woods. And surely, after all the dark distances that you have come, you are not afraid to follow."

It had never been within Cha-kwena's nature to refuse a challenge. He followed Trickster, hurrying on and on until he lost all track of time. It seemed a day passed, and then a night, and then another day. He must have rested, eaten, slept; it all seemed a blur. On and on he went, taking hold of the little white mammoth's ear when it faltered, urging it on until at last the base of the great gorge lay ahead and he stopped. A coyote uttered a high, yapping cry that sounded too much like laughter. Then all was still. The yellow wolf had vanished into the trees. And Cha-kwena stood stunned by yet another Vision.

A boy . . . and a bear standing upright in alarm.

In the mist and the rising wind they stood, the great bear of the shaman's dreams and the wild and willful boy. For a moment Cha-kwena could have sworn that he looked upon himself. And in that moment he was young again, following his grandfather, Hoyeh-tay, into the far forests of his distant homeland to the secret salt spring, where the sacred mammoth came to drink and where the warriors of the People of the Watching Star, led by Masau, had found the sacred herd and slaughtered them to the last . . . save for one.

Cha-kwena stared ahead.

The boy stared back at him. So did the bear.

Did either move? Or breathe?

Cha-kwena was not sure, but suddenly he knew the boy! This wild and scar-faced yet intensely handsome boy with eyes as long and black and sharp as obsidian daggers! "Warakan!" he exclaimed in amazement as he recognized the features of Masau in the boy and saw . . . the sacred stone of the Ancient Ones around his neck!

The boy's face twisted. His right hand tightened around three slender bone staves. "Cha-kwena . . . Yellow Wolf . . . and the totem!" The words bled out of his mouth. "Someday is now! And now you will die!"

And then a stave was flying.

Cha-kwena ducked and raised his spear to deflect the missile, but he failed to anticipate the boy's ability to hurl another so quickly or so accurately from his left hand. Even as the first clattered to the ground at the feet of the little white mammoth, the second struck the calf. The little tusker screamed and bolted blindly into the trees.

"Yah yah!" the boy cried, triumphant. Leaping forward madly, he hurled his last stave at Cha-kwena.

Outraged, the shaman ducked again and felt the lightweight weapon glance harmlessly across his back.

The boy had left him no choice: When he had run forward, the bear had run with him. So Cha-kwena took aim at the high humped shoulder of the monster of his dreams and brought it down before it killed him.

Mah-ree looked up from sorting medicine leaves as a blur of brown burst from the trees at a stumbling run. She screamed and leaped to her feet, but Bear Brother ran past her as though she were not there, "mraawing" pathetically to itself as it slid down the precipitous west-facing flanks of the gorge toward the grassland below.

Jhadel came from the lean-to between the boulders. "What just came through the camp like a whirlwind?"

"Warakan's brother," she told him, staring after the animal. What was that flash of blue and red banding hanging from its shoulder like a ribbon? A spear? Yes. It had looked like a spear. For a moment, it occurred to her that perhaps Warakan had finally made good on his pledge to make a weapon for her—not that she would use it in this land in which she had sworn never again to profane the laws of the Ancient Ones.

And then, suddenly, the colors burned her. They were Cha-kwena's colors! Red for the earth of the Red World of their ancestors; blue for the sacred blue mesas, where the shamans of the many bands gathered to commune with the spirits of the Ancient Ones under the Blue Land of Sky.

"Cha-kwena!" She exhaled his name as a prayer of longing for him.

And in the next moment her prayer was answered.

Warakan came sweated and panting through the trees. "I have speared the totem in the forest, and Yellow Wolf has dared to hurl a spear against my brother! Why do you stare? Get your medicine things, woman of Warakan!" he commanded, looking down, moving forward, following the bloodied tracks of the wounded bear. "Come, I say! You must help me! Bear Brother needs the help of Medicine Woman!"

"You have speared the totem!" Jhadel was pointing a trembling hand.

Mah-ree was staring. "You wear the sacred stone! You have stolen it! Thief! Liar! Give me the talisman! I will bring it to him. And if you have truly raised a hand to wound the totem, we will heal it together and beg the forces of Creation to forgive you!"

"The forces of Creation will soon lead Warakan to its meat! My brother needs the magic of the stone, and the skills of Medicine Woman! Hurry! Follow me with things for stitching and salving! I will calm my brother and make him ready to receive healing at your hands."

He was gone.

Mah-ree stared, shocked, disbelieving as she saw the small, lean form leap and bound down the scree, calling at the top of his lungs for the cub to stop and wait. And then she saw something else: smoke on the horizon. Her heart stopped. "Kosar-eh returns with my band!"

"No." Jhadel had his hand on her shoulder. "West Wind rises. Now it will be as Warakan has foreseen. Those who would hunt us will come across the land."

"Can you be sure, Wise One?"

"If the totem is in the forest with Yellow Wolf, would you put this old man's doubt to the test and risk them both to our enemies?"

He was right, and she knew it. She steadied her nerves. "We will not be here to greet them. Help me to gather our medicine things, Jhadel. Cha-kwena is in the forest! With or without the sacred stone, this woman must go to him, and to the totem! After all that has been between us, he may not want me, but together you and I may help him to heal the totem and—"

"There is nothing between us now."

Mah-ree stiffened as Cha-kwena's voice thrilled through her body. She whirled. He was there, standing at the edge of the forest! Her shaman had returned for her at last! "Ah!" she exclaimed and, breaking Jhadel's hold, forgot everything save the moment as she raced toward him. How much older he appeared, and stronger, with his wide face set against fatigue beneath the beaked extension of his sacred owl-skin headdress. She reached out to him, longed to lay her hands upon his beloved features, to press her body against his, to breathe in the sweet scent of his breath, to caress his mouth and eyelids with her lips. Then all longing died in her. She saw the bloody stave in his hand and stopped dead in her tracks before him. Now, for the first time, she noticed anger in his eyes, and a terrible anguish.

"The totem?" Jhadel's quivering albeit imperative query invaded the moment. "Has the boy slain the white mammoth?"

Cha-kwena was observing the old man uncomprehendingly. "Jhadel of the Watching Star. How come you to this place?"

"I seek that which was painted by a Yellow Wolf within the womb of the world. I seek a white mammoth that has risen from the Valley of the Dead to walk once more upon the earth. I seek the living spirit that alone sustains the heart of the three tribes. I seek you, Shaman, First Man . . . Guardian of the Totem."

Cha-kwena's head went high; his expression was one of pure defensive distrust. His eyes were scanning past and around the Wise One, fixing on the smoke that rose on the horizon. "Where is Kosar-eh and the rest of my band?"

"Long gone from this place," Jhadel informed him. "Into the west wind . . . long gone . . ."

"Yet the sacred stone is here with the wild boy who

walks with a bear!" Cha-kwena exclaimed. He looked at Mah-ree. "You did not return the talisman to them as I commanded."

Mah-ree hung her head. "This disobedient woman was afraid to return alone through the dark wood. She waited for you. Many days. Only when you did not come did she at last find the courage to obey. By then Kosar-eh and the others had gone away and . . ."

Her words ended there. She was in his arms. He held her so tightly that she could barely breathe.

He kissed her face and proclaimed, "Forgive me, Mah-ree. The stone is for another. The Ancient Ones have foretold it! Never again will Cha-kwena allow anger or anything else to come between him and his First and Forever Woman! But now, Medicine Woman, bring your medicine bag and come with me. Together we must find the totem."

"Jhadel will help you to find the way. This wise man is old, but he is still a shaman!"

# 7

It was nearly dark by the time Warakan caught up with his brother. Cha-kwena's spear had worked its way from the wound, and the boy had picked it up and gone on his way with it to where the bear had stopped on a high, grassy hillock. Although Warakan spoke gently, every time he ventured near, his brother warned him away with sullen, menacing growls.

"As you like, but soon Medicine Woman will come, and she will be angry if you do not allow her near, for she will have spurned the shaman to tend your wound!"

But Mah-ree did not come.

And Bear Brother found a position in which, with much straining of his neck, he was able to lick his wound for himself.

Warakan watched the bear. He was relieved to see that the animal had not suffered mortal wounds; the spearhead had lodged in the thick layer of fat that had accumulated high on its shoulders. The wound would heal, no thanks to Mah-ree, and leave no permanent injury.

The boy glowered as the night came down. He watched the stars prick the sky, then brighten and begin their slow but inexorable slide toward dawn until at last he was forced to concede that Mah-ree was not coming. She had chosen the one in whom her loyalty lay, and it was not Warakan or the cub but her cursed Yellow Wolf. "Until the day I make an end of him!" he vowed. Handling the man's spear and thinking of the sweet irony that he would savor on the day he killed him with it, he drifted off to sleep.

It was the smell of roasting meat that woke him. Hungry, he sat up and looked around. Bear was gone. The moon was high. He knew the scent must be coming from the gorge, but strangely the wind was from the west. He shrugged, wondering how this could be, but since he was more anxious for the company of his brother than for a meal, he tracked the cub over the far side of the hill until he found its trail mixing with the fresh spoor from another, much larger bear. Finally both tracks disappeared into an island of trees.

Yielding to discretion for once, Warakan refrained from entering the woods. He called to his brother. He waited. And waited until once again sleep took him. All too soon it was dawn.

He twitched awake and looked around, fully expecting Bear Brother to be lying asleep beside him. With a sigh of profound disappointment, he saw that he was alone. Feeling rejected by yet another member of his family, he was again aware of the scent of roasting meat. Curious, he used the wind to place the origin of the good smell, for it was definitely not coming from anywhere near the gorge. Following his nose, he moved across the hilly land and ascended a long, dry, grassy slope. Suddenly, half shocked out of his skin, he dropped to his knees. A large force of men was fanning out and moving with great stealth toward the source of the aroma of roasting meat: a small encampment of only three lodges, close to the bend in the river.

The colors of the painted hides were vaguely familiar, those of Land of Grass People . . . and from the two distinct patterns on the hides and the close alignment of the lodges, he guessed that they belonged to two small families traveling together.

Warakan swallowed; his mouth was dry with fear. The force of men advancing on the family encampment was his nightmare come to life. Even from his vantage point, he could see that the men were all stripped nearly naked for war, their hair loosened, their skin tattooed. The colors and patterning of their body paint marked their tribal affiliation—warriors of the People of the Watching Star.

He felt sick, yet at the same time he was strangely exhilarated and relieved. They were here! He had been right to fear their coming! They had come with the rising of West Wind! Warakan clutched the sacred stone, grateful that Bear Brother's wanderings had brought him to see his enemies before they had a chance to fall upon him, Mah-ree, and Jhadel, as they were about to fall upon the lodges of the sleeping people from the Land of Grass. It occurred to him that he should turn and run to warn the others, but he was still angry with them for refusing to help his brother, and Yellow Wolf was there to help them now. So he remained where he was, wondering why the warriors of the Watching Star were waiting to attack.

Kosar-eh could not believe his good fortune. Days ago a small flare of sparks and smoke on a distant ridge had caught Tsana's eye, and the chieftain had accompanied a pair of scouts to determine its origin. They had found the encampment that now was before them, and Kosar-eh's heart was afire with dark and wondrous purpose. He had fulfilled his promise to the People of the Watching Star. The gorge lay ahead and beyond that the forest. Soon they would seek Yellow Wolf and the totem

and the sacred stone. For once in Kosar-eh's life the
forces of Creation were on his side.

"Land of Grass people!" Hrak was sure of it.

"A pair of men, three women, a handful of female
children . . . a small band. Who knows why they broke
with the others," said Indeh, looking straight at
Kosar-eh. "But while the absence of small boy moccasin
prints tells us that the son who was stolen from you is
not with them, the men of this band *were* with the raiding party that killed your woman. The footprints of the
giant make it sure!"

"Xohkantakeh!" Kosar-eh slurred the name, trembling with longing to kill as he imagined the giant on his
beautiful beloved, shaming her, hurting her. "I will go!"
he declared. "For my woman . . . I must go! One man
with hate in his hands could finish them all."

"Are you sure you want to do this alone, Black and
White Warrior?" Tsana's tone was one of a man who
did not want to lose a friend.

"It is what I have lived for these past many
moons."

"But if you are slain, we will not have our brother
with us when we take Yellow Wolf and the sacred stone
and the totem!" Hrak protested, unable to suppress his
genuine concern.

"Pity," drawled Indeh with a wolfish smile.

Kosar-eh, in his impatience, chose to ignore the
comment. "We have discussed this before. I have shown
you the way to the gorge." His eyes were on Tsana. "I
have told you how you may find your way through the
forest in the way of Yellow Wolf by following mammoth
sign left by the sacred herd long ago. But on this dawn, I
tell you that the forces of Creation are with me! I will
be slain by no man from the Land of Grass. They will
die by *my* hand. And I will return to fight with you

against their brothers after we have finished with Yellow Wolf."

"After you do to their women and children what they have done to yours . . . if a man from the Red World has the courage for such." Indeh's statement was no statement at all; it was an insult, a direct challenge.

Kosar-eh did not will himself to move, but suddenly he had the tip of his war spear at the man's throat. "I will take their lives and skins as I took the skin of Cheelapat. And then I will bring these skins and the skins and heads of their men as war trophies to Tsana . . . to be staked at the entrance to the Valley of the Dead, along with your own, if you ever speak so to me again!" He withdrew his spear and took a step back, smiling at the sight of the blood running down Indeh's neck until he saw a smirk come to the other man's face.

"Go!" said Indeh. "I see you wear the hair feather of your woman to make you bold. Go. Let us see what Black and White Warrior will do in her name. Bring us the skins of those who had a part in her slaughter. This man will never doubt your courage again!"

There was a general murmuring of agreement.

Tsana was measuring, weighing the moment and the wind. "If the wind turns, Black and White Warrior will lose his advantage. Let this be done now—as he requests, alone. Unai, bring that which I have asked you to carry in the event my brother could not be turned from his need."

Puzzled, Kosar-eh watched as Unai came forward, a wrapped spear in one hand and a massive stone-headed braining club in the other. Unai gave the sinew line a quick tug, and the buckskin wrapping fell away from the head of the spear. It was Tsana's own, tipped by the finest of the white chalcedony spearheads.

"It is for the white mammoth," Kosar-eh protested.

"There are others. Kosar-eh has made this . . .

his best, his finest. Let him use it to speak the language of his heart this day."

And so Kosar-eh went alone, working his way around the encampment until he was downwind of it. Only then did he pause and turn, knowing that West Wind would not betray Death as he came to those who awaited just vengeance below.

As he began his move, his brothers among the hunters of the Watching Star waited and observed.

"Do you think he will appreciate our joke on him?" asked Hrak of the others.

"I hope it kills him," replied Indeh.

"Your rancor is deep, and fitting for a man of the Watching Star," Tsana said with approval, slapping the man fondly on the back. "I have known from the beginning that he was lied to about his woman being slain. I have kept the knowledge from him to make sure that his hate was strong enough to lead us here. Until you found the imprint of the footsteps of a lame female, I was not sure that she was still alive."

Indeh's meaty face was spread wide with satisfaction. "Let us move closer. I want to see him 'pleasure' himself on his own woman this day!"

Neeracheela and Xohkantakeh had made love in the soft, shadowy light of dawn, and afterward both had risen in whispering silence, giggling together like children as they slipped naked into the river to bathe. The water was cold, fast, and deep as it cut a bend through thick cottonwoods. The giant basked like a river otter, but Neeracheela was quickly out of her depth and soon chilled. She left her man to swim alone and perhaps later, as was his pleasure, to enjoy the sport of spearing a few fish or grouse or rabbits.

Shivering, Neeracheela bundled quickly back into her clothes and hurriedly returned to raise the morning fire. She wanted to have the morning meal ready by the time Xohkantakeh returned; this was to be a special morning. She knelt before the fire, working quietly, not wanting to disturb Zakeh and Shan, or Broken Wing and the children. Xohkantakeh would return in good time, cleansed and refreshed by his swim; by then the haunches of the lame little antelope that Zakeh had taken late yesterday would be nearly cooked to perfection.

Neeracheela smiled to herself, thinking how little men saw when they lay with or looked at their women. Last night Moon had risen full again, yet neither Xohkantakeh nor Zakeh had noticed that not one of the three women in their camp had requested a hut of blood to be erected since before the rising of the last moon. Her smile broadened. How could her man not recognize the changes in her body, the swelling of her breasts, the hardening of her lower belly, for what they were? Perhaps it was a condition common to all males, for Zakeh remained oblivious to Shan's pregnancy even though the woman had been trying to end it before he made his decision to walk with Xohkantakeh. Poor Shan. Having outlived all of her children, she had been glad to think herself past bearing. Yet, of late, since coming into the country of yellow grass and dwelling with men who spurned the ways of war, Shan no longer regretted her condition and, thanking the forces of Creation for not allowing her life-unmaking medicines to work, secretly rejoiced as she planned for the infant she would bear soon after the return of White Giant Winter.

Neeracheela shook her head in loving acceptance of her man's blindness when it came to females. This morning she would have to say something. She could not continue much longer to open her body to the passionate thrustings of his wondrously large and competent woman pleaser, nor could she allow such happy roughhousing as they had just enjoyed in the river. Xohkantakeh's life was in her! Neeracheela *knew* it and exalted in the knowledge, which had been hers for two moons now.

She turned the spits that held the haunches, and fat spattered the coals. The fire leaped high. Smoke rose. The smell of roasting antelope filled the air, the scent as delicious as the meat would soon be. Kneeling back, Neeracheela positioned herself so that her body served as a break for the impetuous gusting of West Wind.

One of the wolf pups within the lodge of Broken Wing and the girls began to growl. A soft voice whispered, "Hush, would you wake your sisters?" Neeracheela's smile eased into an expression of tender affection for the young woman who had spoken from within. She hoped that Broken Wing's failure to shed a woman's cyclic blood was due to the fact that she had been nursing a baby prior to the ravaging she had experienced during the first moons of her captivity. The young woman's body had been so cruelly torn by repeated and deliberately brutal rape; she deserved a respite, a time of gentle healing. Xohkantakeh had sworn she would have it. He had vowed that if Broken Wing's man was not found, he would care for her as a daughter until the ending of his days—as he could only hope his own daughter and Zakeh's had been cared for had they survived the brutal winter as captives of the People of the Watching Star.

Neeracheela's heart swelled with pride in her man. She could hear the sure steady race of the river and wondered if he had come from the deeps yet, or if he had splayed himself out happily naked on some wide, flat river rock, bathing himself in the light of morning as he loved to do, or if he was even now coming from the grove.

She drew in a deep breath. What a fine morning it was. The wind from the west was steady and warm, causing the grasses to hiss as it combed through them and set the leaves chattering in the cottonwood grove by the river. The sun was just rising above the high, gorge-cleft hills to the east, bathing the plain in the first rays of day. A new life was beginning for her! A better life than the one she had left behind.

Neeracheela's smile was radiant as she turned her face to the sun. Strange, she had not heard birdsong for some time. And why was the little wolf still growling?

Something snapped behind her, and she winced, startled, then turned to see . . . a man, a spear, an up-raised braining club, and . . .

He struck.

Before she could utter a sound, before she could raise her arms to defend herself, Kosar-eh leveled the blow. One strike, hard, with all of his weight behind it. The sharpened end of the stone head of the braining club came downward against the woman's skull, pene-trating deep into her temple and all the way through her eye to the bridge of her nose before he pulled back and freed the weapon for a second blow. Did she make a sound? He was not sure. Some small exhalation of surprise perhaps? He did not know; he did not care. He struck again, across her neck as she fell forward. Blood spattered, enemy blood. He looked down at the first death that he had made this day.

"What? Did you hear that, Zakeh?"

Kosar-eh started at the voice of another woman coming from the lodge to his left. He stood back, away from the entry, reminding himself that there were two more enemy women in this camp, three children, and a pair of pups . . . and two men, only one of whom was any real threat.

The name "Zakeh" had told him in which lodge he would find the giant. A rush of adrenaline made him shiver with anticipation. He had come well prepared. From his waist thong he took a leather sack of oil and, with a flick of his wrist, hurled the contents onto the two lodges to his right. A scant second latter he had pulled a bundle of grass free from the same thong, dipped it in the cooking fire, then quickly moved to set the oiled hides aflame. In the meantime, a man's head was emerging from the lodge to his left. Kosar-eh whirled and struck another blow for Ta-maya; the man slumped. He struck again, and again, reducing skull and brain to rubble, then jerked the sprawled form forward and waited for the woman within to emerge, curious and unaware. She obliged him. And was dead.

And now, facing the other two lodges, Kosar-eh watched the wind begin to do his work for him. He kicked with the side of his foot, sent embers and sparks flying toward the little shelters. Days of dryness had parched the hides; already fire was licking and beginning to feed upon the skins. In a moment the giant would emerge and end his life with a spearhead through his throat . . . not his heart. He would live long enough to see his children burned alive, his woman ravaged before his eyes, then slain and skinned by his own creation—a man who had once wanted only to live as a hunt brother, a man transformed by the treachery of the People of the Land of Grass into an avenging warrior of the Watching Star!

"Xohkantakeh!" Kosar-eh hurled the name at the lodge. "As you have done to my woman, this man has done to your daughter in the stronghold of the People of the Watching Star! Now! Come! Black and White Warrior will have your death and the deaths of your woman and children as you have had the deaths of mine!"

His heart was pounding. The world seemed red to him, bright. A strange and wonderful thrum was beating in his brain. The scent of wind and fire and burning animal skins was sweet to his senses. Where was the giant? Why did he not come? "Yah hay!" he shouted in contempt, and leaped forward to swipe at each of the two burning lodges with his spears.

And suddenly the small frightened form of a child came scurrying on its knees from one of the lodges.

Kosar-eh heard a woman scream from within, "No! Wait! Ika, pull her back. Wait, Lana, wait!"

His brow came down. Another form was following the first. A wolf pup? Revulsion toward the animal and child burst inside him. Ka-neh was dead, and Klah-neh stolen! And this spawn of the men who had robbed him of his sons lived on to enjoy the pleasure of a pet! Instinct compelled Kosar-eh's hand. Through the blood-red pall of killing madness, nothing was focused, yet his senses were sharper, more keenly felt than anything he had ever experienced. A great and terrible darkness seemed to be hemorrhaging inside his head, intruding into the redness that burned behind his eyes, and a heartrending sound ripped from his soul and ululated on the wind like the howl of a dying wolf.

"For Klah-neh, my son who has been stolen! For Ka-neh, my son who has been slain!" He knew in that moment that he was no longer Kosar-eh of the Red World, nor Man Who Spits in the Face of Enemies among the tribesmen of the Land of Grass, nor Black and White Warrior of the People of the Watching Star. The blood of Ranamal and Cheelapat burned behind his eyes. He could taste it in his mouth. And now a man and two women were already dead at his hand. He had become Death—and nothing mattered except his need to finish what he had so long yearned to begin.

He was so close to the child. He need not even

bend to use his braining club; one hard strike with the butt end of his spear, and its head would be shattered. But the wolf pup was at one of his ankles. Irked, he raised his foot and crushed it under his heel, then turned his attention back to what would soon be a more meaningful killing.

"Aiee! Man of My Heart, no!"

The words did not penetrate the red and black pounding need of the moment. The cries of a woman were only that, a pathetic feminine appeal for him to stop, to show mercy; he could not remember the last time he had yielded to such a plea. He would not yield now. The voice itself, and the long-unheard love name of his beloved, failed to touch him.

A woman was emerging from the tent with a frenzied, hobbling gait. She paused, barely able to maintain balance as she stood protectively before a shrieking little girl and another, older female child, who held yet another dazed pup. There was a skinning dagger in the woman's hand, held in the way of a weapon, not of a tool. The wind was whipping her hair before her face. He could not see her features, but he could see her eyes moving between the wind-lashed black strands, taking quick inventory of the encampment and then, wide with horror, looking straight at him.

"You . . . it *is* you!" Her exhalation was a soft and twisted whisper that made him wonder if somehow her spirit was not pouring from her mouth and unraveling on the wind. "You . . . you cannot do this!" She was stammering breathlessly, shaking her head. Tears welled in her eyes. "Please. Throw aside your spear. Step away from the child. Please!"

Her plea brought a laugh from him. He moved in easy and quick defiance of her absurd behavior. He would make an end of the child, and then of the woman and the other two spawn of those who had slain his own precious young. It was in that moment, as a man's anguished roar came from well behind, that he remembered the giant.

Kosar-eh whirled, instinctively positioning both spear and braining club to do their worst. Xohkantakeh was bigger than he remembered, and he was coming at a full run with a spear of his own ready to be released in the instant he closed to the proper range. And that moment was now. Kosar-eh did not hesitate. He levered back and—

"No! Kosar-eh, no!" screamed the woman. "Xohkantakeh, hold!"

And at the very instant the two men released their weapons, Kosar-eh's throw was ruined. The magnificent shaft with its head of gleaming crystal flew awry. He heard it fall and go skittering forward. Something had come up hard against his back. Distracted, he was shocked to realize that the woman had flown at him with a speed and strength he would not have thought possible. She was on him now. He could hear her weeping, feel her knife deep in his shoulder, her weight working to turn him and force him from the path of Xohkantakeh's oncoming spear; she was too late.

Stunned by the force of the blow, Kosar-eh staggered back, barely realizing that he had, in fact, been struck until the strength went out of him and he dropped to his knees. The braining club fell from his hand. An amazing coldness expanded across belly and lower back. He stared down and was shocked to see that his hands clutched at the shaft of a weapon that had penetrated straight through his midsection.

The woman screamed, "No! Aiee, no!"

And then, suddenly, everything was quiet and bright. So bright! He listened. The red and black were fading within his head. The thrumming was gone. Slowly, he became aware of the sound of the river, of the wind moving through leaves and grass. Then, gradually, other sounds filled the quiet—the weeping of a woman, the gasping sobs of a terrified child, the soft whining of a pup, and the slappings of a man beating flames from his lodges with his bare hands.

And then the man was before him—a giant, blocking the light of the sun, casting a long and heavy shadow. Kosar-eh stared, unblinking, remembering other shadows—cast by ravens and teratorns circling high over another ravaged camp.

A shudder went through him. *He* was the raven who had come circling this camp this day. *He* was the teratorn who had come to feast on Death in the light of the rising sun. Yet observing the deaths that he had made, Kosar-eh found no satisfaction in them. A man and two women whom he barely remembered from the days and nights he had spent among Shateh's people; so much blood, something pitiful about the way the bodies lay. He was swept by a wave of something hurtful, something that felt too much like remorse as the sound of the weeping child penetrated his senses as cruelly as the spear had penetrated his flesh. It was ugly, this vengeance; he found no pleasure in it, only the all-too-familiar emptiness and now a deep aching pain where the stone projectile point of the giant's spear had made a ruin of him.

He slumped down hard on one hip; the resultant pain was overwhelming, but only for a moment. When it passed, he realized that his limbs had gone numb; he could not have risen if he tried. His entire body felt strange to him, heavy, unnaturally centered in his gut and loins, bleeding inward and somehow disconnecting from his spirit. He shivered, certain that the wounding Xohkantakeh had given him was a mortal one. He was glad.

"Now, man who boasts of slaying the daughter of

Xohkantakeh, as you have given to Zakeh . . . his hunt brother will give to you!"

Kosar-eh looked up. The giant was about to brain him with his own war club. A quick death would be welcome; it was more than he would have given were the situation reversed.

"No!" the woman sobbed. "No more! Be it given by your hand or his, Xohkantakeh, this woman will not see more of Death this day!"

Kosar-eh frowned. The woman's voice was torn by anguish—and so familiar that his heart lurched. A terrible bitterness touched him as he realized that the forces of Creation were taunting him even now, for surely he could have sworn that he heard the voice of his beloved coming from the mouth of one who had just helped to slay him. She had been checking the bodies that he had made. Now she had the child that he had come so close to killing hefted on her hip. The wind still blowing her hair across her face, she came limping forward to stay the giant's hand just as it was about to fall.

"Please, Xohkantakeh," she cried. "I beg you, no!"

Kosar-eh saw his own impending death in the eyes of the man, but for all his size, the giant was weak when it came to the will of his woman. He lowered the war club. Contempt for the other man filled Kosar-eh. The woman sobbed and handed the child up to her man as she dropped to her knees beside Kosar-eh, head bowed, the fingers of one hand moving to a hesitant exploration of his wound. Her touch roused pain, and her murmurings of despair annoyed him. He slapped her hand away. "You cannot heal this wound that you and your man have made, woman," he snarled.

"My man?" The query was a small breathless gasp, but somehow the turning of the words changed the woman's posture. She had been slumped forward over his wound, her shoulders sagging and trembling with every sob. Now she stiffened. As she knelt erect and raised one hand to draw her hair from her face, she looked at him, and Kosar-eh felt the world shift beneath him. Even before he focused for the first time on the small, feather-festooned bone hairpin that she wore and realized with a start that it was mate to the one he wore, he saw her face.

"Ta-maya!" he exclaimed, and for what seemed an endless space of moments in which he could neither move nor breathe, he looked upon her face and dared not blink lest she vanish before his eyes. Her face was set, the features drawn wide and as tightly composed as though carved into some sort of smooth and unyielding stone. Her beauty was marred now, scarred about the mouth and high across her cheeks, the result of beating, he was sure, but she was alive. *Alive!* And he had nearly killed her with his own hands! Confusion stung him.

"Ta-maya!" He cried the name of his beloved again. "Woman of My Heart, how can this be?"

She caught her breath as though his words had struck her. A moment later she was on her feet, standing rigidly at Xohkantakeh's side. There was no love for Kosar-eh on her face when she spoke. "Yes. How *can* this be?" Her voice broke. Her chin and the corners of her mouth were quivering. Her eyes were huge; tears were spilling down her cheeks as she spoke. "This woman does not know this man! The man of this woman's heart could not wear the tattooing of the People of the Watching Star. The man who has given this woman's spirit the will to live through all these long bloody moons, because of his gentle kindness and love for his children and the children of others—he could not have done . . . this!" Again a sob tore from her throat, but this time it was not for him. "Neeracheela! Shan! Zakeh! My sisters, my brother! You have slain them, and would have slain this child if I had not stopped you!"

The older of the two girls who had come to stand close at Ta-maya's side was glaring at him. She held the surviving little wolf close to her breast. "Kill him, Xokeekokee! He has killed my pup!"

Ta-maya shivered as though against a gale. "As he would have killed us all if Xohkantakeh had not returned to stop him!" Bereft, she ripped the feathered bone pin from her hair and threw it in Kosar-eh's up-turned face. "Why did you not come for me? Over all the long hills, through all the many snows, I waited. I bore everything! I risked everything to try to find you! And always I knew you were alive. I . . . I . . ." Her face contorted. "Aiee! Look at you! You have become one of them, the *worst* of them!"

"Ranamal . . . Before I killed him in your name, he told me that he had seen you die."

"And you believed."

"I—"

"Do you imagine that I was not assured of your death? I would not believe it! I *could* not believe it! I felt your life in me . . . a part of my spirit, beating in my heart! And even if I had seen your bones with my own eyes and given up all hope of seeing you again in this world, do you imagine that Ta-maya, after all of the sadness that has touched her in this life, would have set her grief to harm others—to kill women and children— in the name of lost love?"

He wanted to explain. He wanted to tell her of his anguish. He wanted to tell her how his heart had twisted at word of her death and that of her little sister, Tla-nee, and of Ka-neh, and at word of little Klah-neh's abduction. He wanted to tell her of all he had suffered and endured to keep his surviving children alive, of how he had felt himself dying without her, slowly, day after ruinous day, night after violent night. He opened his mouth to form the words, but the wind was suddenly gusting hard in his face and all around him . . . not West Wind, but Four Winds, each the living breath of the forces of Creation . . . turning his thoughts until his mind was ablaze with images of a vast firelit cave and a man assuaging his grief on the willing bodies of other women and in the pain of others.

Kosar-eh could smell and taste more than his own blood welling at the back of his throat. It was the blood of Cheelapat and of Bhandi—the tall, frightened daughter of the giant—who had preferred to drown in the black pool of her own blood rather than face another ravaging at his hands.

He closed his eyes. Again he shivered. He felt weak and tired, so tired. Had he done these things? Flayed one woman's body and the spirit of another unto death? Yes. And reveled in his action, as he had reveled in the killing of the occupants of this camp.

He opened his eyes. The wind carried tiny particles of grit across the miles, stinging his face and hurting his eyes. Suddenly angry, he felt a flicker of self-justification stir in him as he looked up at the giant and, ignoring the barely contained killing rage that congested the man's face, said to Ta-maya, "This man . . . this raider who has slain my child and your sister . . . he now keeps you as his slave? He will understand the way of a man's need of vengeance, a man's need of women in the long dark night when grief gnaws at his spirit like a wolf chewing the bones of the dead."

Ta-maya stiffened. "It was Ranamal who took the name of Wolf, wore the skins of that animal, and led the raid of Axwahtal's men against our camp! Perhaps, when you killed that man, his spirit came to live in you."

Kosar-eh was too stunned by the premise to speak.

Ta-maya spoke on. There was a change in her now.

His last pronouncement had set a coldness loose within her; it touched her face and her words. "Xohkantakeh and Zakeh had no part in the killing of Ka-neh or Tlanee! After the raid, Xohkantakeh saved this woman's life, put her good above his own, and turned his back on his tribe for her sake—and with the family of Zakeh and these parentless children that he has made his own, has chosen to pursue a life free of war and killing. Not once has he slaked his man need on this captive in all the long moons since she has dwelled in his encampments! He has respected the way of her heart toward another. He has promised that if our two bands should come together in this land of good hunting, gladly would he name Kosar-eh of the Red World as his brother." She paused. There was inestimable sadness in her eyes as she looked at him, and a tremor went through her. "You—man of tattoos and blood and killing madness in your eyes. Not once have you asked about Klah-neh. Not once have you cared to know if that small, brave son was alive or dead! Aiee! Perhaps he is better off with Axwahtal and the others, because now this woman sees that Kosar-eh *is* dead! You are not my man! Xohkantakeh is Ta-maya's man, from this day until the ending of her days . . . always and forever!"

The shriek of a war whistle seared the moment.

Kosar-eh saw the giant tense, and for the first time since leaving them, he remembered Tsana and the others. "They will come now . . . the warriors of the Watching Star . . . my brothers. Take this Woman of My Heart and go, Xohkantakeh, or truly this man will have brought you death this day!"

They ran.

Ta-maya wept as she hurried forward, forcing herself to a pace that she had not thought herself capable of, especially with her one good arm holding Xree fast against her side. There was no time to mourn the dead, no time to lament the wounding of Kosar-eh. Her heart felt torn asunder. *Man of My Heart . . . I do not understand, will never understand. Aiee! Neeracheela . . . Shan . . . Zakeh! May your spirits follow and forgive us for leaving you behind!*

"My pup!" wailed Ika as she ran, pulling a screaming Lana along. "I dropped her! My pup is still back there, Xokeekokee! We cannot just leave her! She has no mother, no—"

"Do not look back for what is lost and can never be retrieved!" the giant commanded, snatching both girls effortlessly into his massive arms as he hurried forward into the cottonwoods and toward the river. "Now! Into the water!" he declared, setting the girls down and commencing to unfurl the thong snare lines he had thought to fetch from in front of the lodge before they left.

Ta-maya looked at the racing deeps and paled. "It cannot be! The water spirits will—"

"Carry us to safety!" he insisted.

Ta-maya was frightened, not for herself but for the little ones, and despite her resolve not to do so she could not help but think of the man they had left behind. Her heart ached; her spirit bled for him. "His wound was bad . . . beyond healing?"

"A death wound," the giant confirmed, and raised a telling brow as he began to loop and knot the snare thongs into a harness with which he would bind the children to his body as he swam with his woman out of harm's way. "Mourn the other dead in that camp, Broken Wing. Mourn for my hunt brother and your sisters and the new life that I know they carried. As for Kosar-eh, soon his brothers will be with him, and he will die with them the death that he has chosen for himself!"

\* \* \*

"Ah . . . it seems that in this camp things have not gone as either of us expected, Lizard Eater," Tsana observed drolly as he knelt beside Kosar-eh after examining the bodies. "Is your woman one of those? The one with the ruined face, perhaps?"

"What . . . what do you ask of me?"

"I asked if you slew your own woman, Lizard Eater." He smiled at the dazed expression on the dying man's face. "She was here with this band—a lame woman, the same woman whose moccasin tracks I saw in the snow before I brought you and your lizard-eating family into the stronghold of the Watching Star."

"W-what . . . ?"

"Ah, the lizard eater is surprised that we have enticed him to kill his own woman. But, then, what can we expect of his kind? Easily lured and led. Tattoos and war paint cannot change a man!"

"They have fed themselves to the river!" announced Indeh, trotting back from the cottonwoods with Hrak.

"The water runs deep and fast," reported Hrak. "They are dead by now, I think!"

"Ah . . . did you hear that, Lizard Eater? It seems your vengeance has worked the way we planned, after all. Although we were hoping that after all the nights and days we allowed you on our women, we could have enjoyed a little time on yours." Tsana smiled. How he was enjoying the moment! It was even better than he had hoped for.

"Is this spear offending your belly, Lizard Eater?" Indeh came close and, taking hold of the shaft, worked it cruelly from side to side and cried "Yah hay!" when Kosar-eh screamed and retched blood, and more.

Tsana gestured the man back. "Do nothing to hasten his end. This wound will keep him days and nights at his dying—unless the stink of it and the blood of those he has slain draw meat eaters." He rose, waited for the speared man to cease retching, then said, "As you die, know that it is you, Black and White Warrior, who has brought Death to your woman. The totem lives. Your shaman did not lie. You should have listened to him. Now, because you have betrayed him, the warriors of the Watching Star will soon be invincible in the power of the sacred stone and the blood of the totem. Now we will move our war camp to the base of the gorge to which you have led us. We will pass the night hidden in its shadows. We will invoke the spirits of our ancestors. Tomorrow they will be with us when we enter the forest to begin the hunt for Yellow Wolf. And we *will* claim his power and that of the totem and sacred stone. Our success is assured in the blood and meat of Shaman's Sister, shed and consumed by my people on the dawn of the rising of the Morning Star as Kosar-eh of the Red World led us forth from the Valley of the Dead with spears that he had made—and did not look back in concern for the living sacrifice that he had brought to us!"

Warakan had crept as close as he dared. He had seen it all. The colors and patterning of the painted lodges marked them as belonging to two hunters whom he remembered from his days among the People of the Land of Grass. Zakeh and Xohkantakeh had been keepers of the sacred smoke and fire of the chieftain's sweat lodge. He held no strong feelings for either man, but both had been loyal to his grandfather, and he had been glad to see the giant manage an escape through the trees and into the river with his woman and children. Perhaps they would survive. The river spirits had been kind to Warakan once; he wished on the sacred stone that they would be kind to the giant and his family.

SHADOW OF THE WATCHING STAR    477

And now, at last, it was over. After a brief, terrible
howling that sounded as though it came from the throat
of a gutted wolf, the warriors of the People of the
Watching Star had helped themselves to whatever the
first woman to die had been cooking, then had knocked
down the smoking lodges and gone their way, some of
them headed toward the gorge, others trotting in the
opposite direction toward a camp that Warakan could
see hidden within the curve of the western hills. They
had left the body of the black-and-white-painted warrior behind, among the dead, with the spear that had
killed him protruding from his belly and the one that he
had thrown at the giant still lying underneath the collapsed drying flame where it had skidded after it was
thrown wide.

*Two spears!*

Warakan could not believe his luck. The power of
the sacred stone must indeed be working for him! With
some minor refinishing of the shafts, so that the origins
would not be identifiable, Mah-ree would be impressed
by him yet! But dared he take time to go after the
spears while nearly half the fighting force of the warriors of the Watching Star was headed toward the
gorge?

He stared after the tattooed warriors. They did not
appear to be in any hurry, and the gorge was far away.
If he moved quickly, he could take the spears and then,
circling wide of the Watching Star people, with the
power of the sacred stone giving wings to his feet, easily
make it back to the others at a run, in plenty of time to
alert them to danger—if the howling and smoke from
the burning lodges had not already done so.

Heady with intent, Warakan raced for the ruined
encampment. Death was no stranger to him. He had
seen the remains of war raids before. Nevertheless, he
kept one hand on the sacred stone as he slowed his

steps and came into the camp. He told the spirits of the
dead that he was only a boy in need of spears and that
he meant them no disrespect. They did not speak to
challenge him as he moved toward the fallen warrior
and paused close to the body. The man lay on his side,
curled inward around his wound; there was much blood
and a stench that spoke of a gut piercing. Warakan
made a face. Removing the spear would not be pleasant. He pulled in a deep breath and, turning his back to
the corpse in which the heavy shaft was embedded,
went to drag the second weapon from beneath the drying frame while he worked up the courage to take the
first.

The haft was barely visible. No wonder the men of
the Watching Star had not taken it with them. He knelt,
took hold of the butt end of the spear, and drew it out,
delighted to see that the wood was smooth and un-
adorned. He would soon have his own mark on it, and
Mah-ree would never guess that he had not fashioned it
himself. Feeling happier than he had a right to in such
surroundings, Warakan forced himself not to smile. A
moment later he had the entire spear off the ground
and upright, but with the sun sparkling on the head of
the stone, he could not see it clearly. It was only when
he held it out and down that he nearly dropped it in
shock.

"White stone!" He stared. *A spear with which to kill
the totem! Truly, the sacred stone has given this gift to me!*
He cocked his head, ran his hands over the projectile
point, and even though the edges sliced his fingertips
and made them bleed, he smiled. He had never seen or
touched anything so beautiful. Not even Mah-ree would
have this spear. It was his, a gift from the forces of
Creation. She would have the other, the one still embedded in the fallen warrior . . . after he cleaned it, of
course.

The whining of a pup caused him to turn. Startled, he saw a little furry face peeking from beneath one of the fallen lodges. Resting his treasure upright against his shoulder, Warakan advanced and, kneeling before the lodge, to his amazement found a wolf pup in his lap. He remembered the howling. "Surely that sound could not have come from you." The animal licked his face.

Warakan frowned, wondering what a wolf pup was doing in this camp. Surely he was having enough trouble with one pup and did not need another, even if it was only a wolf and would never grow to the proportions of a bear. Yet when he noticed that windblown sparks from the felled lodges and unattended fire pit had started small fires in several areas of grass close to the corpse within the camp circle, he picked up the pup and, after freeing the sacred stone so that it hung by its thong well down over his collarbone, inserted the tiny animal, bottom down, into his tunic. Its little tongue licked at his chin. He ignored it. The fires worried him. Lest they be transformed into a larger blaze that might endanger Bear Brother as he wandered with his new bear friend, Warakan set himself to stomp them out.

The last thing in the world the boy expected was to have his ankle grabbed by a dead man.

"Leave them . . . let them burn to seed a wildfire that may deter the ambitions of those who have betrayed me and slain the children who trusted me!"

Warakan stiffened at the corpse's garbled but intensely spoken command, then jumped straight up and out like a startled hare, broke the grip of the dead man's hand, and came down hard on both feet, ready to sprint, or to spear if need be—but too amazed and curious to do either.

The dead man had propped himself up on an elbow and was staring at the boy out of a tattooed face. "Warakan . . . foundling of Shateh and son of the

Watching Star . . . I see that at least a portion of your stones have come back to you."

The boy stared, incredulous, as recognition dawned. "Man Who Spits in the Face of Enemies?"

"Once. Now they spit at me . . . with this. . . . Here, draw it out."

Warakan's mouth dropped open. He stared at the spear's point of entry and shook his head. "If I take it, you will die."

"I have been dead a long time."

Warakan shook his head. The corpse was no corpse. "I do not believe you."

"Judge for yourself." Slowly, in broken phrases, the man told of how he had come to this place, and why.

Warakan was still shaking his head when the last word was spoken. "You must not tell Mah-ree these things," he said. "She will blame herself. She will say that if she had returned the sacred stone to you, as Yellow Wolf commanded, none of this would have happened and—"

"Mah-ree is with you? Cha-kwena commanded . . . that the stone was to be for me?" Kosar-eh was breathing hard from the exertion his words required.

"Until he could make the totem return through the forest so that you could see it with your own eyes, as I have done!" And now it was the boy's turn to speak of how he had come to this place, of how a spirit of the forest mists had proved to be no spirit at all but a young woman, awaiting the return of a shaman so that she might beg his forgiveness for her disobedience and place into his care once more the sacred talisman of the Ancient Ones. "He has returned with the totem as he promised. He is in the forest now, just beyond the gorge. But, like you, I do not believe in his power. Look! I have stolen the sacred stone! With its power I will make him pay for all the bad magic he has worked against the People. And with this spear, Warakan—grandson of Shateh and son of Masau—will finish the totem. Together you and I will eat its flesh and drink its blood. Then, Kosar-eh, your wound will heal, and we will both be invincible against our enemies! And if your woman has escaped down the river, we will find her, and she will be yours again, and everything will be as it was! Look . . . here . . . the sacred stone! Touch it and you will be well!"

A moan went out of the man. He sagged around the spear. "Do not speak to me of magic, Boy. . . . There is none left for me. But I will tell you now that at the end of this day, the Four Winds will conspire together and will turn and blow down from the heights . . . it is the way of the forces of Creation in this land. So run now! By the time you reach the base of the gorge, the wind will have turned. Fire the grass there! Create a barrier of flame to drive our enemies back into the land of West Wind. . . . If the Woman of My Heart still lives, allow her and her new man to find safety at last! Find Cha-kwena, Boy, and return to him the sacred stone of our ancestors. . . . Tell him to take Mah-ree and flee with the totem, beyond the edge of the world, into the face of the rising sun . . . where men like I . . . and boys like you . . . will never find them!"

Warakan was shaking. "The stone is mine! I will *not* give it to Yellow Wolf! And how can I set fire to the grass when my Bear Brother will be in the path of the flames?"

"For the sake of those who await your return, how can you not? Your Bear Brother will know to run for the river ahead of fire, Boy! But if the warriors of the Watching Star find those whom you have abandoned, Mah-ree will fight to the death beside Cha-kwena to save the totem. . . . Jhadel will be slain as a traitor

. . . by those to whom he was once shaman of the Watching Star."

Warakan was torn. The stone was curled tightly in one hand, but the talisman yielded no insight, no clear way to decide the right thing to do. "I . . . I . . ."

"Choices . . . ah . . ." The man's eyes rolled back in his head. His body spasmed as he willed himself to focus his vision on the boy. He fought for every word that he now spoke. "My choices have brought me to this place . . . to this ending. What you do now, Warakan, in consideration or disregard of others, will place you on the way in which your life will lead you from this day. May you not come to your last breath in a place like this and look back on all your days with sorrow. . . . Perhaps, when all is said and done, you are not Son of the Watching Star, not Grandson of Shateh of the Land of Grass, but a son of the People . . . of all the tribes. Take the sacred stone back to Cha-kwena, Boy! Turn your back to vengeance and war forever. Go. Rejoin those who care for you. Tell them to remember Kosar-eh as you help them to lead the totem to safety . . . and away from . . . this."

Warakan was stunned to hear Jhadel's hopes pour out of Kosar-eh's mouth along with the dying man's last breath. Clutching the talisman and ignoring the presence of the pup, he closed his eyes and knew that, in this moment, he had only one choice. Bear Brother *would* run for the river. He knew this in his heart as surely as he knew that he would not allow his enemies to make an ending of the lives of Jhadel and Mah-ree. There was a great, hot lump in his throat as he realized just how much he loved them both . . . more than Bear Brother . . . more than life itself!

And so, with the bewildered pup still stuffed into the top of his tunic, Warakan quickly searched out an adequate piece of hide in which he could carry the makings for quick fire. When this was done, he withdrew the spear from the body of Kosar-eh. He thought about cleaning the spearhead in fire and taking it with him, but he did not want it anymore, not after what it had done. Besides, the man it had slain was a warrior. For all of Kosar-eh's talk of weariness of war, the boy knew he would need a spear in the world beyond this world, for surely his spirit would walk the wind among many enemies. The boy laid the weapon beside the man. And then, after backfiring the little camp and asking Fire and Wind to take the life spirits of the slain and the slayer to the world beyond this world in honor, if not in peace, he turned his back on Death and ran.

Unseen in shoulder-deep grass, under the circling shadow of a golden eagle, Warakan ran. With the sacred stone around his neck, the white-headed spear in his hand, and the flight feather of an eagle in his hair, he knew that the spirits of Shateh and Masau and Kosar-eh were with him and would give him strength and will to speed well ahead of his enemies. At last, in the lengthening blues and mauves of late afternoon, he reached the base of the gorge.

There, for the first time since leaving the encampment, he paused. Kosar-eh had been right. The Four Winds were gathering. Warakan waited, felt their power rising and whipping all around, until suddenly the mating of the forces of Creation was done. The winds blew together from the east now, blew hard and hot, driving the sun to die in the west, so that tomorrow it might be born again, renewed.

"Who among my enemies will be there to see it?" The boy spoke the words aloud, wanting the Four Winds and the forces of Creation to hear them as he ran again, boldly, angrily setting a line of fire in the grass between the gorge and the advancing warriors of the Watching Star.

"Run, Bear Brother!" Warakan shouted into the Four Winds. "Run for the river, you and your kind, for what Warakan does now he must do for his own!"

# 8

The sky burned.

Warakan slipped and fell as, halfway up the gorge, he collapsed. The spear clattered to the stony ground. Exhausted, he drew it close and lay on his belly for a moment, allowing his body and lungs a chance to rest before trying to rise and scramble on again. The wolf pup complained against his weight. He turned and lay flat on his back. Absently fondling the pup with his burned fingertips, he stared up and out, eastward, all across the plain. The world was burning, and the sky above his head seemed to be burning with it.

The boy's breath snagged in his throat. Not since the night of the Northern Dancers had he seen such a sky. And, as on that night, he saw his nightmare through the fire. In body paint and war feathers, with their ankle-length hair loosened for battle and streaming in the wind, the tall, tattooed warriors of the Watching Star were advancing toward him. . . . No . . . they were fleeing *from* him . . . and they were screaming as they were being burned alive.

Warakan sat up. "May it be so for them!" he cried into the night and the fire, the tears stinging his eyes as he wept. "Bear Brother . . . be safe! Be alive and with your own kind in the river this night!"

He closed his eyes, his fingers straying from the little wolf to the sacred stone. Suddenly he felt a sharp jolt of intuition as he saw through his closed lids a river of stars pouring out across forever. And in that river a bear "mraawed" and waded happily, snouting up star mist with another of its kind. Far to the south, along a bend of the great Sky River, a giant of a man sheltered a weeping woman and three small children in the embrace of his strong arms. Farther still, a little girl hugged a buckskin doll to her meager chest as she trudged beside a woman carrying a blind child close to her great breasts. The woman spoke to the little girl. Her voice flowed out across the great Sky River, and Warakan heard the low scrape of her whisper.

"Come . . . Yes, it is good that you have chosen to arise and follow me, Shaman's Sister. . . . Let us go, you and I, into the darkness, for in the shadow of the Watching Star we must leave this Valley of Death. Come with me now, girl, if you would see the dawn. The power of the stone and the totem and the shaman Chakwena are with us still! All that is good is rooted in them. Come, I say! Ban-ya of the Red World is *not* your enemy. I have watched and waited for our chance to escape those who are. Come! Did you think I would let the carnivore eat any more of my children? We will find our way back to the Red World together."

Warakan opened his eyes with a start. The Vision had been strong. "They are safe . . . *all* of them!" he said, and in response the wolf pup pawed its way up his chest, straight over the hand that held the sacred stone, and licked his nose. Warakan smiled and licked the pup back. "Yes, you are safe, too. Boy Mother of Wolf will take care of you! But come. In case any of our enemies have made it through the fire, we must warn the others.

And I think Jhadel will be glad to know that Warakan is still alive, although what he will think of you . . . well . . . we will soon see!"

They were gone.

The camp on the heights of the gorge was deserted. Warakan sat down, stunned. They had left him! Jhadel and Mah-ree had known he was out there on the plain, searching for his brother, and they had left him.

"Warakan?"

Relief flooded the boy, then trepidation. He leaped to his feet and stuffed the pup down his tunic. Jhadel was coming through the trees, leaning on his staff, his head held high, his form aglow in the light of the fire that burned in the world below. He had the strangest expression on his face. Warakan tensed, wondering if perhaps he had killed the totem and the old man was coming from the forest to disown him forever.

"I have seen the totem!" Jhadel's voice trembled with joy in this revelation. "Life Giver *has* been reborn!"

"I did not kill it?"

"A glancing blow, no more. It *is* totem, after all, you know. Someday it will be as the one that walked before . . . a great white mammoth with shoulders that pierce the clouds, and tusks as long and wide as great trees, and a voice that will echo like thunder in the sky. Until that day Mah-ree and Cha-kwena have taken it deep into the forest, ahead of those who would follow to destroy it."

"I think I may have stopped them," said Warakan, giving a backward nod to indicate the burning sky.

"For how long?"

Warakan could not answer.

"Cha-kwena will not risk the totem again. He has told this shaman that he is confident at last in the purpose to which the power of the Ancient Ones has called him. He will be Guardian of the Totem forever. And now, with Medicine Woman strong in the healing knowledge and wisdom that Jhadel has given her, she will be able to keep herself, her man, and the mammoth safe and well in the days to come as they journey beyond the edge of the world to a place where no men will hunt them."

"You were wrong when you said that she was to be my woman," Warakan said. The statement hurt, badly, but in this moment he knew that he was at last man enough to make it. "But she and her shaman cannot walk without the sacred stone. We will bring it to them!" The sudden burst of altruism amazed him. It actually made him smile. "Come! I am ready. Which way have they gone?"

"You may not follow them, Warakan."

"Of course I may! And will! I have a spear now. I am not afraid. I—"

"You are never afraid. This is not a good thing. Nor is the spear with the white head that gleams red as blood in the light of the fire you have made. A white spearhead . . . to kill a white mammoth!"

Warakan shrugged. "It need not be."

"Bury it."

"I—"

"Bury it, or return into the land of death from which you have come! I do not want to know how it came into your hand. But I tell you now that the one who carries that spear does not walk with me."

*Choices.*

Kosar-eh's word returned to haunt Warakan. Keep the spear and return alone into a burning land of enemies. Bury it and return to the confidence of a friend, even if that friend was Jhadel. The boy exhaled a sigh of begrudging acquiescence. At this moment, with Wise

One his only friend in all the world, he knew what he must do.

And so, with the grass fire illuminating the night, Warakan buried the spear while the old man spoke quietly of what must be. "Together we have been chosen to protect the sacred stone of the ancestors. The spirits of First Man and First Woman of all the generations reside within the talisman. They have spoken to Cha-kwena. Now they will speak through you. The stone is the heart link with the time beyond beginning, the one thing that will make the tribes remember in coming days of war that there is another way . . . another hope. The fate of the People is now in the hands of Cha-kwena as he walks with Life Giver and returns with Mah-ree through the dark forest to the far land of ice, where they will live together in the way of First Man and First Woman forever, Father and Mother of a new generation and a new band. In time their children will come from the forest. They will seek the stone. In the care of those who will come after you, Warakan, it will be waiting—the heart link that will make the People one again."

Warakan rose. His hands hurt. The pup had rooted downward through his tunic and was now on the ground, nipping and tugging at the laces of his moccasins.

"What is that at your feet?" asked Jhadel.

Warakan shrugged and, knowing there was no way to avoid the truth, picked up the pup and held her out for the old one's admiration. "Behold, Sister Wolf."

"An animal . . . *again*? It will seek its own kind in time."

"So will I."

The old man shook his head as though the boy were beyond all understanding. "So be it then. Come. We too must go into the forest to hide ourselves away from the rising winds of war. The spirits of the stone will guide us. We will find a safe place beyond the green mists to raise a new sanctuary within which this man will teach you all he knows. Come. My time is short. And you have much to learn."

Warakan sighed. As the old man turned and walked on his way, the boy inserted the pup into his tunic and took a long last look at the burning sky and land below. Bear Brother was out there somewhere . . . as were the survivors among the People of the Watching Star and the People from the Land of Grass. Somehow he knew that he would see them again.

With Sister Wolf close to his heart, the sacred stone of the Ancient Ones around his neck, and the golden eagle feather of a war chief fastened securely in his hair, Warakan—grandson of Shateh and son of Masau, the Mystic Warrior—followed Jhadel the Peacedreamer into the forest under a bloodred sky.

# AUTHOR'S NOTE

Some months ago, while returning home from sleuthing in the halls of the Hermitage and across the hinterlands of Russia for the roots of the first Americans, I found myself on a daytime transpolar flight across Greenland and the vast expanses of northeastern Canada.

On a clear night, when seen from an aircraft, these vastnesses seem an inversion of starless sky. Now and then a thin silver sparkle will shiver amidst the blackness, then disappear. A town? A village? Perhaps only a hunting camp. How many souls look skyward? No matter. Light defines human presence in an immensity of darkness. Somehow, staring down out of a winged cocoon of air that slices through the upper limits of the atmosphere at six hundred miles per hour, the sight—regardless of how meager or transient—is comforting.

Daylight, however, brought another aspect. Awe inspiring. Chilling. I was forced to remind myself that it was May of 1994. In Saint Petersburg, linden trees were budding along bustling Nevsky Prospect. In Moscow, tulips were in bloom, and Lenin remained on display in Red Square. In the mountains of southern California, to which I was bound, aspens were greening the walkways of Big Bear Village, and lilacs perfumed the high country with the scent of spring. But below, the vast subarctic barrens and boreal forests of Labrador remained in the grip of "White Giant Winter." With no roads or towns visible, it appeared as though the Age of Ice still lingered upon the world.

Lakes. Rivers. Snow-whitened land. The dark furring of trees. All lay frozen below me. Scars left by the retreating Laurentide Ice Sheet were easily seen from thirty thousand feet—moraines and drumlins, eskers and kames, the resultant risings and fallings of a land scraped, gouged, and "dumped on" by the comings and goings of a relentless, miles-thick mass of ice that has more than once sprawled midway and across this continent from coast to coast.

In the intermittent glare of the sun, the Laurentian Plateau appeared exhausted if not humbled by an Ice Age scouring that, in geologic time, ended only yesterday. Over ten thousand years have elapsed since the last of those cold, Pleistocene dawns, time enough for the civilizations of man to rise and fall, but not time enough for weather, lichens, and climate-stunted vegetation to create soil out of the hard crustal shield of the barrens, or for deciduous trees and grasses to intrude into the dark, evergreen heart of the taiga.

Nevertheless, in that moment, flying over what seemed endless miles of postglacial desolation, the ghost of a dead epoch lingered in my mind. Had I not just glimpsed a manifestation of its lingering presence asleep within the sprawl of the Greenland ice cap? Was the Age of Ice not still alive somehow despite the passage of millennia? Was it not lying patiently sprawled across the top of the world, awaiting some subtle fluctuation in the radiant energy of the sun, or some as-yet-to-be perceived perturbation in the orbit of the earth or some distant star to trigger its inevitable rebirth? And then, like a great white bear rising from hibernation within the earth—or like Wíndigo of northern Cree and Ojibwa myth—would that cannibal giant with a heart of ice not move out of the north to once again "consume" the land?

I sat closer to the window, staring down at a landscape that, prior to leaving for Russia, I had been attempting to describe in the book you have just finished reading. As the author of seven novels set in the North American Ice Age, I had, of course, experienced and written of tundra, taiga, and glacial barrens before; but in that long, sunlit airborne passage across Labrador it struck me that I was seeing the barrens for the first time. Without a horizon to anchor my imagination to earth, the immensity of the desolation left in the wake of the ice sheet was not impressive—it was shattering. And, all at once, it was wonderful!

This was the land as Cha-kwena would have seen it when he came through the great forest and into the barrens that lay at the edge of the world. It was as though I looked back through time to the days of the three tribes when scattered bands of the People left the cool grasslands that lay within the rain shadow of the Rockies to hunt a white mammoth beneath the shadow of the Watching Star. The Laurentide ice sheet was centered on Labrador in those days—an awesome albeit shrinking mantle of conjoined glaciers beneath which all of northeastern Canada and Greenland lay buried. Retreating glacial lobes protruded into the newly forming Great Lakes while most of Minnesota, North Dakota, Manitoba, and Saskatchewan lay at the bottom of a prehistoric lake of such monstrous proportions that its dimensions numb the imagination. And all along the receding frontal wall of ice—from New England, across the Midwest, and northward onto what is now the Great Plains—lay a belt of tundra as bleak and desolate as the land over which I flew.

Beneath broken cloud cover, the appalling distances of Labrador's tundral barrens and boreal forest stretched on and on until it seemed that no man could ever have found reasonable cause to commit himself, much less his family, to a landward crossing of such life-threatening immensities. And yet, since time beyond beginning, in keeping with the great Northern Hunting tradition of all subarctic Paleolithic peoples, native Americans have, in the way of their Paleo-Siberian ancestors, followed migrating herds of game to the very limits of those barren lands and into those primordial forests.

Based heavily on the ever-growing archeological record, as well as on old journals, monographs, and the wondrous lore of the People, this novel has attempted to depict the lifeways of vanished tribes and, through plot and characterization, reveal a possible metamorphosis for the roots of native American mythology.

Ongoing research continues to prove that "folks is folks" wherever you find them. Consequently, wars have been fought over hunting territory, as well as "for the hell of it," since time beyond beginning. Ritual sacrifice and cannibalism associated with the Morning Star ceremony date into the mists of antiquity and were recorded and witnessed on the Great Plains by travelers and ethnographers among the Pawnee and Arikara well into the nineteenth century.

I like to think that Warakan might well be the ancestor of the heroic and intractable Stone Boy of Lakota myth, or perhaps of Ish-na-e-cha-ge, First Born of Santee legend—all at once man and animal, darkness and light, provider of the feast and demolisher of it.

The legend of Bear recounted by Jhadel is drawn from several native American fables that speak of Bear's unique relationship to and with Man. And Chakwena, as Guardian of Animals and of the totem, is progenitor of a shamanic line that exists to this day among the hunting cultures of the far north, where people worship the land and sky as well as the animals they hunt—none more so than Bear.

Great Paws, Grandfather, Walks Like a Man, Brother!

Strong One, Grandmother, Grizzly Bear Woman!

Bear was and continues to be a metaphor for Man, for reincarnation, for birth and rebirth, a transcendent symbol of the human ideal of power and gentleness combined and also of all that is terrifying and bestial in human nature, both male and female.

As with all of the previous novels in The First Americans series, the author would like to thank the incomparable staff at Book Creations, Inc., for seeing the project through to deadline—especially Pamela Lappies, editorial director; Elizabeth Tinsley, copy editor; and also, but never an afterthought, Sally Smith for all the emotional support and cheering along the way!

WILLIAM SARABANDE
*Fawnskin, California*

## THE SAGA OF THE FIRST AMERICANS

*The spellbinding epic of adventure
at the dawn of history*

## by William Sarabande

# THE EDGE OF THE WORLD

___56028-X  $5.99/$6.99 in Canada

___26889-9  BEYOND THE SEA OF ICE      $5.99/$6.99 in Canada

___27159-8  CORRIDOR OF STORMS      $5.99/$6.99 in Canada

___28206-9  FORBIDDEN LAND      $5.99/$6.99 in Canada

___28579-3  WALKERS OF THE WIND      $5.99/$6.99 in Canada

___29105-X  THE SACRED STONES      $5.99/$6.99 in Canada

___29106-8  THUNDER IN THE SKY      $5.99/$6.99 in Canada

*Also by William Sarahande*

___25802-8  WOLVES OF THE DAWN      $5.99/$7.50 in Canada

-------------------------------------------------

**Ask for these books at your local bookstore or use this page to order.**

Please send me the books I have checked above. I am enclosing $____(add $2.50 to
cover postage and handling). Send check or money order, no cash or C.O.D.'s, please.

Name _____

Address _____

City/State/Zip _____

Send order to: Bantam Books, Dept. DO 1, 2451 S. Wolf Rd., Des Plaines, IL 60018
Allow four to six weeks for delivery.

Prices and availability subject to change without notice.          DO 1  5/95